THE
NINTH
TALISMAN

Tor Books by Lawrence Watt-Evans

THE OBSIDIAN CHRONICLES
Dragon Weather
The Dragon Society
Dragon Venom

LEGENDS OF ETHSHAR
Night of Madness
Ithanalin's Restoration

Touched by the Gods
Split Heirs (with Esther Frieser)

THE ANNALS OF THE CHOSEN
The Wizard Lord
The Ninth Talisman
The Summer Palace

THE FALL OF THE SORCERERS
A Young Man Without Magic
Above His Proper Station

THE
NINTH
TALISMAN

VOLUME TWO OF THE
ANNALS OF THE CHOSEN

LAWRENCE WATT-EVANS

A TOM DOHERTY ASSOCIATES BOOK

New York

TOR®
fantasy

THE NINTH TALISMAN

Copyright © 2007 by Lawrence Watt-Evans.

Edited by Brian Thomsen

A Tor Book
Published by Tom Doherty Associates, LLC
175 Fifth Avenue,
New York, N.Y. 10010.

www.tor-forge.com

Tor® is a registered trademark of Tom Doherty Associates, LLC

The Library of Congress has cataloged the hardcover edition as follows:

Watt-Evans, Lawrence, 1954–
    The ninth talisman / Lawrence Watt-Evans.—1st ed.
        p. cm.—(Annals of the chosen ; v. 2)
    "A Tom Doherty Associates book."
    ISBN 978-0-7653-1027-9 (hardcover)
    ISBN 978-1-4299-5030-5 (e-book)
    1. Fantasy fiction. 2. Fantasy fiction, American. I. Title.
    PS3573.A859 N56 2006

                                                              2007298417

ISBN 978-0-7653-3804-4 (trade paperback)

Tor books may be purchased for educational, business, or promotional use. For information on bulk purchases, please contact Macmillan Corporate and Premium Sales Department at 1-800-221-7945, extension 5442, or write specialmarkets@macmillan.com.

First Edition: May 2007
First Trade Paperback Edition: October 2014

Printed in the United States of America

10 9 8 7 6 5 4 3 2 1

Dedicated to Susan Carscadden,
for all the help she's given my family through the years

ACKNOWLEDGMENTS

Thanks to Brian Thomsen, Russell Galen, Kristin Sevick, Deborah Wood, and Terry McGarry for making this series better than it might otherwise have been, and again, my thanks to Timothy S. O'Brien for essential aid in world-building.

THE BALLAD OF THE CHOSEN
(as sung by the soldiers of Winterhome)

When day turned dark and shadows fell
Across the broken lands
And madness turned to taloned claws
Our ancient ruler's hands
Then eight were called by whims of fate
To save us from our doom;
The Chosen came to guard us all
And lay evil in its tomb

[chorus]   If a Wizard Lord should turn
          Against the common man
          These Chosen eight would bring him down,
          Bring peace to Barokan!

The Leader shows his bold resolve
Confronting every foe
His words would guide the Chosen as
He told them how to go

The Seer sought the comrades out
And gathered them to fight
Nor could their foeman hide from her;
She has the second sight

[chorus]

The Swordsman's blade is swift and sure
His skill is unsurpassed

If any stood against him, then
That stand would be his last

A lovely face the Beauty has,
And shapely legs and arms
She distracted evil men
And lured them with her charms

[chorus]

There is no lock nor guarded door
That can stop the Thief
He penetrates the fortress dark
To bring the land relief

Every song and story told,
The Scholar knows them all
He knew the wizard's weaknesses
To hasten evil's fall

[chorus]

The Archer's missiles never miss;
His arrows find their mark
He struck at evil from afar
To drive away the dark

The Speaker harks to every tongue,
Of stone and beast and man
She found the Dark Lord's secrets out
So no defense could stand

[chorus]

When in the Galbek Hills there was
A monster come in human shape

The Swordsman struck the evil down
To save the land from magic rape

And thus the last of evil's spawn
Was driven out of Barokan
Never more will madness come
To trouble Barokan

No new Wizard Lord will turn
Against the common man
These Chosen eight shall keep him wise,
Bring peace to Barokan—
Yes, the Chosen guard us all,
Bring peace to Barokan!

THE
NINTH
TALISMAN

[PROLOGUE]

His true name began Erren Zal Tuyo kam Darig seveth Tirinsir abek Du, but the people of Mad Oak, in Longvale, did not use true names, for fear of the power they granted. He had grown up with the nickname Breaker, but after he took on the role of the Chosen Swordsman even his family and closest friends came, in time, to call him Sword. He was a big man—"Breaker" had reflected not his temperament, but his awkwardness before his coordination caught up with his growth—but now that he had reached his full height and become comfortable with his size, he moved with speed, grace, and assurance.

Some of that grace doubtlessly came from his magic, of course. The *ler* of muscle and steel had made him the world's greatest swordsman as part of the complicated pact that gave the Wizard Lord authority over all Barokan, and that gave the eight Chosen the right to remove the Wizard Lord, by any means necessary, should he violate the limits set upon his power.

He had played his role as Swordsman, and had slain the Dark Lord of the Galbek Hills, a Wizard Lord gone mad. He had played his part, and then he had returned home to Mad Oak.

And now, three years after the Dark Lord's death, Sword sat in the pavilion talking with Younger Priestess, one of the three individuals in the town who could communicate with the spirits of land and life and thereby keep Mad Oak habitable. Without Priest, Elder Priestess, and Younger Priestess, there would be no one to coax the soil into yielding crops, no one to convince game to allow hunters to kill it, no one to keep the wild *ler* beyond the borders from encroaching on the town.

That sometimes meant that the priestesses had little time to spare to talk to other humans; talking to the *ler* kept them busy. For the moment, though, on a cold night in early winter, after most of the town's inhabitants had gone home to huddle in their beds, Younger Priestess had found time to speak quietly with Sword in the town's deserted pavilion.

After all, human souls were *ler,* too, and sometimes needed a priestess's attention.

The two of them sat on the edge of the great stone hearth, the remains of a fire flickering amid the ashes behind them, keeping the worst of the winter's chill at bay. Most of the lanterns had gone out; a few still glimmered by the door, but most of the vast interior was dim and shadowed. The glowing sigil on the priestess's forehead, the sign of the *ler*'s favor, shone vividly gold in the darkness.

They sat quietly for several minutes after the last other people had left, but eventually Younger Priestess broke the silence.

"You don't seem happy, Sword," she said. "Your soul is clouded."

He shrugged without looking directly at her. "I am well enough," he said.

"Well enough? No more than that?"

He turned to face her directly. "Should I be more than that?"

"Why not? Your sisters are more than just well enough. I see Harp's soul shining like the dawn when her fingers are on the strings and the drums are beating, or when she thinks about the child she is to bear. Fidget's soul leaps like a flame when she watches the boys at play, and Spider's dances in delight when she runs through the streets with her playmates. Your mother is still weighed down by your father's death, and by your role among the Chosen, and the knowledge that you aren't happy, so hers is clouded as well. Time will help with her sorrows, but yours? I don't know what causes them, so I don't know if time will disperse or thicken them. I would like to dispel those clouds, if I can."

"I doubt you can," Sword said, turning away again. "After all, I killed a man; shouldn't my soul be darkened forever by such an act?"

"But he was a murderer and a madman, a Dark Lord who deserved nothing but death," Younger Priestess said. "You played your role well."

"A role I no longer believe should exist," Sword said.

"Oh?" Younger Priestess frowned. "You think you should pass the role of Swordsman on to another?"

"No, I didn't say *I* shouldn't be the Swordsman; I said the role shouldn't exist at all. I don't think there should *be* a Swordsman."

Her frown deepened. "But then who would slay a new Dark Lord, should one arise? Do you think the Archer and the other Chosen could do as well without a Swordsman?"

"There shouldn't be any Chosen. There shouldn't be any Dark Lords. There shouldn't be any more Wizard Lords."

"No Wizard Lord? But then who would keep the *other* wizards in check?"

"No one. The other wizards are no longer a threat. There hasn't been a rogue wizard in centuries."

"Because we have the Wizard Lord to prevent them!"

"But there are so few wizards left, we don't *need* a Wizard Lord!"

She stared at him for a moment, then said, "You don't know what you're talking about."

Startled, he turned and stared back.

"Haven't you learned your ballads?" she asked him. " 'The Siege of Blueflower'? 'The Slaughter at Goln Vleys'?"

"I know the songs," Sword replied, a trifle sullenly. "That was a long time ago. There were hundreds of wizards back then; there aren't even two dozen left today."

"One is all it takes to cause trouble."

"How much trouble can one ordinary wizard cause?"

Again, she stared at him in silence for a moment. Then she said, "Did you know that a wizard once came here, to what's now Mad Oak, intent on carrying off women for his harem? One wizard, and that was enough to cause havoc."

Startled, Sword said, "A rogue wizard came here? Is there a song?"

"No, no song. No story. Just a memory, from long ago, before there was any Wizard Lord to protect us."

"What? A memory? But there have been Wizard Lords for seven hundred years."

"And this happened perhaps eight hundred years ago, before the Council of Immortals chose the first Wizard Lord, centuries before the Mad Oak first grew, when the village here had no name of its own."

"Then how can there be a memory? No one lives eight hundred years."

"No person does, but *ler* can, and *ler* can be made to pass along memories, from one priestess to another. One of my ancestors, the one who defeated that wizard, thought it was important that the story should be passed along, and she had no faith in human storytellers. She feared they would clutter the truth up with dashing heroics and grand speeches, so instead she gave her memories to the *ler* of the hearthstone in the village shrine, and each priestess since has received them from the stone in her turn."

"So this lone priestess defeated a rogue wizard? That hardly makes it seem as if he was much of a threat. What happened?"

"I told you my ancestor did not trust human storytellers; I will not betray her trust by playing the part of one. If you would like to know what it was like, what she did and thought and felt, then come with me now, down to the shrine, and I will let you remember it for yourself."

"You can *do* that?"

"I think so, yes. Perhaps not for just anyone, but you are one of the Chosen, bound to *ler,* so I think the hearthstone will let you receive it."

Sword tried to look into her eyes, to read the expression there, but the surrounding darkness and the glow of the mark on her brow made it impossible to see anything there but blackness.

"All right," he said. "Show me, then."

Fifteen minutes later he knelt before the shrine, his forehead touching the bitterly cold stone of the unlit hearth, as Younger Priestess spoke quietly in a tongue not meant for human ears. He was beginning to regret agreeing to this when suddenly the cold vanished, the winter night disappeared, and he was walking between trees, walking in daylight, walking with an unfamiliar gait, with hips not his own, hips that swung in a way a man's did not. His shoulders were suddenly narrower, his arms weaker, his chest pulled forward.

He was a young woman, returning from a ritual placating the game spirits in the forest northeast of town. He was a priestess named Tala. . . .

Tala brushed the dirt from her skirt as she walked out of the grove, and straightened the bow on her shoulder. Then she looked up at the village, squinting slightly—her eyes were unaccustomed to the bright sunlight after so long in the shade of the trees. A strong breeze stirred her hair, but she paid it no attention.

Something looked odd—or perhaps merely *felt* odd; she could never be entirely sure where her own perceptions ended and the influence of the local spirits began. She shaded her eyes and peered, and opened herself to the *ler,* but even then it took her a moment to realize what was wrong.

All the men were gone. There were women working in the fields, and children running about, but the men of the village were nowhere to be seen.

"Oh, now what?" she asked no one in particular.

The men are gone, something replied. She was unsure which *ler,* which spirit, had spoken, but she didn't particularly care. They were all connected in any case.

"I can see that," she said. "*Why* are they gone?"

To defend the village.

The "voice" came from the earth itself, she realized, rather than any lesser spirit. The essence of the village's soil knew everything that happened within its bounds, a broad oval stretching from the far ridgetop to a point a little over half a mile into the forest she had just left, but it wasn't an especially bright being by human standards—or perhaps it simply didn't understand humans well enough to apply whatever intelligence it might have. Tala was fairly certain it was not going to volunteer any further explanations. Getting useful information from it was possible, but required asking exactly the right questions.

Tala did not have the patience to properly interrogate the earth-spirits just now, after spending three days and nights in the wood dealing with the stubborn forest *ler.* She was tired and hungry and her back was sore from sleeping on the hard ground, and once she got home she could ask Mama or Broom or Tanner what was happening. She did not ask any more questions, but began trotting toward the village.

She did say, "I thank you, spirits of my homeland, for your aid and answers," as she took her first steps. She wasn't about to forget the necessities in her hurry.

The path seemed straight and true before her, despite the wind rippling the barley in the fields, so she knew the *ler* had accepted her thanks and were not offended that she had not bothered to kneel. The earth-spirit was usually reasonable about that—not like the haughty, demanding spirits in her father's metal that only the smith's hammer could beat into submission, or the foul-tempered *ler* of the riverbank.

She saw her mother, up on the hillside with Tala's younger sisters, and waved, but her path did not lead in that direction. She could have turned aside, but the village was closer, and there would be someone there who could explain.

She could feel the *ler* around her with every step; something had disturbed them, she knew, though she could not guess its nature.

A moment later she passed the marker shrine into the village proper, hurried past the Carver family's house, and found a clump of half a dozen women talking quietly in the sunlit meeting common, their arms wrapped around themselves to protect them from the warm wind.

(Somewhere, Sword marveled at the sight of what he recognized as the town square, but without a single building he knew around it. There was no pavilion on the ridge, none of the houses he had grown up among—but then he realized that he could see the village shrine, and the hearthstone he now lay against, in the correct spot, though exposed to the elements, without their familiar shelter.)

"What's happening?" Tala called as she approached.

Her voice was almost lost in the murmur of the wind, but six worried faces turned toward her, her aunt Tanner among them.

"Priestess!" Tanner said. "There you are! We were beginning to worry."

Tala glanced up at the sun. "I'm not late," she said. "It's not yet noon."

"But . . . well, we thought you might have heard and cut your ritual short."

Tala ignored the foolishness of suggesting the ritual could be shortened; if she had been so disrespectful as that, the forest would have allowed the village no venison, no coney, no walnuts, not so much as a mushroom for the next year. "Heard *what*?" she asked. "Where are the men?"

"They're at the border," Tanner replied, gesturing in the general direction of the ridgetop.

"An attack is coming," Redlocks added.

"An attack? What kind of attack?"

"Armed men. From another place."

That made no sense. Armed men could not simply walk through the wilderness to attack the town. "But nobody would . . . But how? Why? How do they know these men are coming?"

"Priest said so. He was walking the bounds, and the spirits warned him. He came and got all the men, and they left about an hour ago to meet the enemy at the border, just over the ridge."

Tala was still puzzled. She had never heard of such a thing. No one had ever threatened the village before. "Who's attacking us?"

"We don't know," Tanner said. "Priest said the warning just said it was many men."

"*Ler* generally can't count very well," Tala commented.

"He said he had asked if there were more men than we had in the village, and the spirits said there were about that many, maybe a few more or a few less."

"So all the men went out to fight them off?"

The women nodded. "That way," Tanner said, pointing. "Across the ridge."

"They took spears," Greeneye said.

"And bows," Redlocks added. "Smith wanted to bring one, but of course you had his with you."

Tala tugged at the bow slung on her shoulder. She had been showing it to the game spirits in the forest, so they would know what would strike down their creatures. "My father couldn't hit anything with an arrow anyway." That was due as much to his occupation as anything else; something of the fire and iron clung to him and disturbed the *ler* of bow and arrow, making it reluctant to do his will. Tala had tried to teach him a little of the archery spirit's true name, so that he might force its cooperation, but he had laughed and said he saw no need. The village had enough hunters without him, and no other smiths.

"But it would look that much more fearsome, a big man like that with a bow," Chitchat said.

"They want to frighten the attackers off, not kill anyone," Tanner offered. "It wouldn't matter whether he could hit anything."

"Priest said he would arrange some surprises," Redlocks added.

And of course, Tala knew, he would. He would talk to the *ler* and make sure that every sharp pebble found its way under an invader's foot, that muddy earth would be more slippery than it looked, that birds and rabbits would startle at just the right moment, that sawgrass would cut at the foe's ankles and branches would whip at their eyes. The defenders would be untouched by these hazards, perhaps protected behind cooperative bushes or friendly trees. All the local spirits would come to the aid of their own people, and help drive away the intruders. The village, human and *ler* together, was a single community.

And the invaders must *know* that. Tala frowned. *Every* village had its own patron spirits to protect it.

Something didn't make sense. A large group of men? Who in all of Barokan would be stupid enough to make such an attack? How could they get there? What could they hope to accomplish?

And how could the spirits have *known* that these strangers intended to attack the village?

Tala knew there was no point in asking the village women; none of them knew much of anything about *ler*. Only priests and priestesses, the men and women born on a midsummer's night when the full moon was in the sky, could hear the spirits' voices and learn to bargain with them.

Which, at the moment, meant Tala, whom the villagers called Little Priestess, and Dein, generally known as Priest—naturally they did not use even the shortest fragments of their true names in the course of normal events. They were the village's only contacts with the spirit world, needed to coax the crops to grow and the game to draw near, to regulate the rain and keep the frost away until the harvest was in, to calm the river when the spring floods raged.

Dein was almost twenty years older than Tala, and had been her mentor throughout childhood, introducing her to the *ler,* teaching her their names, explaining the long-standing agreements the priests of previous generations had negotiated. She was grown now, and taking on a larger share of the priestly duties, including the three-day annual ritual of meeting with the inhabitants of the forest to bargain for the right to hunt there. And she was beginning to suspect, from some things the spirits had said, that she was already better at the job than Dein had ever been. Sometimes Dein seemed to just go through the motions, without *thinking* about what the *ler* told him.

Had he thought to ask how the spirits of the village lands knew the attackers were coming? By their very nature, most of the spirits could not travel beyond the bounds—they were confined to their own territory, and in fact the village lands were *defined* by the territory where this particular community of *ler* dwelt. The priests of one village could not command the *ler* of another; the very laws of nature, the rules by which the spirits operated, varied from one place to another. Dein could not have spoken to any *ler* outside his own village, so spirits inside the village must have warned him—but how? They could not have seen the invaders approaching.

Tala tried to find sense in it. Why would anyone attack the village? How could Dein have been warned of their approach?

She had already had a lifetime of practice in asking such questions, in order to deal with the *ler* and their inhuman logic. Their behavior often seemed strange and irrational, but there was always a reason for what they did. She just had to figure out what it was.

A spirit had told Dein an attack was coming, but *was* anyone actually attacking? What if the warning had been false? What did someone hope to accomplish?

Well, what *had* it accomplished?

It had sent all the men and weapons to the far side of the ridge, leaving only unarmed women and children and a few old men in the village itself. If she had been here, instead of in the forest, she would undoubtedly have gone along as well, leaving the women and children without even a means to hear any warnings the *ler* might give.

That was surely what their actual foe had intended.

"Oh," she said. "Oh, spirits, defend us!"

We stand ready, a chorus replied. *The air is troubled and hostile, and we are ready to face whatever it may bring.*

"What is it?" Tanner asked. "What's wrong? Did the spirits say something?"

"No," she said, not entirely accurately. "I just thought of something." She looked around.

Several of the village women were working in the surrounding fields, soothing the *ler* of earth and plant with the simple chants that had been passed down through the generations, driving away birds and insects, checking to see how soon the crops would be ready to harvest. Others, her own mother among them, were tending children, scattered across the fallow fields on the hillside.

Gathering them all together to organize a defense might take an hour or more—and a defense against what? Tala was certain the attack that had drawn the men away was a fraud, a feint, a distraction, and that the real attack would be made on the village itself, but she still did not know what sort of an attack it might be. The spirits' reference to troubled air could mean anything.

The village had no enemies, no treasures worth stealing. Their lives were comfortable, but not luxurious, and their possessions were the ordinary substance of everyday existence. No one could steal the land itself; the fields would be barren, the game elusive, the water foul, without the services of a priest or priestess to coax cooperation from the *ler*, and only a priest who had been born here could serve.

The only things worth taking, she realized, were the villagers themselves.

And *that*, she knew, was all too possible. There were places where people kept slaves. There were landless rogue males who wanted women as wives or concubines.

And there were said to be *ler* that demanded human sacrifices. Oh, not in the immediate area, but there were stories about communities in the flat country to the south, or in the marshlands to the west. Their raiding parties were said to roam far and wide, abducting travelers and dragging them back to die on bloodstained altars.

Someone had lured the men away by giving Dein a false warning, and now the real attackers would descend on the undefended village . . .

"What is it?" Tanner asked. "What did you think of?"

"How could anyone give a false warning?" Tala said aloud.

The warning came on the wind, the earth told her.

"Well, they *couldn't*," Tanner said. "That's how Priest knew . . . Priestess, what's wrong?"

"There are people who could give a false warning," Tala said.

"But the *spirits* warned Priest, not a person."

"And who told the spirits?"

The warning came on the wind, the *ler* repeated.

The women looked at one another.

"I don't understand," Redlocks said.

"The only people who can command *ler* are priests and wizards," Tanner said.

"I don't think this was a priest," Tala said. "We don't have any enemies among the priests of Longvale. And I have never heard of priests who could command the wind that blows freely from place to place, yet the spirits tell me the wind carried the warning."

A gust of wind rustled blouses and sent skirts flapping.

"Oh, burning fire!" Greeneye said. "You think there's a *wizard* involved in this attack?"

Everyone knew that just as priests learned to control the *ler* of specific places, wizards learned to control *ler* who were not so constrained—the *ler* of air and fire, of heat and cold, of migratory birds and wandering beasts. And where priests were at the heart of their communities, most wizards were outcasts, as rootless and unreliable as the *ler* they commanded.

The wind swirled dust up from the common and whipped at Tala's hair as she said, "I think there's a rogue wizard on his way to the village right now—or perhaps he's already here."

There is a stranger among you, the earth beneath her agreed. *He has not touched me, and so I did not know him until you spoke.*

Tala raised her arms. "Spirits of earth and air, I beseech you, reveal to me any enemy that may be present!"

She could sense a struggle around her as the village *ler* bent their power to the task she had given them; then the wind shifted, and from the corner of her eye Tala saw a flicker. She whirled.

It was as if a veil was blowing away in tattered pieces, gradually exposing the man standing by the village's central shrine. Tala turned to face him directly.

He was tall, and wore crossed leather belts over a blue silk tunic. Loops on the belts held at least a dozen assorted pouches and talismans, and the pockets of his leather breeches bulged with more; rings shone on every finger, each undoubtedly representing a spirit he held in thrall. A blue cap was set jauntily on his head, still securely in place despite the unnatural wind, and he was smiling sardonically at Tala.

And he was hanging in the air, an inch or two off the familiar soil of the village.

"Very good, Priestess," he said.

Redlocks shrieked and ran; Greeneye backed away whimpering. The others stared, stunned, at this apparition.

"The wind was the clue," Tala said. "You made a wind-spirit tell them an attack was coming."

The wizard's grin widened. "Indeed I did, and now they're all thrashing about on the wrong side of the ridge, looking for a nonexistent army, while I have my pick of their women." He glanced around. "I see a few who would suit me."

Tala stared at him for a moment as the others backed away; she was thinking furiously, trying to devise some way to repel this invader and protect her people.

The bow on her shoulder was not strung; in the time it would take to string it, draw an arrow from the quiver on her back, nock, draw, and release, the wizard could unleash a dozen spells. He obviously controlled several wind-spirits, and probably fire-spirits as well; the wind might snatch the bow from her hands, the fire burn it to ash, before she could loose.

Likewise, she could send a message through the *ler* and summon the men of the village home, but even if they ran, the wizard would have a quarter of an hour to work his will upon their women. He could easily pick a few and carry them off in that time.

And the women—well, they could put up a fine resistance, she was sure, but how many would be hurt by wind or fire or other magic? How much damage would be done to houses and crops?

As for the native spirits, what could they do? The wizard could obviously fly above any attack they might make.

Fighting him was not the solution.

But what was? She could hardly let him rape and enslave any of her fellow villagers. Even Felri, who had teased Tala mercilessly when they were children until the *ler* began tripping her repeatedly, did not deserve that.

She had to do *something*. Protecting the village was her job, her role, the task she had been born to. It was a burden she did not always enjoy, but she had never failed to bear it. Even when she had been so sick of the constant demands of the *ler* that she had dreamed of leaving the village and going somewhere she would be just an ordinary young woman, she had never considered doing so until another priest or priestess was born.

But now she could see no way to carry out her duty.

No way but one.

She said, "I'll go. Take me."

A sudden stillness fell over everything; Tala knew she had the undivided attention of the spirits around them.

The wizard's grin vanished. "What?"

"Take me," Tala repeated. "Get me out of this village."

He cocked his head to one side, and one hand closed on a wooden talisman carved into a shape like a candle flame. "Why? I'm not looking for a wife or an apprentice, woman, just a whore, to warm my bed and scrub my floors."

"A slave, of course. And what am I here?" Tala replied. "I spend my days being ordered about by the *ler,* running their errands so that they'll allow the rest of the village to live unmolested. I have no husband—you think that's by choice? The *ler* forbid me to bed a man! No man, no children, no land of my own, no time to do anything but run hither and yon at the spirits' bidding! I spent the last three nights sleeping in the forest, rather than my own bed, at the whim of these spirits! Better to scrub your floors, wizard."

The stillness shattered. *You lie,* a hundred voices said in unison. *You lie!*

Tala turned and shouted at the bare ground, "What do you know about it? What do you know of the human heart? Better a human wizard than a lifetime of you!"

"But, Priestess . . ." Tanner began, and Tala whirled to face her.

"Don't start, Aunt!" she said. "You don't know what it's like any more than the *ler* themselves do!" Then she turned back to the wizard. "Take me with you. I'm so *tired* of this! Let Priest fend off the disease!"

Once again a sudden hush fell, though Tala could feel the earth, the stones and grass and the air itself, listening intently.

"Disease?" the wizard said. Tala could feel the *ler* echoing the question, and hoped the wizard could not sense it as well.

"Don't worry about that!" she said desperately. "*I* don't have it, I promise! I swear, by the spirits around us, I do not have the plague!"

The wizard's gaze flashed from one woman to the next, Tanner to Greeneye to Chitchat. "What about them?" he asked.

"Don't worry about them," Tala said. "The *ler* protect them from its ravages as long as they're here."

"And elsewhere?"

"They don't go anywhere else. No one leaves here. No traders come here. You know that. Isn't that why you chose us?"

"Do they *all* have it?"

"Just take me with you!" She stretched out her arms and took a step toward him.

The wizard drifted back, bumping against the shrine and knocking his hat askew. His face had gone pale.

Then he straightened up and pointed a talisman at Tala. "I think not," he said. "Stay back, Priestess; I have changed my mind. I think I will find another village, one more to my liking." He reached up with his free hand and doffed his cap, then returned it to its proper place. "Your pardon, ladies, but I think I will be going now."

The wind, which had died away somewhat, suddenly rose to a howl, and seemed to wrap itself about him; he flickered and faded and was gone.

"No, wait!" Tala cried.

"Farewell, Priestess," his voice answered from somewhere overhead. Tala looked up, blinking in the sunlight, but could see nothing but blue sky and high clouds. The wind whipped her hair across her face and stung her eyes, and she had to turn away.

Then she pulled the bow from her shoulder, pulling it free of her thrashing hair, and knelt as she strung it.

"Spirits of my homeland, hide me from my enemy," she said, her words inaudible to human ears over the roar of the wind. "Forgive me lies told in your service. Guide me to strike down your foe." The string snapped taut, and she drew an arrow from the quiver on her back. "If you feel it just, drive this shaft of wood from your forests through his heart, so that he may never return to trouble us again."

She was far more concerned about what he might do to other villages, but a return would be possible if he realized she had been bluffing, and she knew that the *ler* of this land really did not care at all what might happen elsewhere.

We forgive your deception.

No word about her intentions—or theirs—toward the wizard. She grimaced. Then she stood, and turned until the direction felt right; at least one of the spirits was guiding her, but whether accurately or not she could not say. She nocked the arrow, drew it to her ear, aimed it upward, and let fly.

The wind seemed to snatch the shaft from the bow; it sailed high and far, and vanished into the air.

And then she heard a brief scream, and the wind abruptly died away as the wizard's lifeless form plummeted from the sky into old Brewer's barley field, landing with a hideous thump.

For a long moment after that the world seemed unnaturally still; then Tanner said, "You killed him."

Tala did not bother answering; she was listening to the spirits. Several were speaking at once, telling her that the men were on the way back, that the touch of the wizard's talismans and bindings upon the field was an abomination that must be removed but that his blood would freshen the earth once they were gone, that she was forgiven her lies.

She wondered whether they realized how close to the truth her lies had been. She had never really intended to accompany the wizard, to become his property; she had had quite enough of feeling herself to be the property of the entire village, and could not see a single master as an improvement. That speech about the endless demands made on her, though, had come from her heart. She had never asked to be a priestess.

But then, she had never asked to be born at all, yet she was very glad to be alive. Sometimes she enjoyed the prerogatives of the priesthood, as well.

She thought for a moment about those talismans the wizard had carried. With those, if she could learn how to use them, she might be able to control the winds as the wizard had, to fly through the sky, or conceal herself from sight. That was tempting.

But really, what would she do with such powers?

For all her life she had had her priestly powers, the ability to bargain with the *ler*, to coax favors from them. What had they gotten her that any other young woman didn't have, and what had they cost her? What would she do with even *more* supernatural power? She looked at Tanner's face, and Chitchat's, and saw that her own neighbors, her own aunt, were frightened of her.

And as her arrow had demonstrated, the wizard's charms would not hide her from the *ler*.

Why bother, then? What had the wizard himself gotten out of his magic? He had come here to steal women—what a miserable, lonely existence he must have led to resort to such brutality!

And with that thought, all temptation to steal the wizard's magic was gone, and the urge to leave the village as well. Think how *lonely* life must be for people who could not speak to every rock or tree!

"I thank you, spirits of my homeland, for your aid and answers," she said, as she unstrung her bow.

Then she sighed and marched toward the barley field to deal with the mess.

Sword straightened up slowly; his back was stiff from the cold.

"You see?" Younger Priestess said. "We need a Wizard Lord to keep such people away! Deception and rape and murder, from a lone wizard!"

"This Tala seems to have dealt quite effectively with that one by herself," Sword said, as he got slowly to his feet. He did not bother pointing out that the long-ago wizard had not managed to rape or murder anyone. "I think that if people organized themselves properly, we wouldn't need anyone to help us against the wizards."

"But think how clever that wizard was, luring away the men! If Tala hadn't been quick-witted with her lies . . ."

"But she was," Sword interrupted.

"But what if she weren't? As long as there are wizards, we still need a Wizard Lord. And as long as there is a Wizard Lord, we need the Chosen. We need *you*."

"Maybe," Sword said. He shivered slightly. "It's late, and I'm cold. Good night, Priestess—and thank you for that little taste of the distant past; it does give me something to think about."

Younger Priestess stared at him for a moment, then gave up. "Good night, then, Sword," she said.

As he walked back toward his mother's house, Sword thought about what he had just experienced, but it was not merely the danger of uncontrolled wizardry he considered. Instead he found himself remembering what it was like to be a woman, with a body that moved differently, always aware that you were vulnerable in ways men were not. And what it was like to be a priestess, bound to the spirits of the land, always surrounded by the inhuman voices of the *ler*.

He had spent months in the company of the Speaker of All Tongues, known as Babble, who heard *all* the *ler,* not just those who cooperated with the local priests; now he had some inkling of what she lived with constantly, the barrage of voices and demands.

But he had also experienced the closeness of Tala's ties to her home. Sword had long felt himself strangely isolated from his fellows; even before he accepted the role of Chosen Swordsman, he had sometimes felt as if he didn't really fit in here in Mad Oak.

Now he knew just how well a person *could* fit in here; Tala had been his opposite in many ways. She had been a part of the town, as he was not—but she had been confined by it, as well as supported.

Everything had its price, had both benefits and costs. That was simply how the world was. All anyone could do was to try to find the right balance.

The existence of the Wizard Lord and the Chosen was a part of the system that had kept Barokán peaceful for centuries, and whether he liked it or not, the system was in place. It was something he had to accept.

At least, as long as there were wizards. If they someday died out, then everything would change.

And there were only about eighteen or nineteen wizards left in all of Barokan. They *were* dying out, slowly.

There might yet be an end to wizards and wizardry and Wizard Lords someday, and no more need for the Chosen.

Someday.

But not today. Not yet.

1

Sword paused on the path below the pavilion, an empty jug in his hand. Standing a few yards past the brewer's house that marked the end of the village's central cluster of homes, he leaned forward, listening.

He thought at first it might just be an echo of someone speaking up in the pavilion, that rambling ridgetop structure that served as the village's communal storehouse and gathering place, but the direction was wrong even for an echo. In all the years he had lived here, all the hundreds of times he had walked this path, he had never before encountered such an auditory illusion.

Then he thought he might be imagining it, or hearing spirit voices rather than anything physical, but no, he could definitely hear something happening far ahead, off to the left, in the trees—not in the pavilion or anywhere else in the village lands, but in the trees beyond the edge of town. It wasn't birds, he was sure, nor squirrels chittering. There were several voices speaking, real ones, human ones, and much rustling and thrashing.

He frowned, wondering what *that* was about. There weren't any homes or fields down that way; the town of Mad Oak ended at the boundary shrine a hundred yards ahead, and the sounds were coming from somewhere well beyond that, in the wilderness.

The voices were human and male, but he had no idea what men would be doing out there. The old path to Willowbank ran through that general area, but no one used it anymore, not since the guide had retired. Even when the Willowbank Guide had been working, no one would have been thrashing about like that. The local *ler,* the spirits of that particular bit of forest, were not likely to appreciate such a disturbance. *Ler* that had made their accommodation with humanity would tolerate it, and a man could generally rattle about in town without worrying about angering the spirit of each branch he brushed aside, or each blade of grass he trod upon, but out in the wild beyond the border the spirits were not so forgiving. Anyone venturing out there was likely to find thorns embedding themselves in his legs, branches lashing at his eyes, and the entire natural world in general trying to kill him.

So who was making all that noise?

Sword looked down at the jug in his hand, and at his empty belt. If he had been wearing his sword he might have decided to investigate, but he had just been going up to Brewer's storeroom under the pavilion to fetch a gallon of beer. He hadn't seen any reason to go armed. He had his silver talisman in his pocket, as he always did, but had not his sword, nor any *ara* feathers to ward off hostile magic; he could almost certainly survive a little jaunt into the wilderness, but it might be unpleasant.

"What's happening?" someone asked from behind him. "Sword, do you know?"

"No," Sword replied. "I don't think it's anything to do with me." He turned to discover that half a dozen townsfolk had heard the commotion as he had, and had emerged from their homes to peer into the underbrush beyond the boundary, trying to make out what was going on.

"They're coming closer." Sword knew the woman who said that as Curly.

"Yes, they are," he agreed. He realized that the others were all watching him expectantly, and he sighed. He knew that they thought that exploring this phenomenon was somehow his responsibility.

Being one of the Chosen, the eight magical defenders of Barokan, was not supposed to mean that he had to check out every potentially dangerous oddity that might happen along, but convincing his fellow townsfolk of that seemed to be impossible. They seemed to feel that if they had a hero living among them, they were entitled to see heroics.

"I'll get my sword," he said. He resisted the temptation to say anything about the beer; after all, he could fetch that any time.

He turned and trotted back through the village to the little house he shared with his mother and younger sisters, where he set the still-empty jug on the kitchen table and fetched his sword belt from the peg by the door. He buckled it in place, making sure the blade was loose in its sheath, then hurried back out, through the village square and along the path below the pavilion.

A score of the townsfolk had gathered at the boundary stone and were staring out into the forest, though none set so much as a toe beyond the marker. Much rustling, thumping, and unintelligible conversation could still be heard out in the wild. Whatever was making the noise seemed to have come a little closer.

As Sword neared the group one of his childhood friends, a big fellow called Brokenose, said, "They've been calling, but we haven't answered. We were waiting for you."

"Thank you," Sword said sourly, and not at all sincerely. He remembered why he and Brokenose didn't spend much time together anymore as he peered out into the trees. Sword was fairly certain he glimpsed movement, though he was not sure what he was seeing. "Has anyone told Priest or the priestesses?"

"Younger Priestess is fetching Elder Priestess from the northern fields," said a man called Flute. "Priest is still ill."

"Ill" was a euphemism. Old Priest was dying, and everyone in Mad Oak knew it, though not all were willing to admit it. "I know he's ill," Sword said. "He should still be told."

"Won't the *ler* tell him?" Curly asked.

"Maybe," Sword acknowledged.

"*Ho, the village!*" came a distant cry. "Can't you hear us?"

Several people turned expectant faces toward Sword, who raised his hands to either side of his mouth. "We hear you!" he shouted back. "Who *are* you?"

There was a mutter of what might have been cheering, and then a voice called, "We'll explain when we get there!"

That triggered a round of murmuring, and Sword sighed again.

"Are you sure we should *let* them get here?" Curly asked.

"I'll go see who they are," Sword said, and with a hand on his sword hilt he marched down the slope.

He paused at the boundary shrine, knelt briefly, and said, "I thank you, spirits of my homeland, and pray that I may return safely to your protection." Then he rose and stepped past, into the wilderness.

He could feel the change instantly as he left behind the familiar, accepting *ler* of his village and stepped into the territory of the wild *ler* that dwelt outside human bounds. The air seemed suddenly hot and hostile, rather than warm and comforting. The gentle breeze turned harsh. Weeds tore at his trousers.

Most people in Mad Oak would never have dared to set foot beyond the shrine without a guide and the protection of *ara* feathers, but Sword, as one of the Chosen, was immune to most magic. Wild *ler* might harass him, but were unlikely to do him any serious harm. Except for the bloodthirsty Mad Oak itself, up on the ridgetop to the southwest, he did not think anything near the village posed a real threat to him, and even that terrible old tree had failed to lure him in the one time he had gotten close to it. Putting his hand on the hilt of his sword had been enough to alert the *ler* that protected him and break the oak's spell.

He kept a hand on his sword's hilt, just in case, as he marched boldly down into the birch grove.

He did not have to go far; as soon as he passed the first line of undergrowth that bordered the grove he could see the strangers, fifty yards away among the birches. There were at least a dozen of them, all big men in matching attire. They wore broad-brimmed, cloth-covered helmets crowned with *ara* feathers, and despite the heat they were clad in thick quilted jackets and leggings striped with dense rows of *ara* feathers—jackets and leggings that showed signs of hard use, with hundreds of little slashes and tears, patches of mud and smears of green, thorns and briars everywhere. The feathers were crumpled and broken in many places.

Clearly, these men were not appeasing the wild *ler*, nor dodging them, as a guide might, but were simply bulling their way through, relying on their strange clothing to protect them from lashing branches, stabbing thorns, and the claws and teeth of small animals. Heavy leather gloves held sticks and shovels and machetes, and the men were hacking and digging their way through the undergrowth. The damage to their protective clothing made it clear that the undergrowth and its *ler* had not yielded without a fight.

Sword had never seen anything like this before, nor heard of such a thing. The people of Barokan had always respected *ler,* always tried to cooperate with the spirits of the land and sky and forest. Every town and village had made accommodations with its own *ler,* usually through a priesthood that negotiated with them, and the land between the scattered communities had been left alone.

Until now. These men were clearly not leaving the wilderness alone.

Sword kept walking into the birch grove, watching the men intently. He didn't recognize any of them. None were from Mad Oak, nor were any of them guides he knew.

This whole scene was unspeakably bizarre. Whole gangs of men simply did not venture into the wilderness like this, and ordinarily *nobody* would tear up the natural landscape in such a brutal fashion, so utterly heedless of the *ler.* The normal thing to do would be to either try to slip through without disturbing the *ler,* or to appease them as best one could, but these men appeared to be deliberately antagonizing the wilderness spirits.

"Who *are* you?" Sword demanded, as soon as the strangers noticed his approach.

The slashing, chopping, and shoveling stopped as the entire party turned to look at him. "The Wizard Lord's road crew," one of them called back. "Who are *you,* coming out here unguarded?"

"I'm called Sword," Sword replied. "What do you mean, road crew?"

"Sword? The Swordsman? Really?" Several voices spoke at once, as the entire party lowered their tools and turned to stare.

"The Swordsman, yes." Sword drew his weapon and let it hang loosely in his hand. "Now, who are you people, and what are you doing here?"

"He told you, we're a road crew," a man called. He reached up and doffed his helmet, revealing sweat-matted hair and a long, half-healed slash across his forehead that seemed to indicate that at least one *ler* had put up resistance. "We're cutting a road through from Willowbank to Mad Oak."

Sword blinked and lowered his blade further. "Cutting a road?"

"That's right. You don't have a guide for this route anymore, so we're cutting a road, and if it's properly maintained you won't *need* a guide, ever again."

Sword struggled for a moment with this concept.

He knew that in the Midlands the towns were often so close together that they were connected by broad roads, wide enough for two carts to pass, where no guide was needed to protect travelers from the untamed *ler* of the wilderness; he had been there, and seen it for himself. But that was in the *Midlands,* where one town was only rarely separated from the next by more than a mile, and where the land between was as likely to be open grassland as forest. There were no open roads in Longvale, where a good ten miles of thick woods and marshland divided Mad Oak from Willowbank; there were only narrow, winding paths that required a skilled guide to navigate safely.

Or rather, there *had been* only narrow, dangerous paths until now. Looking past the self-proclaimed "road crew," Sword could see that they had indeed cut a broad, straight path through the forest—a strip of bare, sun-dappled brown earth stretching away as far as he could see, with mounds of chopped greenery lining either side. He could smell the rich scent of fresh soil, an odor he associated with fields, rather than forests.

Bits of leaf fluttered about those side mounds in ways that had nothing to do with the faint breeze that found its way through the birches, and little glimmers of light and color moved through them where no sunlight could reach; the *ler* of the plants and other things that had been cleared away were obviously still active, and struggling to respond to the disruption of their home.

The road itself, though, seemed clear and untroubled. Sword pointed at it. "That goes all the way to Willowbank?"

"Indeed it does," said the man who had first told him he faced a road crew, glancing proudly back over his shoulder. "Oh, it's not all as straight as that, as we had to route it around the bogs, but it's a good road. And before that we cut a road from Rock Bridge to Willowbank, and from Broadpool to Rock Bridge."

"You did?"

"We did. And if the other crews have done their jobs, you can now walk from here all the way to Winterhome without a guide, so long as you stay on the road and wear a few feathers."

That was more than Sword could comprehend all at once. "Winter-home?"

"Winterhome. That's where the Wizard Lord lives, after all."

Sword nodded. "Of course," he agreed.

He had heard that the current Wizard Lord had chosen Winterhome as his home. He had vaguely wondered why, since he knew the Wizard Lord was not a native of Winterhome, but he had not pursued the matter. After all, a Wizard Lord could live anywhere in Barokan that he chose; if the current one wanted to live at the foot of the Eastern Cliffs, in the town where the Uplanders wintered, that was his business, and none of Sword's concern.

But Winterhome had to be a hundred miles away. Could there really be a highway all the way there, through all that wilderness? He stared at the road.

After a moment's awkward silence, the apparent crew chief turned and called, "All right, now, we have work to do! We want this cut through to Mad Oak while it's still light—with luck we'll dance with the girls in the town's pavilion tonight!"

A murmur of agreement sounded. The men lifted their tools and resumed hacking at the underbrush, extending their road through the birch grove.

Sword shifted his gaze from the road vanishing into the forest to the hands swinging machetes and hoes. He stared for a moment, then turned without another word and headed back to town.

This was all strange and new, and he had no idea how to react to it, but it did not seem to call for hostility. The road crew was not breaking any laws, so far as he knew. It was not *customary* to disturb all those wild *ler,* but there was no formal stricture forbidding it. As long as the men stopped at the boundary shrine, and did nothing to upset the town's own *ler,* there was no obvious reason to interfere.

Besides, Sword had no real authority in Mad Oak; he wasn't a priest. He would go back and let the rest of the town decide what to do.

As he neared the boundary he could see a score of his townsfolk waiting for him just beyond the shrine—not just those who had been there before, but more. Elder and Younger Priestess had joined the party, and looked unhappy; the sigils of office on their foreheads seemed to be pulsing and glowing red, rather than their usual pale and steady gold. Sword waved to them to indicate that all was well, but he was not actually sure that was true.

"What's happening?" Younger Priestess called. "The *ler* are upset!"

"They're building a road," Sword called back. "All the way to . . . to Willowbank."

The priestesses exchanged glances; then Elder called, "They're doing *what*?"

"Building a road," Sword repeated, though he was close enough to the border now that he no longer needed to shout. "They're clearing a path through the wilderness, so we won't need guides anymore."

"Can they *do* that? What about all the *ler*?" Younger Priestess asked. Her hand reached up to rub at her forehead.

Sword shrugged. "The men don't appear to be having any real problems. A few cuts and scratches. They're wearing protective clothing and carrying *ara* feathers."

"They *are* disturbing the *ler,* though," Elder said. "Many, many *ler.* We can hear them."

"And feel them," Younger added.

Sword glanced over his shoulder at the flashing machetes and thumping shovels. "They don't seem to care."

"Well, they don't need to live here!" Younger exclaimed. "Those are *our ler* . . ."

"No," Elder said thoughtfully. "They aren't." She looked at Sword. "They'll stop at the border?"

"I assume so. One of them said something about dancing in our pavilion tonight. I don't think they mean *us* any harm, nor anything in Mad Oak."

"They're disrupting many spirits, though—earth and leaf and tree. And those won't just quietly vanish."

The light and movement in those mounds alongside the road had told Sword as much. "What *will* they do?" he asked, genuinely curious. "I've never heard of anything like this."

The priestess frowned. "Well, they'll dissipate *eventually*—a *ler* like that without a home, without a solid object to bind it to our world, fades away in time."

"Not all *ler* are tied to objects, though," Sword protested, looking down at the sword in his hand.

"The *ler* of the land are," Elder said. "Any *ler* a priest can deal with is. The so-called higher *ler,* the abstract *ler,* they're the domain of wizards, not priests, and I doubt they're being disturbed by this. These men aren't defying wind or fire or strength or warmth or any of those, they're uprooting branch and stalk, and turning earth."

"So the disturbed *ler* will dissipate . . ."

"Eventually. But until then they'll strike out in any way they can. They'll form into misshapen ghosts to strike at their attackers, they'll look for things they can possess, new homes they can claim."

"But the men are protected," Sword said. "They're wearing *ara* feathers, and good sturdy clothes."

"Then they may be safe enough, but I won't walk that road they're building any time soon. And I think we may want to keep a close watch on the livestock and the children for the next few days, and be wary of bad dreams." She looked Sword in the eye. "Did they say who began this? Whose idea it was, to battle the natural order in this way?"

"The Wizard Lord," Sword said. "The Lord of Winterhome."

"Ah," Elder said. For a moment no one spoke; then she added, "Do you think you may need to kill him?"

The question was not as bizarre as it might seem, and Sword took it very seriously. The Wizard Lord was selected by the other wizards of Barokan, the so-called Council of Immortals, to rule over all the land from the Eastern Cliffs to the Western Isles, and was given great magical power to do so. The Wizard Lord controlled the weather, and had power over wind and fire, over disease, and over many of the beasts of the wilderness. He was empowered to serve as judge and executioner of any wizard who misbehaved, and any criminal who fled from the towns into the wild.

And as a check on the dangers of such great power, eight ordinary people were chosen to take up special roles and receive limited magical powers of their own, and it was the duty of these eight to remove any Wizard Lord who proved himself unfit for his high office.

Sword, the Swordsman, was one of the Chosen. The silver talisman he always carried in his pocket bound him to the *ler* of muscle and steel and ensured that he was the world's greatest swordsman, unbeatable in single combat. In the past, when Wizard Lords had gone bad, it was usually the Swordsmen of the time who eventually slew them.

This particular Swordsman had thought the job was ceremonial when he first accepted it, as more than a century had passed without any known misbehavior by a Wizard Lord, but that long streak of good fortune had already been broken once. Several years ago Sword had struck down the Dark Lord of the Galbek Hills with a single blow to the heart.

But that Wizard Lord had slaughtered a village; this one was merely building roads. How could building roads be a crime punishable by death? Yes, it disturbed the natural order, but who did it really harm?

And if the Wizard Lord had not gone mad, and was not harming anyone, nor trying to exceed the powers allotted him, then he was not a Dark Lord and did not need to be removed. The Chosen were not responsible for maintaining order, but only for ridding Barokan of Dark Lords.

Elder was waiting for a reply.

"I hope not," Sword said. "I very much hope not."

2

The road crew did indeed reach Mad Oak before dark—well before, in fact. The sun was still a hand's breadth above the ridge when the overseer looked at the swath they had cut right up to the boundary stone, a ten-foot swath of bare brown earth, and called, "Tools down!"

The crowd of villagers watching from safely inside the border burst into applause. They had been calling greetings, questions, and encouragement for some time as the road neared the town, and now that the job was complete they welcomed the road crew across the boundary with cheers, shouts, handshakes, and claps on the back. The idea of an open road all the way to Willowbank had captured their imaginations, though Sword was not entirely sure just what benefits they thought it would bring. After all, no one from Mad Oak had ever traveled much; the loss of the Willowbank Guide had been considered an inconvenience, but hardly a great tragedy.

Still, most of the town seemed to think the road was a wonder that would somehow make the world a better place, and had greeted the road-builders as heroes.

The two priestesses, however, had had to withdraw to the pavilion; the disturbed *ler* beyond the boundary shrine were making them both ill. Younger had been frighteningly pale when she withdrew, her sigil of office resembling a smear of blood. Elder's color had been better, but she was not steady on her feet, and Sword had helped her up the path.

Sword had gone back out for another conversation with the road-builders at one point, asked a few questions about the project and the Wizard Lord's actions elsewhere, and how other priests and priestesses had handled the resulting discomforts, but then he had come back up to the pavilion to check on the priestesses.

They were obviously suffering, but insisted there was nothing he could do. When Sword had spoken to the road crew they had expressed sympathy, but said that the pain would pass off in time, with no permanent harm done. The Wizard Lord had been building roads for four years now, and all those myriad displaced wild *ler* had not yet killed a priest; the tame *ler* had always protected their patrons.

Sword had left the priestesses in the rocking chairs by the unlit hearth, and had gone out to the pavilion terrace to watch the celebration begin. He leaned over the rail and peered down as the road crew finished their work, and the cheering started.

He remembered once before when he had stood leaning on this rail, seven and a half years before, looking out across the trees below. That had been the night of that year's barley harvest celebration, when the Old Swordsman and two wizards had arrived in Mad Oak, seeking a volunteer to replace the aging member of the Chosen.

But that had been different. It had been a quiet evening at dusk, not a bright afternoon, and he had been looking straight out at the valley, not across the fields to the borders; enjoying the weather and thinking about his future, not watching what might be a change in the very nature of the town's existence. The crowd had been up here gathered around Brewer that night, drinking up the summer beer to make room for fresh wort, not down by the boundary shrine marveling at a new road.

Surely, he thought, he must have stood out here since then, but he could not think of a time when he had. His training in swordsmanship, his daily practice, the unhappy year he had spent traveling, his sour disposition upon his return—he had not spent much time in the pavilion at all, really. He recalled a few gatherings and meetings inside, including the conversation with Younger Priestess three years before that had led to his odd experience with the memories trapped in the village shrine, but he could not remember a single occasion when he took a moment to come out on the terrace and simply look down at the valley.

Seven and a half years ago he had agreed to become the Chosen Swordsman, and that had led in not much more than a year to his meet-

ing with the Dark Lord of the Galbek Hills, atop that crude tower outside Split Reed. He had slain the Wizard Lord, avenging the murdered
innocents of Stoneslope, and then he had come home to Mad Oak, hoping to never again have reason to leave.

And until now, he hadn't. The new Wizard Lord had done nothing to
attract his attention or cause him concern, nor had any of the other
Chosen visited to discuss anything. There was absolutely no evidence
that the present Wizard Lord had murdered anyone or otherwise broken the strictures that he was expected to obey. The few reports that
had reached Mad Oak had all seemed quite favorable.

But building roads, disturbing countless ler—while hardly a crime,
that was not what was expected of the Wizard Lord. It was completely
unanticipated, a thing that had never happened before. It might even be
a sign of madness.

If the present Wizard Lord had gone mad, like the last, then he, like
the last, must be removed. There had never been two Dark Lords so
close together, Sword was fairly sure, but that did not mean it could
never happen.

But building roads—if that was mad, could there be such a thing as
beneficial madness? Those cheering townspeople down there clearly
didn't see anything wrong with new roads, no matter what the wild ler
might think. It wasn't as if anyone liked wild ler; they were a dangerous
nuisance, something to be respected, but never loved. The loss of any
link with Willowbank when the old guide retired had been an annoy-
ance to many of the town's inhabitants, and they seemed delighted to
have a new connection.

The two miserable priestesses, on the other hand, whatever they
might think of the road itself, were suffering from its effects on the natural spirits of the land. Both seemed very ill, though they were somewhat vague about the exact nature of the illness. Younger Priestess had
said the pain was in her soul, not her body.

If Elder Priestess was right about the road's creation releasing malig-
nant ghosts into the community, then Sword thought others might also
come to regret the road's arrival, as well.

But those effects would be temporary, wouldn't they? And when the ghosts were laid and the disturbed *ler* scattered and harmony restored, the road would still be there. Anyone who wanted to would be able to walk to Willowbank in half a day.

And the road crew had told him that similar roads already stretched the length of Longvale, and all the way to Winterhome, under the cliffs east of the Midlands. Other roads were being built out to the coastal towns to the west, and into the southern hills. These projects had been under way for years. Surely, building any of those would have cast out *ler* just as much as this one had, yet road construction had continued. The aftereffects could not be so very dreadful, then.

The crowd of villagers and laborers was moving now, heading up to the pavilion to celebrate properly; Sword could see Flute and Fiddle hurrying to fetch their instruments, and probably to rouse Drum and Sword's sister Harp. There would be music and dancing, and someone would undoubtedly convince Brewer to roll out a barrel or two of his best.

Sword had not done much dancing of late. His experiences as one of the Chosen had not given him anything to dance about.

Perhaps, though, that was a mistake. Perhaps it was time he cheered up. This road—it was a change, certainly, a big one, but wasn't it a change for the better? Couldn't a Wizard Lord use his power not just to protect Barokan from storms and outlaws, but to improve life for ordinary people?

Sword did not remember hearing of any Wizard Lord who had ever done that, but why not?

Those disturbed *ler* and the discomfort they caused the priestesses would fade soon enough, while the road would remain. Anyone who wanted to travel to Willowbank or beyond could do so, even though the last Willowbank guide had retired without training a successor. Oh, a few *ara* feathers might be a good idea, to ward off hostile *ler* to either side, but there would be a *road,* a clear and open route to follow. And presumably it would, in time, have *ler* of its own, and as with nearly all man-made things, those *ler* would be cooperative and helpful. *Ler* always reflected the nature of the objects they ensouled, so that a hammer's *ler* helped it strike hard and true, a knife's *ler* helped it cut, and a road's *ler* would, it must be assumed, guide travelers' feet to their destination.

Of course, a knife's *ler* sometimes thirsted for blood, since that, too, was in the nature of a blade; Sword's mother had thrown away at least one outwardly good knife because it insisted on nicking fingers at every opportunity. A road's *ler* might have some unwanted aspects, but really, they could hardly be as dangerous as the wild *ler* of the forest.

Perhaps the *ler* of the road would coax people to travel, to wander, to hunger to see what lay beyond the next bend.

In fact, Sword found himself thinking now, when surely the road's *ler* could be only half-formed at best, that it was time he did some more traveling himself. And it was obvious where he would go—down the new road to Winterhome, to talk with the Wizard Lord, and perhaps meet with some of the other Chosen.

He had briefly seen Winterhome before, years ago, during the reign of the Dark Lord of the Galbek Hills. Likewise, he had met the Wizard Lord before, when the man was simply the Red Wizard, an ordinary member of the Council of Immortals. The Red Wizard had even visited Mad Oak, when Sword was preparing to claim his place among the Chosen.

It would be interesting to see how both Winterhome and the wizard had changed.

And then the cheering crowd was spilling into the pavilion, shouting and laughing, and the time for serious thought was past; this was a time to join in the celebration. Within minutes a barrel was rolled out, cakes were fetched, and the music began.

Sword made a halfhearted effort to join in, but did not dance much. He took a few quick turns with Younger Priestess in an attempt to take her mind off the disturbed and scattered *ler*, but she quickly regretted the motion and insisted on returning to her chair. He danced one gavotte with young Potter, who had only recently finally escaped her childhood nickname of Mudpie. Mostly, though, he stood and watched, and the sword on his hip was enough to deter anyone who might have tried to intrude on his thoughts or drag him into the festivities.

The men of the road crew were pleasant enough company, and while they were eager to dance with the village women they took no unwelcome liberties, so far as Sword could see. Perhaps they were too tired to make trouble after the day's labor.

The idea that some of them might be seriously interested in taking Mad Oak women as wives occurred to Sword. That would be . . . odd.

Normally, people in Longvale married within their own village, since there were so few people who traveled, but with this road open that might change. It would be easy for men from Mad Oak to go courting in Willowbank, or men from Willowbank to come to Mad Oak, and everyone knew that strangers were more interesting than the same old people one had grown up with. That exotic appeal had meant that the local girls had often flirted with guides and bargemen, but only rarely had such flirting led to marriage; the unsettled life of such men held little appeal for most people.

A road that let ordinary folk travel between towns might be very different, though. A farmer from strange and distant Willowbank might seem more attractive than a farmer from dull old Mad Oak, and the road would make it easy for such strangers to visit. Strangers had been rare before, but that might be about to change.

In fact, this road crew was probably the largest group of strangers ever to be seen in Mad Oak. Sword wondered whether they themselves realized that.

He did not speak to any of the road-builders directly, having asked his share of questions earlier and having no desire to spoil anyone's fun, but he listened with interest when any of their conversations happened to take place nearby. He did not hear anyone mention any changes in courting behavior, but he *did* hear some of the foreigners talk about traders bringing goods up from the south or west.

He had not thought about that, but of course it made sense. The roads in the Midlands allowed wagons to pass easily between towns, vehicles far larger than any of the carts used in Mad Oak, so that things grown or made in one place could be sold in another. There were often entire marketplaces devoted to such business, and the Midland towns all used coined money to simplify such commerce.

Mad Oak's only trade heretofore had been the handfuls of jewelry or spices that the guides brought in their pockets, or the limited variety of goods the bargemen brought along the river, and payment had been made in goods and services—mostly beer and barley—so that the town had no currency of its own.

That might be about to change. Sword was unsure whether that was entirely a good thing.

At one point he found himself standing between old Brewer and Little Weaver, neither of whom seemed to be participating in the festivities. He glanced from one to the other, then asked, "And what do *you* think of this new road?"

"I'm not sure," Brewer said. "All this talk of traveling merchants— what if they bring that southern wine?"

"What if they do?" Sword asked, puzzled.

"Well, then they won't need my beer, will they?"

Sword was one of the few people in Mad Oak who had ever actually drunk wine, when traveling in the Midlands and the southern hills. "It's not the same," he said. "I think people will still want good ale, especially in the summer."

"Will they?" Brewer did not seem very reassured.

"I think so, yes. After all, the bargemen always seemed happy to take your beer in trade. And perhaps you could take some down to Willowbank yourself, and sell it there—you might do very well for yourself."

"Don't they have their *own* beer in Willowbank? The barges come from the north, but Willowbank isn't north, it's south."

"I don't know," Sword admitted. "I've never visited Willowbank. But the barges go both ways."

"My mother's worried about whether people will still need our weaving," Little Weaver said. "One of the road-builders was talking about the fine fabrics he's seen in the markets of the south."

While the local woolens were of excellent quality, Sword remembered some of the fine linens and woven cotton he had seen while traveling. "She may have a point," he said.

"And what's this going to do to the guides?" Brewer asked. "Who's going to pay the Greenwater Guide if he can just stick an *ara* feather in his cap and stroll down the road to Willowbank?"

"I don't know," Sword replied. He looked at the dancers, whirling happily across the floor. "I suppose they'll have to find new occupations. Perhaps they can become traders."

Brewer made a wordless noise that clearly meant he was unconvinced, then turned and stamped off.

The others watched him go, then looked at one another.

"I think I'd like to dance again," Little Weaver said. "Sword?"

"Thank you, but no," Sword said. "Perhaps later."

Little Weaver frowned, then shrugged, and hurried away, leaving Sword to his thoughts.

As the evening wore on and the musicians began to tire, some of the older women who had been supplying food brought bedding instead, and those visitors to Mad Oak who did not make other arrangements, or who drank too much to go elsewhere under their own power, slept comfortably enough in the pavilion. The festivities did not so much end as gradually fade away, but in time the last of the music trailed away, the last steps were danced, and the townspeople drifted off to their homes, leaving the outlanders to themselves.

Sword made his way back to his mother's house long after his mother and younger sisters had gone to bed. He took a seat in the kitchen and sat with the door open, looking out at the night sky, for a time.

A road to Willowbank—and if he had heard and understood some of the chatter at the dance correctly, the plan was to extend the road farther north, out beyond Mad Oak to Ashgrove or Reedy Bend, and perhaps to build *another* road leading south from Mad Oak to Birches.

No one had said anything about a road to Greenwater, perhaps because that would mean crossing the ridge from Longvale into Greenvale and finding a route past the Mad Oak itself, but Sword supposed that might happen in time, as well. Or perhaps someone would build a bridge across the river, or establish a ferry, and then build a road east into Shadowvale—after all, why not? If the Wizard Lord wanted it done, why not? There were roads all through the Midlands; why not in the vales?

And why had none been built in all the centuries before? Why was this happening now, in the reign of the Lord of Winterhome, when it had never happened before? What had prevented it? What had changed?

Was it simply that no one had *thought* of it before? Had everyone assumed it would be impossibly difficult, and never attempted it?

Perhaps no one had dared defy the wild *ler*. The roads were disturbing *ler,* obviously, and upsetting priests everywhere; one of the road crew had said the Priest-King of Willowbank had not liked the idea at all at first, but had been brought around by the first caravan of trade goods from the Midlands. Since most towns were effectively ruled by their priests, and the priests would suffer the most from any road-building, that might have been enough to deter any experiments up until an even higher authority, the Wizard Lord, ordered it done.

But surely there was more to it than that. There had to be a story, and Sword knew who he could ask about stories. There was a man in Barokan who knew the truth of all the old stories—the Scholar, one of Sword's fellows among the Chosen. He called himself Lore, as a general thing; Sword had heard his true name, but could no longer remember it with any certainty. Did it start with Olmir? Olbir?

It didn't matter. Whatever his true name, Lore would be able to answer some of Sword's questions. And perhaps the Wizard Lord, or his representatives, could answer a few, as well.

Sword had returned to Mad Oak six years ago after killing the Dark Lord, and had kept mostly to himself since then, working in the barley and bean fields, helping his mother tend the family home. He had thought he had had his fill of the world outside Mad Oak, when he came home disillusioned. He had once thought of the Chosen as heroes, of the Wizard Lord as a larger-than-life figure, but they had not lived up to his expectations. Some of the Chosen had refused their roles or proven useless, and one had been an outright traitor, while the Dark Lord had, despite his magic, proven to be a selfish little man who died easily when a sword pierced his heart.

And the Council of Immortals, the band of wizards who chose each new Wizard Lord, had been arrogant and unwilling to listen to anything Sword might have to say about how he thought the whole system was unnecessary. He had tried to tell them that the time for Wizard Lords had passed, that the system did more harm than good and it was time to change, and they had ignored him—but perhaps the Red Wizard had been listening after all. Perhaps, now he was the Wizard Lord, he was making these changes, building these roads, because he saw that Sword had been right.

It would be very satisfying if that were the case, but the only way Sword could ever know for certain would be to ask the Wizard Lord himself. And even then, the man might lie.

On the other hand, the roads might somehow be a threat to the peace and safety of Barokan, part of some bizarre wizardly scheme. Sword could not imagine what such a scheme might be, but if there *were* one, then that would mean that the Wizard Lord of Winterhome was a new Dark Lord, and it was the duty of the eight Chosen to remove Dark Lords.

Sword was fairly certain there had never been two Dark Lords so close together as this; after all, if he remembered correctly there had only been nine in the seven centuries the system of Wizard Lords had existed. Had any Chosen Swordsman ever faced two Dark Lords in his lifetime? Sword had thought, when he came home from the Galbek Hills, that he had served his purpose and would not be called on again; had he been wrong?

It seemed unlikely. But then, it had seemed unlikely that the Lord of the Galbek Hills would turn out to be a murderous madman.

The more Sword considered the situation, the more certain he was that he had to go to Winterhome. He wanted to speak to the Red Wizard, and find Lore, and meet with the new Seer, whatever he or she was called, and perhaps with some of the other Chosen, to discuss it all and decide what, if anything, they should be doing.

It might well be that despite the doubts of the priestesses and weavers and old Brewer these new roads were a fine thing, something that should have been done centuries ago, and if so, then perhaps Sword and the other Chosen would see what they could do to assist the Wizard Lord. After all, even if their primary purpose was to remove Dark Lords, why not use their magic for other purposes? Why not help the good Wizard Lords, as well as remove the bad ones?

He would head for Winterhome, he decided. Not at once, not the next morning, but soon, when he had had time to review and prepare, when the *ler* had calmed and the roads had had time to recover from the violence of their creation. He would head south, at least as far as Willowbank. He might decide there was no need to go all the way to Winterhome, but he would definitely walk the new road as far as Willowbank.

Soon, he told himself.

Soon.

3

It was four days later that Sword hoisted his pack to his shoulder and set out on the road south.

During that four days the people of Mad Oak had been haunted by nightmares and ghosts. Some of the livestock had been skittish and intractable, half the milk in town had soured, and at least one barrel of beer had been mysteriously skunked, but the road had apparently stayed open, though no one from Mad Oak had yet dared to use it.

Nor had anyone more from Willowbank or farther south arrived. The road crew had returned to Willowbank after just a single night in Mad Oak, taking their tools and their padded, *ara*-feathered suits with them. They had talked about a possible return to extend the road north, but no one had seemed very certain of the details, and as yet there was no sign of any such continuation.

They had also spoken about opportunities for ambitious young men and women in Winterhome and the Midlands, and along the roads; it seemed that road-building was not the Wizard Lord's only project, though details were scarce. Sword was eager to learn more about those other projects, and how this business of recruiting people to work outside their homelands functioned. He had always been told that most people were bound by their own *ler* to their native land, and that people who tried to relocate often sickened and sometimes even died.

The Chosen, of course, were immune to such things, protected by their magic, and guides and bargemen were people who either had never formed ties properly or were able to break them and survive, but *most* people were alleged to have these magical ties. How, then, could the Wizard Lord be gathering people from all over to build his roads and work on his other schemes without condemning them to suffering and possible death? Had he developed some magic to deal with the problem? Or had it all been a myth all along?

There was so much to ask!

Sword did not want to rush off while the displaced *ler,* or Mad Oak's own *ler* that had been upset by the whole thing, were rampaging about. He had waited a few days to be sure that the disturbances would pass.

Indeed, the road's disruptive effects had faded with each passing day as the priestesses gradually coaxed and wheedled the town's *ler* back to their usual complacency, and chased the foreign *ler* back past the boundaries. Sword had chatted with Elder Priestess on the third day, as she rested up after a particularly difficult negotiation with the *ler* of the paths through town, and from what she told him he concluded that the worst was over, and there was no reason for him to linger. Soothing the *ler* was not his job in any case, nor anything he knew how to attempt, and the priestesses seemed to be handling things well enough.

With that settled, he had gathered a few things and said his farewells, and now he was marching south toward the road to Willowbank.

It felt odd to be leaving Mad Oak without a guide, but that was the whole point of the new roads—to let ordinary people travel from one town to the next unaided. Sword, of course, was not technically an ordinary person, but he had nonetheless followed the Greenwater guide when last he left Mad Oak, and had assumed he would do the same should he ever leave again.

Instead he had his sword on his belt, his talisman in his pocket, and three curling *ara* plumes in his hat, but he was alone, with no one to show him the route or protect him from hostile *ler*–he needed only to follow the road to reach Willowbank, and then Rock Bridge, and then Broadpool, and on along the length of Longvale until he emerged into the eastern Midlands, and then up across the downs to Winterhome, there beneath the Eastern Cliffs.

He stepped past the boundary shrine, unsure what to expect. Ordinarily, when he crossed from an inhabited area into the wilderness, he could sense the change immediately, as he moved from the presence of familiar, accepting *ler* into the territory of wild, often hostile ones. This road, though, had been torn out of the wilderness, forced through without the consent of the *ler*. The old *ler* had been dislodged, and new ones would evolve in time, and everyone seemed to assume that the new would accept human traffic as natural and right—but did they actually know that? And the new *ler* would not be fully formed yet . . .

When he passed the shrine and set his foot on the new road he felt not the hostility of the wilderness, but a disorientation and confusion, as if he had suddenly been turned around. He took another step, then paused.

The *ler* here were disturbed, unquestionably. Even he could feel it, despite the magic-deadening *ara* feathers in his hat, and he was no priest or sensitive. He swallowed, steadied himself, and began walking.

It was a very odd sensation. He knew that physically, he was simply walking straight ahead along a broad, straight, flat path, a good seven or eight feet wide, but mentally, spiritually, it felt as if he were balancing on a wobbling edge. He remembered what one of the road crew had told him about maintenance—if the road were not used regularly, it would close up, turn hostile, become perhaps even more dangerous than the wilderness it replaced. Physical maintenance, keeping it clear of obstructions, was relatively simple; spiritual maintenance, keeping it fit for human use, was more difficult. People had to walk it as if they belonged there, and force the road's new *ler* to accommodate human needs, rather than allowing the *ler* the upper hand. If the *ler* ever became dominant the road would require its own priesthood, like a village.

He could feel that the *ler* here were still in turmoil, and he tried to think *at* them, to impose upon them the idea that this road was *his* place, not theirs.

It seemed to help—or perhaps he was adjusting as he moved, or the *ler* were less distraught farther from Mad Oak. The dizzy, unsteady feeling subsided by the time he had gone half a mile, and he was able to concentrate on enjoying the walk and his surroundings.

The morning sun was well above the Eastern Cliffs, slanting brightly through the trees; the leaves above were vivid green, the undergrowth on either side of the road a tangle of green and brown and gray. Birds sang somewhere nearby, though he did not see them.

Willowbank lay perhaps ten or twelve miles south-southeast of Mad Oak—a long walk, but by road it should be easily done in half a day.

When the old Willowbank Guide had been leading people between the towns he had taken a safe but more circuitous route, and the journey had required almost a full day, typically starting before the sun had cleared the cliffs and arriving just before sunset.

Sword studied the wilderness on either side of the road, trying to guess what dangers the old guide had found it necessary to avoid, but he could see nothing that looked especially hazardous. There were deadfalls and hanging vines, uneven ground and scurrying squirrels, flickers of light and movement that appeared to have no natural cause, but no obvious threats.

But then, why would they be obvious? That was why people needed guides in the first place, to warn them of *hidden* dangers. He heaved his pack a little higher on his shoulder and marched on.

Perhaps four miles from Mad Oak the road took its first real departure from a direct line between the two towns; up until now it had shifted slightly to one side or the other to avoid the largest trees, but had generally been straight. Now, though, the land ahead grew marshy, and the road veered to the right to stay on solid ground. Sword knew the Longvale River lay beyond that marsh, and he peered off into the wilderness, but was unsure whether he could see it, or whether he was imagining it. He could definitely hear splashing, though, whether it was frogs in the marsh or fish in the river or something else entirely.

He stayed on the road, and resisted any temptation to investigate. That was wilderness out there, and he was on his way to Willowbank and Winterhome, not just out exploring. Not that any sane person would go exploring in the wild merely on a whim in any case, even with *ara* feathers and the protection conferred by his status as one of the Chosen.

He paused at roughly the halfway point to eat the barley bread and drink the beer he had brought with him, then looked thoughtfully at the earthenware bottle he had just emptied. He knew that if he dropped it in the wilderness it would anger the *ler* enough to cause him bad dreams and minor misfortune, but what if he dropped it on the road? The *ler* there were still in flux, unformed. They might not know yet that castoffs were something they could and should object to.

But why risk it? Why encourage bad habits? And why throw away a perfectly good bottle? Its weight wasn't enough to justify discarding it on a journey of this length. He pushed the cork back in and stuffed the bottle into his pack, then marched on.

The sun was halfway down the western sky when he knelt at the boundary shrine and asked the *ler* to make him welcome in Willowbank.

Several villagers had already spotted him, of course, and were waiting just inside the border to welcome him. They looked much like the people of Mad Oak, but their clothing was subtly different, with odd embroidery and slanting cuffs, and several of the women wore their hair in a style Sword had never seen before, pulled into an off-center ponytail that draped over one shoulder.

"Mad Oak! You're from Mad Oak, yes?" someone called.

"I am," Sword answered, rising.

"The north road works! It's safe!"

"He has *ara* feathers in his hat . . ."

"But he didn't have a guide, and he came alone! Who cares about the feathers?"

"He has a *sword*," a girl pointed out.

That silenced everyone for a moment, as they stopped, turned, and stared, verifying the girl's observation.

"He *does* have a sword."

"He's the Swordsman, then. Of course he was safe."

"Are you the Chosen Swordsman?"

"Yes, I am," Sword replied, stepping across the boundary.

The air suddenly seemed still, the light brighter, colors sharper, the ground beneath his feet steadier, as he left the half-formed *ler* of the road for the mature spiritual community of Willowbank. He took a deep breath and tasted the air, smelled the village's crops and livestock and cooking fires, the faint whiff of a distant tannery, the hot breeze from a blacksmith's forge. Apparently, he thought, it was not so much that the *ler* had become so very much less confused as he traveled, but that his own senses had adjusted, and now that he was back among healthy, friendly, and experienced *ler*, everything seemed preternaturally clear.

"Welcome to Willowbank!"

A man in a long white shirt stepped forward and held out a hand. "I am Toru an Sallor, acolyte to the Priest-King. Welcome to Willowbank!"

Sword took the hand. "Erren Zal Tuyo," he said. "The Chosen Swordsman."

The priest tilted his head. "I thought the people of Mad Oak did not use any part of their true names."

"We don't. But I'm not in Mad Oak, and the Swordsman is part of all Barokan. If you tell me a part of who you truly are, it might be considered rude not to reciprocate. What's custom in one village is a crime in the next, after all, and I have no desire to displease the *ler* of Willowbank."

When Sword had last gone traveling he had avoided the use of any of his true name as much as possible, as it had made him uncomfortable to hear it spoken, but in the intervening years he had thought it over and decided that was just habit, not reason, and that he should make more of an effort to suit his actions to the customs of the places he visited. After all, thousands of people in Barokan used parts of their true names every day without suffering any ill effects. Villages that totally avoided true names, as Mad Oak did, were scarce.

Saying the name aloud still made him uneasy, though, even if the priest did not seem to have noticed.

"Very good. And why have you come to Willowbank? Are you testing the road, as some of us assumed? Because it seems to me hardly a fair test to send one of the Chosen."

"No one sent me. In truth, I'm merely passing through, on my way to Winterhome. With the roads open, this route is undoubtedly faster than following the Greenwater Guide down to Valleymouth and then finding my way through the Midlands."

"Winterhome?" The priest dropped Sword's hand. "Surely, you don't mean you're on your way to kill the Wizard Lord?"

"No, no!" Sword hastily raised both hands in protest. "Of course not—unless you know of some reason I should. I do want to speak with him, if he's willing, but I have no reason to wish him harm." He gestured at the road. "I came here from Mad Oak by myself, unguided, in just half a day. If anything, I owe him my thanks."

"Yes! Yes, we're very excited about these roads—though I must say, the construction was quite painful for myself and the other priests. Even the king felt it. For myself, I lay sick in bed for four full days, and

I still can't eat certain foods without dire consequences. When we saw you coming we had hoped it was the start of regular trade with Mad Oak."

"I'm sorry," Sword said. "It's just me. But if you want to trade, I'm sure the people of Mad Oak would be happy to see a merchant's wagon."

The acolyte blinked. "A what?"

"A merchant's wagon. They use them in the Midlands—it's like a farmer's wagon, but closed in, and full of things to sell or trade."

"Oh! Those! Three of them came down from Rock Bridge, with all manner of wondrous things, when the road first opened. That was what convinced our king to let more roads be built. But we don't have anything like that *here*," Toru said.

"Of course you don't, not yet. Foolish of me. But you might see about building one, or bringing one of your own up the road from the Midlands."

"Oh," Toru said. "Oh!"

"Can we do that?" someone said. The little crowd had been listening to the entire conversation, of course.

"I don't see why not; would your *ler* forbid it?"

"The *ler* of Willowbank obey the Priest-King, just as we all do," Toru said. "If he wants us to build wagons, we will build wagons."

"I see." Sword had encountered such places before, where humanity had gained ascendance over nature—or rather, where the priests had. Not all of them were pleasant. He hadn't realized Willowbank operated on that model. "If I might ask, how far is it to Rock Bridge? Could I reach it before dark?"

Toru glanced at the sun. "I doubt it," he said. "Not unless you ran the entire way."

"In that case, is there somewhere I could stay the night? I don't want to inconvenience anyone . . ."

"Nonsense! The slayer of the Dark Lord of the Galbek Hills is always welcome in Willowbank!" Toru hesitated after completing this fulsome sentence, then added, "That is, I believe so, but of course, the king's word is final."

"Of course. What is the proper etiquette for asking his permission?"

"I'll see to it myself, if you could wait here for a moment."

And with that, the acolyte turned and trotted toward the village proper, leaving Sword surrounded by eager villagers asking questions about the road, Mad Oak, the Dark Lord he had slain, his sword, and every other remotely relevant subject they could think of. Sword did his best to answer them all politely, even if only to say, "I'm afraid I don't know anything about that."

A few moments later the priest returned, with instructions to escort Sword to guest quarters in the Priest-King's own mansion. Escaping the eager little crowd was a relief.

The relief was short-lived, however. Once he had entered the great shadowy central corridor of the mansion, rather than taking him directly to his room, three more acolytes descended on him and hurried him to an ablutory; the Priest-King wanted him to freshen up, and then present himself for an audience. Refusing was out of the question, so half an hour later, after he had had his hands and face thoroughly scrubbed and his hair and beard vigorously brushed, after his boots had been polished, and after a flimsy white robe had been draped over his dusty traveling clothes, Sword was led into the Priest-King's throne room.

The room was large and moderately luxurious without lapsing into ostentation; carpets covered much of the floor, and the beams supporting the ceiling were carved and painted. The Priest-King himself slouched in a welter of cushions on an oversized chair atop a broad, low dais at the far end, a nimbus of golden light flickering around his head; Sword swept off his hat, bowed deeply, and awaited instructions.

"Come here, come here," the king said, beckoning from his slouch.

Sword obeyed, rising from his bow and approaching with head bent, as the acolytes had instructed.

He had never seen anyone with a halo before, though he had heard of such things; the effect was impressive, far more so than the sigils worn by Mad Oak's handful of clergy. It left little doubt that this man was indeed favored by the local *ler*.

"What brings you to Willowbank?"

Sword stopped and said, "I am only passing through, on my way to Winterhome to talk to the Wizard Lord."

"Just talk?"

"I hope so." He raised his head. "I intend to ask him a few questions about these roads he has ordered built, and perhaps other projects. I don't expect anything serious or unpleasant to come of it."

That halo was fascinating; it did not behave like ordinary light. It cast no shadows, and although it appeared fairly bright, it did not seem to illuminate at all anything more than a foot or so from the Priest-King's head. Sword found himself staring at it.

"Ah! So what do you think of the roads? How was the walk from Mad Oak?"

Sword answered as best he could as the Priest-King barraged him with questions, just as the villagers out by the boundary shrine had. He found himself recounting the story of how he and the other Chosen had slain the Dark Lord of the Galbek Hills—though he left out a great many details he did not think the king needed to know.

At last, though, the king seemed satisfied; he swung himself around and rose from his throne. He was a tall man, a bit plump, a bit soft, with long curling brown hair that reached halfway down his back, and a close-trimmed beard streaked with gray; Sword did not think he would have been considered especially handsome were it not for that ethereal glow that surrounded him and flattered his features.

"You must be hungry," the Priest-King said. "Come take supper with me."

This invitation, like any other the Priest-King gave, had the force of an order, so Sword followed without argument, and found himself seated at a great carved-oak table weighed down with delicacies of every sort. Half a dozen lovely young women in low-cut dresses waited on them as they ate and drank, making sure neither of the men had to reach for anything, and that no goblet ever stayed empty for more than a few seconds.

As they ate, the king asked more questions, and Sword noticed that the serving maids listened intently to the answers, that in fact the Priest-King appeared to be timing his questions so that the women could hear Sword's responses. That undoubtedly explained why the king deliberately repeated certain questions Sword had already answered in private; they were matters the Priest-King thought were of general interest, and his staff would spread the answers throughout Willowbank.

The food was excellent, as might be expected at the Priest-King's table, and dish followed dish almost endlessly—thick soup and fine bread and assorted fruit and grilled meat and a stew of spiced vegetables, until Sword felt as if his belly were bulging and his sword belt had become uncomfortably tight.

At last, though, the meal was done, and the king sent Sword off to the appointed guest room, with a serving wench carrying a candle to light his way. It had been a long day, and Sword was ready to sleep, but when he reached his room he discovered that his hosts expected one more thing from him—the serving maid did not leave once his own candle was lit. He hesitated, then decided he was not *that* tired.

In the morning she fetched his breakfast, and carried his polite farewells to the Priest-King. As the sun cleared the Eastern Cliffs, he set out down the road to Rock Bridge.

The journey was uneventful, and Council of Priests in Rock Bridge made him welcome. They asked his opinion of the new roads; he answered truthfully that he had not yet formed an opinion. The roads certainly made travel easier, but they also disturbed the natural order of things, and he had not yet decided whether the benefits outweighed the damage.

The road from Willowbank to Rock Bridge was far less disorienting than the one from Mad Oak to Willowbank; it had had longer to recover from its creation, and the difference was obvious.

From Rock Bridge, Sword continued the following day to Broadpool. That stretch of road already showed traces of wagon ruts, and though he did not meet any traveling merchants in either town, the inhabitants of both towns were happy to tell him that some had been there, selling strange foods and fabrics and a variety of other wonderful things.

In Broadpool several of the witches, as the local priestesses were called, took turns interrogating him in various odd ways; the evening was well advanced before he realized that they were competing to see whose bed he would sleep in. He announced that he was exhausted and would sleep alone, and the questioning abruptly ceased.

In the morning he found every door in the village locked against him, and his pack placed beside the boundary shrine where the road led south; he took the hint and did not linger.

From Broadpool he had a choice of roads, to his astonishment. He took the more easterly route, to Beggar's Hill, where he found lodging with a woodcarver turned innkeeper who went by the name of Nicker.

It was in Beggar's Hill, as he was about to head up the stairs to his room in Nicker's Public House, that the big brown hound by the hearth raised its head and said, "Hello, Swordsman."

Sword stopped and turned.

The half-dozen other occupants of the taproom were staring at the dog in astonishment and fear, but Sword knew what was happening. He had encountered talking animals before, when he and the other Chosen went after the Dark Lord of the Galbek Hills; the Wizard Lord could see through the eyes of lesser creatures, and control their actions, even to the point of making beasts speak. It was a convenient way for him to communicate over long distances, a trick of which no other wizard was known to be capable.

"Hello, Wizard Lord," Sword said calmly.

"Are you coming to see me?" the dog asked. Its voice was rough, not remotely human, but the words were clear enough.

"Yes, I am," Sword replied.

"I thought so. I can only see your exact location at night, for some reason, but your route seemed to be headed this way."

"Yes. I'm coming to Winterhome," Sword agreed.

"Why can't I place you clearly along the way?" the hound asked. "Is there something wrong with the roads?"

"I don't think so," Sword said. "I assume it's the *ara* feathers on my hat. Which I take off at night."

"Oh, I see. Yes, that would explain it."

"I don't entirely trust the roadside *ler*, as yet," Sword said.

"Sensible of you. Then I'll see you soon?"

"Yes."

"Good. I'm looking forward to it—and the dog is getting upset, so I'll speak with you when you get here."

"As you please," Sword said with a bow.

At that the dog started, getting quickly to its feet and letting out an unhappy yip. Then it shivered and trotted away toward the kitchens, whimpering.

The unnatural silence that had filled the room during the magical conversation suddenly burst into a murmur of hushed voices, and every eye in the room was focused on the Swordsman.

Sword paid the observers no attention. He watched the dog go, to make sure there would be no last-moment afterthought, then turned and continued upstairs. It was useful to know that the Wizard Lord was taking an interest in him, he told himself. Useful, but as always, a bit disconcerting.

It was the morning after, as he was raising his head after making his farewell prayer to the *ler* of Beggar's Hill, that he looked up at the sun clearing the Eastern Cliffs. He had already taken a step past the boundary shrine onto the road, but now he stopped dead in his tracks.

"What is *that*?" he asked, pointing.

His host, Nicker, had escorted him to the border, as the town's *ler* were wary of unaccompanied strangers. The innkeeper had started to turn back just short of the shrine, but upon hearing the traveler's voice he paused. "What is what?" he asked.

Sword pointed. "That," he said.

Nicker looked where the Chosen Swordsman was pointing.

Something stood atop the cliffs far to the southeast, a broad structure of some sort. It did not appear particularly remarkable, though details could not be seen at so great a distance and with the morning sun behind it, but it was not the architecture that had caught Sword's eye. It was the location.

There *were* no permanent structures atop the cliffs. Everyone knew that. The Uplands were a vast windswept prairie, and the Uplanders who lived there most of the year were nomads who lived in tents as they followed the great flocks of *ara*, the gigantic flightless birds that provided them with meat, magic-resistant feathers, and the beaks and hollow bones they used to make their tools.

The Uplanders did not build multistory buildings right at the cliff edge.

"I don't know," Nicker said. "They started building it two or three years ago; I think it's finished now."

"*Who* built it? The Uplanders?"

Nicker shrugged. "I don't know," he said. "I don't think so. The ru-

mor is that it's another of the Wizard Lord's projects. I'm pretty sure
one of the road crew said it was."

"Projects? What sort of project is it?"

"I don't really know."

Sword did not like that. The Wizard Lord was the mystical overlord
of all Barokan and could go anywhere in his realm that he pleased, but
the land atop the cliffs was not part of Barokan. The cliffs were the
eastern boundary, just as definite as the boundaries of the towns within
Barokan. The Wizard Lord had no business doing anything in the Uplands, and certainly shouldn't be *building* anything up there; that was
intruding into the Uplanders' territory. Building roads through the
wilderness within Barokan was one thing—all Barokan was within the
Wizard Lord's purview—but building something in the Uplands?

And who knew what the Wizard Lord might be building elsewhere
in the Uplands, too far back from the cliff edge to be visible?

"Did that road-builder say what it is? What it's for?"

"Well, he had a name for it," Nicker said, glancing up at the cliff-top
structure. "At least, my niece said he did."

"What was that? Did she say?"

"She said it's called the Summer Palace."

Sword blinked at him, then turned to stare at the building atop the
cliffs. "Summer Palace"—just what did that mean? Some Wizard Lords
had built palaces and lived in them, probably more than hadn't, but a
Summer Palace?

And surely the Wizard Lord couldn't intend to *live* in it, to dwell outside Barokan!

He definitely needed to speak to the Wizard Lord!

4

As he followed the roads to Winterhome, Sword gradually approached the Summer Palace, watched it grow nearer, then passed it and saw it recede again. It stood a few miles northeast of Winterhome along the cliff edge.

He could still see it clearly, though, as he passed the boundary stones and saw the immense guesthouses lining the road ahead of him. It was hard to be sure at so great a distance, but he believed it to be two or three stories in height, with broad sloping roofs, and fairly large, perhaps as large as the guesthouses the Host People of Winterhome maintained for the Uplanders.

The guesthouses, of course, were empty at this time of year. The Uplanders had long since made their annual climb up to the plateau and would not return for months, but their clan banners still flew from each guesthouse that Sword passed, fluttering from a pole at the southeast gable of each, the gable nearest the path that led up from Barokan to the Uplands. Each guesthouse stood three stories high—two stories of massive stone, and a third of wood and plaster, beneath broad, overhanging roofs. The doors and windows were shuttered and barred for the summer; the dormitories were abandoned until autumn.

Sword knew there were three avenues of these structures, leading into the heart of Winterhome, the streets where the Host People lived year-round; he was coming in along the road that led northwest from that central core. He marched on, seeing no one—but that was to be expected in the late spring.

But then he came within sight of the great central plaza, and stopped dead.

He remembered well what the plaza had looked like six years before—a broad open space with five streets radiating out to north, south, west, northwest, and southwest, while the east side ended in the steep stony slope at the foot of the cliffs, the rough road to the plateau winding up from the center of that eastern edge. This was the one spot in all Barokan where enough of the Eastern Cliffs had crumbled that people could climb a path winding its way for several miles across broken stone and jagged outcroppings to the Uplands, and the plaza of Winterhome had been built around the foot of that path.

The loose, mossy, gray stone had been left untouched for centuries, and the town had been built on the gently rolling land just to the west. The eastern side of the plaza had been open to that steep, rocky wilderness.

Now, though, the entire eastern side of the plaza was occupied by a palace, and the entrance to the road up the cliffs was a great stone arch that led *through* that palace.

The plaza was bustling with people, the vast majority of them in the distinctive all-black garb of the Host People. None of them seemed to be paying any very special attention to the palace—that is, unless one counted the guards at the various entrances, standing comfortably in their places, with their red-and-black uniforms and ornate eight-foot spears. Most people seemed to be huddled around various wagons, but Sword paid those no attention. He focused entirely on the palace.

Sword had never gotten a very clear understanding of how the local priesthood operated, or whether there was a secular government in Winterhome at all; he had been concerned with other matters when he visited the town before. He was fairly certain that there was no king or archpriest who could have ordered the building of such a palace, though.

And that presumably meant that the Wizard Lord, the Lord of Winterhome, had built it.

That was normal enough in itself. Each Wizard Lord was expected to construct, or oversee the construction of, a fortress or mansion of some sort, to indicate his mastery of the land's resources. Every Wizard Lord for seven hundred years had built himself a castle or palace or tower.

Sword had never seen one like this, though. It was certainly nothing like the stronghold of the Wizard Lord's predecessor; that had been a small, crude tower in the Galbek Hills, far to the southwest. This one was larger than any of the ruins or converted palaces Sword had encountered elsewhere. It was, in fact, immense, perhaps the largest single building Sword had ever seen, dwarfing even the temples and pavilions that dominated some towns; it was as big as three or four of the guesthouses put together. Gray stone walls rose to various heights, the central block as high as five stories above the plaza. Broad wooden eaves extended out on all sides, and several elaborate doors and gateways, and dozens of windows, pierced the stone in elegant patterns. The doors and shutters were painted red, the frames black; some were further decorated with painted flowers and carved, gilded rosettes.

It would seem the Wizard Lord of Winterhome did many things on a grand scale, not just build roads.

And it would appear that Sword would not need to ask directions if he wanted to visit the Wizard Lord; that palace was hard to miss. Sword picked up his pace and marched down the last few yards of street and across the great plaza, dodging the crowds and wagons, aiming his steps toward the largest and most ornate of the several doors.

Heads began to turn and eyes to follow him as he made his way toward the palace gate. He was not the only foreigner in sight, by any means, and his white shirt and brown leather pants were not especially distinctive, but he *was* the only man around with a sword on his hip, and the only man marching alone toward the palace.

Two guards were waiting with lowered spears when he reached the door, and a dozen or more of the Host People were staring. "Hello," he said cheerfully to the guards. "I'm the Chosen Swordsman, and I'd like to speak to the Wizard Lord, if I might. Is he in?"

The guards exchanged glances. "He's here, but I don't know if he'll want to see you right now," one of them said.

"I believe he's expecting me. Could you tell him I'm here?"

The guards looked at one another again, and then the one on the right said, "Wait here." He opened a door and stepped inside—not the big, ornate door, but a small, very plain one to one side. He had to maneuver carefully to get his spear through the opening, and he left the door slightly ajar behind him.

Sword waited, and in a moment the guard reemerged, once again angling his spear carefully.

"I've sent a messenger," he said. "We should have word soon."

"Thank you," Sword replied. He looked around.

Several Host People were still staring at him. The heavily bearded men wore baggy black tunics and long, loose breeches, tied tight at wrists and ankles, while the women were hidden in huge tentlike garments, with scarves wrapped around their faces; that made it hard to tell one from another, and Sword was not sure whether he had ever seen any of these people before.

He probably had not. He had not been in Winterhome for years, and had met few of the Host People even then.

The weather was warmer than when Sword had been here before, much warmer, so many of the men did not have their hoods pulled up to hide their hair and faces, and the women wore gauzy summer scarves rather than the heavy woolen winter ones, but they were still all covered from head to toe in black fabric. Telling the local men apart could be challenging. Identifying the women was impossible, and that was quite deliberately. The garments were designed to hide the women from the visiting Uplanders in the winter, so as to pose as little temptation as possible for their bored young men.

The Uplanders were not here, but up on the plateau, far away; Sword was mildly surprised to see that the Host People women still hid their faces so carefully. He wondered whether they stayed so thoroughly covered in summer's full heat. Judging by the thinner scarves, he guessed they made some concessions to the climate but remained largely concealed.

The palace guards wore uniforms cut much like the Hostmen's clothing—loose-fitting garments with baggy sleeves and legs, but bound tight at wrists, elbows, knees, and ankles to keep the excess fabric from getting in the way. The difference was that their tunics were bright red, rather than black—though the breeches and garters were all black.

There were a lot of guards, Sword thought. He had only seen one Wizard Lord's home before, and the Lord of the Galbek Hills had only had half a dozen serving maids staffing his tower, no guards at all—but the Dark Lord of the Galbek Hills had been dangerously insane. He had feared that any male servants would be seduced by the Beauty into turning on him, and had instead relied on magic and treachery for his defense, rather than guards.

Sword knew that previous Wizard Lords had had guards; he had just never heard any clear numbers. Perhaps it was perfectly normal for a Wizard Lord to have a dozen guards at the doors to his palace.

The small door opened, and a short man leaned out. "Swordsman?" he said.

"I'm here," Sword replied, straightening.

"Come in, then. The Wizard Lord is eager to speak with you."

The guards stepped aside, and Sword followed the man inside.

The little door opened into one corner of a broad hall. The grand entrance that Sword had originally headed for also opened into it, but was barred tight at the moment. Woven rush mats covered the stone floor; a few tapestries broke up the monotony of the long white plaster walls. Light came from a few scattered windows, and much of the hall was in shadow. The interior was pleasantly cool after the uncomfortably warm square.

"This way," the man said, beckoning. He was short and thin, with brown hair and a loose white tunic bound at wrists and elbows with black garters, and Sword wondered whether that was his usual garb, or whether he was a Hostman who wore a white tunic at the Wizard Lord's insistence, or whether he had taken up the garters after arriving here, in an attempt to adopt local custom.

He led Sword around a corner into a corridor, then through a gallery, and into an antechamber where more guards waited. There they paused.

"You'll have to leave your sword here," the short man said apologetically. "And any other blades or weapons you may be carrying."

"I haven't come to kill him," Sword protested.

"Nonetheless, I'm afraid we must insist," the man said. "You are a man appointed by the Council of Immortals to hold the power of life and death over the Wizard Lord; surely, you'll understand that he prefers to take a few precautions before meeting with you."

Sword hesitated.

"You are free to refuse, of course, but in that case I'm afraid the Wizard Lord will not speak to you in person. If you feel you *must* speak with him while armed, he can arrange to converse through a proxy—perhaps a cat?"

Sword remembered the miserable whimpering of the hound in Beggar's Hill after the Wizard Lord had released it. "That won't be necessary," he said, reaching down to unbuckle his sword belt.

Besides the recent exchange with the present Wizard Lord through the innkeeper's dog, Sword had spoken with the Dark Lord of the Galbek Hills through animal intermediaries several times—a rabbit, a raccoon, an ox, a crow, and others, including a cat. The memories were not pleasant ones, and besides, he knew that serving as the Wizard Lord's proxy was not a pleasant experience for the animals involved, either. Their throats were not designed to produce human language, and their *ler* were not meant to be constrained in such a fashion. He therefore preferred not to deal with this new Wizard Lord that way.

Giving up the sword was not really a problem; after all, the *sword* wasn't magic; *he* was. He had the talisman of his office, the Talisman of Blades, safely tucked away in a hidden pocket, and as long as he had that, he could wield any swordlike weapon better than anyone else alive—a stick or knife would serve, if no sword was available. He was never truly unarmed.

He wasn't foolish enough to *say* that, though. He tugged the sword belt free.

One of the guards stepped forward to accept the sword as he removed it. "Handle it carefully," Sword said.

"Of course," the guard said, bowing.

The little man bowed as well, then opened another door and gestured for Sword to precede him.

Beyond the door was the Wizard Lord's throne room.

Sword had seen throne rooms before, in various temples, although the Dark Lord of the Galbek Hills had not bothered with one. He had not, however, seen anything as elaborate as this. Gilt and red enamel were everywhere, and every vertical surface seemed to have been carved, painted, or both, the bright colors gleaming in the sunlight that poured in through two high rows of clerestory windows.

Sword looked up at the windows far above, then around at the ornate furnishings in amazement, until his gaze fell on the dais at the far right end of the room. The man formerly known as the Red Wizard, now the Wizard Lord, sat in an absurdly elaborate red-and-gilt throne on that dais, smiling happily at Sword.

Sword recognized him immediately. His face was unchanged by the six years since they had last met, his straight black hair was still worn long and loose, and he was attired in similarly gaudy red robes, trimmed with green and gold embroidery. His ears were still adorned with gold rings, his throat with a cord bearing several talismans, and the same staff he had carried when he first visited Mad Oak stood propped against the side of the throne.

There were several guards and clerks scattered around, but only three men on the dais. The Wizard Lord was on the throne at the center, the other two standing to either side and slightly behind—and to his astonishment, Sword recognized both of them.

Just behind the Wizard Lord, at his right hand, stood Lore, the Chosen Scholar, in his usual garb of brown leather and white linen.

And behind the Wizard Lord's left shoulder stood a third man Sword knew instantly—the former Leader of the Chosen, the man who had betrayed the Chosen in a conspiracy with the Dark Lord of the Galbek Hills, the man Sword had ordered to pass on his talisman and title or die.

"What are . . ." Sword began, as he stopped dead in his tracks. Then the words stopped, as well, as he realized he did not know what he wanted to say first.

"Sword!" the Wizard Lord called. "How good to see you! Come over here where we can talk without shouting!"

It took a surprising effort to force himself to move, but Sword managed to put one foot in front of the other and approach the throne. At last he stood before the dais, on a vividly red carpet at the foot of two low steps.

"Wizard Lord," he said.

"Call me Artil," the Wizard Lord said.

Sword's mouth opened, then closed.

"I understand you wanted to speak with me," the Wizard Lord said.

"I . . ." For a moment, Sword struggled to make sense of what he saw, to find words to express his confusion, but then he gave up and resorted to his original plan. "Yes," he said. "I wanted to ask about some of these projects of yours."

"Which ones?"

Sword was still too discomposed for subtlety. "The roads. And the Summer Palace."

The Wizard Lord smiled brightly at him. "Do you like them? How are the roads working out up in Longvale? I haven't heard much from that direction yet. Are there many traders out there?"

"I . . . am not sure yet. I have heard of caravans, but not seen any. And I have some doubts about the wisdom of disrupting the natural order."

Artil's smile broadened. "The *old* natural order, you mean. We're making a new one, but it's just as natural, or it will be when it's done. Really, there's nothing untouchable about the old ways; we've been meddling with *ler* for centuries with our priests and magic. I'm just doing it faster, and in a more organized and useful fashion."

This response threw Sword even further off his stride, and his next words were chosen almost at random. "I suppose you are putting the guides out of work."

The Wizard Lord waved that aside. "Not really," he said. "They just don't need to work as hard. They can still carry messages and merchandise, much as they always have."

"And it's been hard on some of the priests."

The smile dimmed. "I hope not *too* hard; I know there were some headaches and the like, and I do regret causing anyone such discomfort. Has there been anything worse up in Mad Oak?"

"Well . . . yes."

The faded smile abruptly vanished, replaced with a look of honest concern. "What's happened?" the Wizard Lord asked.

"Oh, nothing *really* bad," Sword admitted. "Some queasiness. Bad dreams, specters, soured milk, a few kegs of ruined beer."

"Is it . . . will it pass? Could your priestesses say?"

"They thought it would," Sword said. "There was already some improvement when I left."

"But then that's nothing, surely, compared with being able to walk to Willowbank in what, a few hours?"

"Half a day," Sword said.

"Half a day, then. Isn't that worth some discomfort, then? A little inconvenience? And it *will* pass, I'm certain. I'm sure the milk and beer and dreams will all be back to normal within a year."

This conversation was nothing Sword had expected; he had thought that he and the Wizard Lord would sit down in private somewhere and discuss matters gravely and cautiously. Instead he was in this immense room with at least a score of people listening, and the Wizard Lord was bubbling with enthusiasm, not seeming to hold a thing back. Sword glanced around uncertainly.

Everyone was simply standing there, listening, saying nothing. This was apparently all perfectly ordinary for them. Guards were standing ready, clerks were taking notes, but no one seemed at all surprised by any of it.

And those two other men standing silent on the dais, to either side of the throne—what were *they* doing there? Why were Lore and Farash inith Kerra here, apparently acting as advisors? Lore's role as one of the Chosen was to keep the Wizard Lord in check, not to aid him in whatever schemes he might pursue, and the former Boss surely ought to be living in quiet disgrace somewhere far away.

But there they were.

Asking them to their faces why they were there, in this crowd, seemed indelicate. Sword resolved to stay on the subject of road-building for the moment. "Why . . ." he began; then he stopped, cleared his throat, and rephrased the question he wanted to ask. "How is it you came to order the construction of these roads?"

"Well, it's something *you* said," the Wizard Lord said, smiling again. "At the council in the Galbek Hills, when I was chosen to be the new Wizard Lord. You asked whether we really needed a Wizard Lord anymore, since there are no more rogue wizards to be controlled. You said we should see what would happen without one."

"I remember," Sword said cautiously. "But they chose you as the new Wizard Lord anyway."

"Indeed they did, and at the time I thought that was wise. But after further consideration I finally decided that you were right—it's time to change the whole system. It's outlived its original purpose. I don't need to spend my time hunting down murderers and guiding the weather. Ordinary men and women can hunt down outlaws, with a little guidance. And for the most part, the weather can take care of itself, though I don't mean to imply I'm neglecting it. I'm doing my job and guiding the wind and rain, don't worry."

"I wasn't worried," Sword said.

"But you see, here we have this immense concentration of magical and political power in the person of the Wizard Lord—at the moment, in *me*—and we aren't doing anything with it except maintaining an old system that's long since outlived its purpose. So I decided to see what *else* we could do with it, to make Barokan a better place for all of us. I talked to my advisors, and we thought of extending a system of roads out from the Midlands—the Midlands are the wealthiest part of Barokan, and the only obvious reason for that is the relative ease of trade and travel, so that seemed the single best thing we could do."

"Your advisors." Sword blinked, and looked at the former Boss, on the Wizard Lord's left.

The Wizard Lord noticed the direction of his gaze.

"Yes, I decided to ask Farash inith Kerra for advice. I know you two had some sort of falling-out during the campaign to remove the Dark Lord, but still, he was the Leader of the Chosen for a dozen years. I thought he might have some useful insights. And he was eager to share his ideas."

"I'm sure he was," Sword said dryly.

Farash inith Kerra, when he was known as Boss, had made suggestions to the previous Wizard Lord, as well, and had tried to betray the other Chosen into traps in the Dark Lord's dungeon. He and the Dark Lord had planned to set themselves up as the absolute rulers of Barokan. Even before that conspiracy began, Boss had used the magical persuasiveness of the Chosen Leader to set himself up as the master of the town of Doublefall, complete with a palace and a harem of slave girls.

But Sword had not bothered to tell anyone that. He had forced Farash to give up his role and magic, and he had thought that would be enough to render him harmless.

But apparently he had been wrong.

Had the new Wizard Lord not heard what Farash had done? Had no one from Doublefall spread the news? Sword had assumed that the story would be all over Barokan in a matter of months.

Now that he thought about it, though, he had heard no hint of it back in Mad Oak. And *he* hadn't said anything; he had not wanted to be bothered with memories of his adventures.

Had Farash somehow contrived to keep it all secret, even after he gave up his role among the Chosen? Or did Artil, the Red Wizard, the Wizard Lord, simply not *care* that one of his advisors had magically enslaved a town?

And Lore—what was the Chosen Scholar doing up there?

As if guessing his thoughts, the Wizard Lord said, "I also found Lore, to tell me what had been attempted before and what had not, and to make sure I did not transgress any of the boundaries set on my authority. I don't want to be called a Dark Lord, and either killed or forced into retirement. Since it's up to the Chosen to determine whether I have followed the rules, it seemed like the simplest sort of common sense to *ask* you whether my ideas were acceptable, rather than try them out and *then* worry about a sword in the gut or an arrow in the eye. So I consult with Lore on every major decision, and he assured me that building roads and bridges and ferries and canals did not violate any of the established strictures."

"I'm sure it doesn't," Sword agreed. "I just . . . well, I was worried about whether there might be unforeseen effects."

"Oh, nothing major, I'm sure! The *ler* are disturbed, of course, which will cause some temporary problems, and I know it can be uncomfortable for the priests who communicate with the *ler*, but I can't see how it would do anything dreadful in the long run."

"And the Summer Palace? Is it—why is it called that?"

"I would think *that* would be obvious," the Wizard Lord said. "Especially when you're standing here in the Winter Palace on a warm day." He dabbed a finger against his brow, and Sword could see a faint sheen of sweat.

"Then it's for *your* use?"

"Yes, of course. I'm tired of sweltering-hot summers, and as for using magic to keep myself cool—well, you'd be amazed how difficult it is, and how much it disrupts the natural patterns, and the fact is, I'm trying to use as little magic as possible. It's much simpler to just go somewhere that's cooler to begin with, and the high plateau is definitely cooler. Not to mention the breeze, and the spectacular view. You can see a hundred miles from up there! So I've had the Summer Palace built. In fact, we'll be leaving to go there for the season in a few days; you almost missed me. It's only been completely finished this year, and this is the first time I'll be using it properly. Until now I've only visited."

"But it's in the Uplands," Sword protested.

"Yes, it is. But the Uplanders agreed to let me build it there."

That missed the point, and Sword tried again. "But it's not in Barokan!"

"Yes, I *know* that," the Wizard Lord said gently, as if talking to a child.

"But you are the Wizard Lord of *Barokan!*"

"And I can see more of it from up there than I can down here. I'm hardly going to be abandoning my duties just because I'm on top of the cliff instead of below it. I can ride on the wind, remember, and fly down here if some emergency requires my presence."

"But . . ." Sword groped for words. Building a palace atop the cliff did not break any laws, so far as he knew, nor did it harm anyone, but it didn't seem *right*. This was all so strange!

He knew there was some simple, basic reason that the Wizard Lord should not leave Barokan for the Uplands, but before he could put his finger on it, the Wizard Lord spoke again.

"If you'd like to see it, I'd be happy if you would accompany us there," he said.

Again, Sword was caught off-guard; he stared at the Wizard Lord for a moment, then at Farash, and then at Lore, trying to read their expressions.

He saw Farash was nervous, Artil welcoming, and Lore . . . pleading? But why? Farash probably feared having his past revealed, and the Wizard Lord clearly wanted a chance to show off his accomplishments and ensure that the Chosen approved of them, but why were Lore's eyes so desperate? What did the Scholar want to tell him, or want him to do?

Well, accompanying them up the cliffs would give Sword a chance to talk to them all, to learn more of just what was happening, not to mention that seeing the Uplands was an experience he had never had. And he did wonder what the view would be like from up there. Even the view from an ordinary ridge could be beautiful; what would it be like looking down from thousands of feet above Barokan?

The Wizard Lord was watching him expectantly, waiting for his reply.

"I would be delighted," Sword said at last.

[5]

"It's natural enough for the Wizard Lord and the Chosen to avoid befriending each other," the Wizard Lord said, as he flung aside a well-gnawed bone. "After all, the Chosen may find themselves called upon to kill the Wizard Lord, and you can't expect an executioner to seek out the condemned. But if you think about it, natural or not, there's a great deal to be gained if we work together."

"Oh?" Sword said, reaching for his mug of beer. He had the impression that wine was more commonly served at meals in Winterhome, and suspected that the beer was in his honor, since he came from a barley-growing community.

They were seated next to one another at a long wooden table, in a grand dining hall hung, for reasons Sword could only guess at, with the banners of various Uplander clans; Sword recognized several he had seen flying over the great guesthouses to the west of Winterhome's heart. Sword sat on Artil's left; to the Wizard Lord's right was Lore, and beyond him sat Farash inith Kerra. Various other courtiers and officials were seated to either side of this central party, as well as along the far side of the table; all in all, Sword estimated there were about thirty diners present, with at least a dozen young women in the Wizard Lord's red-and-black livery waiting on them, and guards standing at every door.

"Of course!" the Wizard Lord said. "The eight of you have some amazing magical talents that could be put to good use in improving life in Barokan, but because of the traditional separation you don't *use* them for anything except removing Dark Lords, on those unfortunate occasions when they arise." He picked up his own beer and took a sip before continuing, "I mean, think about it. Lore, here, remembers *every true thing he has ever been told!* He's better than a thousand-volume library! And the Archer—he can put an arrow in any target he can see, more or less. That could be used to send messages or documents across rivers, or to carry small objects from one place to another faster than a man can run. The Leader is supernaturally persuasive—she could be of great use in questioning outlaws, don't you think?"

Sword was too distracted by the pronoun "she" to respond coherently, and the Wizard Lord continued, "I haven't quite arrived at any constructive use for *your* particular talents, unfortunately—well, not unless you wanted to be captain of my guard, and I suspect that wouldn't fit well with your ordained duties as one of the Chosen. I admit it would make *me* nervous!" He laughed.

Sword smiled reflexively, but he did not really think it was funny; in his present mood he did not think he would find *anything* funny.

It was not that the Wizard Lord was doing anything *wrong*, exactly; it was just that he was doing everything *differently*. A person in Barokan had a role to fill, a place in the world, a way to fit into the great intricate pattern of life that the *ler* created; people knew what to expect from one another. But this Wizard Lord was not doing *anything* in the way Sword expected a Wizard Lord to act.

He had mentioned several times now, first in the throne room and then again here at the supper table, that he was trying to minimize his use of magic, and that baffled Sword. Why would the man who controlled more than half of all the wizardly magic in Barokan be reluctant to use it? And he was constantly talking about ways to *improve* Barokan. The Wizard Lord's role had traditionally been to protect and *preserve* Barokan, not improve it.

And now he referred to the Leader of the Chosen as "she." Sword had not known the new Leader, Farash's replacement, was female; that, too, hardly seemed traditional. The Leader was supposed to *lead* the Chosen against the Dark Lords, and that was traditionally a man's role. Half of the Chosen could be either sex—there was no reason to restrict the Scholar, the Seer, the Thief, and the Speaker to either sex. The Beauty had to be female, of course, and the Swordsman and the Archer had to be male to be strong enough for their roles, and Sword had always thought that the Leader, too, should be male.

But he could not say why, really. He had great respect for female leaders—Elder Priestess back in Mad Oak, the high priestess who ruled Greenwater, and others—but he had still assumed that the Leader of the Chosen should be male.

He was not sure whether he was more bothered by the new Leader's sex, or by his own reaction to learning of it.

And he could not help wondering if this determinedly untraditional Wizard Lord had influenced the choice, for his own reasons.

"I am a little surprised that you keep Lore so close at hand, in that case," Sword said. "After all, he may not carry a sword, but he is still one of the Chosen."

"Oh, but I'm not at all worried by the presence of the Chosen *as* the Chosen! I've done nothing wrong, and if you ever did decide I had become a Dark Lord, I would choose abdication over death. But if *you*, dear Swordsman, were at my side *with* a sword in your hand, I might worry that perhaps instinct would get the better of you should I do something of which you disapproved, and you might act before giving me a *chance* to abdicate."

"It doesn't work that way," Sword said.

"Doesn't it?"

"No."

The Wizard Lord glanced over at Lore, who confirmed, "It doesn't. The very essence of the Swordsman's ability is control, not violence."

"Indeed? I'm pleased to hear that!" Artil sat back, grinning.

"You would find the sword at your throat, awaiting an explanation or further threat, not in your heart," Lore continued calmly.

The Wizard Lord's smile was suddenly less steady.

"That's assuming I drew it at all, rather than just asking," Sword said hastily.

"And wouldn't you?" Artil asked him, turning to look him in the eye.

"That would depend on the circumstances," Sword said truthfully. "I don't draw it frivolously."

"No? The legends about the Chosen would seem to imply otherwise."

Sword was puzzled. "I earned my living while traveling by doing sword tricks, if that's what you mean."

"No, I was thinking about tales of duels and executions and so on."

Sword blinked. "Are there such tales?"

"Indeed there are."

"I don't remember any," Lore offered.

The Wizard Lord turned to him. "No? You're saying they're all lies?"

"All that I have heard."

"*All* of them?"

"I can't be sure I've ever heard any," Lore replied.

"Oh, but you must have! There are dozens. Not just the usual sorts of stories; besides the supposed bits of history, they range from jokes about jealous husbands to stories where our friend the Swordsman is used as a threat, a monster to terrify children into behaving themselves. I've been hearing them all my life, and surely you have, as well! While I knew they were exaggerations, I had always assumed they had some basis in fact. They're so widespread—you *must* have heard some!"

"I don't remember any," Lore replied.

"Then *every* tale I've heard about the Swordsman or the Archer killing people in duels or contests, or executing people other than Dark Lords, was false?"

"So it would seem," Lore replied. "I don't remember a one."

"Really! That's astonishing." The Wizard Lord turned back to Sword. "Tell us, then, honestly—how many men have you killed?"

Sword stared at him, astonished. "One," he said.

"Just one?"

"Your predecessor."

"Ah." The Wizard Lord seemed discomfited. "No one else?"

"No." Sword found himself too baffled by the Wizard Lord's surprise to be really offended. He hesitated, testing his own resolve, then asked, "How many people have *you* killed?"

"Oh, well . . ." The Wizard Lord waved the question away.

"Fewer than your predecessor, I trust."

"Yes, of course! I haven't killed anyone."

Sword nodded a wordless response.

The Wizard Lord gazed at him silently for a moment, then leaned back in his chair and took a swig of beer. "As the Chosen Swordsman, you could probably kill your enemies with impunity," he said. "*I* certainly couldn't do anything about it, since I am forbidden to harm you.

I find it interesting that you don't seem to have even considered the idea."

"I have no . . ." Sword began, and then he noticed Farash, seated three places down the table and listening intently. "I have only one living enemy," he corrected himself, "and I deliberately chose to spare his life."

"Ah! No rivals in love, no one who teased you as a child, no one who stole from you, or bested you by trickery?"

Sword shook his head. He had always been big and strong for his age, and had had a fairly pleasant childhood; really, the only ones to ever tease him, or play tricks on him, had been his sisters and his friend Joker, and he had never held any grudge for any of that. "None I haven't long since forgiven and befriended."

"You are a forgiving man, then."

"I would like to think so."

"Wise of you, I'm sure—but a curious trait in the man chosen to be the Council's executioner."

Sword frowned, and peered into his beer mug. "I am not exactly an executioner," he said. "My role is a little more complicated than that, just as yours is more complicated than simply ensuring that the rains fall on schedule."

"I'm sure it is." Artil's voice did not convey any conviction whatsoever.

Sword looked up and met the Wizard Lord's eye. "And if I might, Artil—just what *do* you see as your role? You said you were trying to use as little magic as possible; why is that? Isn't magic what the Wizard Lord is *for*?"

"*Controlling* magic, my friend, not *using* it," the Wizard Lord replied, leaning forward again. "That's what you taught me out in the Galbek Hills that night. The Wizard Lord's original job was to bring wizards under control, to put an end to the rogue wizards who were rampaging across Barokan, raping and pillaging at whim. The Wizard Lords were given all the magic that could be gathered in order to achieve that goal, because what else could be used to fight wizards? And it worked, and there have been no rogue wizards in *centuries* now, and you looked at that and asked why we still need a Wizard Lord at all. At the time we paid no attention, but when I *became* the Wizard Lord I thought long and hard about that, and I concluded that we do *not* need a Wizard Lord any longer to hunt down rogue wizards or stamp out banditry. But then, was there something *else* that a Wizard Lord could do, that no one else could?"

"Regulate the weather," Sword said.

"Pah! That's nothing." He waved it away. "The weather in Barokan was never any great problem, even before there were *any* wizards. Ask Lore here, he'll tell you; our ancestors came here and settled because the climate was gentle and the land was fertile, and the priests could bring the *ler* to heel and coax forth crops. We don't need a Wizard Lord for *that!* And with less than a score of wizards left in all Barokan, most of them living quietly in odd corners so as not to attract the Wizard Lord's anger, it seems plain to me that we don't actually need wizards' magic at all, for anything. It's a dying art, an aberration, a relic from another time."

"But then . . . All right, what *do* we need a Wizard Lord for?"

"Well, we don't, really, but we can *use* one," the Wizard Lord explained. "You need to look at the *other* part of the title. I am not merely a wizard, but a lord, a ruler. I am, effectively, the ruler over all Barokan. My rule is limited—as it should be, I'm not objecting—by the Chosen, who will remove me should I do harm to my people, but otherwise, who can challenge me? I can do what I please, so long as I do no harm. Why not do *good,* then? Why settle for merely maintaining things as they are? Barokan has changed over time, become a peaceful and prosperous place; the old days of wild wizards and wild *ler* are gone. Why shouldn't we make it even *better,* now that the old evils are defeated? I said it was prosperous, but it's not as prosperous as it might be, because trade is so limited by the wilderness separating our communities, so I set out to build roads connecting them. And many things that could be done aren't, simply because there's no one to organize people to see them done, so I organized people. I organized the road-builders, and the canal-diggers, and the bridge-builders. The construction crews that built my two palaces can now go on and build other structures for the various towns, build bridges and markets and temples. I've organized the palace guard here, and I'm training them to keep the peace in a somewhat more efficient fashion than the old magistrates and priesthoods—they don't just guard *me*, they guard everyone. And I'm doing all this without using magic any more than I must, because I want it all to function *without* me." He spread his arms wide, taking in all the dining hall and the lands beyond. "I want to create a Barokan that *really* doesn't need a Wizard Lord, that uses good old common sense to regulate matters instead of whimsical magic, so that someday, when we last few wizards are retired or dead, it won't all fall apart."

"That's . . . that's an ambitious scheme," Sword said uncertainly.

"I suppose it is." The widespread arms fell to the arms of his chair. "Do you like it?"

"I don't know," Sword said, sincerely. "I need to think about it a little."

"Oh, *do* think about it! I'm sure you'll see what a grand thing it is. Your compatriot has." He gestured at Lore, then at Farash. "And your former leader."

Sword did not find that as comforting as the Wizard Lord probably thought he should. "Have you spoken to the other Chosen?" he asked.

"I spoke to the new Leader—Boss, she calls herself, as I suppose the Leaders always do. She felt it would not be appropriate for her to work closely with me, but she said she thought it all sounded very promising."

"That sounds sensible."

"The Beauty refused to speak to me, and I have not yet approached the others. I've been busy with other matters."

"I see."

"I'm hoping to locate them soon, though. You've saved me some trouble by arriving unasked, as you have."

"Oh?"

"Yes! Seriously, Swordsman, I want all the powers in Barokan—the Wizard Lord, the Chosen, the Council of Immortals, and all the scattered priesthoods—to work together to make our homeland a better place. I want you all to join me, to make suggestions, to help with my projects and advise me on how best to aid our people."

"You apparently didn't feel any need to consult us before building your roads and palaces, though."

"Well, honestly, Swordsman, if I had tried to get everyone to agree to my projects beforehand, do you think it would have worked? We'd all still be arguing about who should speak first and how the votes would be counted. No, I took the initiative so that everyone could *see* the benefits of cooperation. Once the wagon's rolling it's easier to push."

"I . . . May I speak frankly, Artil?"

The Wizard Lord leaned back and waved grandly. "Oh, by all means! Please do!"

"At first glance, your plans seem wonderful, but young as I am, I have still lived long enough and traveled far enough and seen enough of the world to know that things are not always what they first appear to be. I am not ready to leap up and proclaim your ideas to be the start of a magnificent future; I must reserve judgment until I have seen more."

The Wizard Lord again gestured broadly. "Fair enough! Just give me a chance, and you'll see that I have only the best intentions, and that I'm ready to change anything that does more harm than good." He turned, and pointed at a newly arrived platter that held half a dozen hideous, dead, spidery creatures. "Try one of these, won't you? They're called crabs; they come from the shallow seas near Northmarsh. I had the roads to Northmarsh given priority so I could have these shipped in, and not have to fly out there any time I wanted them—the *ler* of the air are among the hardest to handle, you know; flying is not something even the best wizard can do very often."

"Crabs?" Sword eyed the platter warily.

"Yes, crabs. You crack them open and suck out the meat and juice. They're a delicacy on the coast and the Western Isles, but until the roads were built there was no way to bring them this far inland. They don't keep, they have to be transported alive in a barrel of seawater and then boiled, and that just wasn't possible until there were roads and wagons. Really, try one—they're delicious."

Sword looked at the ghastly things and shuddered. "No, thank you."

"As you please," the Wizard Lord said, clearly disappointed. He reached out and tore a leg off one of the creatures with a brittle crunch. He snapped it open with his hands and, just as he had said, sucked out the meat, with evident enjoyment.

Sword gulped beer, wiped his mouth, and said, "There's one more thing,"

"And what would that be?"

"I would like to speak to you privately—and to Farash, and to Lore, each in turn. There are things I want to say that I am not comfortable saying before so many people." He gestured at the table, where two dozen clerks and courtiers were eating as well as the Wizard Lord, the two advisors, and himself, then extended the gesture to take in the guards at the doors and the maids serving the meal.

"Well, how privately do you mean?"

"I mean alone with each of you. No guards, no servants, and your word that you will not use your magic or any devices you may have built into this place to eavesdrop when I speak to the others."

The Wizard Lord considered that for a moment, then beckoned to one of the guards, who stepped forward.

"Swordsman, this is Azal ori Tath, the captain of my guards," the Wizard Lord said, as the guard came to the table.

Sword nodded an acknowledgment.

"Captain, you heard him?"

"Of course."

"What do you think?"

The captain eyed Sword judiciously, then said, "If he will strip naked, and enter your presence wearing only a garment we provide, and in a place of our choosing where we are sure no weapon has been hidden, and if you go armed, then I think the risk is acceptable."

"My word that I will not harm him is not sufficient?" Sword asked.

"No, it is not. Not when my master's life is threatened."

"I mean him no harm," Sword said.

"Then you should have no objection to the terms."

"Oh, I'll accept the terms," Sword said with a sigh. "I just think it's a good bit of unnecessary trouble. After all, you surely don't force *everyone* who comes near him to follow such rules!"

"You are not 'everyone,'" the captain said. "You are one of the Chosen."

Sword nodded. "Indeed, I am. Very well, then. After dinner, then?"

"A time will be arranged," the Wizard Lord said. "More beer?"

[6]

The time was arranged, as promised, and that evening Sword was summoned from his chamber. Since he knew what was expected he wore only a simple robe and carried nothing with him but the silver talisman that gave him his status as the Chosen Swordsman—he could not safely leave that behind. If he were to be separated from it for more than a few minutes he would become ill, as he knew from unhappy experience.

The search for hidden weapons was distressingly thorough. The talisman was found and deemed sharp enough to be a potential weapon, but Sword was able to convince the guard accompanying him to let him carry the talisman and leave it on the floor just outside the door, where it would, he hoped, be close enough to satisfy the *ler* while distant enough to not threaten the Wizard Lord.

At last, that done, he was escorted into a small, bare room where he found the Wizard Lord waiting.

The Wizard Lord was sitting in the only chair.

"I'm afraid you'll have to sit on the floor, or stand," he said apologetically. "The captain feared you might use any other furniture as a weapon."

Sword sighed, and settled cross-legged to the floor near the door, tucking his thin white robe under him. "If I really meant to harm you," he said, "I could use my bare hands, or twist this robe into a garrote."

"I have a knife," the Wizard Lord said, "and of course my magic."

"I could take the knife away from you and gag you with the robe— but Artil, I mean you no harm. That I tell you these possible methods, and thereby give up any element of surprise, should tell you as much."

"It is your sacred duty to kill me should you think I am unfit to be the Wizard Lord," Artil replied warily. "I think it only reasonable to take precautions."

"Of course. But honestly, I *don't* think you're unfit, and I do believe you when you say you would choose abdication over death."

"I don't particularly want that, either."

"I wouldn't expect you to. Honestly, though, I don't want to harm you or force you to abdicate."

"What else could you want to discuss privately with me? After all, Sword, we don't know each other; we've met just twice before today. What connection is there, other than your duty as one of the Chosen? And what could that be, except my removal?"

"Oh, this is another matter entirely, though I won't say it's completely unrelated."

"And what would that be?"

"Farash inith Kerra."

"Oh?" The Wizard Lord leaned back in his chair, looking puzzled.

Sword sighed. "Wizard Lord—Artil—do you know *why* Farash is no longer the Leader of the Chosen?"

"I know that the events surrounding my predecessor's death . . . well, no; I don't. I asked him, of course, but he said that you had found him negligent in his duties, and he had agreed to give up the role in consequence, but he had sworn not to discuss it further."

"He swore no such oath to me. He hasn't explained further because he did not want to tell lies when Lore was around, and he didn't dare tell the truth."

The Wizard Lord frowned uneasily. "What are you saying?"

"I am saying that Farash inith Kerra, Leader of the Chosen Defenders of Barokan, was a traitor. He had allied himself with the Dark Lord of the Galbek Hills and deliberately sabotaged our actions. He convinced us to let the Thief refuse her role, he led us to the Dark Lord's refuge with no plan or preparation, he did what he could to demoralize and delay us, he conspired with the Dark Lord to ensure that the Speaker was wounded so that half our team stayed behind to tend to her, and finally he lured Bow and myself into traps in the Dark Lord's dungeon. I was able to free myself with my magic—you will forgive me if I don't give the details; I may need that trick again someday—and take him and the Dark Lord by surprise. I slew the Dark Lord, as you know, and I forced Farash at swordpoint to promise he would relinquish his role in the Chosen." He sighed. "It did not occur to me to wonder what he would do after that, and I could never have guessed he would become your advisor. I would have thought that seeing one ally killed before his eyes would have discouraged that."

As Sword gave this speech, Artil's eyes first widened, then narrowed to slits. He leaned forward, elbows on knees. "He . . . he *betrayed* you?"

"Yes."

"But . . . but why?"

"Because he had made an arrangement with Galbek Hills. Working together, they would capture as many of the Chosen as possible, hold us prisoner so that we could neither use our magic nor pass it on, and then, with the seven of us out of the way, the two of them would rule Barokan as if it were their personal plaything, enslaving the population. Farash had already used his magical persuasion as the Leader to enslave his home town of Doublefall—he told me he had a palace there, and a harem."

"But he . . . Did he really? Have a palace, I mean?"

Sword shrugged. "I never saw the palace or the harem, but I heard him conspiring with the Dark Lord, heard him admit to his crimes, heard him suggest that he and I should join with the Dark Lord's successor—with *you*—to rule Barokan."

"He did? And you—you clearly rejected his proposal, but then why didn't you kill him? Surely, you had sufficient reason!"

"It was not my place. I am chosen to defend Barokan against evils committed by the Wizard Lords, not against the other Chosen. I thought that with his magic gone he would be harmless, and . . . and I don't *like* killing. It's wrong. Sometimes it's necessary, but it's still wrong."

Artil tugged at his lower lip and stared at Sword. "So that's . . . Farash is your one enemy, that you mentioned earlier? The one whose life you spared?"

"Yes. Exactly."

The Wizard Lord sat back in his chair and stroked his pointed beard. "That's very interesting," he said. "Very interesting indeed."

"Wizard Lord," Sword said, "of all I have seen since leaving Mad Oak a few days ago, the single thing that most worried me was that man standing by your shoulder on the dais. The roads are a surprise and I fear they may yet have unforeseen consequences, the Summer Palace troubles me because it is outside your proper domain in Barokan, your alliance with Lore is against all tradition, and I wonder why you have so many guards and such elaborate defenses, but that man's presence is the only thing that has genuinely frightened me and made me doubt the sincerity of your good intentions. I fear that even without his magic, he has a persuasive tongue and can mislead you." He spread his empty hands. "And I sit here defenseless before you because I *do* believe your intentions are good, and that you wish to rule Barokan wisely, long, and well, and for that reason I felt I had no choice but to warn you."

"He may have changed, you know," the Wizard Lord said thoughtfully. "He may have learned a lesson from the failure of his previous conspiracy. He may have seen that there's more to be gained from good than evil, that it's better to be loved than feared."

"He may," Sword agreed. "But I doubt it."

"And I don't blame you. You did well to tell me this privately; I appreciate your trust."

"Thank you."

"Was there anything else?"

Sword hesitated. "I'm not sure. I feel as if there is more I should say, as if I should tell you that I have many reservations about the roads and palaces, but I can't think just what I want to say, and in any case I don't need to do that here in private—and I think you already know it, really, even if I don't say another word."

"I think I do," the Wizard Lord said. "I understand your concerns, I do. I'm upsetting systems that have been in place for seven hundred years, and we have no way to be sure that my new systems will be better. I know that, and I see why it worries you, but there is a saying among the fishermen of the Western Isles—a net can snag on the rocks, a snagged net can capsize your boat and pull you under, but if you don't cast the net, you don't catch fish. Sometimes you need to take a chance, and see if it works. If it doesn't, well, you learn what there is to be learned, you clean up the mess, and you go on."

"I hope you're right, Artil."

"And you'll come with us to the Summer Palace, as one of my advisors? Perhaps you could give some of my guards lessons in swordsmanship."

"I could," Sword replied, uncertainly. Something was nagging at him about the Summer Palace, but he could not quite think what it might be.

"And—I have another favor to ask, and I ask it now, in private, so that you can refuse it if you wish without word spreading everywhere."

"What is it?"

"I told you that the Beauty refuses to speak with me. Could *you* speak with her on my behalf, and tell her what I'm attempting? Give her your honest impression. I want *all* the Chosen to understand the situation. I'll be sending envoys to the others, but the Beauty—I think *you* should speak to her."

"Because no man but another of the Chosen can do so without being overcome by lust, and women are prone to envy?"

The Wizard Lord smiled crookedly. "No," he said. "Nothing so devious."

"Then why?"

"Because she trusts you."

"Oh." That caught Sword off-guard, but he could not deny its accuracy. The Beauty did not trust anyone but the other Chosen, that was true enough. "Why didn't you send Lore? He's been here for some time, after all."

The Wizard Lord grimaced. "Years. But he refused."

Sword blinked. "Oh," he said. That was puzzling; why would the Scholar have refused? He had spent months in the Beauty's company, six years ago, and they had gotten along well enough. She trusted him, Sword was sure.

Well, Lore presumably had his reasons. They weren't Sword's. Sword certainly had no objection to seeing the Beauty again. Quite aside from the fact that her role was that of the most beautiful woman in the world, and any man would enjoy looking at her and listening to her voice, he had found her pleasant company. Even with the male Chosen she had been reluctant to let anyone see her or get too close, but in the time they had spent together she had gotten over that to some extent, and he felt as if he had indeed gotten to know her well. She had been cautious, but brave and quick to act when it was called for. She did not waste words, and when she did speak her words were always sensible. Sword had briefly thought their friendship might become something more, but she had put an end to that by pointing out the eighteen-year difference in their ages.

Eighteen years—that meant she must be forty-four or forty-five by now. It was probably time for her to pass her role on to a younger woman.

That was up to her, though.

"I'll need to think about it," Sword said, "but I can probably do that."

"Good! Good!" The Wizard Lord clapped his hands together. "Well, is that it, then? Are we done?"

"I think we are," Sword said. "Shall I leave first? Is that what the captain advised?"

"I believe it is," the Wizard Lord said. "Back the way you came, to recover your clothes."

"Of course." Sword rose in one swift and graceful motion, and bowed to the startled Wizard Lord.

"You moved so *fast!*" he said, clutching at the arms of his chair.

"Good night, Wizard Lord," Sword said. Then he turned and left the room.

A guard was waiting outside the door, and as soon as Sword had retrieved his talisman the guard escorted him to the changing room, where he doffed the simple robe he had been given for the more comfortable and familiar one he had brought with him from Mad Oak. Then he returned to his assigned quarters and dressed himself properly—there were things he wanted to do before going to bed.

He hesitated, then left his sword in his room. He did not want to appear too hostile. His talisman was safely tucked in an inside pocket, of course, but the sword remained behind.

Once he was out in the corridor he realized he had no idea where he was going, but he spotted a guard at one end of the passage; he ambled over. "Excuse me," he said. "I was hoping for a few words with Farash inith Kerra—do you know where I might find him?"

"Who?"

"The Wizard Lord's advisor, the one who used to be the Chosen Leader."

"Oh, Old Boss? Sure, his room is right up there, third on the left." He pointed.

A moment later Sword was knocking on an enamel painting of a waterfall that decorated the door the guard had indicated.

"Who is it?" called a voice from inside.

"The Swordsman," Sword replied.

For a moment there was silence; then Sword was certain he heard a heavy sigh. "Just a moment," Farash called.

Sword waited.

A moment later the door opened, and Farash beckoned him in. "I knew we would need to talk," Farash said. "We might as well get it over with."

"That's very much my own feeling," Sword said, as he stepped in.

The room gave every appearance of being a long-term residence, rather than a mere guest room like Sword's own; there were papers and personal items scattered about, and an open wardrobe held a variety of clothing. Farash gestured at a chair, and Sword took a seat.

Farash did not take the other chair, but settled onto the edge of a writing desk. "Did you come to Winterhome looking for me?" he asked.

"No," Sword replied. "I came to see the Wizard Lord, and your presence here was a complete surprise."

Farash sighed. "I doubt the surprise was any less pleasant for you than your arrival was for me."

"That may well be true." Sword shifted in his chair, then asked, "What are you doing here?"

"I am the Wizard Lord's advisor. There's nothing sinister or underhanded about it; I'm exactly what I appear to be." He grimaced. "This time."

"You have the gall to . . ."

Farash held up a hand. "Don't start that."

Sword glared silently.

After an awkward moment, Farash let his breath out and said, "Fine, yes, I was a traitor to the Chosen, and I sided with the Dark Lord of the Galbek Hills in an attempt to rule Barokan without restraint. I built myself a palace and enslaved a town with my magic. I admit that. It was a bad idea. It was wrong, and it didn't work. I hid the murder of an entire village, and probably caused the spirits of the dead a moderate amount of distress by delaying their rightful vengeance. I interfered with a good many innocent lives in Doublefall, robbed almost everyone there, and you could consider my harem to be an exercise in rape, though I assure you that none of the women thought so at the time. Everyone in Doublefall did what I said because my magic had convinced them that they wanted to, that they were acting of their own free will, and before I gave up my magic I went back there and persuaded them all to forget what I had done. In case you've wondered how I avoided any punishment for my acts, now you know; they only remember bits and pieces of my rule, and don't know I did anything untoward. Yes, I did it to escape punishment, but I also wanted to save *them* any trouble, any regrets or recriminations about how they let themselves be used."

"I did wonder about that," Sword admitted. "About why I hadn't heard any more about what happened in Doublefall, and how you survived and stayed free. I had assumed the story would come out, and you would be disgraced."

"Yes, well, it was obvious I couldn't continue as I had been, once Galbek Hills was dead and you knew what I'd done. So I went home and tried to end it as gently and peacefully as I could. You do realize, I hope, that I could have wiped out the entire town? If I had told them to kill themselves, Doublefall would be inhabited by nothing but dry bones and well-fed rats and crows by now—but I am not the evil heartless monster you seem to think. Those people hadn't hurt me, quite the contrary, and I had no desire to harm them."

"And you didn't know whether someone might investigate," Sword pointed out. "Murdering an entire town might have drawn the attention of the new Wizard Lord, don't you think? And I don't think he'd have made you his advisor in that case."

"Well, yes, I suppose that was part of it. But really, Sword, I was trying to *fix* things. I had tried to do something selfish and . . . well, evil, I suppose, and it hadn't worked out, so I did my best to undo it. Really."

"And then you came here, to Winterhome."

"Yes!" Farash snapped. "What did you think I would do, curl up and die? You left me alive—did you think I would simply wander off into the wilderness and live on roots and berries? You knew I liked wealth and power; where else would I get them? Look around you! I'm living in a grander palace than ever, even if it's someone else's instead of my own. My purse is full of gold, and eager young women compete for my attention. And the best part of it is that I did this *honestly*, without hurting anyone, without breaking any rules. *This* Wizard Lord wants to *help* people, to make Barokan better, and I'm helping him do that, and it's making my life better than my stupid plotting with that idiot in his ugly stone tower ever did."

"And you have no hidden motives, no darker plan?" Sword made no attempt to hide his suspicion.

"No! Why should I? I'm getting everything I want by being *good*, Sword! There's no reason to hide anything. And do you know, you made this possible?" Farash smiled crookedly. "As the Leader of the Chosen I couldn't have worked so closely with a Wizard Lord, or accepted all the privileges I have here; people would have objected, the *ler* would have objected, it wouldn't have fit my role. And what I did get would have come from my magic, not from me, and if I pushed too hard, my *ler* might have turned on me eventually. But you made me give up my role in the Chosen, give up my magic, break my link to the *ler*, and that meant I was free to work *openly* with the Wizard Lord, to *earn* what I want."

His smile twisted wryly. "Do you know, when I was ruling Doublefall, even when I had beautiful girls worshipping at my feet I knew there was something slightly unreal about it all? It wasn't *me* who had brought them there, it wasn't *me* they were worshipping, it was my magic. It was the *ler*, not *me*. It was . . . unsatisfying. Frustrating. Almost demeaning, somehow. And I thought that if Galbek Hills and I ruled everything, that would be better—but really, I don't think it would have been. It would have been even worse, I suspect. But *this*, what I'm doing now—it *is* better! No one is worshipping me, but they respect me, they honor me, and it's *genuine*, it's not magical."

Sword stared at him.

"This is *better*," Farash said. "You did me a *favor* by killing the Dark Lord and making me give up my role!"

"You're serious?"

"Absolutely! I am happier now than I had been since I first agreed to accept the Talisman of Command."

Sword stared at him, trying to comprehend this. He had not imagined this possibility. He had expected the former Leader to live out his life in quiet disgrace somewhere, ashamed and afraid.

But that had been unrealistic, and he should have known as much.

"I still don't trust you," he said.

"I wouldn't expect you to," Farash replied.

"I told the Wizard Lord."

Farash sighed. "Already? I was afraid of that. What did he say?"

"He said you might have changed."

"And maybe I have. Not so very much, really, because I still want much the same things I always did. I just know better now than to try to take them without earning them."

"I still . . . I find that hard to believe."

"I'm sure you do. I probably would, too, in your position, and frankly, you don't strike me as the sort of person who forgives or trusts easily. Sword, I don't expect you to trust me, or to like me, or to forgive me; all I ask is that you give me the benefit of the doubt, and let me go on as I am until you have even the tiniest shred of evidence that I have not reformed."

"I'm not going to just kill you," Sword said. "And I can't force the Wizard Lord to send you away."

"You could still ruin my life quite effectively, though, just by telling everyone what happened six years ago. Artil may be willing to let the past lie; his attention has always been on what lies ahead, not what's behind us. Most people, though, would not be. The women who curry my favor, the men who look at me with respect, would all see me as the miserable traitor who enslaved innocents and let ghosts wander un-avenged. I'd be an object of disgust and derision. And those who *did* find themselves agreeing with me about anything would wonder whether I might be using some lingering magic on them, and would rebel at the thought. You could bring all that down on me with a few words in the right ear."

"Yes," Sword admitted, speaking slowly and thoughtfully. "Yes, I suppose I could."

Farash said, "Sword, I have no right to demand anything of you, but I am asking you to show mercy, and keep the past to yourself. If I do anything evil, betray any trust, harm any innocent, then by all means, do your worst, spread the story from cliffs to coast, come after me with blades drawn if you want—but *until* you see some sign that I have not reformed, I beg you, hold your peace, and let me keep my place here. I am doing good, I swear by all the *ler*. I am working as hard to improve Barokan as I ever did to rule it. Let me atone as best I can."

Sword slumped in his chair and stared up at the former Leader's face. Such a request should be accompanied by a pleading expression, by outstretched hands, but Farash was leaning on the desk with his hands on his hips, and his expression was one of challenge, not entreaty.

"I'm a barley farmer and a swordsman," Sword said at last. "Meting out justice to anyone but a Dark Lord isn't my responsibility."

"I'm glad to hear you say that."

"But I give you a warning, Old Boss," Sword said. "I came here to see whether the Wizard Lord might be meddling in things he should not, and I have not reached a conclusion. If I decide that the Red Wizard has become a Dark Lord and must be removed, I will remove him. And if I learn that it was *you* who made him into a Dark Lord, who suggested whatever evil results in his removal, then I *will* kill you."

"Understood," Farash said, standing up straight. "And fair enough. And with that agreed, I expect to live a long and happy life and die peacefully in bed." He held out a hand.

Sword ignored the hand as he rose from the chair.

"Good night, Farash inith Kerra," he said.

And then he left the room, and found his way to his own bed.

7

Sword had intended to speak to Lore first thing in the morning, but instead he was caught up in the preparations for moving the household up the cliffs to the Summer Palace. The entire palace seemed to be full of hurrying people carrying bundles. Sword found himself lending a hand here and there, or stepping aside to let heavily laden people pass, and did not manage to reach Lore's quarters until the sun was above the cliffs.

The apartment was empty; a guard told him the Chosen Scholar had left an hour or so earlier, and his current whereabouts were unknown.

Frustrated, Sword headed for the throne room, thinking Lore might be there, or that the Wizard Lord might be and might know where Lore was.

The throne room was deserted, though. He turned away from the door, disappointed, and almost collided with his quarry.

"Lore!" he said, stepping back. "You startled me."

"Sword." Lore nodded, straightening his vest as he did.

"I was looking for you," Sword said. He glanced around to see whether anyone else was in earshot, but the passage and throne room both seemed deserted save for the two of them.

"So the guards told me," Lore replied. "That's why I'm here. What can I do for you?"

"You can answer a few questions, I hope."

"That's something I'm usually good at," Lore said, managing a smile—the first one Sword had seen on his face since arriving in Winterhome.

"Well, these aren't about ancient history or old stories, I'm afraid."

"I can guess what one of them is, then," Lore said. "You want to know why I'm here, working with the Wizard Lord."

"Yes. That's the obvious one, certainly."

"Well, what he told you is true. About three years ago he tracked me down to ask whether his plans violated any of the limits the Council placed on him, and whether anyone had ever attempted them before, and if so, why they failed."

"I can see why he would ask you, and why you would answer, but to come and live in his palace and stand at his right hand seems . . ." Sword groped for the right word.

"Compromising?" Lore suggested.

"More or less, yes."

Lore shrugged. "He had *many* questions, and I wanted to keep an eye on him. Remember that the Dark Lord of the Galbek Hills committed crimes that went undetected for five years; I don't want anything like that to happen again. If this one goes mad, we want to know immediately, don't we?"

"I suppose we do."

"And frankly, if you listen to him—doesn't he sound half-mad, sometimes? When he came to me with his schemes for clearing roads and building a community atop the cliffs and draining the southern marshes, I thought he was on the verge of raving. I thought at least one of the Chosen should keep a close watch on him, and he *asked* me to, so here I am. And sometimes I think he *has* gone mad, and other times I think he may be the greatest man to ever live in Barokan, and every day I learn a little more about him."

Sword nodded slowly.

"But whether *you* should stay, whether you should have accepted his invitation to visit the Summer Palace—well, I'm not so sanguine about that. You aren't an advisor by nature, Sword; you're a fighter. I really hope there won't be any need for fighting. And if he decides to find a use for you, well, if you have a mallet, you look for a peg."

"You have a point," Sword acknowledged. "But I want to see more of him, and judge him for myself. As you say, he does seem slightly mad—and I don't trust Farash, either; as long as he's here . . ."

"What *happened* between you and Old Boss, Sword?" Lore asked, interrupting. "I don't remember anything you said about it, and we both know what that means."

"It means I didn't tell you the truth," Sword said. "I didn't tell you much of anything, really. I didn't directly lie to you, that I recall."

"Lying by omission is still lying, isn't it?"

"Maybe," Sword said. "I'm really not sure of that."

"Whether it is or not, I'd like to know what happened."

"Ask *him*, then; he might even admit it."

"That's hardly a satisfying response."

"Well, it's what you're getting, for the moment; I'm just not ready to tell you more yet. Maybe soon."

"It wasn't just that he was careless and overconfident, was it?"

"No."

"Do you think you'll *ever* be ready to tell me?"

"Oh, probably. Just not yet."

"I answered *your* question."

"Confirming what our friend Artil had already told me, yes. Thank you. And I do have another question."

"Oh?"

"The Wizard Lord asked me to talk to the Beauty about his plans."

"Ah. And he told you I'd refused."

"Yes."

"And you want to know why."

"Yes."

Lore contemplated Sword for a long moment, then said, "I'll trade."

Sword sighed. "I thought you might say that."

"And?"

"And I'll do it. Why did you refuse?"

"Have you forgotten the effect the Beauty has on men?"

"No, but . . ." Sword paused.

To some extent, he *had* forgotten the effect she had on men who were not somehow protected from her magic. While she was the most beautiful woman in the world to anyone, himself included, she was even more than that to ordinary men. She was irresistible, a creature whose appearance could cause a man to forget everything else, whose merest whims were commands as long as she remained in sight. Even men who would not otherwise take an interest in women were drawn to her. Women tended to be overcome with envy at the sight of her.

The Chosen and to some extent the Wizard Lord were immune to her magic, though her natural charms were enough that Sword, Lore, Bow, and even Old Boss had found themselves maneuvering to get close to her, listening to the sound of her voice as if it were music, and staring at her without meaning to. Other people could fend off her powers by wearing or carrying *ara* feathers, which blocked or weakened most forms of magic, but most men would be overwhelmed by her presence. That was why she lived alone in Winterhome, where the customary garb for women effectively concealed her charms.

"She couldn't come to this palace," Sword said.

"No. The guards and staff would fall to pieces at the sound of her voice, or if she took the scarf from her face. And before he would permit her into his presence, the Wizard Lord would insist on having her searched, just as you were, to make sure she wasn't planning to stab him with a hidden knife—after all, that was how the Dark Lord of Kamith t'Daru died, with a Beauty's blade in his chest. But who could *do* that? Who could search her safely and effectively? So she can't come here, and can't speak directly to the Wizard Lord; her refusal to see *him* was just common sense."

"He could talk to her through an animal."

"I think he may have tried that. If so, it didn't work. I suppose she refused to talk to him."

"But why won't *you* see her?"

"What good would it do? She won't come out of hiding, and she isn't going to kill him without the cooperation of the rest of the Chosen."

"But what *harm* would it do?"

Lore took a moment before replying. "I don't think you see, Sword, just how precarious my relationship with the Wizard Lord is. Helpful and enthusiastic as I may be—and I am *not* always all that enthusiastic—I am still one of the Chosen, the group charged with the right and the responsibility to kill him if he exceeds his bounds. I don't want to bring him bad news. I don't want to argue with him. I don't want to do anything to remind him of what the Chosen are chosen to do. If Beauty were to sway me and convince me that the Wizard Lord is doing something wrong, what would my choices be? I could tell him that he must abandon his cherished plans, and he would attribute it not to my own good sense, but to the Beauty having seduced me into a conspiracy against him. Or I could refuse to return here, and he would see that as a sign, once again, that the Chosen are coming to remove him. Neither of those is an attractive option."

"Is he *that* worried about the Chosen?"

"Yes."

"But why would she sway you? *You* know far more about his plans than *she* does!"

"It might be that I am too close to them to see flaws that she will notice. Remember also that my perceptions are skewed by my magic—I remember everything I am told that is true, but I can forget lies. That means that sometimes, I remember the good and true parts of someone's plans and forget the errors and deceptions. Oh, it's not common, and I try to guard against it, but it can happen, and it can give me an unjustly favorable impression of a situation."

Sword stared at him for a moment. "I never thought of that," he said at last.

"There's no reason you should, but I live with it every day. All of us among the Chosen have our difficulties, some more subtle than others—poor Babble lives with a constant flood of voices she can't shut out, Beauty must shut herself away from other people, those are obvious, but *I* live with the knowledge that I may be misjudging people because I remember them as more truthful than they really are. The Leader can't trust anyone else's assessment of his decisions—or rather, *her* decisions, now—because her magical persuasiveness makes them much too prone to agree with even the stupidest blunder. And I sometimes think Bow sees everything as a target. I suppose you must have your own problems, though I confess I don't know what they are."

"I'm not sure I do, either," Sword replied. "But still, suppose the Wizard Lord's plans do *not* have any flaws that Beauty has noticed. What then?"

"Subtle again. Why, then the Wizard Lord would expect her to help him, to serve him in convincing others to cooperate with him. And I think it's very obvious how she could do that, if she wanted to."

"Simply by asking them and smiling, in most cases," Sword said.

"And what would happen if she refused to do this?"

"The Wizard Lord would assume she actually opposed him and was preparing to remove him."

Lore nodded and held up a finger. "Exactly. You have come to understand the man's mind, as I have. And *would* she agree to help him by seducing his opponents?"

"No. Never." Sword knew Beauty better than to think she would ever do such a thing; she would never use her magic for anything but its intended purpose of aiding in the removal of a Dark Lord.

"Very good. You understand *her* mind, as well." Lore lowered the admonitory finger. "And besides, Sword, I don't want to see her. It would be an exercise in frustration. I like her, and I'd like to know her better, but that isn't going to happen."

"Oh." Sword felt like an idiot for not having considered that, but then another thought struck him. "But why isn't it going to happen? I'm too young for her, but *you're* not. You're a little older than she is. And you're one of the Chosen, so her magic isn't an insurmountable issue."

"Sword, we traveled together for months, remember?"

"Yes, and Bow demonstrated that he was a boor she wanted nothing to do with, and she and Old Boss didn't get along very well, but I didn't notice *you* having any great problems."

"You didn't notice any great successes, either. *You* were the only man among the Chosen she found attractive, your youth notwithstanding. And yes, I know that part of that attraction may have *been* your youth, and the reputation that goes with your role, and that the attraction wasn't enough to overcome the difference in your ages, but really, Sword, don't you think I'd have seized on even the *slightest* hint that I might have a chance with her, once you were gone?" He shook his head. "She isn't interested in me, and to go to her as the Wizard Lord's messenger and errand boy would not help, and I would prefer not to put myself through that particular form of humiliation."

Sword was not absolutely convinced that Lore's assessment of the situation was correct, but he had no coherent evidence or argument to the contrary to present. He had not seen any sign that the Beauty had any interest in the Scholar, and he had to admit it was a rational enough reason, when combined with the rest of it, to refuse to talk to her.

And the rest of it, the whole discussion of what might come of such a conversation, suddenly struck home.

He had said he would talk to the Beauty, and almost everything Lore had said about the possible outcomes applied to him, just as it did to Lore.

But no, he corrected himself; he had not said he would talk to her. He had said he would need to think about it.

But if he went back to the Wizard Lord and said he would not talk to her, the Wizard Lord would want an explanation. Lore had refused, and had apparently not explained why . . .

"What did you tell Artil?" Sword asked. "When he asked you to talk to her, I mean."

"I said it wasn't my place."

"He accepted that?"

"What could he say?"

Sword considered that. He suspected that if he tried the same thing, and said that after thinking about it he felt it wasn't his place, the Wizard Lord would not appreciate it—especially since he might well know that Sword had spoken with Lore; he hadn't made any attempt to keep this conversation a secret.

He would suspect conspiracy. That would not be good.

And furthermore, Sword realized, he *wanted* to speak to the Beauty—not as the Wizard Lord's advocate, but just for himself. He wanted to see her again, and hear her voice, even if they could never be more than friends and compatriots.

"That's my side of the bargain," Lore said, interrupting Sword's thoughts. "Now for yours."

"Oh," Sword said. He paused and looked around.

They were alone at the door of the throne room; the passage was empty, the throne room deserted.

"Come in here," he said, "where we won't be heard." He took Lore by the sleeve and pulled him into the throne room.

"The Wizard Lord could be listening anywhere, you know, through a spider or a mouse," Lore pointed out. "We don't have the Seer to warn us here."

"Yes, well, I already told *him*," Sword said. "But I don't want rumors running rampant."

"Ah." Lore glanced around as the two of them took up a position in the center of the great empty room, well away from all walls, doors, and windows, as well as the dais and throne.

Sword leaned close and whispered, "I should have noticed something much sooner, but do you remember when we reached the Dark Lord's tower, and Babble was wounded, so you and Seer and Beauty took her to the wagon to be tended?"

"Yes, of course."

"And Bow, Boss, and I went on into the tower, and Boss said the Wizard Lord must be in the dungeons and cellars?"

"Yes."

"Well, Bow and I went down the stairs, and got separated, and there were traps set down there. The Dark Lord had built corridors with hidden doorways and had his maids waiting, ready to slam the doors and entrap us. It worked on Bow, and he was sealed in down there in the dark, but I heard them in time, and caught my sword between the doors before they could close, and forced my way out. If Galbek Hills had used big strong guards like the ones around here I might not have been able to do it, but he only used girls because he was worried about the Beauty turning his servants against him. I was able to overpower the two maids and lock them away."

"Bow had told us part of that," Lore acknowledged.

"Yes, well, when I realized it had been a trap I went back upstairs, looking for Boss, and I realized he had never tried to follow us down at all. He had gone *up,* up the stairs to the top of the tower. And I followed him up there and overheard him talking to the Wizard Lord about how they had fooled us all, and how Bow and I were safely locked away in the dungeon and it was time to call in the others and trap the rest of you as well. He had been conspiring with the Dark Lord all along, plotting to lock us away. They didn't want to kill us, since that would destroy part of the Wizard Lord's own magic, but holding us prisoner would leave the two of them in a position to do anything they pleased, and to enslave all of Barokan, just as Farash had already enslaved Doublefall with his own magic."

"*What?*"

"Oh, yes. Old Boss had a palace and a harem back in Doublefall, and the entire town waited on him hand and foot. And he had deliberately talked the Thief *out* of accompanying us, because he knew she could probably avoid their traps and escape from any prison, but he did it so subtly we didn't even realize he had."

"That's . . . that's . . ."

"So I burst in, took them by surprise, killed the Wizard Lord—and that was enough of death for me. I let Farash inith Kerra live, on the one condition he swore to give up his role as the Leader of the Chosen. Which he did, but now I come here and find him advising the *new* Wizard Lord, and he tells me that before passing on his role as Leader he ensured that the people of Doublefall would forget any harm he had done them and remember only the good." Sword's voice rose from a whisper to a growl on this final sentence. "He swears he has reformed and will never again harm an innocent, but you will forgive me if I am not entirely convinced."

"Does Artil know this?"

"He does now. And so do you, and I trust the two of you will keep watch over him."

Lore nodded, straightening up from the crouch he had assumed while listening. "I will endeavor to do so," he said.

"Good." Sword clapped him on the shoulder. "And *I* intend to go speak to the Beauty, before I lose my nerve."

8

The Beauty's home, a quarter-mile north of the plaza, was much as Sword remembered it—a cozy stone-and-wood house with small, tightly shuttered windows and a blackened oak door. He stepped up and knocked.

The last time he had come here uninvited he had been accompanied by Old Boss and the old Seer, and the Seer had been able to tell them where Beauty was in the house, whether she was coming to answer the door or not. This time Sword had no such magical information, but could only wait impatiently, wondering whether his knock had been heard, whether the Beauty was even there.

He knocked again.

A moment later the door opened a crack, and a scarf-wrapped face peered out. Two beautiful green eyes blinked at him, and then the door was flung wide. "Sword!" she said. "How good to see you! Come in, come in!"

Somewhat startled by this enthusiasm, Sword obeyed. He had expected to be allowed in, but he had not anticipated *this* positive a reception. "Hello, Beauty," he said.

The familiar hearth was cold and dark; no one needed a fire on so warm a day as this. The two rocking chairs still stood to either side, though, and the Beauty gestured for him to take one while she settled in the other. The table was bare save for a wedge of cheese and a paring knife on a cutting board, and there was no sign of the old ginger tomcat.

The vase on the shelf by the mantel was jammed full of *ara* feathers, many more than Sword remembered being there.

"It's good to see you again," Sword said, quite sincerely.

"Then see me properly," Beauty said, pulling the scarf from her face and throwing back her hood, letting waves of dark hair spill free around her face and throat. "It's a pleasure to have someone here who can look at my face and not be overwhelmed by it." She shook her head to clear her hair away.

Sword smiled with astonished delight; he had not expected her to show her face so readily. He tried not to stare too openly. "Oh, even without any magic, it can be overwhelming," he said. "You're still a very beautiful woman." That was no polite exaggeration; even in her forties, the Beauty was incredibly attractive, her skin smooth and flawless, the curve of her cheekbones clean and perfect.

"The most beautiful in the world. I know. But just a woman." She smiled wryly, and Sword felt his heartbeat quicken.

He was flattered that she had uncovered her face; when they had traveled together six years earlier, from Winterhome to the Galbek Hills, she had kept her face hidden as much as possible, even when only the other Chosen were around. He had not seen her as exposed as she was now until the Dark Lord lay dead in his tower. He knew this intimacy meant that she trusted him, and he knew that she would not have done this with most of the others. He was flattered, and felt more honored than he ever had by any other compliment.

He wished there were some way he could reciprocate, but he had no hidden beauties to reveal. He felt awkward as he groped for words.

"How have you been?" he asked at last. "Well, I hope."

"Oh, well enough." She gestured at their surroundings. "I'm still here, just as you see me. And you? You went home to Mad Oak? You've been there all these years?"

"I did," Sword said. "I have."

"How was it?"

He hesitated. "Different," he said at last. "My father had died, and everything was . . . different. They wanted me to be a hero returned from his adventures, not just another barley farmer. You've been shut away so long, hiding yourself, I don't know whether you'd understand . . ."

"I remember," she said quietly. "It wasn't the same for me, because I was *always* a beauty, people had always stared at me and talked about me as if I wasn't a person who could hear them but some sort of gorgeous animal, and boys had lusted openly after me ever since my breasts grew, but when I became *the* Beauty it all became a thousand times worse. I could no longer hold a conversation with *anyone*. Men would not hear my words as anything but a veiled invitation, women would twist them into insults, even children just stared at me with their mouths agape. Until I came to Winterhome and donned the hood and scarf, I never had a moment's peace unless I locked myself away."

"It isn't . . . it hasn't been *that* bad for me," he said. "Nothing like that. I'm only the Swordsman, after all."

"I don't know why I did it," she said. "I was young and stupid, but even so, how could I possibly have thought that becoming even *more* beautiful would make anything *better*?"

"Did you? That wasn't what you said before."

She laughed musically, and Sword found himself blushing for no reason he could explain. "No, that's right, I didn't think it would make it any better," she said. "You're right. I thought I was already so beautiful that I might as well put it to some use, and that it couldn't be much worse. But it was."

"I'm sorry. It hasn't been like that for me; people still talk to me, I can still walk through town without people staring. It's much subtler than that; it's as if they keep *expecting* something of me, but even *they* don't know what it is. But they're disappointed all the same when it doesn't happen."

She nodded. "I can imagine," she said.

He smiled. "There's one thing you can probably appreciate better than anyone," he said. "How the women look at me."

She frowned. "I'm not sure I understand."

"Well, according to legend, my magical abilities extend to wielding anything even remotely swordlike with superhuman skill, including that rod which every man is born with. There may be some truth in it, I don't know, as it isn't a matter that lends itself to open and honest comparison, but certainly the women of Mad Oak have all heard the tales and believe them. They very rarely say anything aloud in my hearing, but I see the way they look at me, the considering glances and curious stares."

"Are they all eager to share your bed, then?"

"No." Sword shook his head. "They all *think* about it, certainly, I can see it in their eyes and hear it in their voices, but I spend as many nights alone now as I ever did. I think they're afraid to test the legend— but whether they fear it to be true or false, I couldn't say. And I think they treat me differently. When they consider me as a lover, I believe they look on me as a possible diversion, not a possible husband. That was never the case before I became the Swordsman." He shook his head. "I would have thought the tales of my skill would make me *more* desirable as a husband, not less."

"A husband doesn't spend most of his time in bed," the Beauty replied. "As one of the Chosen you will always have obligations beyond your family, and your legendary prowess probably makes them think you more likely to stray, less likely to be satisfied with one ordinary woman. Better to enjoy a night or two and move on than to try to hold what you can't."

"I suppose that's it. Is that how men look on you, then? As a brief amusement?"

"No. On the contrary, they want to possess me, to *own* me, as if I were a thing rather than a person. But they're men, and the ones who lust after you are women; our sexes differ in more than the physical."

"I suppose we do."

For a moment the two of them sat in companionable silence; then the Beauty said, "And why are you here, Sword? Surely you didn't come to Winterhome just to share our discontentments."

"No. I came to Winterhome to see what sort of man the Wizard Lord was, and why he had ordered the construction of roads through the vales."

She nodded. "Of course. And that's a very good reason. Have you learned what you sought to know?"

"Not really. Not enough. I've spoken with him, and heard him say he built the roads because he just wanted to help, but there's more to him than I've seen and heard, and I'm not sure I like it."

"I'm sure I *don't* like it, but I can't really explain what troubles me."

"Oh? I know you refused to speak with him."

"I refuse to let *any* man save the Chosen see me without my hood and scarf, and he wanted me to consent to be searched by his guards, to be sure I had no dagger beneath my robes, ready to thrust into his heart."

"I thought that might be it. But he could speak to you through a beast, couldn't he?"

"He tried, but I won't speak to him. I'm afraid I might say something that will turn him against me. I don't trust him."

"Why not? Have you seen any harm come from these grand plans of his?"

"No, on the contrary, the roads have brought traders to Winterhome, and let the Host People travel elsewhere, and so far that's all been good. The priests complain, especially when the roads are being built, but for most people the results are clearly an improvement. It appears this is exactly what the Wizard Lord intended, and it's working well."

"Then why don't you trust him?"

The Beauty studied Sword's face for a moment before replying, "You worry because he built roads where there had never been roads, yes?"

"And palaces where there had never been palaces, yes."

"Yes, his palaces, with guards and servants everywhere—*two* immense palaces, where every other Wizard Lord has been content with one. The moment the first was complete he sent his workers to begin another. He has road crews working their way northward down Longvale and Shadowvale, and up and down the coast, and deep into the southern hills. I have heard he has canals and bridges and other projects under way, as well."

"Yes, so I've heard."

"And you worry about the roads and the palaces—you're a man, you look at the things being built."

Sword frowned. "What? And you do not?"

"No. I'm a woman. I look at the people *building* them. I look at the guards and the servants and the laborers and the designers and the road workers, and I ask myself, where did they come from? Why did they come? Who are they? How does he keep them, and why? He is terrified of being assassinated by the Chosen, you know that, but why doesn't he fear anyone else? Why is he so certain the captain of his own guard won't turn on him over some petty slight?"

"I don't know," Sword said, startled. "I hadn't thought of any of that. But wouldn't his magic protect him from any ordinary assassin?"

"If he has a chance to use it, perhaps."

"Where *did* he get all those people? Do you know?"

"I know about some of them. I know that he visited several towns and called for volunteers. He said he wanted strong, brave young men to help him in making Barokan a better place. He promised good pay and satisfying work and the respect of honest people."

"That seems . . ." Sword paused. "How is that different?"

"Ordinarily, a Wizard Lord or anyone else says what roles he needs to fill, and lets people come to him until all the roles are filled. *This* Wizard Lord went to half the towns in the Midlands saying he would find work for anyone who wanted it."

Sword frowned, puzzled. "That *does* seem odd. What will he do with the extras?"

"That's what worries me, Sword. There *are* no extras. He *does* find work for all of them. I'm not sure how, or where they all go."

Sword's frown deepened.

"I can't say what he's done wrong, Sword, but I don't trust him," Beauty said.

"I can see that," Sword replied.

"And if you tell him that, he'll probably make my life miserable."

"He might, yes," Sword agreed.

"Maybe it's time to give it up, then," she said. "Ask the wizards to find my successor."

That startled Sword anew. He started to speak, to say something reassuring, but then he stopped. The Beauty was in her mid-forties, after all, and handing the role on to a young woman or a girl was a perfectly reasonable thing to do.

But on the other hand, doing it under pressure from the Wizard Lord . . .

Blade, the old Swordsman, had given up his role and turned his place among the Chosen over to Sword in part because he mistrusted the last

Wizard Lord. Although all had turned out well enough in the end, he had been hesitant to do so, and Sword remembered why.

"No," he said. "Then you'll have no defense against him. He'll be able to kill you on a whim."

Beauty stared at him. "Why would he do that? Why would he care about me, if I have no magic?"

"I don't know," Sword admitted. "Maybe he wouldn't—but I don't trust him, any more than you do. He isn't following the traditional models, fitting into the traditional roles; there's no way of knowing what he might do."

"Then what am I to do?" she asked, a note of despair creeping into her voice. "I want nothing to do with him, but will he accept that, and not think it makes me his enemy, to be destroyed?"

"He *ought* to accept it, if it's put to him properly."

"That doesn't mean he will."

"I'll do my best to convince him. And I'll remind him that harming any of the Chosen is one of the things forbidden to him. I'll try to convince him this extends to those who were Chosen, but are no longer."

"Thank you."

It was all Sword could do to remain in his chair and not reach for her, go to her, take her in his arms—she was *so* beautiful, and she was so obviously grateful, so welcoming . . .

But she was too old for him. Or he was too young for her.

"I should go," he said.

"Why?"

"The Wizard Lord is leaving for the Summer Palace soon, and he wants me to come along."

"And you're going?"

"Yes."

"Why?"

Sword considered making up a more noble explanation, but then decided she deserved the truth.

"I want to see it," he said. "I want to see what the Uplands really look like, and what the view from the top of the cliffs is like. I'm told the air is different up there, harder to breathe somehow—I can't imag-

ine how that could be, but I have heard it said. I want to know what
that feels like, what it tastes like and smells like. And I want to see more
of what the Wizard Lord is doing, but mostly, I want to see that
palace."

"I see. I don't blame you, I've often wondered myself what it would
be like to stand up there and look down at Barokan—but don't bother
asking, I'm not coming, and you know why. Maybe someday, when
we're sure this Wizard Lord can be trusted."

"Maybe," he said.

And then he rose, and took his leave.

9

Sword looked up the path ahead, at the lines of guards-men and porters and courtiers making their way up the shadowy slope, and wondered what the Uplanders made of all this. Didn't they resent this intrusion on the lands they had held for centuries? Why had they al-lowed the Summer Palace to be built at all? Had the Wizard Lord made threats of some sort, perhaps said that they would no longer be wel-come in Winterhome if they did not cooperate?

That was probably the reason, even if no explicit threat was made. The Uplanders needed access to Winterhome. It was generally accepted that no one could survive a hard winter up on the plateau, and the Up-landers did not try. They came down into Barokan to escape the wind and cold and snow and replenish their supplies, and the Wizard Lord ruled Barokan.

And this particular Wizard Lord, unlike any of his predecessors, had set up his home and headquarters in Winterhome itself, where the Up-landers couldn't ignore him. They probably didn't feel they could kill him, either, with his guards and his magic protecting him.

Sword wondered whether any Uplanders had tried to contact any of the Chosen. Neither Lore nor Beauty had mentioned anything about such an attempt, and he certainly hadn't met any Uplanders himself, but perhaps one had spoken to Boss—whoever the new Leader might be—or one of the others.

They must *know* about the Chosen. After all, they did spend three or four months a year in Winterhome, and interacted freely with the Host People. They would know that the Chosen were responsible for remov-ing out-of-control Wizard Lords. They could have asked.

Or perhaps they really didn't mind this intrusion, though Sword found that a bit difficult to imagine. If someone built a gigantic palace in any town in Barokan without permission, the townspeople there would be very unhappy indeed. Usable land, land with cooperative *ler*, was too precious to waste.

He glanced to the left, where the land fell away from the path and he could look down on the roofs of Winterhome, and the fields around it, and to the north even the forests beyond that; he and his fellow travelers had already climbed hundreds of feet, and Sword had a completely new and unfamiliar perspective on his homeland. Everything looked *smaller* from up here; he knew that was simply because of the distance, a sort of visual trick, but he could not entirely convince himself that those little black things moving through the streets were full-sized men and women, that the roofs he saw covered full-sized homes and shops, that the bigger buildings on the western roads were actually the gigantic guesthouses where the Uplander clans spent the winters.

The sharp line between the cliffs' shadow and the sunlit lands to the west added to the sense of unreality; it was still morning, and the sun was climbing the eastern sky, so that the cliff face was dim, the sun still hidden from those on the path. Looking out of the shadows at the brightness below added an oddly dreamlike feel—but he knew he was awake. The buildings below were real and solid, and only light and distance made them appear otherwise.

The slope dropping away beside the trail didn't look all *that* steep, but he knew it actually was. If he were to slip and fall he would not stop until he fetched up against the back wall of the Winter Palace, hundreds of feet away, and he would probably be a corpse by the time he got there, battered to death by rolling and bouncing down that long expanse of rocks.

He slowed his pace; the group ahead of him was coming to the next switchback, which was also where the path was steepest, and getting people and baggage safely around the bend meant not rushing anything or crowding anyone. He watched as they all made the maneuver, one by one, and marveled that he had never heard of anyone falling down the cliff to his death in all the years the Uplanders had been using this route.

He would have to ask Lore if that was simple ignorance on his part.

And he would ask Lore for more information about the Uplanders, as well. *Did* they object to the presence of the Summer Palace?

And if they did, did that make Artil a Dark Lord? If he harmed innocent Barokanese that was a crime calling for the Chosen to act, but if he harmed Uplanders, was that any business of the Chosen? They were the Chosen Defenders of *Barokan,* not of the entire world. Uplanders were human beings, and deserving of consideration for that, but they had explicitly set themselves outside Barokan's laws and customs.

Lore might know of some obscure decision on the subject.

Lore, however, was up at the front of the expedition, with the Wizard Lord and Old Boss, while Sword was halfway back, among assorted servants and retainers. A score or so of the Wizard Lord's housekeeping staff had gone on ahead, departing before dawn to get the Summer Palace ready for occupation, but the main party had a dozen guards at the fore, then the Wizard Lord and his contingent, with everyone else strung out willy-nilly behind them, in a parade stretching for miles.

Sword supposed he could try to work his way forward to catch up with Lore, but even on the wider portions of the trail passing anyone seemed unnecessarily risky. He decided his questions could wait, and pressed on.

As he walked he could feel the *ler* of the surrounding rock, hard and still, not quite like any others he had sensed; he had crossed stone before, but never anything so steep and solid as this. When he turned to look down he could also feel *ler* of air and sky, but they seemed oddly distant and detached.

He remembered that he had heard stories long ago that there were no *ler* in the Uplands, that the entire plateau was spiritually lifeless, but Lore had said that was mere myth. That did not mean, though, that the Upland *ler* might not be *different*. He was leaving Barokan, with its familiar magic, behind. . . .

He stopped dead in his tracks, almost colliding with the heavily laden chambermaid behind him.

That was what had troubled him about the very concept of the Summer Palace, that was the little something that had nagged and nibbled at him but that he hadn't identified. The Wizard Lord, along with everyone who accompanied him to the Summer Palace, was leaving Barokan—and *all the Wizard Lord's magic* came from the *ler* of Barokan!

As did all the magic of the Chosen.

Sword stepped to the side as best he could, pressing himself against the rocky cliff to let the chambermaid with her bundle of linens pass him, and then the wine steward with his cart, and a guard, and a dozen others. Several of them glanced at him curiously as they passed, but he paid them no attention as he fumbled in his pocket and found the Talisman of Blades, the little silver device that bound the *ler* of steel and muscle to him and made him the world's greatest swordsman. He pulled it out and looked at it, cupping it in his hand.

It gleamed silver, glowing more brightly than the dim light in the cliff's shadow could justify. Clearly, its magic was still working—and if it continued to work, he reminded himself, that meant that he would need to find an hour to practice his swordsmanship before he slept that night. That was not likely to be terribly difficult, though; he hoped to reach the Summer Palace before full dark. He knew that some of the people making this pilgrimage would need to make camp and finish the journey tomorrow, but he was reasonably certain he could do it in a single day.

He still had his magic.

Was he still in Barokan, then? If the magic still worked, then presumably he was. But didn't Barokan end at the Eastern Cliffs?

He glanced up. He hadn't actually passed the Eastern Cliffs yet—he still had hundreds of feet to go. So far the trail had zigzagged up the pile of stony debris at the foot of the cliffs, and up ahead it ran along ledges somehow cut from a crooked portion of the cliff face itself. Not too much farther above that the path turned east into a break in the cliff's edge, running up a steep triangular valley that led to the surface of the plateau; that turn might be where he would actually leave Barokan and cross into the Uplands.

The Wizard Lord had already turned that corner. Did that mean he had left Barokan, and his magic, behind? Or as the lord of Barokan, did he take its magic with him? Would this path, and the Summer Palace, now become a part of the Wizard Lord's realm?

Was that a deliberate feature of his schemes? Did he intend to expand his empire, spread his reign out across the Uplands?

But why would he do that?

Sword looked down at the talisman in his palm, then closed his hand around it and began walking, inserting himself into the procession between a dancing girl and one of the kitchen boys. He would find out soon enough whether Barokanese magic worked in the Uplands, he told himself, and if he didn't get moving he would get stuck behind some of the slower traffic and have to camp out on the trail when it got too dark to climb.

Hours later, when he was soaked in sweat from the afternoon sun, he found himself at the point where the trail turned from the cliff face into the triangular canyon; at this point the path widened considerably, at least at first. Sword paused, squeezing to one side to let the kitchen boy pass, and took out his talisman again.

It was much harder to see any glow, now that the sun was in the west and shining directly on him; Sword twisted, trying to shelter the talisman with his body.

It did still seem to be glowing, and he still *felt* the same. He put a hand on the hilt of his sword, and felt the weapon's cold, hard *ler,* waiting to be drawn, as always.

He stepped into the canyon, off the face of the cliff—and fell to his knees as *ler* tore at him, trying to pull him back. He almost yielded, but then he caught himself; if he let himself be dragged backward he might well be unable to stop, and find himself plunging off the path and down the cliff. He knelt, struggling, the talisman clutched before him.

Several people made their way around him; he was only vaguely aware of their passage, and saw them only as moving legs and battered boots. He heard murmurs, but paid no attention as he focused all his attention inward.

"Are you all right, sir?"

Sword looked up at a dirty face wearing a worried expression. The kitchen boy who had been behind him on the path for so long had glanced back, seen him fall, and stopped, stepping out of the procession. Now the lad, who couldn't be much older than twelve, was standing over him, clearly concerned.

"I'm not sure," Sword replied. "Don't worry about me, though. I can handle it myself. Though I thank you for your kindness, and bless the *ler* of your house."

"You're certain?" The boy hesitated.

"Certain enough. Go on; get to the palace before dark. You don't want to camp out on the trail." Sword managed to gesture awkwardly with one hand, while still holding the talisman in the other.

The boy did not appear entirely convinced, but after another look around he turned and scampered back into line, several places behind his old position, though that did not matter as much in this stretch, where the canyon was wide enough for half a dozen to walk abreast.

Sword stayed where he was, kneeling on the stone, as he tried to understand just what was happening. He could feel his hands opening and closing, though he was not trying to move them; he could feel muscles in his arms and legs and shoulders and hips trying to flex, to force him to move.

The *ler* of muscle were at work here, plainly—and he knew that the *ler* of muscle were bound to him, as the Chosen Swordsman, through his talisman.

Clearly, the Chosen were not meant to leave Barokan, and whatever the Wizard Lord might think, Barokan ended here, at the foot of this triangular valley.

But the Wizard Lord had gone on ahead, as had Lore.

Sword looked up the canyon, at the lines of people and carts and bundles, then down at the talisman. Perhaps it was only *he* who was not meant to leave Barokan.

But that made no sense; he had to be able to go wherever the Wizard Lord went.

The Wizard Lord had said he wanted to use as little magic as possible, but surely he would not have *given up* his magic? The Dark Lord of the Galbek Hills had said he would rather die than surrender it.

But the Red Wizard, the Lord of Winterhome, was not the Dark Lord of the Galbek Hills; if anything, he seemed to be making a deliberate effort to be the Dark Lord's opposite.

Perhaps he really *had* left Barokan, and his magic, behind, in order to live in his Summer Palace. Or perhaps the palace was somehow a part of Barokan now, even though this canyon was not.

Sword looked at the talisman in his hand and said, "Hear me, O *ler*. I am Erren Zal Tuyo, the Chosen Swordsman, and yes, I am leaving

Barokan and your power behind, but I do so in pursuit of my duty. I swear by my name and my soul that I will return to Barokan and resume my role and my magic when I am satisfied that my duty is done. Will you let me go?"

The world seemed to flicker and swirl for a moment; he felt his muscles spasm, and his hand closed so tightly on the silver talisman that its points dug into his flesh, drawing blood. He tried to open his fist and found he could not; instead he squeezed even harder, and blood seeped from beneath his fingers. He watched helplessly as it dripped onto the stone of the path.

And then suddenly he was free; his hand sprang open, and the talisman would have been flung away if its point had not been dug into his flesh. He snatched it out with his other hand and thrust it in his pocket, then groped for something to use as a bandage.

And as he did he felt the world change around him. The light seemed to dim, the stone around him went dead, the air lost its richness, the smells it had carried suddenly faded. He was no longer a part of his surroundings, but instead a self-contained being, detached and alone and empty.

The *ler* had released him.

He had forgotten what the world felt like without his magic; he was suddenly awkward and uncertain.

But he was also free to continue on up the valley to the Uplands, and he hurried to do so.

Now that he was in the canyon there were rocky slopes rising on either side, rather than a sheer wall on one side and a steep drop on the other, and the sky had narrowed to a long triangle of blue overhead. The path, on the other hand, had widened, but he could see that it narrowed again ahead, so he hastened to find a place in the ongoing procession, this time putting himself between a guardsman and a cartload of bedding.

He almost collided with them, and attempts to adjust required more thought and effort than he expected. He realized that for years now he had had a supernatural awareness of his surroundings and heightened reflexes, and that when he had paid his way across the border from Barokan with his blood, he had also given these up. Now he could stumble not because of hostile *ler* underfoot, but simply because he wasn't watching where he put his feet.

And in fact, he realized that he could no longer sense *any ler* at all. He asked the guard about it, and had his suspicions confirmed—the land here felt *ler*less and dead to everyone from Barokan, not just to him.

He could deal with that; he had been in dead places before. The loss of his own guiding spirits was far more dismaying. He trudged on for hours, marching into the wind that poured down the valley, trying to adjust to his new status, and feeling ever more tired and weak.

He had not thought that so much of his strength came from his magic. He wondered how much of his skill with a blade remained; he had trained and practiced for years now, an hour every single day, so surely he would retain some of his swordsmanship even without any of his magic.

The sun was low in the west, casting long shadows up the path in front of him, when Sword finally neared the top of the canyon. The walls on either side were shrinking, the path rising steeply and narrowing, the sky widening. He could see that much of the party had emerged onto the plateau; he could see some of them staring east in amazement, could see their hair and clothes whipping in the wind, could hear them calling to one another in astonishment, though he could not make out their words.

Others appeared to have collapsed in exhaustion, and now sat or lay by the trail, catching their breath. Sword realized his own breath was coming in pants and gasps, too. It was not so much that he felt terribly weary as that he seemed unable to take a good, deep breath. He looked around, and saw that many of the walkers around him were wheezing, yawning, and otherwise struggling to breathe.

It was not just his lost magic making him weak and breathless; something was wrong with the air itself, he realized.

He had heard that the air was different up on the plateau, but his imagination had never quite matched the reality. Perhaps this was why the Uplanders weren't worried about yielding territory—the air itself guarded them from invasion, its *ler* refusing to properly sustain Barokanese lungs. Although his magic had certainly let *him* know when they crossed the border, they had passed no boundary shrines, no man-

made markers, to tell them when they had reached the Uplands and become intruders; still, anyone would know by now that this was clearly
not Barokan.

And as for the lack of a marker, why would Barokan's customs apply
up here? Who would have built such a shrine? There was no need to
mark the border, and no one to mark it.

The air in the lower part of the canyon had not seemed as difficult to
breathe; perhaps that part of the path was neither Upland nor Barokan,
but something between. Perhaps *this*, then, was where they truly entered the Uplands.

And if so, it was only right to acknowledge it. Sword bowed his
head, did his best to take a deep breath, and said, "*Ler* of the Uplands,
we ask your pardon for any affronts we may have committed against
you; we are ignorant of your ways and mean no harm nor disrespect.
We pray you let us enter into your realm, and breathe freely here."

Several people nearby heard him, and emulated him; a mumble of
prayer and beseeching filled the valley.

Some people, he had noticed, didn't seem to have had any problem
in the first place; others were gasping like dying fish, trying to fill their
lungs with air that seemed unwilling to cooperate. Sword had no idea
why there would be such variation; did some of them have a trace of
Uplander blood, perhaps? Had some somehow offended the *ler* of the
plateau's air?

For himself, he seemed to be breathing a little more easily again; he
shook himself and moved on, up the valley.

And then his head cleared the level of the plain, and he stopped in his
tracks as the wind blew his hair awry. Someone prodded him from behind and he began walking again, but he stared ahead at the plateau.

Even to his dulled senses and deadened sensitivity, the sight was overwhelming. The plains stretched out before him as far as he could see;
with each step lifting him higher, he saw what seemed to be miles farther. There were no hills, no houses, anywhere between the valley and
the eastern horizon; the land stretched out to east and north and south
for what seemed to be forever, utterly flat, far flatter than the Midlands
of Barokan that he had previously thought to be as level as land could
be. Mile upon mile of green grass, shining in the late-afternoon sun, lay

beneath a limitless, cloudless blue sky that seemed vastly larger than the sky of Barokan.

A cool, brisk breeze was blowing from the east, whipping his sleeves and hair, though in his present condition it felt oddly lifeless.

A few strange trees were widely scattered in the distance, each standing isolated and alone; there were no groves, no forests. Far off in the distance to the southeast he could see a flock of birds running across the grass, birds with stubby, undersized wings that could not possibly support them in flight. At first he could not make himself interpret what he saw, as the infinite emptiness provided few clues to scale, but at last he was able to adjust his perceptions and see that those birds, with their absurd little white wings and their long white tails and curling pink crests, were each as tall as a man, perhaps taller.

Those were *ara*, obviously. He had never seen an *ara* before, but he had heard descriptions and seen crude drawings and handled their feathers, and those distant birds could be nothing else. *Ara* feathers and bones and beaks were valuable property down in Barokan; they could be had only by purchasing from Uplanders, since the giant birds could not survive anywhere but the plateau. The birds were famously immune to magic, their feathers shielding them against it, and it was generally believed that meant hunting them would be difficult, since they could not be magically coaxed into giving themselves up to the hunters. It was assumed that the Uplanders were brave and clever, to catch such creatures.

But there were *hundreds* of them in that flock, perhaps thousands! Out in plain sight, for there was nowhere to hide on the highland plateau, no cover, no shelter, just a flat, open surface extending forever in every direction but west.

No wonder the Uplanders always had feathers to sell when they came down to Winterhome. And no wonder they didn't mind giving up a few acres for the Wizard Lord's palace, when they had so vast a space!

There were no Uplanders in sight anywhere, though there were a few odd squarish structures off in the distance, too far away for Sword to make out their function; presumably the nomads were all somewhere beyond that distant horizon.

That meant the plateau was even more vast than it appeared.

Sword had never imagined anything like this. He had pictured a much smaller plateau—though now that he thought about it, he wasn't sure what he had thought would limit it.

The line of travelers was turning left, heading north, toward the Summer Palace, and the plain appeared as infinite in that direction as it had in the east. It was only in the west that it did not seem to stretch out forever, and there it just *stopped,* a few miles away. Beyond the cliffs Sword saw only sky; all of Barokan and the seas beyond lay below his line of sight.

The Summer Palace stood near the cliff's edge to the northwest of them, still a few miles away. Despite the distance he could see it far more clearly here than he had from below—three stories of stone walls and red-painted eaves, with broad verandahs and balconies on all sides. The line of climbers stretched in scattered clumps from the head of the canyon through the gates; Sword saw no sign of the Wizard Lord and Lore and Farash, who were presumably already inside.

"It's the thinner air," someone said, and Sword turned to see a guard supporting a wheezing old man. "You'll get used to it in a day or two."

"Thinner? Thinner *how*?" someone asked. "What does 'thinner' mean when you're talking about air? It's already invisible and almost nothing; how can it be thinner?"

"There's just *less* of it up here," the guard explained. "I don't know why; maybe the air *ler* don't like it here. Whatever causes it, there isn't as much air as there is down in Barokan. There's enough to breathe, but your body isn't used to working so hard to get it."

"Why is it worse for some people than others?"

The guard shrugged. "I don't know," he said. "Ask an Uplander priest, if you can find one."

Less *air*? Sword marveled at the concept; he had never imagined such a thing. He looked around once again, taking in the vast plain and infinite sky, and wondered whether the lack of air might make it all look larger, somehow. *Could* it really be as endless as it appeared?

It didn't look distorted; it merely looked vast. He decided the air had nothing to do with it.

He marched on, at as brisk a pace as he could manage, aware with every step of his own breathing.

 An hour and a half after he emerged from the canyon Sword walked through the lantern-hung gate of the Summer Palace and looked around, marveling at the wonder the Wizard Lord had created. Cooling fountains bubbled on either side of the grand entrance; trellises were arranged to provide shade for the courtyard beyond, though as yet the vines intended to adorn them had not grown up to any useful size. Ornamental stone planters still held as much bare dirt as greenery.

Even in the scattered light of lanterns and torches, with the gardens and planters still raw and with dozens of people bustling about, it was lovely. Whether he had any right to do so or not, the Wizard Lord had made something very beautiful. Sword wished he could still sense the spiritual world, as well as the physical, so that he might appreciate it more fully.

The line of new arrivals was fairly thin by this time but still trickling in, to be met inside the gates by a steward who directed each person to the appropriate entrance to the palace itself. Sword was a guest, with no particular assigned duties in the palace, nothing he was required to do nor anywhere he had to be, so when he introduced himself to the steward he was greeted with a shrug. "I am told you are to do as you please," the steward said.

"Thank you," Sword replied. He stepped aside and watched the steward direct the next few servants around to an eastern entrance, but then turned away. No one paid any attention to him as he wandered from the entry plaza along a verandah to the left; he followed that past an elegant arcade and through an arch, and emerged onto a terrace at the western end of the complex.

And here he found himself looking at something that made his first view of the high plains seem like nothing. The western terrace was built right out over the edge of the great cliff, and from its rail Sword found himself looking out over all of Barokan.

It took him a moment to adjust; initially it seemed a sea of dark blues and greens, like a rolling lawn beneath the last glow of a long summer sunset. Then he grasped the scale, and had to hold the terrace rail to steady himself.

Those little patches of red and brown and white, catching the last pink and orange glimmers of the twilight, were towns. The gentle mounds were the hills and ridges. That flat area ahead and to his left, crisscrossed with roads and covered in dark fields, was the Midlands; to his right were the vales, the long valleys paralleling the cliffs. Far to the left were the southern hills.

He could see the vales *and* the hills, even though they were separated by *fifty miles or more* of the Midlands.

If he leaned out over the railing, ignoring his vertigo, and looked down and down and down and slightly to his left, he could see Winter-home, with the Winter Palace tucked almost out of sight beneath the cliff, and the five main roads radiating out, the guesthouses lined up like blocks in some child's game, all of it shadowy, but speckled here and there with the orange glow of fires and torches and lanterns. To the right was Shadowvale, and beyond that Longvale, and he peered out into it, trying to match what he saw with what he knew of the geography. Ordinarily he could have sensed something of the essence of what he saw, felt a little of the *ler*, but that was gone while he remained outside Barokan, and he had to rely on nothing but vision and knowledge.

That clearing, he decided, was Beggar's Hill, and beyond that was Broadpool, the wide river there faintly reflecting the last light, and he thought he could make out Rock Bridge in the distance. Willowbank and Mad Oak were too far off to be recognized with any certainty, but he was not at all sure they were over the horizon. There was a hazy something on the ridge out at the very limit of visibility. . . .

From up here the Wizard Lord would unquestionably have a better view of the lands he was charged to protect than he could ever have had from within them—though he might not have the magic he needed to protect them.

"Impressive, isn't it?" a voice said from behind him.

Sword was not accustomed to being unaware of anyone's approach; he whirled, leaping away from the railing. His hand fell to the hilt of his sword. Then, as he saw who had spoken, he froze.

The Wizard Lord was standing before him, his red robes catching the lanternlight and flapping gently in the breeze. Something about him looked different, though Sword could not identify it immediately, but it was definitely Artil.

"If you draw that thing, we may have to kill you," he said, and Sword forced himself to release his grip on his sword. Only then did he notice the four red-and-black-clad guards who stood just behind the Wizard Lord, two on either side.

"Sorry," Sword said. "It's instinct. You startled me."

The orange light of the setting sun was striking the Wizard Lord's face from below, but that was not the only difference, nor was it merely the lack of any magical awareness. Then Sword realized that Artil did not have his staff, and the cord of talismans was gone from his neck.

"My apologies for that," the Wizard Lord said. "But it's quite a view, isn't it? I love sharing it with people."

"Even armed people?" Sword asked wryly.

"I hadn't realized you were armed," Artil said. "I might have approached differently, had I known."

"I'm the Swordsman," Sword said. "I'm almost always armed." He started to add a comment on the Wizard Lord's missing staff and talismans, then caught himself. That absence implied that the Wizard Lord had indeed given up his magic to come here, just as much as Sword himself had, but Sword was not yet ready to discuss that. He had not yet thought out what he wanted to say, and admitting that he was no longer necessarily the world's greatest swordsman might be unwise.

"I suppose that's true," Artil said. "That doesn't sound like much fun."

"It's not."

"I see." The Wizard Lord nodded. "But about the view . . . ?"

"It's magnificent," Sword said, glancing back over his shoulder. "Really magnificent. I can't wait to see it by daylight."

"I saw that earlier; I'm looking forward to seeing it at night, the firelights of the towns laid out beneath the stars. If you'll give your sword to one of my guards, we can look at it together and talk."

Sword hesitated for a moment, then shrugged. "I'd like that," he said. He debated unbuckling his sword belt, but instead just drew his sword, tossed it up and caught it by the blade, and proffered it to the nearest guard hilt-first.

He did not mention, though he thought about it, that ordinarily he could have killed all three men with it, if he wanted to, before they could react. Having left his magic behind, he wondered whether he still could. He had still had all those years of practice, but would that have been enough?

The man took the weapon gingerly, clearly unsure what to expect.

"It's not enchanted," Sword told him, guessing at the cause of his apprehension. "*I* am, but the sword isn't."

He saw no reason to mention that at the moment the enchantment appeared to be broken, or at least suspended.

"Oh," the guard said, relaxing slightly and letting the tip of the blade fall to boot-top level.

Sword nodded to him, then turned back to the west. The Wizard Lord stepped up beside him, and together they leaned on the rail and looked out over Barokan.

"It's beautiful," Sword said.

"Very," the Wizard Lord agreed.

"And that's the land you're sworn to protect, spread out down there."

"Indeed it is. And your implication is that I should be down there, instead of up here?"

"It's a question one might ask, certainly."

"I suppose it is." He fell silent for a moment, staring out over the darkening land below; Sword waited.

"Don't you think," the Wizard Lord said at last, "that we can see it better from up here than we do from down there? Don't you think we can be fairer from up here, above it all, than we can down there, surrounded by the distractions of everyday life?"

Sword glanced at Artil, then out across the magnificent landscape.

"No," he said. "You can see *more* from up here, but you can't see it as clearly. You can't see the details, and details matter."

The Wizard Lord's mouth twisted in a wry smile. "I should have known you would not be so easily swayed," he said. "Well, then, I'll tell you the truth. You're quite right that up here, I can't meddle as directly in matters. That's a deliberate choice on my part. I told you that I'm trying to change the system, and that's the truth; I want to set up a *new* system, one that will unite all Barokan into a single people, connected by safe roads and strong government. I want a government of men, not magic; a government where human justice prevails, rather than the whims of wizards or *ler,* or the edicts of priests. I want to make the very role of Wizard Lord archaic and unnecessary. But I can't do that just by ordering it; people don't change their ways as easily as that. The priests and wizards and *ler* are all accustomed to their positions of power, limited only by the Wizard Lord's greater power, and the ordinary folk are accustomed to yielding to the wielders of magic. The traditional balance of power is entirely a balance of magic, priests and wizards and the Wizard Lord and the Chosen each with their own particular magic, their own authority to act in particular ways."

"Yes, of course," Sword agreed. "I don't see . . ."

"I wasn't finished," Artil said, cutting him off.

"My apologies."

"Accepted. Now, as I was saying, for at least seven hundred years, and probably far longer, all power has rested upon the ability to wield magic, to make *ler* do one's will. I want to change that. I want to make *people* the final authority, not *ler.* I want to have a society so strong and confident that when some *ler* says, no, you cannot do that, even the lowliest farmer or housewife, even just a child at play, can tell that *ler* that we will do as we please, and that if it does not yield it will be rooted out and destroyed, like the *ler* that once filled the wilderness where we have now built roads. *Ler* have nature on their side, beasts and plants and earth and sky, but we have our minds, our will, our numbers and organization! A lone man crossing the wilderness is taking his life in his hands, but my road crews, because they have numbers and tools and organization, can cut their way through the wilderness with impunity, driving out any *ler* that try to stop them."

"I see," Sword said.

"But you don't yet see what this has to do with my palace here," Artil said. "Do you?"

"I don't," Sword admitted.

"It's because we must not rely on magic. We must stop organizing our lives around cooperative *ler*. We need to make our *own* rules, without *ler,* without magic. I want to show everyone that people don't *need* magic; we don't need to wheedle and cajole the *ler,* or trick them or trap them, or bind them with oaths, or pay them off with sacrifices. We can make our way without them; *we* can reshape *them*. I want to be master of Barokan because the people *want* me as their master, not because I hold the eight Great Talismans and have a thousand *ler* at my beck and call. I want to show everyone that I don't *need* magic to rule Barokan."

"And so you came here, where . . ." He hesitated; neither of them had yet said this openly. Then he finished, "Where your magic doesn't work."

The Wizard Lord smiled at him. "Exactly. I can look down and see that the land is at peace. If there are catastrophes I'll see them, or messengers will bring me word, and I'll deal with them—if possible without magic, but should it be necessary I can go back down to the boundary on the trail." He gave no sign of surprise that Sword had known his magic did not work outside Barokan, and presumably that meant he knew that *Sword*'s magic did not work here, either.

That was probably why he was willing to speak to one of the Chosen at such close quarters, without forcing Sword to strip bare and be searched. Handing over his sword was enough; here Sword was just an ordinary man.

At least, so the Wizard Lord thought; he did not consider, might not even know, that Sword was a man who had practiced swordplay for an hour or more every day of the past seven years. That acquired expertise had not entirely vanished with his magic.

And he was a man who still had questions. "What about criminals fleeing into the wilderness, or rogue wizards?"

"There have been no rogue wizards in more than a century," Artil replied. "You know that. And I know all my seventeen remaining compatriots in the Council of Immortals; I doubt any of them would ever run amok. If one of them should, though, or if a murderer should escape justice somewhere, then word will be brought to me and the matter will be attended to. In fact, I hope I *will* get a chance to demonstrate that such things can be handled by ordinary men, with a modicum of courage and a sound organization, without resorting to magic."

Sword considered that, looking out at the fading colors in the western sky. "What about the weather?" he asked.

"I have left bindings and instructions upon the relevant *ler,* and matters should proceed quite well without me. The weather may not be quite as perfectly regulated as it would be were I minding it, but it should be good enough. After all, our ancestors got by for centuries before Wizard Lords learned to control the weather."

"So you're trying to demonstrate that we don't need a Wizard Lord."

"Yes! Just as you said, all those years ago in the Galbek Hills, just before I was chosen for the job. I want to be the *last* Wizard Lord Barokan will ever see."

Sword stared out at the darkening western horizon, trying to decide what he should think of this. He *had* said that perhaps the time had come to abandon the system of Wizard Lords, but this was not how he had envisioned it happening. He had not really *had* any clear idea of how it might work, of what could replace the existing system; he had merely been tired and angry at the waste and death and destruction the Dark Lord of the Galbek Hills had spread across Barokan, and certain that there had to be a better alternative.

And now the new Wizard Lord, the only person in a position to deliver it, was offering him exactly what he had said he wanted. Logically, he should be overjoyed, but he wasn't. Perhaps he had changed in the intervening years, or perhaps he had merely had time to recover from his anger and betrayal and realize that the old system had indeed worked for seven hundred years.

He wasn't overjoyed, but he was not sure what he *did* feel.

"You can't stay up here all year," he said.

"No, of course not," Artil agreed. "This is the *Summer* Palace, and I will indeed return to the Winter Palace, and my magic, in the autumn. But spending months up here will show everyone that it's *possible* to run Barokan without the Wizard Lord's magic."

Sword nodded, and did not say what he was thinking—that this might also demonstrate that it was possible for Barokan to function without a Wizard Lord, or any other ruler, and that Artil might some-day find himself deposed without the intervention of the Chosen.

Nor did he mention that one reason the Wizard Lord's scheme made him uneasy was that it removed one of the major holds the Chosen had over him. Traditionally, no Wizard Lord dared to kill any of the Cho-sen because each of the eight was tied to one-eighth of his own magic; killing any of the Chosen would reduce the Wizard Lord's own magical ability by that eighth. But this was a Wizard Lord who did not want to use his magic in the first place; he might well have no compunctions about killing the Chosen, should they threaten him or his power. The loss of a part of his magic might not matter to him.

This was, in fact, the *strangest* Wizard Lord Sword had ever heard of. There was nothing in any of the old songs or stories he knew that suggested any other Wizard Lord had been reluctant to use his magic, or had ever considered setting foot outside Barokan.

It didn't even seem entirely consistent with what little Sword knew of Artil im Salthir's personal history. The first time Sword had ever seen the Red Wizard he had been *flying*, which was hardly something one would expect of someone who didn't like magic. He had been flamboyantly dressed even then, carrying a staff strung with dozens of talismans. . . .

But then Sword realized he had never seen the Red Wizard perform any magic *other* than flying; maybe those talismans and fancy clothes had just been for show. He remembered that the *ler* of Mad Oak had not initially allowed Artil to land in the town; his feet had been held in the air until a priestess asked the *ler* to let him land. Did that have any connection with his present attitudes?

Did it matter?

Really, all that mattered was whether the Wizard Lord was doing more good than harm as ruler of Barokan. If he was a benefit to the land, when all was said and done, then Sword had no business with him; if he was a danger, then it was Sword's duty to remove him. Other than that, his actions were no concern of the Chosen.

And his reasons, his moods and motives, were never any of Sword's business. All that mattered were his actions.

And right now, Sword could not decide whether the Wizard Lord's actions would do more good than harm. His plans were so different from everything Sword had ever thought about that Sword could not judge them.

He would have to wait and see what came of them; that was all there was to it.

"So?" the Wizard Lord said.

Startled, Sword looked up, and realized he had been staring silently over the cliff for several minutes. The landscape below was mostly dark now, the rich colors faded to blacks and grays, though several orange pinpricks showed here and there where people had lit fires and lanterns.

"I'm sorry?"

"So—what do you think of my plan? I want to say, 'Isn't it magnificent?' but for all I know you think it's some sort of ghastly violation of the rules, and you'll try to whack my head off if you can't talk me out of it."

"No, I don't think it's ghastly," Sword said. "I don't know *what* to think of it."

Artil smiled at him. "It *is* different, isn't it? But I think it's the right thing to do. You know as well as I do that things have changed since our ancestors created the first Wizard Lord. The wilderness is less wild than it once was, the *ler* of field and town far tamer than before, and instead of hundreds of wizards roaming about wreaking havoc there are only eighteen of us left. Magic is fading, or at least changing, and we no longer need it to live in Barokan—so why not discard it entirely? Eighteen wizards—and did you know only one of us has an apprentice? We've given ourselves such a bad reputation, put so many restraints on ourselves these past seven centuries, that no sensible youth would want to be a wizard. Oh, we still get a few applicants, but for the most part they're clearly unsuited. They want to be wizards for the sake of petty revenge, or to impress the girls in their villages."

Sword could not help remembering that the man he had killed six years before, the Dark Lord of the Galbek Hills, had been one of those who became a wizard for the sake of revenge. Apparently wizards were not always as careful as they should be about who they accepted as apprentices.

Or perhaps Laquar kellin Hario had just been very good at hiding his true nature.

"We do need to be careful, since we don't want any more rogues or Dark Lords," Artil continued. "We made one mistake that you and your comrades had to remove; we really don't want another. But that means that in another hundred years, even if I don't change a thing, there may not be *any* wizards; the last member of the Council of Immortals will appoint himself the final Wizard Lord, and what will happen when *he* dies? Better to change the system *now,* and remove the wizards from power peacefully, while a few of us are still around to oversee the transition."

"I hadn't thought of that," Sword said, startled.

"Neither had most of my compatriots on the Council, so far as I can tell," Artil said, looking out over the rail as if he expected to see other wizards there. "When we were discussing who would be the new Wizard Lord I tried to bring it up, but no one else seemed concerned."

"I suppose most people don't worry much about things that can only happen after they're dead," Sword replied.

"Perhaps that's it." He stared out into the darkness a moment longer, then clapped Sword on the shoulder. "Come on, let's go in and see if my people have managed to put together any sort of supper. You must be hungry after the long climb."

"I am," Sword acknowledged. He turned away from the rail, and accompanied the Wizard Lord into the Summer Palace.

It was only later, when the tables had been cleared and the Wizard Lord departed, that a guard finally returned his sword.

[11]

Sword remained at the Summer Palace for four days, and with each day he felt the emptiness in his heart grow. With each day he wondered why Lore and Artil were not similarly afflicted. He did not ask them; finding the energy to speak about it, in the thin air and his enervated condition, was beyond him.

He spent most of those four days observing the Wizard Lord, talking with Lore, exploring the palace, or simply leaning on the terrace rail, staring down at his homeland.

He practiced his swordsmanship for an hour each day, even though he was fairly certain it was not magically required of him here in the Uplands. He had definitely lost some of his skill, and the sword often seemed heavy and awkward in his hand, but he could still wield the weapon effectively. On those occasions when other people happened to see him in action, they seemed quite impressed; *he* knew he had lost much of his speed and dexterity, but apparently it wasn't obvious to the casual observer.

He made sure to keep his silver talisman, the Talisman of Blades, with him at all times, even though it now seemed nothing but a lifeless bit of metal. It would not do to get into any dangerous habits.

He also spent a good part of each day just looking at the Uplands. That vast, flat expanse, utterly devoid of any perceptible spirit, did not seem entirely real. The occasional flock of *ara* did not make it any less fantastic, nor did the rare glimpses of the Uplanders in the distance, stalking the giant birds or moving their tents from one spot to another or doing whatever it was they did with those strange frameworks of theirs. Streaks of smoke from their campfires straggled up the eastern sky on the calmer days, but calm days were few. On most days winds whistled through the grass and around the palace eaves. The weather was much cooler than Sword was accustomed to in summer, and the nights were downright chilly.

But then, that was one reason for putting the *Summer* Palace up here in the first place—to escape the heat and humidity of the lowlands.

His diet was rather different than it had been back home. Uplander traders had sold the Wizard Lord what appeared to be several tons of *ara* meat, smoked or salted or dried, and a large quantity of *ara* eggs, which the palace cooks used in a variety of interesting ways. Sword had never eaten *ara* before, and did not particularly like it at first, but soon found himself acquiring a taste for the stuff.

Although a goodly stock of food and other necessities had been laid in before the Wizard Lord moved his household, a steady stream of supplies and messengers trickled up the trail from Barokan, bringing news and perishables. The haulers and messengers generally stayed only a single night before heading back down, so that each morning saw a procession trudging out, and every afternoon found new arrivals appearing from the valley as if rising out of the earth itself.

As promised, Sword became accustomed to the thinner air after a day or two. Adjusting to the absence of his magic took longer; after four days he still felt weak and slow and hollow, even though he was once again breathing normally, and the psychic emptiness was growing worse, not better.

And on the fourth day he asked himself what he was doing there. He had come to Winterhome to talk to the Wizard Lord, to see whether the Lord of Winterhome needed to be removed, and he had done that. The man was different from any previous Wizard Lord, doing new and strange things, but there was no evidence he meant any harm or wished anyone ill, no sign he had any intention of violating any of the rules that bound him. In fact, all his efforts seemed to be directed toward improving the lot of the people of Barokan. He spoke of little else, so far as Sword could determine.

"I'm going home," Sword said to himself on that fourth afternoon, as he stared over the terrace railing at Longvale. "I belong down there, not up here."

There were crops to grow, back in Mad Oak. There were repairs to be made. His family was down there.

His *magic* was down there.

At supper that night he told the Scholar and the Wizard Lord that he was going home to Mad Oak. Artil made a few polite objections, but no serious argument against Sword's decision; Sword thought he was secretly relieved to be rid of the man who might one day kill him.

Lore said nothing; he merely nodded. Sword found that oddly irritating, but did not bother to question the Scholar; he felt too tired, too dull, to press the matter.

The following morning, while the sun was still low on the eastern horizon, Sword walked out the palace gate, his pack on his back, bound for the road down to Barokan.

He stared out across the plateau as he made his way to the head of the canyon, taking in that vast emptiness, and the strangeness of a sun so low in the sky, with no cliffs to ascend before shining on him. A strong wind whipped his hair across his face as he walked, which added nothing to his enjoyment of the journey. High winds were common up here, and he wondered idly whether that had anything to do with the thinner air—perhaps some of the air blew away?

He turned west into the canyon and marched on, ducking his head to gain the shelter of the canyon walls that much sooner.

But as he finally neared the foot of the canyon, Sword hesitated. He knew that he was about to cross back into Barokan, and was unsure what it would feel like. He reached into his pocket and touched the talisman there, while his other hand closed on the hilt of his sword. Although there was no boundary shrine nor any other marker, he could sense that the border was just ahead. He could *feel* the ler, for the first time since he had passed the other way.

He remembered that day when he had first become the Chosen Swordsman; the rush of sensation had been so overwhelming he had passed out. He doubted that it would be so extreme this time, since he had, after all, spent seven years in the role, but he had no idea what it would feel like.

"I suppose I'm about to find out," he murmured to himself. Then, moving slowly and deliberately, he stepped forward.

The numinous rush of magic swept through him; the talisman suddenly burned hot in his hand, and he could feel the cold, feral power of the *ler* in his sword's hilt. The emptiness he had felt was suddenly filled, and the world before him, the land of Barokan spread out below the cliffs, was somehow richer, more real, and infinitely more familiar and welcoming than it had been a moment before. He was a *part* of it again.

"Oh," he said, as he sat down suddenly on the stony trail, overcome by the experience.

That void in his heart had been much larger than he realized. He wondered how he could possibly have not felt, for the past few days, just what he was missing by being separated from his magic and the *ler* of Barokan. By comparison with what he felt now, it was as if he had been dead.

There really weren't any words to do the experience justice.

He sat for a long moment, relishing it, but at last he got to his feet, brushed himself off, and marched on down the path toward Barokan.

When at last he clambered down the final stretch of trail leading to the arch in the Winter Palace's wall, the air of Winterhome seemed oppressively heavy, hot and thick, but even so, Sword thought it preferable to the cool, clean winds of the Uplands. He felt more *alive* here. He hadn't realized how different his very existence had been in the Summer Palace, how drab and empty. He had thought that the thin air had been responsible for much of his malaise, but now he knew that was nothing. What he had really done was to forget what his life in Barokan felt like.

But now he remembered; now he felt it anew.

He could hear voices beyond the arch; in fact, he had been hearing their murmur for some time. He had also seen, all the way from the mouth of the canyon, that the plaza was crowded with people and wagons. Apparently he had chosen a market day for his return, when the farmers and tradespeople brought their wares to be sold.

He took a deep breath, and stepped through the arch into the plaza at Winterhome's heart, into the crowds and bustle, so utterly different from the quiet calm of the Summer Palace. He smiled at startled Host People who turned to stare at his sudden appearance; then he turned his steps north.

His plans were simple; he thought Beauty would probably be willing to share her roof for the night, and in the morning he would head on up toward Longvale. In a few days he would be home. He had long since missed the last of the spring planting, but with any luck at all he would be back in Mad Oak in time to do his full share at harvest.

He looked up at the Summer Palace, perched atop the cliff.

The Wizard Lord was still up there; so was Lore. Sword did not entirely understand how they could tolerate being cut off from their magic, and had to assume that it was somehow different for them than it had been for him.

Well, that was no surprise; they were not much like him in other ways, either.

He looked around at the people of Winterhome, and noticed that their clothes were not quite what he had remembered; the men's cuffs and ankles were not bound up tightly, but fairly loose. The women's garb seemed thinner than he recalled, the scarves not as effective in hiding the faces.

He doubted that they had changed in just four days; he simply hadn't looked closely before. His attention had been on the Wizard Lord, on the other inhabitants of the palace, and on the Chosen, not on the ordinary people of the town.

There were several people in the crowd not wearing the unrelieved black of the Host People at all—travelers, presumably, far more of them than Sword had ever seen in one place before, and clad in a wide variety of attire. The Wizard Lord's roads had presumably brought them in, and ordinarily Sword might have found them fascinating, but just now he was interested in the variations in what the Host People wore. These lighter, looser clothes were clearly adaptations to the summer heat, which he had to admit was unusually fierce. He thought it really *had* gotten noticeably hotter during his brief absence. He wondered whether the Wizard Lord had known this heat was coming, and whether that might have contributed to his decision to build his airy cliff-top retreat.

Or might the Wizard Lord be *responsible* for the heat? After all, he did have fairly extensive control over the weather.

But why would he do that? It made no sense. It was probably just a coincidence that Barokan was so hot just now. It might not last, in any case; in a few days it might be pleasant and cool.

Sword was not going to wait around to see if the weather improved, though. He wanted to get home. He took a few steps, then glanced at the merchant's cart he was passing and stopped in his tracks.

"Ah, I see you've noticed my merchandise!" a man said cheerfully. His accent was nothing like the Winterhome lilt, and it finally registered with Sword that many of the merchants in the plaza, rather than the customers, were the ones not wearing Host People garb. This man, a portly fellow a few years past Sword's own age, wore a purple-and-gold vest over a fine white shirt, despite the heat; Sword suspected that this bright clothing might be a deliberate advertisement. The man's cart was half-full of the most brilliantly dyed fabrics Sword had ever seen.

He could not immediately identify all the fabrics, either. He knew wool and various hides and felts, which were the standard materials in the vales, and he was familiar with linen and cotton from his travels in the Midlands and the southern hills, but there were bolts of cloth here that were like nothing he had seen before.

"What *is* that?" he asked, pointing at a shimmering blue fabric.

"Fine silk, from the southern coast. Never seen it before, have you? Beautiful stuff, isn't it? It's been traded up and down the coasts and islands for a hundred years, but never brought this far inland until now."

" 'Silk'?"

"And this is cashmere. That's velvet, and chiffon . . ."

Sword stared. The materials were almost dreamlike in their beauty, and in the variety of textures. He reached out and touched the burgundy-colored stuff the merchant called "velvet," and marveled at the feel of it. He knew that he was unnaturally sensitive just now because of his recent reconnection with the *ler* of Barokan, but even so, he thought this fabric was almost magical.

"But it's not black," he said, as he pulled back his hand. "What would anyone here in Winterhome want with it?"

The merchant smiled, leaned forward, and whispered, "You don't know what they wear in their own homes, do you? Or what the women wear *under* those tents of theirs?" Then he straightened up and said, "Not to mention curtains and cushions and the like. But to be honest, you have a point. You'll notice that my cart is half-empty, and I haven't a stitch of black material left in it. What you see here is what remains after selling everything suitable for the Host People's tailors and seamstresses. If you look around, I think you'll see a few women with chiffon scarves."

At that, Sword realized that he had indeed already noticed those scarves; some of the Host People women were not merely adapting to the heat, but showing off their new finery.

The very concept of a Hostwoman showing off finery took a little getting used to, but as Sword glanced around at the crowd it really did seem to be the case.

"I can see you aren't a Hostman," the merchant said. "So even with the black fabric gone, perhaps I can sell you a pretty little something for your lady?"

"I don't have one," Sword said, turning away. It was not so much that he wanted to get away from the cloth merchant as that he wanted to look at the other goods on display.

"No one you'd like to give a bit of finery?" the merchant persisted, leaning around Sword's shoulder as he held out a scrap of shimmering fabric.

"No one," Sword said, as he stared at the bushels of unfamiliar grain in a nearby wagon.

The wagon's proprietor noticed his gaze. "Fine rice, from the coastal marshes," he said. "Boil it for a few moments, and you have a fine meal. Good with any meat, or any of these sauces . . ." He gestured at a rack of bottles.

Sword nodded silently, then moved away and looked at the next wagon, and the next.

Salts and spices, strange fruits, unfamiliar foods of every sort, carvings in exotic woods and rare stones—Sword had never seen anything like this marketplace. The new roads had obviously brought a flood of new merchandise. He strolled slowly through the plaza, taking it all in. He listened to the merchants hawking their wares and talking among themselves, and heard a dozen accents he did not recognize, and two or three unknown languages.

And the Host People were buying eagerly. Clearly, the Wizard Lord's roads had brought welcome changes here. Sword remembered what the road crew back in Mad Oak had said, that the Priest-King of Willowbank had been unhappy about the roads until the first caravan arrived, but that had been enough to sway him; apparently that was not an unusual reaction. The Host People were obviously thrilled with this bounty. A few priests might have headaches and stomach cramps, and plenty of *ler* had been dislodged, but the roads would appear to be very popular indeed.

He glanced up at the Summer Palace, perched on the cliff's edge. Did Artil know what he had accomplished here? Did he realize how successful at least one of his schemes had been?

He probably did; surely, this sort of market hadn't sprung up over the past four days. Sword's own brief prior passage through Winterhome had not happened to coincide with any market days, but this level of trade had probably been developing for years.

Sword looked around at the market, at the smiling merchants and laughing customers, at the Host People women in their new chiffon scarves, their children eating exotic candies. They seemed *happy*, and he had rarely seen anyone in Winterhome openly happy.

Artil had done this. Artil had brightened all these lives, transformed an entire population.

Sword really hoped he would never have any reason to kill the man who had brought such a change about.

He certainly had no reason *now*. The Wizard Lord had done no wrong, which meant there was no need for the Chosen. It was time to go home. He hoisted his pack back into place and began trudging northward.

As he neared the edge of the plaza, though, he slowed, then stopped.

He had been traveling for weeks, and there was no reason to return home empty-handed; he could bring his mother a little something, at the very least. He turned to look at the merchants' wagons.

An hour later he headed north again, with his pack a little fuller.

The Beauty did not answer his knock, to his surprise; he debated waiting for her return, but decided against it—she might be anywhere, might not return for days or months. Instead he walked on, leaving Winterhome behind, and slept that night in a guesthouse on the edge of the town of Shadetrees. He was utterly exhausted by the time he reached it, and had spared not a moment for a glance at the town.

In the morning, though, he discovered that the roads had brought exotic goods here, just as they had to Winterhome. Oh, the selection was far less impressive in this smaller community, but it was still a bit shocking to Sword. He browsed a little, then made the expected obeisance at the town's temple and continued on his way north.

By the time he reached Broadpool the shock had worn off. *Every* village now seemed to have merchants peddling their wares from carts and wagons, selling things as mundane as raisins and as exotic as silk brocade, or as strange as sea creatures resembling nothing Sword had ever seen before, pickled in spiced vinegar. He could not imagine what the creatures were intended for; it wasn't until he heard the vendor explaining how to cook them that he realized they were food.

After Broadpool he continued on, through Rock Bridge and Willowbank, until he finally arrived home in Mad Oak, only to find that even in his hometown traders were exchanging spices and seashells for beer and barley.

And everywhere, the buyers expressed their admiration for the Wizard Lord who had made this possible. Everywhere, Sword was greeted with comments, ranging from lighthearted jests to dead-serious admonitions, to the effect that he had better not kill *this* one as he had the last. A few priests still grumbled about headaches and indigestion, and bemoaned the confusion and dismay of the *ler*, and some women chattered about nightmares even as they looked through the merchants' wares, but everyone else was openly delighted by the new roads and the commerce and freedom they brought.

Sword noticed that the roads had already become more welcoming; the dizziness and disorientation he had felt when he first headed south were almost entirely gone. The *ler* had settled into their new arrangements, aided by the passage of dozens of travelers.

Sword watched and listened and took it all in, and when he sat in his mother's house, watching her run a few yards of fine velvet through her fingers and rave about the fabric's beauty, he reached a conclusion.

Even if the Council of Immortals were to come to him and tell him that Artil had violated the rules, even if the Wizard Lord were arbitrarily killing an occasional troublemaker in his campaign to reshape Barokan, even if the new Leader, whoever she was, wanted Artil dead, Sword had no intention of killing him. The man was indeed replacing the old ways with something better, something more popular, something that made life better for everyone.

Oh, there were things the Wizard Lord might do that would go too far—if he exterminated an entire village as the Dark Lord of the Galbek Hills had, for example—but it would take something very drastic indeed to overcome the obvious benefits he had bestowed on Barokan.

And that meant that Sword's role as the Chosen Swordsman was not needed.

Unless something utterly unexpected happened, unless Artil died or went mad, Sword expected to spend the rest of his days as a farmer here in Mad Oak, raising barley and beans.

He smiled at the thought, but it was an unsteady smile that quickly faded.

[12]

The wind coming over the ridge from the west was cold and damp, and pulled the leaves from the trees into sodden brown heaps. Autumn was well advanced, and as Sword sat in the pavilion looking out at the raw weather and the mostly bare trees he thought that he would not be at all surprised to see the first snow almost any day now—though not today; it was still too warm.

The moisture in the air, and the heavy clouds building up overhead, made it obvious that it was going to rain soon. Sword assumed the rain would not fall until after dark; after all, the Wizard Lord controlled the weather, when he wasn't up in his cliff-top retreat, and it had been the custom for centuries to allow rain only at night.

That custom had suffered somewhat during the summer; Artil might have instructed the weather *ler* to behave themselves, but they had not entirely obeyed. The summer had been unusually hot, and three or four times rain had fallen in daylight. Some people had found that upsetting; Sword had discovered, to his surprise, that he rather liked it, despite unfortunate past experiences with unnatural rain. The summer rains had been gentle and cooling, nothing like the ferocious, punishing downpours that the Dark Lord of the Galbek Hills had unleashed in his attempts to deter the Chosen.

But then reports arrived that the Wizard Lord had descended the cliff and settled back into Winterhome, and the weather had begun behaving itself again.

At least, until now. Going by the long streaks of shadow and light the sun was still above the ridge, but those clouds were awfully dark and threatening, the air heavy with moisture. As Sword looked up at the sky through the open shutters, a low rumble sounded.

He blinked.

"*That's* not right!" he said, to no one in particular. He rose from his chair.

The rumble sounded again, louder and closer. There could be no mistaking it.

"That's thunder!" Sword exclaimed.

Around him the half-dozen other occupants of the pavilion were stirring nervously.

"It's what?" Brokenose asked, stepping up beside Sword.

"Thunder! The sound a lightning bolt makes!"

Brokenose stared wildly past the shutters, eyes darting back and forth. "I don't see any lightning," he said worriedly.

"Are you sure, Sword?" Little Weaver asked from her chair ten feet away.

"Yes, I'm sure," Sword said. "I heard it a hundred times when we were on our way to the Dark Lord's tower. Sometimes the lightning is hidden up in the clouds, where you can't see it."

"But the Wizard Lord *protects* us from lightning!" Potter wailed. Sword glanced at her, remembering when she had been a skinny girl known as Mudpie; she had certainly grown up over the last few years, but that unhappy wail was little Mudpie's voice.

"He's supposed to, certainly," Sword replied.

"There hasn't been a thunderstorm in Mad Oak in hundreds of years!"

"I know." Sword squinted up at the clouds. "He has to have brought this one here deliberately. I wonder why?"

"Go ask him!" Potter called.

Several people laughed at that. Sword replied gently, "I can't get all the way to Winterhome before this storm breaks, Potter."

"Well, how do you know he's *in* Winterhome? Maybe he's here, bringing the storm with him!"

That actually had some sense to it, and Sword shrugged. "Let me go up on the ridge and take a look around," he said. "After all, I'm the one person here that lightning can't strike. If the Wizard Lord *is* here, maybe he'll talk to me and explain what's going on."

There was a general chorus of agreement, and Sword turned toward the south door, the one that opened on the trail up to the ridgetop. He had half-expected some of the others to follow him, but they did not; they stayed where they were, seated or standing, and watched him go.

He wondered, as he walked, what the Wizard Lord was up to. Sword had thought, after seeing the changes that the roads had brought to every town from Mad Oak to Winterhome, that Artil had been sincere in his desire to do nothing but improve life for the people of Barokan, but there could be no question that this storm had the Wizard Lord's consent, even if it were not actually of his making.

How could a thunderstorm benefit anyone?

Sword could not think of anything good that lightning might do. If this really was a deliberate thunderstorm, and not a miscalculation of some kind, it seemed depressingly possible that Artil had gone mad, like his predecessor, or perhaps given in to the evil counsel of that traitor Farash inith Kerra.

Sword pulled open the pavilion door and stepped out into the wind, which snatched at his jacket and whipped his hair across his face, roaring in his ears. He blinked, brushed the hair away with one hand while the other clutched at his jacket, then took a few steps and looked up.

The clouds were black and ominous, hanging low over the ridge— but they were not all that large; he could see clear sky in the distance to the north and west, and the setting sun shone orange beneath the overcast, bathing the whole scene in eerie light.

And he could also see, hanging motionless beneath the clouds, a human figure, so high above him that he could see almost no details, could not determine its sex or age, let alone identity. It held a staff, and wore a long red cloak that flapped wildly about it, catching the orange sunset.

That, Sword thought, was almost certainly the Wizard Lord. He was flying there, supported by *ler* of air and wind, and presumably guiding the storm—but why? He wasn't directly over the town or pavilion, but a little to the southwest, directly above the ridge, just outside the borders.

Sword's gaze fell from the wizard to the ground beneath him, and the immense old tree that stood there, and another piece of the mystery fell into place. The Wizard Lord was hovering directly over the great Mad Oak that gave the town its name, the horrific tree that had created a small zone of death beneath its branches.

Whatever Artil was doing up there, it was directed at the tree, not the town.

And then the lightning bolt flashed from sky to earth, blinding Sword for a moment; the crack of thunder deafened him, and the wind seemed to snap at him like a maddened animal for an instant.

Another smaller, sharper crack sounded, as his ears and eyes cleared, then a crackling, and he saw a limb tear loose from the Mad Oak's upper branches and smash its way down through the branches below.

Lightning flashed again, and again thunder rolled over Sword as a second blue-white bolt struck the tree. This time Sword saw flames appear in the oak's crown. The tree, after the fashion of oaks, still had most of its leaves even this late in the season, though all were dry and yellow or orange-brown; ordinarily they would have fallen a few at a time until well into the winter, before the branches were completely bare.

Now, though, the remaining leaves were blazing with more than just autumn color. Fire spread from leaf to leaf, branch to branch.

The Wizard Lord hung in the sky above the burning tree, watching.

Sword stood at the pavilion door, watching.

The wind abruptly died, dropping from a gale to a gentle breeze in seconds, and the world suddenly turned quiet. The howling of wind through the trees and around the eaves of the pavilion, and the rustling of leaves, simply vanished. As Sword's ears adjusted to the relative silence, he could hear the crackling of distant flame as the Mad Oak burned. The fire had spread through the entire tree now, turning it into a gigantic, misshapen torch that sent a column of smoke spiraling upward.

And above the smoke the clouds were parting, thinning, scattering; the storm had served its purpose, and now the Wizard Lord was dispersing it. No rain had fallen, and Sword was sure that none would until the oak had entirely burned. There had been no flicker of lightning, nor the slightest rumble of thunder, since the tree began to burn. Those two great bolts had been the storm's entire purpose.

"Sword, what's happening?" a woman's voice called from somewhere behind him, and for the first time Sword realized that he had left the door open. He turned.

Several faces were gathered in the doorway, looking out at him.

"The Wizard Lord blasted the Mad Oak," he said. "That's what the storm was for." He pointed, then began walking up the ridge.

"What?" Three or four people pushed their way out of the crowd and followed Sword up toward the ridgetop, to where they, too, could see the burning tree.

The little group stood, silently watching, as the flames ate away the last lingering leaves, sending a black mist of ash coiling upward. The branches were now solidly ablaze as well, the great twisted trunk blackened and starting to scorch.

The Wizard Lord had moved aside, to avoid the smoke, and now he seemed to notice his little audience. He turned and swooped downward toward them like some great red bird.

Sword stood calmly waiting, but the others backed away. Potter turned and ran, but Brokenose, Little Weaver, and Coldfoot stood their ground just a few feet behind the Swordsman.

The flying figure came nearer and nearer, and Sword could see that it was indeed Artil, with his embroidered red robes and black hair flapping, the familiar cord of talismans around his throat, his staff in his hand.

He had not carried staff or talismans when Sword had last seen him, up at the Summer Palace, but here he was working magic, so of course he had them.

"Hello, good people!" the airborne figure called.

"Hello, Artil," Sword called back.

"Sword! What a pleasure!" The Wizard Lord waved a greeting. "I knew you lived in Mad Oak, of course, but I hadn't thought I would be fortunate enough to see you here tonight." His descent halted a foot or two above the ground, perhaps six feet away from Sword. Sword could not believe that Mad Oak's *ler* would still refuse him admission, now that he was the Wizard Lord, but perhaps he simply didn't care to press the issue.

"And I had not expected to *ever* find you in Mad Oak," Sword replied. "What brings you here?"

"That tree, of course," Artil replied, gesturing with his staff toward the burning oak. "It was blocking the route of the planned road connecting Greenwater and Mad Oak, not to mention being a hazard in its own right. It should have been removed long ago; the ground beneath it is *covered* with the bones of its victims!"

While Sword knew that to be true, he was not particularly impressed; most of those victims had been deer or squirrels. No human being had been foolish enough to be caught in the oak's spell in years.

In fact, the last person that foolish had been Sword, when he first dared venture outside his hometown seven years before, and he had been saved by the Greenwater Guide and his own magic, keeping his bones safely inside his flesh.

"You're building a road from Greenwater?" Sword asked.

"Well, *I'm* not, but my men are," Artil said. "I do need to keep them busy, and a western route into Longvale would be helpful for the merchants from the coast, wouldn't it?"

"I hadn't given it any thought," Sword said. "The road from Willowbank seems to serve fairly well."

"Oh, but another, shorter route will be even better! You'll see. In any case, I see no reason to leave anything as malevolent as that tree alive, anywhere in Barokan. I know my duties officially only require me to remove human outlaws, but I don't mind expanding my role a little, if it makes life a little better for everyone."

"So now you're eliminating any menaces you can find, regardless of where and what they are?" Sword asked.

"More or less, yes. I'm just one man, of course, even with all my magic, so I'm limited in what I can do, but I'm taking them on one at a time, as my schedule permits. I'm *determined* to leave Barokan a better place than I found it, Sword!"

"I see." Sword heard Little Weaver murmuring something behind him, but he could not make out her words and did not turn around. "That's admirable."

"Thank you," Artil replied.

"Thank *you*, Wizard Lord!" Little Weaver called.

"You're very welcome, my dear." He turned, arms folded across his chest, to watch the tree burn.

Sword stood a few feet away, watching the conflagration.

It appeared Artil had found another way to improve Barokan, and this one did not bother Sword at all. The Wizard Lord was using his magic, rather than abandoning it, and was not interfering in anyone else's business; he was simply removing existing problems.

That seemed very much in keeping with his role, where organizing work crews and building roads did not. More than ever, Sword hoped Artil would not overstep his bounds; a Wizard Lord with the imagination to do this sort of thing was a treasure.

"So have you destroyed many such menaces?" Sword asked.

"Oh, two or three dozen, I suppose," Artil answered, turning back. "A whirlpool here, a monster boar there, and the like. Killer trees are unusual, though, and I think this was the worst I've found."

"I'm not surprised," Sword said. "And I'm sure the new road will be useful."

"Wizard Lord," Little Weaver called, "where are you going next?"

"Back to Winterhome for supper and a good night's sleep, my dear," he replied. "And before anyone makes any flattering offers I would have to refuse, let me say that I want to get home before true nightfall, as flying is far more dangerous in the dark and I have a busy day planned for tomorrow."

"What are you doing tomorrow, then?" Brokenose asked, startling Sword.

"Discussing matters with my officers, for the most part," Artil said. "Making some changes in my organization. Nothing as exciting as destroying an insane oak tree, I'm afraid."

"Ah." Brokenose nodded knowingly.

The talk about his "organization" dampened Sword's enthusiasm somewhat. "We won't keep you, then," he said.

"Thank you. And Sword, feel free to come and visit me again someday. I know you feel it's your responsibility to keep an eye on me."

"Thank you," Sword said. "I'll do that."

The Wizard Lord smiled, then gestured with his staff. He rose swiftly, and this time did not hover, but soared off to the southeast.

For a moment the four townsfolk simply stood, watching the red-clad figure recede; then Sword shivered and turned back toward the pavilion.

"That was the *Wizard Lord!*" Little Weaver said. "We met the actual Wizard Lord!"

"Yes," Sword agreed.

"He *spoke* to us!"

"Yes."

"And he *knew* you," Brokenose said, pointing at Sword.

"Well, yes. We've spoken before."

"He killed the oak," Coldfoot said, staring at the tree, which had lost most of its branches by this point. Just then one of the major limbs cracked, and a large chunk crashed burning to the ground.

"Yes, he did," Sword agreed, glancing at the blazing oak. It occurred to him that it would be a very bad thing if the fire spread to any of the surrounding trees—but presumably that was why the wind had dropped.

Still, it was careless of Artil, he thought, to not stay and watch until he was sure the fire did not get out of control. Perhaps he had some sort of magical monitor in place, or had ordered the local *ler* to see that nothing untoward happened. Perhaps he should have had some of his "organization" standing by to prevent the fire from spreading.

But the fire *wasn't* spreading, so maybe Artil had known exactly what he was doing.

"Will we have to change the town's name, do you think?" Brokenose asked.

"Don't be ridiculous," Sword replied.

"He killed the oak!" Coldfoot repeated.

"He's *wonderful!*" Little Weaver said, clasping her hands over her breast.

Sword glanced at the woman, then at the dwindling speck that was the Wizard Lord.

"Yes, on balance, I suppose he is," Sword said thoughtfully.

A little over a year after his return from Winterhome, a few months less than a year after the burning of the Mad Oak, Sword was plowing a recently harvested bean field in the river bottom, hoping the unusually warm weather might hold long enough to get a second crop in, when the stranger came marching up.

The new arrival was a rather slender young man of moderate height, scarcely more than a boy, clad in a flowing green-and-gold silk cloak that was absurdly out of place out here. His long black hair was swept back in a ponytail and adorned with three long *ara* plumes, and he strode along boldly as he emerged from the patch of boggy woods that separated this field from the heart of Mad Oak.

"Ho, farmer!" he called, raising a hand in salute. "I seek Erren Zal Tuyo, the Chosen Swordsman!"

Sword called to his ox and gave the plow a jerk, setting it hard in the ground; he had been planning to take a break at the end of the furrow in any case, so there was no harm in being polite and seeing what this little popinjay wanted. He rubbed his aching hands together, then turned to address the stranger.

"Why?" he called, as the young man approached.

"I have a message for him," the stranger said as he stopped at the side of the field. Sword was relieved that at least the fellow had the sense not to simply walk out onto freshly turned soil; he looked like a bit of a fool. That cloak was excessively gaudy, even by the new standards brought on by the sudden availability of exotic fabrics and dyes, and his manner was absurdly pompous.

"Where is he?" the stranger demanded.

"I don't think the Swordsman is expecting any messages," Sword replied, amused.

"Well, he'll get this one all the same," the messenger said cheerfully. "At least, if he's still alive and fit."

"Fit enough," Sword said. "What's this message, then?"

"Are you his secretary, perhaps? Why should I tell *you*?"

Sword grimaced. "I'm no one's secretary," he said. "I'm Erren Zal Tuyo, the Chosen Swordsman. What's the message?"

The messenger looked suddenly uncertain. "You're the Swordsman?" he asked.

"I'm the Swordsman. What were you expecting, then? Do I not match the description they gave you?"

"They gave me no description," the stranger said. "But you hardly look like a great swordsman. You're not much older than I am, and I expected someone more . . . lithe. Besides, you don't have a sword."

Sword judged the age difference to be at least a few years. He sighed deeply.

"Nonetheless, I am the Chosen Swordsman. Why would I carry a sword while plowing?" He frowned. "You know, I don't think I'm interested in your message after all. I should get back to work."

"Oh, I think the Swordsman will be interested in *this* one," the young man said, puffing out his chest. "Now, can you direct me to him?"

"I told you, I'm the Swordsman."

The messenger waved a hand dismissively. "Show me some evidence of this unlikely claim, then. To me, you appear nothing but a half-witted young farmer amusing himself by attempting to fool me."

Sword grimaced. "*Why* would I do that?"

The stranger shrugged. "Boredom, perhaps? Or curiosity about the nature of the message I bring."

Sword was, in fact, becoming mildly curious. "Who's this message from? What do they want?" he asked. He was quite sure the message was not from the Wizard Lord; Artil would have used an animal, rather than a human messenger. Everyone in Mad Oak knew him by sight, and would have come in person. That left the other Chosen, the wizards, or people who had some foolish idea that the Swordsman worked as a hero for hire.

Any of those was possible, though.

"That's for the Swordsman to know. Now, if you'll pardon me, I think I'm bound back up to the village, to find a more honest informant—I've clearly been misdirected."

"No, you haven't. I really am the Swordsman. Anyone in Mad Oak would direct you back here."

"I do not believe that."

Sword frowned again. He looked along the verge of the field, and spotted one of the sticks used to support the bean crop, half-buried in the earth. It had been cast aside, presumably, when the last crop was harvested, and left lying there. "Do *you* have a sword?" he asked. Even now, with the availability of cheap northern steel and the scattered reports of bandits on the roads, very few people carried swords, but Sword thought he had seen something under the messenger's outer robe, and the man certainly gave the impression of being the sort of braggart who would go armed. "Or some other weapon?"

In answer, the messenger flung back his cloak. A broad belt of fine black leather circled his waist, and a gold-trimmed hilt thrust up from a black scabbard. "If you think I'm fool enough to give you my sword, and leave myself unarmed so that you can rob me . . ."

"I don't want your sword," Sword interrupted. "But if you'd throw me that stick, I'll show you I'm the Swordsman." He pointed. Then he caught himself, and laughed. "Though I don't know why I bother. It would serve you right if I let you ramble about the countryside looking for some other Swordsman for the next half-month."

The messenger frowned at the farmer, then took four steps over to the stick. He kept his eyes on Sword as he bent down and picked up the discarded beanpole.

It was a peeled branch a little less than three feet long; the messenger could see nothing strange about it. He tossed it gently, and Sword snatched it out of the air.

"Choose the order," Sword said, as he tested the stick to make sure it hadn't rotted much. "Knee, elbow, belly, throat—which one first?"

"What?"

Sword brandished the stick. "Choose one," he said. "That'll be the first place I touch you."

"And what will that prove—that you're quick with a stick?" The man's pompous manner had faded considerably.

"Pick one," Sword insisted. "Then draw your sword and try to stop me."

"Belly," the messenger said, clearly annoyed. "Belly, knee, elbow."

Sword nodded. "Three each, right-left-right. Now draw your sword."

"This is ridiculous. I might hurt you."

"You won't," Sword said. "And if you do, it serves me right."

"Well, *that's* the truth!" the messenger said. He reached across and slid his blade from its sheath.

Sword watched the way the man moved, watched the way his hand turned as he drew, watched the sunlight sparkle on the polished steel blade; he waited until the man fell into a halfhearted guard position.

Then he attacked, moving in low and outside, coming up under the messenger's guard, poking the stick into the man's belly.

Startled by Sword's speed, the messenger reacted awkwardly, bringing the sword down far too late to stop a second jab.

Then Sword's stick swung clear, tapped the back of the sword simply for emphasis, and struck at the messenger's right leg, tapping hard just below the kneecap.

The sword moved, but the stick had already gone, sliding down past the messenger's hand and wrist, tapping him on the inside of his right elbow.

"You forgot the throat," Sword said, as he brought the beanpole up and around and under the messenger's chin.

The messenger stepped back, sword flailing. Sword made two more quick jabs to the belly, one from below and one from above, then went for the left knee.

"Wait!" the messenger said, finally managing a parry that delayed Sword's strike at his left elbow for perhaps half a second. That startled the Swordsman; the messenger was faster than he looked. Ignoring the request, Sword did not wait, but finished his second series with a slash across the messenger's throat that would undoubtedly leave a mark.

"Blast it!" the messenger said, trying unsuccessfully to counter.

The messenger was very quick, and now that he had focused on the action he had a knack of moving in ways Sword did not expect; presumably the *ara* feathers dangling from the back of his head helped with that by blocking his spirit from Sword's magic. As a result the third series of touches took a few seconds longer, but the end was never in doubt. Sword finished it off with a flourish by touching the messenger on each cheek, then whipping the stick around his wrist and knocking the sword from his hand.

Then Sword straightened up, his beanpole raised in salute, as the disarmed messenger stared at him.

"How did you *do* that?" the young man demanded.

"Practice," Sword said. "Or magic, if you prefer. Now, what's this message?"

The messenger blinked at him. Clearly, there could be no further question that this was the man he had been sent to find. He hesitated, clearly unsure whether to retrieve his sword, then decided it could wait.

"The Leader of the Chosen wants to see you."

Sword grimaced and tossed the stick aside. He had been afraid of that. "Oh, plague and ague," he said. "You're sure?"

"Well, yes," the messenger said, startled. "Of course. I'd hardly say so if I weren't."

"You're certain it was her, and not some fraud?"

"Absolutely. Who could make a mistake about such a thing?"

"You'd be surprised," Sword said. "What does she want, then? Has the Wizard Lord done something terrible?"

"She didn't tell me," the messenger said. "I mean, she didn't explain why; she just said I should come to Mad Oak and fetch you. Tell you that she's in Winterhome and wants you to meet her there."

Sword snorted. "It's the Wizard Lord, of course—what *else* could it be?"

"I don't know," the messenger said.

An unpleasant thought struck Sword. He had been avoiding the traders in the village square, and the merchants in the pavilion, so it was entirely possible he had missed some important news—or perhaps this message *was* the news. "Is it still Artil?" he asked.

"Is what still what?"

"Is Artil still the Wizard Lord?"

The messenger blinked. "I . . . I believe that's the Wizard Lord's name, yes. I don't really know, I always just called him by his title. . . ."

"He hasn't died and been replaced in the past year?" Sword demanded.

"I . . . um . . . no, not lately," the messenger said, obviously confused by the question. "Not for years, not since you killed the Dark Lord of the Galbek Hills."

"Then what's he done? Carried off unwilling young girls, or buggered the wrong priests? Slaughtered a town or two, as Galbek Hills did? Please don't tell me she thinks there's something unforgivably wrong with building roads and bridges, or killing monsters."

"I don't know," the messenger said, a trifle desperately. "Really. She just told me to fetch you."

"Damn," Sword said. He turned to look at the ox, waiting patiently in the traces. He sighed again. "Let me finish up here," he said. "I'll meet you at the pavilion this evening, and we can leave in the morning."

The messenger hesitated, then nodded. "Thank you," he said.

Sword nodded back, jerked the plow free, and returned to his work. The messenger stood watching silently for a moment, then turned and left, looking greatly deflated.

When Sword arrived at the pavilion the sun was low in the west and Younger Priestess was lighting the lanterns, murmuring a quiet invocation to the *ler* of fire and light as she did so. A few traders sat along the west wall, their goods displayed on cloths laid on the plank floor, talking quietly among themselves; no customers were in sight. A young couple sat on the terrace bench by the south door, heads bent toward each other, the man whispering in the woman's ear. Sword did not recognize them immediately, and guessed they were travelers of some sort.

The messenger in the green-and-gold robe was nowhere to be seen.

Mildly puzzled, Sword leaned on the terrace rail, looking out over the valley, wondering where the man was. That bright cloak of his ought to stand out almost anywhere.

The far ridge was vividly green in the late-afternoon sun, and seemed to sparkle with gold; Sword was unsure whether that was *ler* moving among the trees, or merely a trick of the light. The Eastern Cliffs were a dark line in the distance, the sky above them intensely blue, and he remembered those vast plains atop them. He leaned out and peered to the southeast, wondering whether he could spot the

Summer Palace from this distance. He never had yet, but he kept thinking it should be possible.

Then he heard a rustling and shuffling, and he turned, hoping to see the messenger's bright cloak. Instead he saw that the couple from the bench had risen, and were walking toward him. He turned to greet them, then blinked.

The young man was the messenger. He had removed his gaudy robe, rearranged his hair, and dressed himself in plain linen and brown leather, and had somehow acquired a female companion, but now that he was upright, his face no longer hidden, Sword recognized him.

It was more than just the change of clothing and position, Sword realized; the man had shifted his stance, the way he held himself, the shape of his shoulders and angle of his neck. Sword remembered also how the young man had moved during the earlier display of swordsmanship. A suspicion began to stir, and Sword quickly reviewed certain roles. He glanced at the woman, then back to the man.

He was still not entirely certain, but Sword bowed to the couple as they drew near. "The Thief, is it?" he asked.

The young man bowed in return. "Indeed," he said quietly, with a quick glance around the room to see that no one else was listening. "They call me Snatcher."

Sword turned to the woman. She had a round face, and was just a little on the plump side; her hair was cut square at her shoulders, dark and straight.

"And this would be—the Seer, perhaps? Or the Leader?"

The Thief turned his head, waiting for his companion to reply. For her part, the young woman studied Sword's face intently before saying, "The Seer." Her voice was soft, and not entirely steady.

"That seemed the most likely," Sword said. "You would know where I am; the Leader would not. So you were sent to find me—but why was it the Thief who came to the fields alone?"

He had addressed the question to the Seer, but it was the Thief who replied, "She thinks I'm the braver of us."

"It takes courage to speak to me?"

"Indeed it does. You are something of a legend, after all, as the man who slew the Dark Lord of the Galbek Hills. It was you who demanded that our predecessors yield up their roles among the Chosen, and whose demands were all met, for reasons we don't understand. You would seem to have something more to you than merely the ability to wield a blade."

Sword took a moment to absorb that, then looked at the Seer.

She turned her eyes away.

Sword did not press the issue; instead he asked the Thief, "Why are you here at all? Why did she not come alone?"

"I was afraid," the Seer murmured, before the Thief could reply.

"She doesn't go anywhere alone," Snatcher added.

"But why you? Why not a hired guide? There are plenty of them eager for work." Now that roads connected so many places, the old guides were no longer really needed simply to get a person safely from one town to the next, and their knowledge of the displaced local *ler* was useless, but many of them were still escorting travelers along the highways, serving as guards and advisors.

"She doesn't trust anyone but the Chosen."

"And you were available, while Bow was not? Or Lore?"

"Lore is once again at the Summer Palace, and she doesn't trust Bow. Boss is busy in Winterhome, Beauty doesn't like to travel, and I suspect Babble, wherever she is, is too busy listening to the voices to be any use."

Sword had not intended to bother asking about the female Chosen; he knew that many women didn't like to rely on other women to protect them, though he did not entirely understand that attitude. He glanced at the Seer, whose eyes were still turned down and away.

He did not bother asking why she distrusted Bow; he remembered enough of the Archer's past behavior to see why she might not. "Then everyone else is already gathered for whatever this mysterious purpose is?"

"Five of us are; not you or Lore or Babble. We'll be fetching Babble next."

Sword leaned back against the terrace railing and asked, "Why?"

The Thief and the Seer exchanged glances. "Why what?" the Thief asked.

"Why are we gathering? Has the Wizard Lord done something terrible?"

"Not that I know of."

"Then why are you here, asking me to go to Winterhome?"

Snatcher cocked his head. "Because Boss told us to," he said.

"And is that reason enough? Has she told you why she wants us to attend her?"

A trace of a smile appeared on Snatcher's face. "You haven't met her, have you?"

"No."

"Then perhaps I'll just suggest that you might want to. Purely out of curiosity. And *she* wants to meet *you*."

Sword frowned and looked at the Seer. "Do *you* know what's going on?"

"We came to bring you to Winterhome," she murmured. "You're the Chosen Swordsman; we want you to help us."

"That doesn't answer the question."

"It's what I know."

Frustrated, Sword began to wonder if he had been too hasty in believing this pair to be the new Thief and the new Seer. When last the Chosen had been gathered there was no doubt about why, and the Seer had been only too happy to explain that the Wizard Lord had killed several people, and had lied about who they were. This pair seemed determined to keep their reasons to themselves.

Could these two be impostors, trying to lure him somewhere?

But who would want to do that? No, they were probably just who they claimed to be, but young and inexperienced. They had obeyed the Leader without thinking.

But she might have told them something, or the Seer might know something herself. "Has the Wizard Lord killed someone?" he asked the Seer. Part of her magic was that she would *know* whether he had, just as she always knew where in Barokan all the Chosen were, and where the Wizard Lord was.

She lowered her gaze again and shook her head. "Not yet, that I can see," she whispered. "Not himself."

Sword stared at her for a moment. It was not the actual words that swayed him, but how she said them.

"All right," he said. "We'll leave in the morning. You can sleep here in the pavilion, or in my mother's loft, whichever you prefer."

 Both of them chose the loft.

Sword had intended to introduce them to his mother and siblings honestly, but the Thief forestalled that by pushing forward and bowing over his mother's hand as she stood in the kitchen door, studying the unexpected new arrivals.

"I am delighted to meet the famed White Rose," Snatcher said, in an unctuous tone completely unlike either the pompous messenger or the quiet young man he had been heretofore; Sword saw that the little man had straightened himself up, thrown back his shoulders, and adopted an entirely different stance. "I am Desrem dik Taborin of Spilled Basket, come to fetch your honored son to aid us."

White Rose cast a sideways glance at Sword, but before either of them could speak the Thief continued, "We have a problem with bandits, you see—a problem beneath the notice of the Wizard Lord himself, busy as he is with other matters in his home in the Summer Palace, and we thought the Chosen Swordsman might be able to help us."

"Oh," White Rose said. She looked questioningly at Sword.

Sword had not intended to lie, but he could see why the Thief might want to. Any mention that the Chosen were gathering was likely to stir up rumors about the Wizard Lord, and at this point it was probably better not to do that. Artil was quite a hero here; the road from Greenwater had been cut through, up by the charred stump of the Mad Oak, just a month before, bringing a whole new wave of traders and travelers.

He still did not want to tell any actual falsehoods, but it was easy enough to tell the truth while still giving the impression the Thief's explanation was correct. "I *thought* holing up in the Summer Palace might cause problems," Sword said. "Anyway, this messenger came to fetch me and I've agreed to go. I offered them the loft bed here; it's a little more comfortable than the pavilion floor."

"Oh," his mother said again. "And who is this? Your wife?" She looked from the Seer to the Thief and back.

"A friend," Snatcher replied. "She knew the way better than I did, and agreed to guide me."

"She did?" White Rose frowned. "But I've never seen her in Mad Oak before."

"I've never been here," the Seer said quietly. "But I've studied maps."

"Really?" The frown vanished. "I've never seen a map. I've heard about them—they're like pictures, but of entire towns?"

"Sort of," the Seer answered uneasily.

"Are you from Spilled Basket, too?"

The Seer didn't reply; instead she threw the Thief a quick glance, and he stepped up. "Yes, she is," he said. "Of course."

"That's a long way."

"Yes, it is."

She turned to her son. "Then will you be gone long?"

"I really don't know, Mother," he said. "I hope it won't be *too* long."

"And you won't kill anyone?"

"I don't know, Mother. I certainly hope not." Killing Artil would make him a pariah, he knew. Killing anyone else would be a crime.

"And this doesn't have anything to do with the Wizard Lord, or his lovely roads?"

"Mother, I promise, I have no intention of going up the cliff to the Summer Palace to harass the Wizard Lord. I'm just doing what this man's asked me to."

"Well, all right, then. Be careful."

"I will." He turned to his guests. "This way," he said.

The rarely used loft room was reached by a ladder through a trap-door; Sword climbed up enough to open the trap and set a candle on the floor by the opening, then descended and gestured for the others to climb.

The Thief hesitated with one foot on the ladder. "I'd like a word with you about our plans," he said.

"I'll be right up, then," Sword assured him.

He watched as the two visitors climbed, and then followed them.

A moment later the three sat around the trapdoor, and Sword asked, "What did you need to say that couldn't wait until morning?"

"I wanted to make sure we understand each other," Snatcher said quietly, as he closed the trap. "I lied to your mother just now, and you knew it and didn't say anything."

"You didn't want to worry her," Sword said. "I understand that."

"I didn't want her to try to stop us," Snatcher said. "Whether she worries or not—well, I see no reason to make anyone needlessly unhappy, but I don't go out of my way to avoid upsetting strangers. But right now, I doubt your mother would want to hear that the Chosen are gathering."

Sword knew exactly what the Thief meant. The Chosen gathered for only one reason. "Not *everyone* is enamored of the changes the current Wizard Lord has made," he said, though he was no longer sure this was true.

"But *most* people are. And even those who aren't know that most of their neighbors prefer the new Barokan to the old. Your mother would probably not be pleased to know you might be called upon to kill the Lord of Winterhome. Whatever she thinks of him herself, she must know it would make you a very unpopular man."

"So you didn't want to worry her," Sword repeated. "And you probably didn't want to risk the possibility that word might somehow get back to the Wizard Lord that the Chosen are gathering, either."

Snatcher smiled crookedly. "Ah, you *do* understand!" He opened his leather vest to display half a dozen *ara* feathers, sewn into the garment's lining. "It's very convenient that so many travelers still carry these to ward off hostile *ler*," he said. "It means we can wear them without arousing the Wizard Lord's suspicions."

"Oh, he's probably suspicious," Sword said. "But he can't really do anything about it." He glanced at the Seer to see if she was going to display her protective feathers as well, but she made no move to do so. Sword supposed they were under her generous skirts.

"So you think he knows we're up to something?"

"He might, yes."

"But you still intend to come with us to Winterhome to meet Boss?"

"Yes. I agreed to be the Chosen Swordsman; I think that means that when the Leader of the Chosen summons me, I should at least see what she wants."

"And if she *does* want this Wizard Lord dead?"

"I'll listen to her reasons, and if I find them unconvincing I will try my best to talk her out of it. And I may need a great deal of convincing."

"Fair enough; I'm not in any hurry to become widely loathed, either. Incidentally, my true name is not Desrem dik Taborin of Spilled Basket; rather, it's Taborin dik Desrem, and I was born and raised in Bayshead on the Soreen Coast, where I was called Ferret. Let us have no lies between us."

Sword nodded. "In that case," he said, "tell me, did you ever really doubt I was the Swordsman?"

Snatcher grinned. "Not seriously, no. I wanted to get your measure, though."

"And did you?"

"Well enough, I think. You didn't just chase me away, and you didn't try to kill me. That little show with the beanpole was quite impressive."

"I'm glad you liked it," Sword said. He glanced at the Seer, who had not said a word since mounting the ladder. "Do you have anything to say about any of this?" he asked.

She shook her head.

Sword stared at her.

"There will be time on the road," she whispered at last.

Sword snorted. "You certainly aren't much like the last Seer," he said. "She talked far more. Did she tell you, when she passed on her role, why she was retiring?"

"She was a coward," the Seer whispered. "She would not enter the Dark Lord's tower with you, even though she had been the one who started the campaign against him."

"She *did* tell you, then."

"Yes."

"And did she think you would do better? You, who didn't dare meet *me*?"

"I *will* do better," the Seer said, no longer whispering. She raised her eyes to meet Sword's gaze.

"Can you be sure of that?" Sword asked gently.

"Yes," the Seer said flatly. Her eyes did not waver; she stared directly at him.

Sword stared back at her. "Oh?"

"Yes," the Seer repeated.

"Sword," the Thief interjected, "I would not argue with her."

"Oh?" Sword turned his attention to Snatcher. "If you will forgive me, she seems a frail and timid little thing, unsuited to a role among the Chosen. Why do you have such faith in her courage?"

"She's from Bone Garden," Snatcher said.

Sword's gaze leapt back to the Seer.

"Her manner isn't timidity, exactly," the Thief explained. "She was taught to be quiet and deferential from infancy, and it's a habit now, but it's not really fear—just habit."

"Bone Garden?" Sword asked.

Ever since he first began traveling in Barokan, Sword had heard tales of the hideous things that were done in Bone Garden—or more often, not so much heard tales as heard hints and implications. Even in the very few towns he had visited that practiced human sacrifice, such as Redfield, where an innocent child was ritually murdered every spring and his or her blood spread on the fields to appease the *ler*, the customs of Bone Garden were spoken of with disgust and horror.

"Bone Garden," the Seer said. "I can show you the scars, if you like. I not only survived there, against the express wishes of the priests, I *escaped*. Do you still want to question my courage?"

"No," Sword said. "But . . . the stories. . . ." He glanced at the Thief. "The stories I've heard about Bone Garden . . . are they true?"

"I don't know what stories you've heard," Snatcher said.

Sword grimaced, unsure where to begin. Before he could say more, though, the Seer looked up and spoke again, in a low, flat voice.

"My mother was called Breeder," she said. "But that was no real distinction; so were a few dozen other women, including some of my sisters—or half-sisters, of course none of us knew who had fathered us.

We weren't permitted to know our true names. Generally, if one of the priests wanted one of us, he wouldn't bother with a name; he would just point or beckon."

"Oh," Sword said.

"It's getting late," the Thief interrupted. "We'll have plenty of time to talk on the way to Winterhome."

"Is that the sort of story you meant?" the Seer asked, staring into Sword's eyes.

"Yes," Sword said. "I'm sorry."

The Seer did not answer; she simply continued to stare at him.

The Thief, too, fell silent.

After a long, awkward moment, Sword said, "I'll be downstairs, then. I'll see you in the morning." He turned and lifted the trap.

The other two sat, silent and motionless, and watched him clamber back down the ladder. His head had scarcely cleared the opening when the trap was lowered back into place. At the foot of the ladder he stood and looked upward for a moment at that closed door.

These two were very different from any of the other Chosen he had known. They were the first to be younger than he was himself, and that really did affect how he perceived them; he was accustomed to thinking of himself as the brash young upstart of the group, but those two made him feel old and stodgy.

He wondered how Merrilin tarak Dolin had found this new Thief, and how the old Seer, Shal Doro Sheth tava Doro, had ever ventured to Bone Garden for her replacement. She had been too frightened to set foot in the tower in the Galbek Hills, yet she had gone to the most feared community in all Barokan to find her successor? Maybe she had been trying to prove something to someone—herself, perhaps. Maybe she had wanted to show that she was not a complete coward.

He would ask the new Seer about it at some point. As she said, they would have time on the road.

That reminded him of the brief bit of description the girl had given when he asked her about Bone Garden. She hadn't said anything about herself, really, only about her mother and her poor nameless sisters, all treated as interchangeable baby makers. Some of the lurid stories he had heard had touched on that. The priesthood of Bone Garden was said to treat the rest of the population as slaves, using them as their playthings, or as beasts of burden. The *ler* reportedly demanded payment of blood or flesh for every crop, for every bit of cooperation between humanity and nature; they did not recognize anyone but the priests as worthy of even the most basic consideration. Rumor had it there were no families in Bone Garden, not as the word was understood anywhere else; even the priests were not permitted that sort of connection with their fellows. Supposedly the town's boundaries were marked out not with shrines of stone or wood, but with a fence made of human bones, a fence that grew higher every year. That was said to be where the town's name came from.

Who could live like that?

And how could someone from such a place have become the Seer?

And why hadn't someone done something about the existence of such a town? If the Wizard Lord was burning killer trees and slaughtering monster boars, perhaps he should take the time to do something about Bone Garden—and perhaps Redfield and Drumhead, while he was at it. If he really wanted to make Barokan a better place, those towns would need to change.

How *had* someone from Bone Garden become one of the Chosen? It didn't seem as if the priests there would have allowed it.

Well, he would have plenty of time to ask the Seer about it on the way to Winterhome. He turned away from the ladder and headed to bed.

The three set out on the road from Mad Oak to Willowbank without incident, and conversation was limited to casual chatter about supplies and weather and the like until they were well along the way. Sword and Snatcher did most of the talking; the Seer preferred to walk silently a step or two behind the two men.

Once the sun had topped the Eastern Cliffs golden sunlight dappled the road ahead, and a gentle breeze rustled the leaves overhead. Every so often a merchant's wagon would come creaking northward, and they would wave polite greetings as it passed, but mostly they had the road to themselves, and simply walked along enjoying the day.

After a time, though, Sword asked, "How did you become the Thief? Merrilin tarak Dolin lived near Quince Market, in the eastern Midlands, not out on the Soreen Coast."

"And did the old Swordsman live in Mad Oak, or anywhere in Longvale?" Snatcher asked.

"No," Sword admitted. "He was from Dazet Saltmarsh. He and a couple of wizards found me."

"And the old Thief found me in, I suppose, much the same fashion, though in her case she was traveling with her husband and two children as well as two wizards."

"All the way out on the Soreen Coast?"

The Thief brushed away a butterfly that had wandered near his face. "Well, no," he said. "They found me at an inn in Crooktree, actually. I left Bayshead when I was fourteen, a few months after my mother died. My aunt had taken me in, but her heart wasn't in it, and I decided to save her the trouble of looking after me. I packed up a few things and paid the guide to take me to Greycliff, then made my way from there."

"You're an orphan?"

"For almost ten years now." A squirrel scampered through the undergrowth beside the road, and Snatcher idly tossed a pebble at it.

"And you . . . where do you live, then?" Sword asked. "Bayshead or Greycliff or Crooktree?"

Snatcher shrugged. "None of them, really. I travel around. It's much easier now, with the new roads."

"But how do you support yourself?"

Snatcher grimaced. "Plague, man, I'm the world's greatest thief! How do you *think* I support myself?"

"But . . . oh."

"I was a thief even before I was Chosen, you know. That was *why* I was chosen. The old Thief hated her role, so she sought someone for whom it wouldn't be a problem." He smiled. "It isn't a problem for me, I assure you."

"But that's . . . that's wrong, stealing for a living!"

Snatcher shrugged again. "I'm sure it is. I didn't have much of a choice at first, though—stealing or begging were about the only options once I left Bayshead, and I decided that if I was going to take other people's money and food and other belongings, I'd rather take them from the stingy than from the generous, so I preferred stealing to begging. Now that I have magic, as well as my native skills, I can be very particular about what I take from whom, and I assure you, I never rob the needy, and I try not to be unkind to the kindly. A coin here, a loaf of bread there, from the rude or greedy, and I appease the *ler* of my talisman, keep my belly filled, and satisfy my own sense of justice."

"But it's still not . . . not *right*."

Snatcher shrugged. "Was it right for my father, whoever he was, to abandon my mother, and for my mother to die young?" He jabbed a thumb over his shoulder. "Is it right that Bone Garden exists, and no one does anything to change it?"

Sword frowned.

"The world is full of things that aren't right," the Thief continued. "The *ler* aren't concerned with what's right and fair, only with following their nature, and we who live among them must accept that."

"I know," Sword said, with a glance back at the Seer. "I know."

With that, the conversation trailed off to nothing.

Later, though, when a northbound wagon loaded with bright fabrics had rolled past and reminded him, Sword asked, "Why did you wear that ridiculous cloak when you came to find me?"

"I had to ask your townsfolk where I might find you," Snatcher explained. "Seer was exhausted and needed to rest, and I didn't want to wait for her to recover. The two of us traveling together wouldn't interest anyone, but someone asking for the Chosen Swordsman might, so I dressed up a little. I knew that way no one would remember my face, or anything about me but the cloak and the officious manner. No one would ever think of that absurd, self-important messenger as the Chosen Thief." He shrugged. "I use disguises fairly often, in my line of work. When we reach Winterhome I'll be in Host People black."

"No one would know you, you thought, including me," Sword suggested.

"True enough. As I said last night, I wanted to get a look at you before you knew who I was." He rubbed his throat, remembering. "That was quite a display of swordsmanship."

Sword did not bother to reply to that.

"And you figured out who we were more quickly than I expected," Snatcher continued a few steps later. "Bow didn't recognize us at all until we told him."

That did not particularly surprise Sword, but again, he did not answer, and the conversation died.

They arrived in Willowbank around midday, where they paid their respects to the Priest-King. That was a quick and perfunctory event, very different, Sword thought, from the excitement when he had first visited the town, shortly after the road had first opened. The steady flow of trade and travelers had removed all novelty from any new arrivals, even the Chosen Swordsman.

The other two did not admit their identities; Snatcher once again claimed to be a messenger from Spilled Basket, and the Seer refused to identify herself at all.

Before the road opened, a stranger who gave no name and stated no purpose would have been viewed with extreme suspicion, but now no one seemed to care; the Priest-King simply shrugged and ignored her.

After the presentation they bought a good lunch from the traders in the town square, and then headed on to Rock Bridge. In the old days, with a guide leading them by a roundabout route through the wilderness, dodging hostile *ler*, the journey from Mad Oak to Willowbank would have been a full day's effort for anyone, but now it was no great feat to make the additional trip to Rock Bridge.

There, however, they stayed the night. The Council of Priests had had a large hostel built to cope with the sudden increase in visitors, and even with the several merchants in town there were plenty of beds for the three of them.

Beds, but not rooms. "We don't want to discourage anyone from opening a proper inn, or ordinary people from renting out rooms," a young priestess explained. "If you want privacy, you'll have to pay for it. But we didn't want anyone sleeping in the market, either."

"Do we want privacy?" Sword asked, looking at the others.

"I have no coin to pay for it," Snatcher said with a shrug. "If you do . . ."

Sword turned to the Seer. "And you?" He caught himself before calling her "Seer," and realized he had no other name for her.

"I don't care," she murmured.

"Then we'll save our money," Sword said. "Thank you, priestess."

Later, as the three of them were walking in the twilight, Sword asked the Seer, "What should I call you?"

"It doesn't matter," she said. "Anything you like."

He glanced at the Thief. "What do *you* call her, when you aren't admitting she's the Seer?"

"Oh, whatever whim strikes me," he said. "Pudding, or Fumble, or Prettyfoot, or Skinny, or Silence. Or I make up a bit that sounds like a true name—Dinzil or Kuri or something."

Sword grimaced at the idea of calling the Seer skinny; she wasn't. "You don't know any of her true name?"

"*She* doesn't know any of her true name," the Thief pointed out.

"You haven't met Babble?"

Startled, the Seer looked up at him as the Thief replied, "No. Why? What does that have to do with her name?"

"Babble calls everyone by true name," Sword explained. "I don't think she can help it; *ler* are constantly barraging her with true names. When she meets someone his soul announces his true name to her before he can speak aloud, and repeats it frequently, so she finds true names much easier to remember than what we call ourselves."

"So she can tell me my name?" the Seer said, suddenly intent.

"Oh, yes. Of course. But wait—when you became the Seer, didn't the wizard who bound you to the talisman use your true name?"

"She may have," the Seer said. "I don't remember. The shock—the whole *world* changed when I became the Seer. Everything I see and feel, everything I know—I don't remember much from the transition. I must have heard my true name, but . . . but it's gone. I remember a sound like a knife, but nothing more."

"Ah," Sword said. "It was quite an experience for me, too, but not so much that I forgot anything."

"You and I, our magic is largely physical," the Thief said. "Hers is perceptual. It's different, I'm sure."

"Of course," Sword agreed.

"The Speaker can tell me my name?" the Seer asked again. "You're sure?"

"Yes," Sword said, startled by her insistence. "I told you she can. I'm quite sure."

She looked at the Thief. "We need to find her."

"We will," he said. "But first we bring the Swordsman to Winterhome. It's almost on the way, in any case."

The Seer blinked. "Is it? She hasn't moved." She pointed to the southwest. "She's that way, about a hundred and twenty miles."

"In Seven Sides?" Sword asked.

"I don't know," the Seer said. "Is she?"

"I don't know," Sword said. "I think that's the right general area, though, and she likes it there, as there's a place with no *ler*. Her home I think would be more *that* way, and a little farther." He pointed a little more to the west than the Seer had. Then he looked around, at the fading glow in the western sky and the black line of cliffs in the east, and at the unfamiliar buildings of Rock Bridge, and spread his empty hands. "Or I could be wrong. I may be misjudging completely."

"Wherever it is, we need to find her," the Seer said. "Winterhome is that way." She pointed to the south and a little east. "Are you sure there isn't a more direct route?"

"We need to deliver the Swordsman first, Skinny," Snatcher replied. "And there aren't many roads across the ridge into Greenvale, in any case. The nearest might be back in Mad Oak."

"But she can tell me my *name*," the Seer said.

"You've lived all these years without it," the Thief said. "You can wait a little longer."

"But . . ."

"Winterhome first. Then the Speaker."

"I could come with you to fetch her," Sword offered. "She knows me; that might be useful."

"She'll know us on sight, won't she?" the Thief asked.

"Well . . . yes," Sword admitted. "She'll hear your souls telling her who you are."

"And Boss told us to bring you first, *then* go get her, so we'll bring you first, and *then* go get her. It's settled."

"I want my name," the Seer muttered.

"Why is it so very important to you?" Sword asked. "Isn't it enough to be known as the Seer?"

She hesitated, then said, "That's what I'm called, but I don't think of it as my *name*. I still think of what I was called in Bone Garden as my name, and I don't want to. I want that gone. I want to know my true name, instead."

"Why?" Sword was confused. "What were you called in Bone Garden? You said you weren't a Breeder, but you . . ."

"Sword," the Thief interrupted, "I don't think you . . ."

"*No*," the Seer said, cutting him off. "*You* don't decide, Snatcher. *I* do."

"Of course, Seer, I know, but I . . ."

"You don't decide. You don't choose what I allow to hurt me."

"I . . ." Snatcher looked baffled, then surrendered. "As you wish," he said.

She glared at the Thief for another few seconds, then turned her gaze on Sword, meeting his eyes.

"You know that in Bone Garden, names are just descriptions, don't you?" she said. "Just words, just facts, like calling a chair 'Chair,' or a tree 'Tree.' They're never whimsical or . . . what's the word? Metaphorical. They aren't, ever. Your mother is called White Rose, but in Bone Garden that isn't a name. It's not possible. You understand?"

"All right," Sword said, confused. He had known nothing of the sort, but was perfectly willing to believe it.

"The most common names are Farmer and Priest, but sometimes there's someone chosen by the *ler* for something special, and that becomes his name—or hers. A child born to be sacrificed to freshen the soil might be called Blood, for example, because that's the only part of him that will matter, the only thing he lives for. I knew two people named Blood in my household."

"Oh," Sword said, unhappily.

"You understand?"

"I think so."

She paused, as if working up her courage, and then said simply, "*My* name was Feast."

For a moment, Sword was unable to comprehend her words; they seemed like meaningless sounds. Then he understood.

"Oh," he said again. He swallowed, and his mouth tasted of bile.

"That's why I still have all my fingers and toes and ears," the Seer said, almost casually. "No one wanted to waste any. Whipping and cutting didn't bother anyone, that heals up, so I have my share of scars, but they kept me intact. And of course no one worried about mistreating me in other ways, since I wouldn't be around for very long to seek revenge, and the *ler* would not permit me to bear children who might seek it for me. I wasn't allowed clothing except in winter, but I was very well fed. I was quite plump. You'd hardly know it, now that I've been doing all this walking and only eating when I'm hungry, with no one trying to fatten me up."

"Stop," Sword said, feeling ill. "Please."

The Seer continued as if she hadn't heard him. "But then the old Seer came and stole me away and saved me, a few months before I was to be used. She told me she had asked the *ler* to help her; she wanted the person in all Barokan who most needed a new role, someone for whom being Chosen would be no hardship at all, and that was me."

She smiled up at him.

Sword grimaced in response, and for a moment no one spoke. Then the Thief broke the silence.

"So now you know," he said. "I get protective about her. Any time I start to feel angry about *my* life, I remember hers."

"Boss doesn't trust Bow with me because she thinks he might see no harm in treating me as the men of my hometown did," the Seer said. "I already survived years of it, after all. He might see the damage as already done."

"I hope she's wrong about that," Sword said, but remembering what he had seen of Bow he could not say with any certainty that she *was* wrong.

The Seer waved a hand. "It wouldn't matter," she said. "I *did* survive years of it. A little more, with just a single man, would be no great hardship. But Boss has her own concerns, and she wouldn't stand for it."

Sword shuddered. "I'm going back to the hostel," he said. "I don't feel well."

"As you please," the Seer said. "Snatcher?"

"I think we'll walk a little more," the Thief said.

Sword nodded silently and miserably, then went back alone, and crawled unhappily into his assigned bed, where he lay staring at the fresh planking of the ceiling for some time.

How could anyone speak so calmly of such abuse? The Seer was a strange little person, but given her background it was astonishing she could function at all. Sword found himself almost overcome with admiration for her. No wonder she wanted a new name, her true name!

It did not seem right that a place like Bone Garden could exist in Barokan. The Council of Immortals had created the Wizard Lords to keep wizards from harming innocents, and to keep outlaws in check, and had then created the Chosen to keep the Wizard Lord himself in check; why, then, had no one ever done anything to suppress the evils of Bone Garden?

But who would? Priests had no power outside their own native boundaries, and why would wizards concern themselves with one town in particular? How would it benefit *them* to purge Bone Garden of its horrors?

And could they? The current system was the result of the agreements made between the people of Bone Garden, and the *ler* of the land it was built upon. There were other towns where the *ler* demanded blood sacrifices of one sort or another, like Drumhead and Redfield and Barrel, and there was little anyone could do about it so long as those towns were inhabited; if the demands of the *ler* were not met the crops would not grow, the wells would run dry, the beasts of the forest would not allow hunters to slay them, the fish in the streams would avoid nets and spears and hooks. In Mad Oak the *ler* yielded to the constant coaxing and admonishment of the priestesses, in Willowbank they chose the Priest-King as the ruler of both themselves and the town's human population, and so on, through a thousand towns and a thousand systems.

In Bone Garden the *ler* required abominations. Without them, the town would be uninhabitable.

Sword thought it probably *should* be uninhabited—but it was not his place to decide that.

The Wizard Lord had been perfectly happy to defy the *ler* in the path of his roads, and the *ler* of the Mad Oak and the other monsters in the wilderness, but the *ler* of a town were another matter. Sword knew that—but all the same, he wished Artil would ignore the laws and traditions, and do something to save all the other innocents trapped in Bone Garden.

Maybe someday he would. And if that happened, might the Council of Immortals demand that the Chosen remove the Wizard Lord, for exceeding his authority?

The idea of killing Artil for daring to destroy the tyranny of Bone Garden's priests was almost as sickening as what those priests had planned for the Seer.

He sank at last into an uneasy sleep, only vaguely aware when the Thief and the Seer finally returned and settled into their own beds.

[16]

The remainder of the trip was made without trouble, and without any further major revelations—though the Seer did report, as they neared Beggar's Hill, that the Speaker was no longer anywhere to be found. When last sensed she had been moving east, but now she had vanished from the Seer's magical awareness, presumably by carrying *ara* feathers.

"She may know she's wanted, and be heading for Winterhome," Sword said. "The *ler* could have passed the news along."

"Maybe," Seer said with a shrug.

All in good time Sword found himself and his companions ambling past the Uplander guesthouses and into Winterhome proper.

He was slightly startled when the Thief steered him directly along the main road toward the central plaza fronting the Winter Palace; Sword had assumed that they would be gathering at Beauty's home on the north street, but that was not the route they were taking.

"Where are we going?" he asked.

The Thief cast him a glance. "I'm not really supposed to tell you," he said. "I'm supposed to say that *they* will find *us*."

"Ah—Boss doesn't trust me?"

"Exactly."

"But the gathering is here in Winterhome?"

"Shall we just wait and see who's in the plaza to meet us?"

"I suppose we could," Sword admitted. He glanced at the Seer. "She knows where they are, I suppose."

"No," the Seer said. "They're hidden from me."

Sword nodded; he should have realized that they would be, since they would hardly want to advertise their whereabouts to the Wizard Lord. He wondered just who would be waiting, but he did not bother to ask. He would see for himself soon enough. He followed instructions without further argument, making his way quickly through the busy street until the three of them reached the plaza.

There was no sign of anyone waiting for them; the plaza was full of traders, merchants, travelers, and Host People, all going about their business, and none of them paying any attention to the three strangers. Snatcher led them quickly across the plaza to a jog in the facade of the Winter Palace, where he turned and said, "Wait here."

Sword shrugged, glanced around, and leaned back against a stone wall, expecting to have a few minutes before their compatriots arrived.

"Swordsman," a quiet voice said.

He turned, startled, and found two women standing a few feet away, with their backs against the wall of the Winter Palace. Despite the heat, both wore the shapeless black robes of Host People women, with black hoods pulled up and veils across their faces.

The nearer pulled her veil aside, though, to reveal a familiar face.

"Babble!" Sword said, pleased. He had not seen the Speaker in seven years, but he recognized her immediately. Her face had perhaps acquired a few more wrinkles, but was otherwise not much changed.

"Erren Zal Tuyo kam Darig seveth Tirinsir," she said. "The *ler* of muscle and steel are relieved you have returned."

"And I'm glad to be back," he said, as something inside him quivered at the sound of the first few syllables of his true name. "I thought you weren't here yet!"

"*Ler* warned me I was wanted," she said. "I came at their call and arrived last night." Then she turned to the Seer and said, "Azir shi Azir ath Lirini kella Paritir jis Taban, I am honored to meet you, and to give you the start of your name. May it free you forever from the foul *ler* of your former home."

The Seer stared at her. "Say it again," she said.

"Azir shi Azir ath Lirini kella Paritir jis Taban," the Speaker repeated.

The Seer shivered, and closed her eyes. "Azir shi Azir . . ." she said. "It's beautiful."

Sword smiled at the two of them. Then he looked at the other woman, the one who had called him Swordsman. This was not the Beauty; he could tell that much. It had not been the Beauty's voice he

heard. Besides, she was too short, and even through the concealing garments he could see she was simply shaped wrong.

The Thief, who had hung back as Babble spoke, now stepped up beside him and bowed. "Hello, ladies," he said.

"It went smoothly?" the short woman demanded, in a surprisingly
low, strong voice. It was definitely she who had called him "Swordsman."

"Well enough," Snatcher replied.

"Good. We'll split up and meet you at the house—I'm with the
Swordsman, you're with Babble, Seer can please herself."

"Azir," the Seer said. "Call me Azir."

"If you like, but we're still splitting up. We don't want to be notice-
able."

That comment reminded Sword that there were several guards in the
plaza; he looked around, but did not see any near at hand. Three or
four were visible on the far side of the plaza looking at something
Sword could not see, but oddly, none were near the palace wall where
the five Chosen stood.

The short woman noticed his gaze. "I persuaded them that they
needed to investigate an unusual rathole," she said. "But it won't take
them much longer to decide they've done their duty there, so come on."

"I take it you're the new Leader," he said.

"I'm relieved to see you aren't a complete idiot," she replied. "Not
that I was in much doubt, from what I've heard of your previous ex-
ploits, but it's good to be reassured. Now, hurry!"

Sword hurried, following her diagonally across the plaza toward the
northwest road, and only then noticed that Snatcher, Babble, and Seer
were already well on their way toward the north road.

"You brought Babble so I'd see a familiar face," Sword said, as he
caught up with the short woman.

"Yes."

"But why did you come out to meet me yourself, instead of waiting
at the house? Why meet in the plaza at all?"

"Remember the guards? I thought they might be watching for you,
and I didn't want you leading them to the house. In the plaza I could
spot them all, and make sure their attention was elsewhere. Try to not

let that sword of yours be too obvious, would you? Besides, I wanted to meet you, and have a few words alone before we reach our destination." She slowed her pace, and let Sword walk beside her.

"Ah."

"You're brighter than Bow, I see. Beauty said you were."

Sword had no idea how to respond to that, so he said nothing.

"Can you be trusted?"

"That depends what you want of me," Sword said.

"I want you to do what's best. To fulfill your role as one of the Chosen Defenders of Barokan."

"You can trust me to do my best, but I can't promise that my best will always be good enough."

"No one could. I understand you've visited the Wizard Lord in his cozy little eyrie?" She jerked her head toward the clifftops to the northeast, where the Summer Palace stood.

"Yes," Sword said.

"Lore is up there, so far as you know? We've been told that he is—do you know otherwise?"

"He's probably at the Summer Palace, yes. He was there last summer."

"Why?"

"Because he wanted to keep an eye on the Wizard Lord, and the Wizard Lord wants him there. There's never been anyone like Artil im Salthir before, and Lore is fascinated by him."

"You think that's all? He's fascinated?"

"Well, that, and I think Artil might find it suspicious if Lore suddenly left. He's wary of the Chosen." He thought, but did not say, *as you obviously know.*

"But he let you visit, and he lets Lore live in his palace?"

"He's wary of the Chosen as a group, but as individuals we interest him. He's made Lore one of his chief advisors, and he's hoping to persuade us all that he's doing good things for Barokan."

"He's trying to keep us fragmented."

Sword almost stumbled at that; he swallowed, and said, "Perhaps he is. I don't know."

"Good." She nodded. "What do you think of our Wizard Lord, then?"

"I don't really know. I think he genuinely means well, and wants to make Barokan a better place. I don't think he's a Dark Lord; if I did, if I thought he should be removed, I would have come looking for you months ago. Right now I think he's doing well. His roads have done wonderful things, he's removed some hazards, and while the Summer Palace worried me at first, this is his second year up there and it doesn't seem to have done any real harm. The weather hasn't been as pleasant as it might, but that's nothing more than a slight inconvenience."

"An inconvenience?"

"Yes." He threw her a glance, but her face remained hidden behind her scarf. "Since you're gathering the Chosen, I take it you think he's dangerous. Perhaps I'm missing something; I know Beauty was worried by his actions. He baffles me sometimes. He's doing things that are unlike anything I've ever heard of, unlike anything Lore remembers, but I don't see any real *harm* in anything he's done."

"Have you spoken with him about his plans?"

"Yes, of course! I was his guest for a few days. We spoke several times."

"And he told you—turn right here—he told you his plans?"

"Some of them, yes. Not everything," Sword said, turning down the alley the Leader had indicated.

"And did any of them worry you?"

"Uh . . . perhaps a little."

"Only a little? Then I agree that he didn't tell you everything. Did he tell you why the weather is so *hot*?"

"Uh . . ." The alley wiggled past fenced-in yards, then narrowed to squeeze between two stone walls. "Well, he's not controlling the weather directly; I suppose it's been hot because that's what the *ler* want."

"It's not his doing?"

"No, I don't *think* so. He told me that he instructed the *ler* in what to do during his absence, then left them to do it—his weather magic doesn't work in the Uplands."

"It doesn't?"

"No; he left all his magic behind when he left Barokan, just as Lore and I did." They emerged from the alley onto the north road, and Sword wondered why they had taken such a roundabout route—did the Leader *really* think someone might be watching them, or following them?

"Did you? *All* of it?" She pointed to the left.

Sword turned his steps in the indicated direction. "All of *mine*, certainly; I can't be sure of the others, but I don't see why they'd be any different. You hadn't known?"

"We weren't *sure*. The Speaker said that was what had happened, and of course the Seer couldn't tell where you and the Scholar and the Wizard Lord were when you were up there, not even the vague idea she has when we carry *ara* feathers, so she thought it was true. I wasn't completely certain it wasn't a trick of some sort."

Sword nodded. "It seems insane, doesn't it? Deliberately giving up his magic?"

"Yes. And removing insane Wizard Lords is one of the duties of the Chosen. *Is* he insane?"

"I don't know! Honestly, I really can't be sure. I don't think so. If he is, it's a far subtler insanity than that of the Dark Lord of the Galbek Hills."

"You'll tell us all about it, then, and we'll see if we can't decide. This way."

As he had expected, they were heading toward the Beauty's home. The familiar door opened as they approached, a man in the black garb of the Host People beckoning them inside. It took Sword a few seconds to recognize him as Bow, the Chosen Archer.

Snatcher and Babble and the Seer—Azir—had taken a more direct route, and were already seated in the chairs by the hearth as Boss and Sword stepped in. Beauty was nowhere to be seen. Babble had doffed her veil and hood. Sword nodded politely to them.

"Sit," Boss told him, pointing at the edge of the hearth; she was already settling down onto the bricks herself. Sword sat.

For a moment everyone was quiet; Boss reached up and pulled down her hood and scarf, revealing an astonishingly young face framed in thick black hair. Sword was looking at her, trying to think what he should say, when Beauty emerged from the back of the house. She was unmistakable, even with her hood up; the very way she walked marked her.

"We're all here, then," Boss said. "Except Lore. Seer, would you do me the courtesy of confirming that everyone is indeed who he should be?"

"My name is Azir shi Azir," the Seer said.

"Oh; sorry. Azir, is everyone who he should be?"

"Everyone here is Chosen," the Seer said.

"Good. Does anyone need any introductions? Sword, you know everyone?"

"Well enough for now," Sword said. "I have only just now met you, and only recently the Seer and the Thief, of course."

"So we know one another. Good. Sword, you spent some time in the Summer Palace, yes?"

"Just four days, but yes. Last summer."

"And you observed the Wizard Lord there? You spoke with him?"

"Yes."

"You told me that he's no longer controlling the weather, that he's relinquished control of the elements by leaving Barokan."

"Yes."

"You're certain?"

Sword glanced around at the others; their full attention was focused on Boss and himself. "Well, he says so," he said. "I've had no reason to doubt him; I know I lost my own magic while I was in the Uplands."

"So the heat and the rains coming in the wrong times and places, and that thunderstorm in Talltrees aren't anything he's doing deliberately?"

"I don't know anything about it," Sword said. "A thunderstorm? There was . . . the Wizard Lord paid Mad Oak a visit last autumn and used lightning to dispose of a nuisance, but that was nowhere near Talltrees, and I hadn't heard of any other storms. We don't hear a great deal from the Midlands up there. What heat? What rains? What storm?"

"The heat that's made the Midlands unbearable this summer," Bow replied.

"And the rains that have left some crops stunted and dying from lack of water, while others are drowning," the Seer said. "Rains that fall by day more and more often, rather than at night as they should."

"And there's been a report of a storm with lightning and thunder that frightened everyone in Talltrees half to death, though the lightning doesn't seem to have hit anything," Boss added.

"I don't know anything about that," Sword said. "There hasn't been anything like that in the vales since last fall, beyond a few afternoon showers that most of us rather liked. I hadn't heard much beyond ordinary complaints about the heat."

"Life-loving *ler* tell me that wind and water and weather run wild, untamed and untethered, doing whatever they will, unmindful of what harm they cause and what help is withheld," Babble said, in her familiar singsong. "The spells that bind them are still twined about them, but no one holds the strings, no one pulls them as they should."

"Oh," Sword said. He looked at the faces surrounding him; their expressions were grim.

"So the Wizard Lord said nothing to you to justify this neglect?" Boss demanded.

"Not specifically," Sword said. "He spoke to me about wanting to give up magic, and run Barokan without it, but he said he had left instructions for the weather *ler* to behave themselves and maintain the usual patterns."

"They haven't," Boss said.

Sword shrugged.

"He hasn't said why he allows these *ler* to run loose?"

"Well, he . . . he has this idea that we should give up magic entirely, that it's growing weaker and we don't need it anymore and would be better off without it." Even as he spoke, Sword knew he was not doing the Wizard Lord's position justice. The words had sounded so much better when Artil said them!

"Why?"

Sword hesitated. "I don't . . . I don't *entirely* know," he admitted. "When he was chosen to be the new Wizard Lord I asked whether we really *need* a Wizard Lord anymore, since there haven't been any rogue wizards in centuries but there have been Dark Lords, and no one seemed to listen to me, but he says now that he thought about my words and decided I had a point. He thinks the old ways are doomed. The wizards are dying out, and he said that other magic is weakening as well, that we would all have to live without magic eventually and we might as well learn to do it now, rather than wait until we have no choice."

"So the Wizard Lord who is charged with protecting Barokan with his magic has abandoned his magic to go live in the Uplands?"

"I suppose he has, yes. In the summers."

"And do you see any reason we should not see this as neglecting his sworn duties, and cause to remove him from office?"

Sword had seen that coming, but had not managed to ready a good answer. "He isn't neglecting his duties *entirely*," he said. "He has his men doing things to maintain order. He's still giving orders; he just isn't using any magic."

"But *he* is sworn to protect Barokan," Boss said. "Not to send others to do it for him."

Sword had no reply to that. He glanced around at the others, but they were all watching silently; they obviously felt this conversation was between Sword and Boss, and not something they were all participating in.

Well, they had probably discussed it with Boss before.

Boss pressed him. "Can you honestly say that you don't think he's guilty of dereliction of his duties as Wizard Lord?"

Sword thought for a moment, but finally admitted, "I can say I'm not certain either way."

"But if he *is* guilty, then you know what *our* duty, as the Chosen, is."

"No," Sword said. "I don't. We're supposed to protect Barokan, but not to just blindly follow a lot of outdated rules. He hasn't directly harmed anyone, or broken any of the rules save by omission, has he? Shouldn't we give him a chance to make it right, and take up his duties properly?"

"Perhaps, if it were just the weather," Boss said. "There's more to it than that."

"There is?" Bow asked, startled out of his silence.

"There are the bandits . . ." the Seer said, uncertainly.

"Much more. And much worse. I wouldn't have gathered you if there weren't."

The other Chosen exchanged glances, then all turned their attention to Boss.

"All right," Sword said. "What else?"

"You said he thought wizards were dying out, Sword? Well, he's been helping them along. He's been murdering wizards."

"No, he hasn't," the Seer objected. "He hasn't killed anyone, not directly. He hasn't used his glamour to compel anyone else to kill, either. I'd know."

"He *can't* kill anyone when he's up in the Summer Palace," Sword said. "Not magically, anyway."

"He isn't doing it magically. He's giving orders to his men and sending *them* to kill wizards. That doesn't take any magic at all. And he's doing it while he's up in his Summer Palace, where the Seer—where Azir won't know."

"Are they rogue wizards, then?" the Beauty asked. "The people he's had killed?"

"Who has he killed?" said the Archer.

"Why would he hide it, if they're rogues?" Azir asked.

"How many were there?" asked Sword.

"How do you know?" asked the Thief.

"*He* says they were rogues, of course," Boss said. "Four that I know of. And I know because one of the other wizards told me, before going into hiding. After all, isn't that how the Chosen are intended to operate? The Council of Immortals tells us when the Wizard Lord must be removed, and we remove him."

"Sometimes," Sword said. "But we use our own judgment, we aren't the Council's slaves."

"Which is why I'm explaining this, and not simply telling you to go kill him," Boss replied. "You're absolutely right. We make our own decisions. And I've brought you here so we can make this one."

"Shouldn't Lore be here, then?" Beauty asked.

Boss turned to her. "I don't think so," she said. "Not necessarily, anyway. I think he may have fallen under the Wizard Lord's spell, and we're better off reaching a consensus without him. We'll talk with him before we do anything drastic, of course, but I want you all to know the situation first."

"He can't be under the Wizard Lord's spell," Bow protested. "We're immune to his magic, and besides, Sword said magic doesn't even *work* in the Uplands!"

"Barokanese magic," Sword corrected. "The Uplanders may have their own."

"I didn't mean it *literally*," Boss snapped. "I mean he's under the Wizard Lord's sway; he believes in him and his plans for a better Barokan, his plan to sweep away a system that's kept us safe for seven hundred years."

"A system that doesn't seem to be needed anymore," Sword said. "I think Artil's right about that. His roads have done amazing things! Every town I've seen in the past two years seems far richer than before."

"Does that give him the right to murder his fellow wizards? To leave Barokan unprotected against malevolent *ler*?"

The others looked at one another uneasily. Finally Sword spoke.

"How certain are you that he really *did* order those wizards' deaths? Couldn't the wizard who told you be lying? Or if he's not, how does *he* know?"

"And how did anyone kill the wizards, anyway?" Bow asked. "It's not as if they don't have magic protecting them. They're not just farmers."

"When did this happen, anyway?" Snatcher wanted to know. "Why haven't any of the rest of us heard about it?"

Boss sighed.

"Make yourselves comfortable," she said. "I'll tell you the whole story."

17

"I was traveling along the coast," Boss said. "I set out to see where the roads went, and got as far as Kurias Saltmarsh, where I got my first look at the ocean, and when I saw it I knew I wanted to sail on it, but the only boats in Kurias are the little skiffs they use for fishing and crabbing. They told me that I could find real ships in Blackport, so I was on the coast road, walking south toward Blackport, when a wind came up out of nowhere."

"Sea breezes can do that," Snatcher remarked.

Boss shook her head. "This wasn't an ordinary sea breeze. This was a whirlwind. I tried to take shelter under some trees overhanging the road, hoping they wouldn't mind, but then a man fell out of the sky and landed in a heap in front of me."

"A wizard," Seer said.

"Of course," Boss replied. "A wizard. One I hadn't met before, an old man. He lay there on the road, and I could hear him breathing, deep rattling breaths, but he didn't say anything, didn't move.

"I was cautious, but I approached him and knelt beside him and said, 'Are you all right?'

"He just moaned.

"I took his shoulder and tried to roll him over, but he was heavier than he looked, the way old men sometimes are, but he pushed himself up so I could see his face, and there was blood smeared in his beard and across the bottom of his nose, and one eye was blackened.

" 'I think my leg may be broken,' he said, and I looked, pulling up the hem of the blue robe he wore, and there was a bruise on one leg from knee to ankle, starting to turn purple, but I didn't see any swelling or dislocation. 'I think it's all right,' I told him. 'It doesn't *look* broken.' "

"Can you really tell from just a look?" Bow asked.

"Usually," said the Seer. "Go on, Boss."

"Well, anyway, we got him straightened out and sitting up, and discussed his leg, and I said, 'You're lucky I was here,' and he said, 'It wasn't luck. I was looking for you.'

"I didn't like the sound of that, and said, 'What do you mean?'

" 'You're the Leader of the Chosen, aren't you?' he asked, and I admitted I was.

" 'Then I was looking for you,' he said. 'The Wizard Lord has gone mad and started killing innocent wizards!'

" 'How do you know they were innocent?' I asked.

" 'Because he tried to kill *me!*' the old man said. 'And while the Blue Lady might have done something, and Kazram could have gone rogue, I know *I* had done nothing at all but go about my own business as I always have.' "

"He could have been lying," Sword said.

"Of course he could," Boss agreed. "Though it was a little hard to think of this old man with a bruised leg as some dire scheming monster."

"But . . ."

"Did I say I believed him?"

"Uh . . . no."

"In fact, I reserved judgment, and asked him to explain himself. Which he eventually did.

"As the old man told it, he had been minding his own business in his home in the southern hills when a group of about twenty men in red-and-black uniforms, with *ara* plumes on their sleeves and helmets, came marching up to his house. Their leader pounded on the door, demanding to speak with him, and when he answered he found this man there while four others stood behind him with swords drawn, five more behind them with spears raised, and the other ten farther back with bows ready and arrows nocked, spaced out so that a single air elemental could not reach them all before they loosed.

"He asked what this was about, and the man who had knocked on his door announced that they had come on the Wizard Lord's orders to inquire after certain forbidden objects. He asked the wizard to step outside to discuss the matter.

"The old man claims he had no idea what they were talking about, but he didn't like the look of all those weapons, so instead he dove back inside and slammed the door.

"The spokesman tried to coax him out, but he refused, whereupon the men set fire to his house. He extinguished the fire, since he commanded several fire *ler*, but he decided not to stay around and argue; instead he climbed out an upstairs window and flew away.

"The archers shot at him as he fled, but his aerial *ler* were able to deflect all the arrows—though only with great difficulty, since they were all fletched with *ara* feathers."

"Can you *do* that?" the Archer asked, with sudden intense interest.

"So he said," Boss replied. "I don't really know."

"They aren't as stiff as flight feathers," Bow muttered, "since *ara* don't fly, but maybe . . ."

"Go on," Sword said, cutting Bow off. "Then what? He flew to find you?"

"Oh, no," Boss said. "He flew to find one of his friends and fellow wizards, someone named Kazram of the Bog. And he found him, all right—or at least his head, stuck on a pole in front of the burned-out ruins of his mansion. The rest of him wasn't anywhere to be seen."

"Charming," Snatcher muttered.

"He asked a nearby farmer what had happened to Kazram, and the man told him that a group of the Wizard Lord's soldiers had come and killed him because the wizard had been stealing from the local priests. '*Was* he stealing?' the old man asked, and the farmer shrugged and said, 'I suppose he must have been.' He didn't seem at all upset that his neighbor had been killed."

"In my experience, wizards aren't very neighborly," Bow remarked.

"Nobody likes wizards," Sword agreed, remembering his experience with Young Priestess four years earlier.

"Go on," Beauty said waving for Boss to continue.

"So he flew on," Boss said, "and found out that three others were also dead—one he called the Blue Lady, one he called the Cormorant, and one he called Brownleg. The Blue Lady had been hanged—I was somewhat surprised that a wizard can be killed by something as simple as hanging, but he assured me that it was possible for those whose magic does not include any sort of flight, nor anything that might sever the rope. Or in some cases, those whose talismans had been removed or destroyed might be unable to use any magical defenses. Brownleg and the Cormorant had been beheaded and staked, like Kazram, though in Brownleg's case there was apparently a fire involved somewhere as well, and the head on display was little more than a scorched skull."

"Was he absolutely sure it was the wizard's, then?" Sword asked.

"He seemed certain of it, and I didn't argue," Boss replied.

"So then he came looking for you?"

"Not exactly; he found four dead wizards, but he also found two live ones—he didn't tell me which. And they didn't believe him when he said the Wizard Lord was murdering wizards for no good reason. 'They must have done something,' they said. 'Perhaps they were plotting together, the four of them.'"

"Perhaps they were," Bow said.

"The old man didn't think so, and he insisted that *he* certainly hadn't been plotting anything, and the soldiers had come for *him*. 'Well, perhaps you were a mistake,' the other wizards said. 'And here you are, safe and sound.' They wouldn't listen when he tried to convince them something was wrong. Neither would any of the ordinary people he spoke to, the neighbors of the dead wizards; they all seemed to think that if the Wizard Lord said those four were rogues, why, then, those four were rogues, and killing them had simply been the Wizard Lord doing his job."

"But the Wizard Lord didn't kill them," the Seer said softly. "He didn't. I would have felt it."

"His men did, the wizard told me. His soldiers in red and black. No one claimed the Wizard Lord himself did it."

"But even then, I should have felt something when he gave the orders," the Seer said.

"Really?" Sword asked. "Does it work like that?"

"I *think* so," the Seer said, uncertainly.

"Even if he gave those orders last year in his Summer Palace atop the Eastern Cliffs?" Boss asked.

". . . oh," the Seer said quietly. "No. I wouldn't sense anything then."

"But why would they *obey* him, if he didn't have his persuasive magic?" Bow asked.

"Because he's the Wizard Lord," Sword said. "That's all he needs; no magic is necessary."

"Sword's right about that," Boss said, and Sword thought he heard a trace of bitterness in her tone. "People are generally quite happy to do what they're told, magic or no."

"Willing, anyway," the Seer said. *Her* bitterness was undisguised. "I don't know about happy."

"At any rate," Boss continued, "the soldiers had reportedly all said the Wizard Lord sent them, and they had marched openly out to the various wizards' lairs, they made no effort to keep their actions secret. The possibility that the Wizard Lord had *not* sent them certainly occurred to me, but it also seemed perfectly reasonable that he had indeed decided to kill several wizards, for one reason or another. And the old man had done the appropriate thing by coming to me, as the Leader of the Chosen, and asking me to investigate.

"So instead of going to Blackport I began to gather the Chosen, and to investigate what I could along the way, and here we are."

"What happened to the old wizard?" Sword asked.

"I don't know for certain," Boss said. "He flew away. He said he was going to the Western Isles, and would find a ship and flee Barokan until he received word that the Lord of Winterhome was gone."

"Sensible," Snatcher said.

"Not very brave," Bow said.

"No one ever said wizards have to be brave," Sword replied.

"What puzzles me, if this story is true," Beauty said, "is that none of the dead wizards' neighbors said a word to protest their deaths. Didn't any of them have any friends to speak for them?"

"Probably not," Snatcher said. "Wizards aren't generally the most pleasant people."

"Nobody likes wizards," Sword repeated. "And those people all love the Wizard Lord. He's brought Barokan together, made everyone wealthy with his roads and bridges, found work for all the bored young men who might have made trouble otherwise, removed dozens of annoying little problems like the Mad Oak. Who wants to argue with him, on behalf of some scruffy old wizard living in the wilderness?"

"Especially since wizards have a tendency to get their living through theft, threats, or blackmail," Boss said. "Most of them don't earn their way with their magic like priests, they just take what they want. Oh, they're not as bad as the ones in the old stories, they don't openly rape and plunder anymore, but they don't exactly win anyone's love or gratitude, either."

"But they must have had *family*," Beauty insisted.

"I suppose that's so," Boss said. "For all we know, their brothers and sisters *did* object—but what could they do, once the wizards were dead?"

"They could have asked the Chosen to avenge the dead," Bow suggested. "Isn't that what we're for?"

"But everyone loves the Wizard Lord," Sword reiterated. "They don't *want* us to kill him, even if he *is* murdering wizards."

"Killing him won't make the roads go away," Boss pointed out. "They're there to stay, and now we all know how to build them."

"They probably *believe* him when he says the wizards were plotting against him," Snatcher said.

"They might even be right," Bow said.

"They might be," Boss said. "I don't know what really happened. I talked to people all the way here, but no one knew anything about any wizards, alive or dead. I don't know for certain that these wizards are really dead. If they are, I don't know who killed them. If the Wizard Lord's soldiers did kill them, I don't know whether the Wizard Lord ordered it or not. And if he *did* order it, I don't know whether he had a good reason."

Sword shifted uncomfortably, debating with himself as to whether he should speak up. He had a theory as to why the Wizard Lord might have killed innocent wizards, but he had no real evidence for it.

And he had already told the Leader that the Wizard Lord was trying to eliminate magic; she must surely have made the same guess he had, that Artil wasn't just passively waiting for magic to fade away or die out on its own.

"That's why I've gathered us here," Boss continued. "To find out what *did* happen, and why. Sword, you said the weather is running wild because the Wizard Lord deliberately let it go when he went up to his summer home."

"Well, he . . . Yes."

"Did he say anything about killing wizards? Anything that might possibly be related?"

"Uh . . ." Sword thought back, trying to remember everything he and Artil had discussed during those conversations over a year before. "I don't *think* so," he said. "Except that he thought Barokan didn't need magic anymore."

"But you only spoke with him off and on for four or five days."

"Over a year ago. Yes."

Boss nodded. "Well, then, all of you—have any of you seen any wizards in the past year, alive or dead? Spoken with them?"

The others exchanged wary glances, but heads shook and voices murmured, "No."

"But I never see any anyway," Beauty said.

"Few and furtive are the wary wizards," Babble said. "I don't . . . yes, yes, I don't see . . ." She didn't finish the sentence, but instead stared at the chimney piece with a baffled listening expression.

"I don't think *any* of us see wizards very often," Sword agreed. "Except for the Wizard Lord, I haven't seen a wizard in four or five years. After all, there are only about a dozen and a half left in all of Barokan."

The Seer looked at him, startled, at that. "That few?"

"Fewer, now, if the story Boss heard is true," Snatcher said.

"Azir, you can't sense wizards the way you sense the Chosen and the Wizard Lord?" Boss asked.

"Not unless they're either nearby, or looking for me," the Seer replied.

"And Speaker, you haven't heard anything from the *ler* who talk to you?"

"No tales have been brought to me," Babble answered. "*Ler* speak of their own concerns, of fitness and patterns and place, not of wizards or death, or news from afar."

"So the Wizard Lord may be killing off the other wizards," Boss said. "He may be killing wizards plotting against him, in which case he's entirely within his authority, or he may be trying to destroy Barokan's remaining magic, which is probably *not* something he's permitted to do. And he's left the weather largely unconstrained while he absents himself from Barokan, which also may or may not be acceptable. You all agree with that?"

There were nodding heads and noises of assent.

"So we need to find out what he really *is* doing, whether these wizards are dead, and if they are, why they died."

Again, general agreement.

"And once we know, we need to decide what to do about it."

"We know what to do about it," Bow said.

"We know what to do if he's broken the rules, yes," Boss said. "But the rules here aren't all that clear. That's why I want to talk to Lore, as soon as he comes down the cliffs. He knows the rules, the history, and the precedents better than anyone else. Maybe the Wizard Lord hasn't done anything wrong. But if he has, then we know what to do."

"Ask him to resign," the Seer said.

"Yes. But if he won't resign . . ."

"He told me once that he would abdicate, rather than fight us to the death," Sword said.

"But he may not have meant it," Boss said. "He may have changed his mind. And if he has . . ."

"We kill him," Bow said.

18

"The Wizard Lord won't be down for a month or more," Beauty said.

"I know that," Boss snapped. "That means we have a month to get ready for him, and to find out what's been happening."

"We could go up the cliff and get him," Bow suggested.

"No, we couldn't," Sword said. "We have no magic up there."

"We could go up anyway."

"Bow, *we have no magic up there*. We're just seven ordinary people, and he's got dozens of guards."

"We aren't going to confront the Wizard Lord outside Barokan," Boss said flatly. "I'm not suicidal. Sending a message, though, to let him know we want to speak to him when he comes down, might be useful."

"I think we'd do better not to give him that much time to worry and plan," Sword said.

"Hm." Boss frowned. "Well, you know him better than the rest of us."

"You said you wanted to talk to the Scholar," Snatcher said. "Perhaps we could go fetch *him* down."

"Or just send him a message, asking him to come," Sword suggested. "Really, it's not pleasant for one of the Chosen to cross Barokan's border."

"Then why does the Scholar do it?" the Seer asked. "This is the second year he's gone up there with the Wizard Lord."

"I know," Sword said. "I don't understand it."

"It may not be as bad for him as it is for you," Beauty suggested. "Each of us is different, with different magic."

"Sending Lore a message sounds good to me," Boss said. "Bow, Sword, Beauty, Babble, which of you knows him best?"

The four older Chosen exchanged glances.

"Probably Sword," Beauty said.

"The old Seer knew him better," Sword said.

"She's not here," Boss pointed out.

"Boss, none of us know him all that well," Sword said, "and sending any of us up the cliff is likely to be uncomfortable and draw unwanted attention. Couldn't we send someone other than one of the Chosen?"

"Of course we could," Boss said. "We will. But I want one of you to write a note for the messenger to deliver."

"Oh!" Sword relaxed. "I can do that, I think. If someone helps me with the pen—I never got the hang of cutting quills."

"I can help," Beauty said.

"Good," Boss said. "Do it tonight."

"Should I mention anything about dead wizards?"

"Absolutely not. Just tell him we need to talk to him."

Sword nodded.

"What are we going to do about the dead wizards, meanwhile?" Snatcher asked. "Did the old man tell you where any of these killings took place?"

"He said he lived in the southern hills, and implied that the dead wizards all lived in the southwestern part of Barokan," Boss answered. "Beyond that, no."

"The southern hills are a . . . no, be still! Go, yes. I mean, they cover a very large area," Babble said.

"Yes."

"Well, we can't just wander around them randomly asking about wizards!" the Archer said. "That would take *years*, and we only have a month or so."

"I know," Boss said. "I was hoping someone might have an alternative to suggest."

"Well, I think . . ." Sword began. He stopped, unsure of whether he wanted to complete his thought.

"Think what?" Boss demanded.

"Well, there were other people there besides the locals when the wizards were killed, after all, and some of them might be here in Winterhome," Sword said. "They would know more about it."

"What? What people?" Bow asked.

"The killers, of course," Boss said. "Good. Clever. So you think we should talk to some of the soldiers at the Winter Palace?"

"I would," Sword said, "except that word would get back to the Wizard Lord, wouldn't it? I don't think that would be . . ."

"I can take care of that," the Leader interrupted.

Sword looked at her. "You can?"

"Yes. My magic. I can make sure nobody remembers talking to us, or sees any reason to mention it to anyone."

"Oh. Oh, yes. Farash mentioned that last summer," Sword said.

Boss suddenly went very still. "Farash? Farash inith Kerra das Bik abba Terrul? The Old Boss? You spoke to him?"

"Yes," Sword said, startled by her reaction. "We spoke last year, and he said that he'd been able to do that when he was the Leader, make people forget things."

"*Did* he? And you spoke to him about this *last year*, not when you were fighting the Dark Lord of the Galbek Hills?"

"Yes, when I came to see the Wizard Lord," Sword said, still puzzled.

"He was *here*? In Winterhome?"

"Yes, of course," Sword said. "He's the Wizard Lord's chief advisor. He was in the Winter Palace when I first came here, and went up to the Summer Palace with the rest of the court. I assume he's up there now."

"He . . ." The Leader was trembling; Sword stared at her in amazement. "Chief advisor?" she demanded. "Farash inith Kerra is the Wizard Lord's chief advisor?"

"Yes. The Wizard Lord thought his experience as the Leader might be useful. Boss, how do you know . . ."

"Do *you* know," she said, cutting Sword off, "what he did?"

Sword blinked. "I know several things he did," he said, dropping any pretense of ignorance. "Which one do *you* know about?"

"I'm from Doublefall," Boss said through gritted teeth. "Do you know what he did *there*?"

"Some of it," Sword said, comprehension slowly dawning. He glanced around at the other Chosen, who clearly had no idea what he and Boss were talking about. "The palace, the harem, and so on. I never saw it, just heard about it."

"I *lived* it," Boss said, clearly struggling not to shout. "I was *in* his harem. He took me from my parents when I was fourteen, and *none of us saw anything wrong* with that! We thought it was an *honor!*"

Sword stared at her in astonished horror. "But . . . but then why would he . . . why did he choose you . . . ?"

"He thought it was *funny*," Boss shouted, giving up the struggle. "He thought it was just hysterically funny, choosing the smallest, youngest, weakest girl in his harem to be the next Leader of the Chosen. It was a little bit of revenge on *you*, Sword, and Beauty and Bow and Babble and Lore, giving you the most useless and ineffectual person he could find as your new Boss!"

"But you *aren't* ineffectual," the Seer protested.

Boss whirled to face her. "You're right, Azir, I'm not! I swore I wouldn't be. I swore that I'd prove him wrong, that I'd be the best Chosen Leader ever, to get *my* little bit of vengeance for what he did to me!"

For a moment everyone sat or stood in stunned silence; then Boss swallowed and forced herself into the appearance of calm.

"I'm sorry," she said. "There's no need for me to shout."

"Shout if you like," Beauty said. "But I don't understand what this is about. Old Boss had a *harem?*"

"Yes," Boss said.

"And you knew about it?" Snatcher asked Sword.

"Yes," Sword admitted. "That's why I insisted he give up his role as Leader of the Chosen. He'd used his magic to enslave the entire town of Doublefall."

"Not just enslave," Boss said bitterly. "We weren't just slaves. We all *loved* him. We *adored* him. We thought we were doing everything to please him because we *wanted* to. He persuaded us, with his magic, that catering to his every whim, no matter how sordid or perverse, was natural and right. I spent months stark naked, begging to be his plaything. When he went off to meet with the Chosen I *wept* that I couldn't go with him."

"I had no idea," Beauty said quietly. "His magic could *do* that?"

"It hardly seemed as if he *had* any magic," Bow said.

"He was hiding it," Sword said. "I think *most* of us might have more powerful magic than we realize."

"Why would he *hide* it?" Bow asked.

"You think he wanted any of us to know what he'd done to Double-fall?" Sword asked. "Remember, we're immune to it—he couldn't make *us* think it was a good thing that he'd taken over a town."

"How did *you* find out?" Boss demanded.

"He told me, in the Dark Lord's tower," Sword said. "He offered to let me share it. I refused." He considered, for a moment, whether or not he should reveal the whole truth, that Farash had betrayed the Chosen entirely.

As yet, it did not seem necessary to go that far.

"You refused," Boss said, staring at him. "But you didn't *tell* anyone, did you?"

"No." Sword thought he was going to say more, that he would explain that he hadn't known Farash could hide the truth, that he had been drained and weary after killing the Dark Lord, but then he stopped.

He hadn't said anything. The reasons didn't really matter.

"Sword made him give up his talisman," Beauty said. "None of us knew why; we thought it was very strange."

"He made the Thief and the Seer give up theirs, as well," Bow pointed out. "*They* didn't enslave anyone, did they?" He glanced at Sword. "*Did* they?"

Sword shook his head.

"No," Beauty said. "But we *knew* how they had failed us. We never knew what Old Boss had done in the tower."

"You didn't tell anyone," Boss repeated. "And you let him live."

"I don't like killing," Sword said. "I'd had my fill, killing the Dark Lord."

"You're the Swordsman; killing is your *job*."

"My job is to defend Barokan from Dark Lords. Killing anyone else isn't my responsibility."

"But you could have *told* someone!"

"Yes, I could," Sword agreed. "I probably should have—but I didn't know he could hide it. I didn't know he could erase memories. I hadn't realized how much we didn't know about his magic. And who would I tell? The Council of Immortals didn't care; they ignored everything I told them. The other Chosen were tired and just wanted to go home. *I* was tired and just wanted to go home. Who would I tell? The new Wizard Lord couldn't harm him; he was the Chosen Leader, and the Wizard Lord is forbidden to harm the Chosen. Really, who could I have told? I thought the truth would come out soon enough, and the people of Doublefall would deal with him. I didn't know until last summer that he'd been able to conceal what he'd done."

"How *did* he conceal it?" Snatcher asked. "I don't understand that part."

"Oh, that was easy," Boss said. "While he still had his magic, before he told the wizards he'd found his replacement, he simply told everyone in Doublefall to forget anything he'd ever done wrong, to remember only the good things he'd done. He told them his palace was the village meeting hall and the temple of the town's *ler*, that he had lived humbly there among us. It worked; we all believed it. We remembered that he'd lived there, that we had made him comfortable, but all the details were just *gone*. I couldn't remember what he'd done to me any more than I can remember suckling at my mother's breast."

"But you remember it now," Snatcher said.

"Oh, yes. *Oh,* yes! Because he chose me as his successor, and the wizards came, and the ritual was performed, and I became the new Leader, and then of course I was immune to the magic of the Chosen, including *his* magic. My memory came back, all of it, the moment my talisman came alive. I remembered the feel of his hands on me, and how he'd laughed at the joke of making a little girl the new Leader, and how I'd stood naked before him displaying myself as if I were a merchant showing her wares, and how he had made my father give me away as if I were a bit of bread handed to a hungry guest, and the pain I felt when he used me but that I wouldn't admit I'd felt, even to myself. I remembered *all* of it."

The Seer whimpered. Sword glanced at her, then quickly looked away, embarrassed—she had her eyes tightly closed, with tears leaking out. She obviously understood all too well what Boss was talking about.

It suddenly struck him as very odd that two of the new Chosen were abused young women, but one had been selected in an act of kindness, to save her from a horrible death, and the other had been picked in an act of cruelty and petty revenge. How could such opposite motives lead to such similar results?

"But by the time I recovered from the transferral," Boss continued, "by the time I could walk and see and talk again, he was gone, and he never came back to Doublefall."

"Could you have reversed his magic?" Beauty asked. "Could you have made *everyone* remember, as you did?"

"Probably," Boss said. "But why should I? What good would it do? They're happy; why make them remember all the pain and humiliation?" She shook her head. "No, I didn't make anyone else remember anything. I left Doublefall instead, and I haven't been back since. I couldn't stand being among my own people, watching them smile fondly at their memories of that lying monster, and think of his rule as the best years of their lives. That's why I was wandering along the coast, heading ever farther away from Doublefall." She shook her head. "I have no home anymore."

"I wonder whether he *knew* you would remember," Sword said. "I don't think he did, or he wouldn't have done it. It can't benefit him to have someone who hates him be the Leader of the Chosen."

"I don't care whether he knew it," Boss replied. "I want him to pay for what he did to my town, and you, Sword, you let him get away with it."

"I'm sorry," Sword said. "I didn't know."

"And now he's the Wizard Lord's chief advisor, and you let him do *that*? You still didn't tell anyone?"

"I told the Wizard Lord," Sword said quietly. "Last year."

For a moment the room was silent as everyone absorbed that.

"And Old Boss is still his chief advisor?" Beauty asked.

Sword nodded.

"Suddenly I like this Wizard Lord much less than I thought," Snatcher said.

"Farash claims to be trying to atone for what he did," Sword said.

"Do you believe him?" Boss demanded.

"No," Sword said. "But I'm not certain enough of my disbelief to condemn him. He asked me to keep his secrets, but made no threats or offers. I thought the Wizard Lord needed to know, so I told him, and I told Lore, as part of a private conversation, but otherwise I have said nothing until now. I've been giving Old Boss his chance to redeem himself—but only one chance."

"Well, what harm can he do now, with no magic?" Bow asked.

"He has the Wizard Lord's ear," Boss said. "That may be magic enough."

"Do you think he was the one who suggested killing the wizards?" Beauty asked.

"I don't know whether anyone needed to suggest that," Boss said. "I don't even know whether it happened, whether any wizards are really dead. That's what we intend to find out. Tomorrow I'll talk to some of the soldiers in the Winter Palace about it."

"Just you?" Sword asked.

"No, now that you mention it, you're coming with me," she replied. "Another set of ears, another person thinking of questions to ask, and someone to watch my back. Someone who knows Old Boss and Lore and the Wizard Lord. Not to mention that having a man along will make it less likely that anyone will take me for a whore come to service the soldiers. Will that suit you, then?"

"Completely," Sword said.

"Good." She rose, brushing a bit of fireplace ash from her skirt. "And tonight you'll write that letter to Lore, and tomorrow we'll get that on its way up the cliff. For now I think it's time we all had some supper. Beauty, whose help do you need?"

And with that, the meeting broke up.

19

Sword and the Seer had been sitting by the hearth trading jokes when Boss returned from sending a messenger up to the Summer Palace. They had begun simply by exchanging greetings, but when Sword called her "Seer" instead of "Azir" she had replied with a sarcastic retort, he had responded in kind, and they had quickly found themselves laughing and telling jokes.

When the door opened to admit Boss and a curl of morning mist they fell silent and turned to look at her.

"Your letter's on its way to the Summer Palace," Boss said. "Which means, Sword, that it's time for us to go talk to a few soldiers."

Sword nodded, and rose. He took the Seer's hand for a moment and said, "It's been a delightful start to the morning, Azir shi Azir."

She seemed startled, and only managed a whispered, "Yes," before Boss took Sword's arm and led him away.

A moment later Boss and Sword were strolling south down the street, trying to look like an ordinary pair of Host People; Boss wore the billowing, all-encompassing black robe and scarf, while Sword wore black tunic and trousers, with snug garters at wrist and ankle. The sun was still at least an hour short of topping the cliffs, and Winterhome lay in deep shadow, but the sky overhead and to the west was bright blue strewn with wisps of white cloud.

The plaza was already crowded, despite the morning gloom; merchants were setting up their displays, opening out doors and unfolding tables from their wagons. Early customers were strolling about, looking at the goods offered, but few were buying yet; the time to spend their money, or trade their own goods and services for what they needed, would come later. Sword and Boss made their way through without stopping, but without visibly rushing, either.

There were guards at the doors of the Winter Palace, as always—though since the Wizard Lord wasn't there, Sword was not entirely sure why. Today only one guard stood by each door, while there were usually two when the Wizard Lord was there, so at least there was *some* acknowledgment of his absence.

Together, the two Chosen ambled casually up to the nearest guard. They stood silently beside him for a moment, until they were certain he had seen them and decided they were harmless. Then Boss said, "So is it a good life, being one of the Wizard Lord's soldiers?"

The soldier glanced at her. "It's all right," he said.

"My brother was thinking about joining up," Boss said.

The guard looked at Sword, and Boss snorted. "Not him," she said. "Look at the size of him! You think a tiny thing like me would have a brother that big? No, he's a friend; my brother's back home."

The guard's mouth quirked into a half-smile; he glanced at Sword, then turned his attention back to Boss. "He's a big fellow, yeah. Your brother isn't?"

"Midway between us, I'd say."

"Well, size helps if he wants to join the guards, but he doesn't need to be as big as your friend here."

"I've seen that some of the guards aren't all that big," Boss agreed. "*You* aren't as big as Erren, after all. My brother's almost your height, not as broad in the shoulders."

"Should be big enough, then."

"Good. So what's it like, being a soldier?"

The guard shrugged. "It's not bad. We eat regularly, the food's pretty good, the pay is less than I might like but I get by."

"Is it exciting?"

He snorted. "No," he said. "I mostly just get to stand around all day looking dangerous."

"Oh, but you soldiers go other places, I've seen you!"

"Well, some do," the guard said, "but I'm not one of them. I've been stationed right here in Winterhome ever since I finished my training."

"Really? I'm sure I saw a group of soldiers marching somewhere—at least a dozen of them. I wondered where they were going; some of them had bows and spears, but they weren't just hunting, were they?"

"I don't know anything about that, I'm afraid."

"Is there someone here who does? Because I was very curious about it."

"I'm sorry, but I . . ." He stopped.

Sword felt something, though he couldn't have said what, or where he felt it. It was something immaterial, something numinous.

Ler. He knew he was sensing *ler* doing something.

The Leader's magic, he realized.

"I'd *really* like to know," Boss said, in a tone like nothing Sword had heard from her before, a rich but somehow demanding voice that reminded him slightly of the Beauty's. "Surely, you can find me someone who might know more?"

To him, as the Chosen Swordsman, her voice was attractive, slightly compelling, but hardly irresistible. To the guard it was obviously far more.

"I'm forbidden to leave my post," he said, "but I can fetch the sergeant of the guard; perhaps he can tell you more."

"I would appreciate that."

"Hold on." With that, the guard turned, opened the door he was guarding, and called inside, "Sir! There's someone here you need to speak with!"

He and the two Chosen waited, and a moment later another guard appeared. "Yes?" he said.

"We had a question or two about the guard's actions," Boss said.

"Oh?" The sergeant glanced at the door guard, obviously wondering why this pair had been deemed worthy of his attention.

"If we could come in and speak to you for a moment?" Sword said. He had observed that people were beginning to notice their conversation, and preferred to take it out of the public eye.

The sergeant looked at the door guard, who half-nodded, half-shrugged.

"All right," the sergeant said. "Come into the wardroom, then." He beckoned.

A minute later the three of them were seated around a small table in a small room, lit by a single small window. A rack of spears hung on one wall.

"Now," said the sergeant, "what's this about?"

"We saw a group of soldiers marching out into the southern hills," Boss said, her voice more or less returned to normal. "We wanted to know what they were doing."

"I don't see why it's any of your business," the sergeant replied pleasantly.

"Well, we heard rumors that they were . . . that the Wizard Lord didn't know they were there. That they were doing something they shouldn't."

The sergeant frowned. "Oh?"

"If you could reassure us that they *were* there on the Wizard Lord's business, and that they were not looting . . ." Boss said, a tinge of her power in her voice. She let the sentence trail off, unfinished.

"Looting?"

"That was the rumor, yes."

"I haven't heard anything about any looting."

"But there were soldiers sent to the southern hills?"

"Oh, we've sent squads all over Barokan, chasing bandits and dealing with rogue wizards. When was this, exactly?"

"It would have been early spring, right around the equinox," Boss said.

"That could have been one of the expeditions sent to handle a wizard," the sergeant said.

"A wizard? What were they doing with wizards?"

"That's not my business," the sergeant said. "I only concern myself with matters here in Winterhome."

"Is there someone we could speak to who *was* involved?" Boss said, and that strange richness was back, stronger than ever. Sword felt the air stir around him.

"I don't . . . I . . ."

"Surely, you see how important it is that we learn all about it," Boss said, and her voice seemed to ring back from the walls.

"Of course I do!" the sergeant said, slapping his hands on the table. "Of course! I'll . . . wait here, I'll find someone."

He rose, and hurried out of the room.

Sword watched him go, then leaned over and whispered, "Will he stay convinced when you aren't there to talk to him and look at him?"

"For a time," Boss murmured. "If no one questions him, anyway. If someone starts him really thinking, that can break the spell."

"What if someone just tells him that you've tricked him?"

"Oh, that won't work; then he'll get defensive, and my hold will be stronger than ever. It's only if people ask him questions, ask him why, and he realizes that he doesn't know. Or if he gets distracted and does something else for a while, when he remembers what he meant to do he may realize something's wrong." She glanced at him. "Didn't Old Boss ever tell you this?"

"No. Old Boss never let any of us see his magic in action at all. Remember, he was keeping secrets from us. He acted just enough like a leader that we never really questioned him, but he never did anything that would actually help us."

"There was more going on than just what he'd done to Doublefall, wasn't there?"

"Yes." He looked at the door; there was no sign of the sergeant's return. "He was working with the Dark Lord all along. He thought that together they could do to all of Barokan what he'd done to Doublefall."

"And you let him live."

Sword had no reply to that.

A moment later the sergeant reappeared, accompanied by a soldier whose red tunic bore a gold stripe on the shoulders. This new arrival held out a hand in greeting. "I'm captain of the Third Expedition," he said. "I understand the Wizard Lord sent you with some questions about our work?"

Sword shot Boss a quick look, but she paid him no attention as she said, "Yes, Captain. Is there somewhere we could speak privately, and let the sergeant get back to his work?"

Half an hour later Sword and Boss were sitting comfortably in the captain's personal apartments, drinking a fine red wine and listening as the captain explained.

"It's all some complicated magical conspiracy, apparently," he said. "I don't know all the details, because the Wizard Lord says they aren't anyone's business, but I know what our orders were, and how we carried them out." He set his glass on a table. "We were sent to find one particular wizard, a woman called the Blue Lady, and question her regarding this forbidden talisman someone had stolen."

"A talisman?" Sword asked.

"Yes."

"What sort of talisman?"

The captain shrugged. "I have no idea," he said. "We were told that no one knew what it looked like, or what it did, but that the wizard would understand what we meant."

"But if no one . . ." Sword began.

Boss cut him off with a raised hand. "Let me handle this part, Erren."

Sword frowned, and sipped wine.

"Captain," she said, with a certain depth to her voice, "if the talisman was stolen, how is it no one had a description?"

"*I* don't know," he said, irritated. "It's all magic. Nasty, untrustworthy stuff. It's a damned good thing we have the Wizard Lord to protect us from it, and it'll be a good thing when it's gone."

"Had the talisman been transformed, perhaps?"

"It might have been. I told you, I don't know."

"Wizards all use a variety of talismans; how was this Blue Lady to know which one you meant?"

"It has a name, more or less," the captain said. "The ninth talisman, it's called. That's what we were told to ask her about, at any rate—the ninth talisman. What became of the first eight, or whether there was a tenth or eleventh, I have no idea. I'm not a wizard, I'm just a soldier; I'm told what to do, and I do it."

Boss and Sword exchanged glances; both of them understood now. Sword's hand brushed at the pocket where his own talisman was tucked away.

The Scholar had explained this to him, long ago. Originally there were only three Chosen: the Leader, the Seer, and the Swordsman. After the first Dark Lord, the Dark Lord of the Midlands, was defeated, the Council of Immortals had added the Beauty. After the Dark Lord of Tallowcrane was slain, the Thief became the fifth of the Chosen. The

Scholar had been added after the Dark Lord of Kamith t'Daru, the Archer after the Dark Lord of the Tsamas, and the Speaker after the Dark Lord of Goln Vleys.

Three Dark Lords had resigned peacefully, and those had not resulted in an additional member of the Chosen, but whenever a Dark Lord was killed by the Chosen, another role was added, so that future Wizard Lords might be further deterred from evil.

And seven years ago, Sword had killed the Dark Lord of the Galbek Hills.

It had not occurred to him until now that the Council of Immortals might have added a ninth; certainly, no one had told *him* about any such addition. There had been no reason to think there might be a new member of the Chosen. Previous additions had not been kept secret; everyone had known the Speaker existed long before the Wizard Lord of the Galbek Hills went mad.

But the Wizard Lord apparently thought there might be a ninth—and if there were, then the Wizard Lord would have a corresponding new talisman in his own collection, so he was in a better position to know than anyone else.

That didn't seem to make sense, though, to have a ninth member of the Chosen that the other eight didn't know about, but the Wizard Lord did.

Except the Wizard Lord didn't seem to know *much* about the ninth, or he wouldn't have had to send his soldiers out to talk to wizards. Yes, the wizards would know if a ninth existed, since it would have been the Council of Immortals that created the role and the talisman, but hadn't Artil been a member of the Council?

And questioning wizards did not mean *killing* them . . .

"So the Wizard Lord thought this wizard had stolen this ninth talisman?" Boss asked.

"No, no," the captain said. "We knew she didn't have the talisman, but she knew who did, and what it was supposed to do. At least, the Wizard Lord thought she did. Our orders were to find her, question her, learn everything we could about this talisman and who had it and where it was, and then report back—but if she didn't cooperate, we were to use any methods we could to force her to reveal what she knew. If we couldn't get her to tell us, or if she harmed any of my men, then we were to consider her to be a rogue, and kill her."

"So she told you?"

The captain sighed. "No, she didn't." He shook his head. "Poor woman."

"What happened?"

"We found her readily enough, just where the Wizard Lord told us she would be, and at first she was cooperative enough. We had a pleasant little talk about the changes the Wizard Lord has implemented—the roads, and the army . . ."

"The what?" Boss interrupted.

"The army. The soldiers. We aren't just guards anymore, so we needed a new name for what we do. We're the Army of Barokan."

"Oh. All right, go on."

"Yes, well, we talked about the army and the roads and the Summer Palace and the Midlands Canal and the Shadowvale bridge project and the Blackport ferries, and we discussed whether she and the other wizards might help out on some projects, and whether she had any ideas for other improvements we might make. She had some interesting theories about what opening up travel this way might do to some of the stranger towns; she thought places like Drumhead might lose most of their population once people realized they could leave, and we talked about whether the priests there might close off the roads to prevent it. And then finally we got down to business, and I asked her about the ninth talisman."

He sighed, picked up his glass, leaned back, and downed the rest of his wine.

"She got upset at that. Downright distraught. She didn't pretend she didn't know what we were talking about; she obviously did, even if *I* didn't. But she said she couldn't tell us anything—not wouldn't, *couldn't*. She was under a spell of some kind that prevented her from talking about it.

"We tried to find some way around it—writing messages, giving clues, something—but we couldn't. And then when we decided to sleep on it and continue in the morning, she tried to escape." He sighed again. "I'm just glad she couldn't fly. We caught her before she'd gone half a mile, and took her prisoner.

"I had my orders. We hanged her, with a short drop and a slipknot, so she strangled, her neck didn't break. I hoped that the spell might break before she died; I'd arranged a way she could signal if it did, even if she was too far gone to talk, so we could have cut her down. I kept a man with a knife ready at the rope, but it was no good—she died without telling us a thing." He stared into the empty wineglass in his hand. "It was ugly. I was tempted to cut her down at the last minute, but I couldn't do it. How would I have explained to the Wizard Lord that we hadn't obeyed his orders? He'd set it all out, how she had to either talk or die, no exceptions, and we couldn't just bring her back to see if he could break the spell himself because she might be carrying some sort of trap or device." He shook his head. "I don't know what this talisman thing is, but it must be very bad to have the Wizard Lord giving us orders like that."

"You killed her?" Sword said. They were the first words he had spoken in almost an hour.

"We *had* to," the captain replied unhappily.

"Didn't she . . . did she have any family?"

"I didn't see any."

"Weren't her neighbors upset, though?" Boss asked.

He looked up from the glass, meeting her eyes. "You'd think they would be, wouldn't you? She seemed like a pleasant person. But no one seemed very distressed by her death; if the Wizard Lord ordered it, then that was that. People love him, you know—and they like *us*, his army. In some of these outlying towns they see our uniforms, and as soon as they realize what they mean, they cheer just at the sight of us. We don't need to do anything; just being the Wizard Lord's representative is enough. He's reshaped Barokan. So if he says some lonely old wizard had to die, people just shrug and say it's too bad." He frowned. "I'm not sure that's a good thing, really, but it's the way it is."

Boss nodded. "I see," she said. She looked at Sword, and then repeated, "I see."

Then she got to her feet, setting her own glass down.

"Thank you, Captain," she said. Her voice shifted tone. "Thank you very much. Now, if you would please forget everything you told us, I would appreciate it."

"Of course," the captain said, rising. "But I thought you wanted to ask me questions about the army?"

"No, thank you; I think I've heard enough."

"But I've hardly said a word!"

"Sometimes a word is all I need," Boss said. "Come, Erren."

20

Sword woke from a nap to hear Azir shi Azir shouting, "He's coming! Lore is coming down the cliff!"

Sword rolled over and sat up. He stretched, then looked around for his boots.

Despite several intense conversations about the mysterious ninth talisman, the slaughter of wizards, and other topics of great interest, the last several days had mostly been dull; Boss had insisted that Sword and Bow should not set foot outside the house, as she considered them recognizable and she did not want their whereabouts to be generally known. The women were sufficiently disguised by their Host People attire, and Snatcher was unknown and in any case had his magical gift for stealth, but the Swordsman and the Archer were somewhat more recognizable.

"But the Wizard Lord will know where I am the instant he sets foot in Barokan," Sword had protested.

"And we don't want anyone to know a moment sooner than that," Boss had replied. "Besides, a few *ara* feathers would mean even *he* couldn't locate you exactly."

Arguing with Boss was rarely productive, and the point about the *ara* feathers was a good one—Boss and Beauty had been filling the house with them and sewing them into everyone's clothing—so Sword hadn't put up much of a fight. He had yielded, and had stayed safely indoors, out of sight.

That had made his daily hour of sword practice a little more challenging, as he had to be careful not to poke holes in the walls or the other people, or to smash any of Beauty's furnishings. That was the good part; anything that made the required session more interesting was welcome. The opportunity to speak at length with the other Chosen was also pleasant enough; he and Azir shi Azir, in particular, spent a good bit of time chatting, though these conversations often ended abruptly when something would touch on a memory of her life in Bone Garden. When that happened the Seer would suddenly fall silent, her face would go blank, and a moment later she would walk away and find herself somewhere private to recover.

Still, despite the company, Sword was beginning to feel shut in, deprived of sunlight and air, and he had gotten in the habit of taking frequent naps simply for lack of anything better to do. Beauty and Babble kept busy managing the household, but had made it clear they did not need or want any assistance—which suited Bow, Boss, and Snatcher, but left Sword and Azir increasingly edgy.

But now Lore was finally coming down the cliff, which would at the very least mean a change in the routine. Sword reached for his boot.

Just then door of the room slammed open, and Boss leaned in. "Is there any reason you should not accompany me to meet Lore?" she asked.

Sword blinked at her.

"Here's how I want it," she said, before he could respond. "The Seer to spot him, me in charge, and a familiar face to reassure him. I think you'd serve best to reassure him, let him know that we didn't murder you for consorting with the Wizard Lord. If you've any argument to the contrary, speak up; if you don't, get those boots on."

"I'll have them on in a moment," Sword replied.

"We'll meet you downstairs, then."

The door was closed again before Sword even saw Boss move.

He sighed, and pulled on his boots.

A moment later he joined the two women at the door, and followed them out onto the street, where they turned right and headed toward the plaza in front of the Winter Palace.

It was late afternoon, and the sun was in the west, so the cliff towering over Winterhome was in bright daylight; Sword looked up at it, and saw the trail winding its way up the cliff face, saw the canyon that led to the Uplands.

From this distance it looked like a small notch.

He turned his head, trying to spot the Summer Palace, but the shape of the cliff was such that it was not visible here; it was around the curve to the north, on a stretch of cliff that had *not* crumbled enough to climb, but was instead a sheer wall of rock, thousands of feet high.

The Wizard Lord was presumably still up there, going about his business, listening to messengers and sending his men on their various errands, mundane or murderous—and that meant he wasn't in Barokan, where he belonged, protecting its people from criminals and the vicissitudes of nature.

On the other hand, he might do less damage up there, if he had really been sending his soldiers out to kill wizards. And no catastrophes had occurred in his absence. Yes, the weather was hotter than usual, rains less predictable, but was that so very important? The Wizard Lord was building roads, organizing people, trying to make life better.

And, it seemed, killing wizards.

But then, the last Wizard Lord had gone mad, and slaughtered an entire town in the southern hills. Killing half a dozen wizards—or even all seventeen besides himself, if that was the present Wizard Lord's intention—was less horrific than that.

After all, the original purpose of a Wizard Lord was to control rogue wizards, and there hadn't been any real rogue wizards in centuries. Traditionalists said that meant the system was working, but Sword suspected it simply meant there weren't enough wizards left to be worth worrying about. Killing the few that remained would certainly eliminate any possibility of future rogues, and every wizard had been warned, when he first took up the study of magic, that the Wizard Lord had the right to serve as judge and executioner, with no appeal, should he use that magic in forbidden ways.

The possibility that the Wizard Lord would abuse that power had never been denied. It was a risk every wizard lived with.

And eliminating wizards would mean that this Wizard Lord would be the last; there would be no one to serve as his successor. Sword thought that might be a good thing. He had no great fondness for wizards; they meddled with dangerous magic and lived like hermits, outside the normal society of the towns and priesthoods. Remembering the story of Tala, he knew that for eight hundred years wizards had been a menace. For seven hundred, they had been restrained by the Wizard Lord, but they were still a potential problem. If they were being exterminated, no one seemed to mind except the wizards themselves; it would remove a danger that had threatened Barokan since the dawn of recorded history.

Given that, did the Chosen really want to depose this Wizard Lord?

Boss seemed to think so. She wanted a Wizard Lord running Barokan, minding everyone's business but leaving the wizards alone, not one hiding in the Uplands while his soldiers disposed of his potential successors, and taking advice from the man who had raped and enslaved her. Perhaps she thought that if the Wizard Lord was doing his job, he wouldn't be listening to Farash inith Kerra, and that if the Dark Lord of the Galbek Hills had been doing his job then Farash could never have ruled Doublefall in the first place.

Or was it perhaps that she wanted an excuse to exercise her *own* power, her own magic, more freely? She had the ability to sway crowds, persuade foes, make snap decisions with unnaturally good odds that they would be the *right* decisions for whatever she wanted to accomplish—and she was only supposed to use these talents to remove Wizard Lords who broke the ancient compact with the Council of Immortals, the agreement that the Wizard Lord would control most of the magic in Barokan in exchange for abiding by the rules the Council had set down over the centuries. This Boss, more than any other, would not want to abuse that power the way her predecessor had—but at the same time, she surely wanted revenge on Farash and any who befriended him.

Maybe she was just looking for an excuse to *use* her magic for its intended purpose, an excuse to remove the Wizard Lord. She wouldn't be the first of the Chosen to feel that way—Bow had admitted, six years before, that he was *eager* to kill the Dark Lord of the Galbek Hills, while Beauty and Babble had both seemed to find the march toward the Galbek Hills very satisfying.

Sword had not been eager or satisfied—yet it had been Sword who slew the Dark Lord while Bow was locked in the dungeons under his tower.

Farash inith Kerra had found another way to use the Leader's power, by subjugating the town of Doublefall and bending its inhabitants to his will, turning them into his slaves. He had betrayed the other Chosen and sided with the Dark Lord in order to maintain his power, and that was why Sword had insisted he give up his role.

But this woman, this *girl* he had chosen as his successor—how fit was she for the role? How sound was her judgment? She herself said that Farash had thought choosing her was a joke; what if he had been right, and she was unsuited to lead the Chosen?

Certainly, she was nothing like Farash had been in the position.

Over the past few days Sword had spoken with the other Chosen. Babble was guided by . . . well, everything; she could hear the spirits, the *ler,* of everything around her, living or otherwise, and said she would do what the *ler* wanted; she did not have a fixed opinion on the Wizard Lord or the new Boss or anything else. Azir shi Azir, on the other hand, practically worshipped Boss, and would do anything she said—though she also seemed devoted to Sword himself, and it was hard to be certain which she would choose should Sword and Boss settle firmly on opposite sides.

Snatcher claimed to have no opinions on the subject but a willingness to abide by the consensus of the others.

Beauty did not trust the Wizard Lord, but hoped his removal could be avoided; she had seen how much her neighbors appreciated the roads and canals, how industrious and happy the young men recruited into the army and the work gangs were.

And Bow wanted an excuse to kill someone, after missing his chance in the Galbek Hills.

Sword wanted to give the Wizard Lord the benefit of the doubt, give him a chance to explain himself. He hoped that Lore would provide a voice of reason, equipped with arguments as to why they should *not* kill Artil, despite the dead wizards.

He was not confident, though, that the Scholar would be that voice. He really did not know what to expect from Lore.

And then there was the whole question of the ninth talisman. *Was* there a ninth talisman, or was it just something the Wizard Lord had invented so that he would have an excuse to have his soldiers kill wizards who refused to talk about it? The captain's account of the Blue Lady's death seemed to suggest that there was such a talisman, but then why hadn't the Chosen known about it? Why hadn't the Seer observed the whereabouts of the ninth Chosen—did this mysterious person always wear *ara* feathers, perhaps? Or might it be an Uplander? The Seer's magic did not extend above the cliffs.

But an Uplander would have been discernible during the winter, when the Uplanders sheltered in the great guesthouses of Winterhome. Azir had said she wasn't completely sure whether a ninth existed or not, because there had been a few occasions when she had thought she might have sensed something, but she couldn't be certain.

Lore might know something about that.

Sword looked up at the cliff again; there were people on the trail, heading down, but they looked like little more than specks at this distance. All of them appeared to be dressed in black, but that meant little—anyone bound for Winterhome might wear black. At any rate, Sword could not identify any of them as the Scholar. Lore might well already be far enough down to be out of sight behind the rooftops of Winterhome.

"Wait here," Boss said, as they neared the edge of the plaza.

"Why?" Sword asked.

"Because we don't want to attract attention and you stand out. Now, shut up and wait here."

Sword glanced at the Seer, who shrugged.

"As you say," he said, and he and Azir stepped to one side, under an overhanging upper story, as Boss advanced toward the gate that led to the path up the cliffs.

There were guards there, of course; there were guards at every entrance to the Winter Palace, as there always were even in the Wizard Lord's absence, and even though that gate did not actually lead into the palace it had a pair of men in red and black standing ready, one to either side.

Sword watched as Boss strolled across the plaza, up to those two guards; he could not hear what she said to them, but he could see them leave their posts, hurrying across the plaza and vanishing into one of the streets radiating from it.

"Is he almost here, Azir?" Sword asked the Seer.

He could not see her face behind the hood and scarf of a Hostwoman, but her voice sounded worried as she said, "Almost. He's on . . . on the slope of broken stone, not the cliff itself, but he still has . . ."

"Shhh!" Sword said. "Look!"

The Seer fell silent and looked.

The other guards had noticed the absence of the two who had been guarding the gate; they were calling back and forth, though Sword could not make out the words.

"They did that once before, when I was here," the Seer told him. "Boss talked *all* of them into going away."

"She did?" Sword looked around. "Do you know how? I mean, what she told them?"

"They all went over to see what was . . . what are they doing?"

Several of the other guards, one from each entrance, were indeed collecting into a group, but they were not approaching the Leader; instead they were gathering at one of the doors, and although it was difficult to see from where he stood, Sword thought the door was opening.

Then several more guards came spilling out, equipped not with swords, but with a mix of spears and bows. One man was obviously in charge—he *did* have a sword, and a polished golden helmet. He raised his blade and shouted, "Earplugs in!"

Each of the other guards then pressed his free hand first to one ear, then the other.

"This isn't right," Sword said, drawing his own blade. He had been hesitant about even wearing it openly on the streets of Winterhome, but Boss had told him to bring it, so Lore would see it and recognize him that much more easily; now he was glad he had. These soldiers were far too reminiscent of the squads that had been sent to question wizards, and which had left the wizards' heads on pikes.

Sword did not want to see Boss's head, nor Lore's, on a pike.

"What's going on?" the Seer said. "This isn't what happened before!"

"Come on," Sword said.

"But Boss told us to wait . . ."

"Boss may be in trouble. Come on!" His sword ready in his hand, Sword marched out into the plaza.

He made no hostile actions, nor any attempt to disguise himself; he just walked out in front of the Winter Palace, making no move to threaten any of the guards. He noticed that Azir had not followed him; he dismissed that as unimportant.

Some of the soldiers glanced at him, but their commander was focused entirely on Boss and didn't notice the Swordsman.

"Leader of the Chosen!" the man in the golden helmet called.

"Leader of the guards!" Boss called back, her voice carrying astonishingly well for so small a woman.

"In the name of the Wizard Lord of Winterhome, I ask you what your business is here, and why you have sent two of my men away," the helmeted guard shouted. He made an odd gesture with his empty hand, waggling two fingers—a signal, Sword realized, as the spearmen and archers formed into two lines.

Hand signals would be the only way to give orders, Sword knew, if those men did indeed have their ears plugged to defend them against the Leader's persuasive magic.

"I am meeting a friend, and did not wish our conversation to be overheard," Boss replied, in a somewhat less stentorian tone. She stood by the gate, hands on her hips.

"Leader, it is our duty to *guard* that gate," the man said. "We cannot do that if you send us away with your magic."

"If I am here, the gate *needs* no guarding," Boss replied.

"Nonetheless, we have our orders—the gate is to be guarded at all times, and none may pass through without the Wizard Lord's approval."

"The Wizard Lord is claiming authority over the Uplanders now?"

"No, but you are no Uplander. You're the Leader of the Chosen."

"And does the Wizard Lord claim authority over *me*?"

The guardsman hesitated. He glanced over his shoulder and saw Sword, as well as the blade he held, and decided that this was getting out of hand. He raised his hand and made a grabbing gesture.

His dozen men began to move toward the Leader, lowering spears into thrusting position and drawing arrows from quivers. "We will talk when you . . ." the commander began.

He did not finish the sentence; instead he stared in astonished horror as Sword sprang into action.

Sword had practiced with the sword for an hour of every day for almost eight years now; he had been trained by his predecessor; and most importantly, he was magically bound to *ler* of muscle and steel who were sworn to make him the greatest swordsman alive. He did not hesitate; he did not even need to think as he went into action, beyond deciding that he was fighting to disarm, rather than to kill. He ran forward, blade raised, one man against a dozen.

The sword came down on the first spear and sliced off its head, leaving the startled guardsman staring at the blunt stick he held in hands that stung from the impact; with his ears plugged, the man had had no warning of the Swordsman's approach. Sword was already whirling on his heel by the time the spearhead fell, and the return stroke of his blade came up from beneath another spear, knocking it from its bearer's hands.

He had surprise on his side, and the fact that his foes had their ears blocked and could not hear his approach or their comrades' warnings; he was able to split a third spear, behead a fourth, snap a fifth, and work his way halfway down the line of spearmen before anyone could react.

But by then the leader of the squad had begun gesturing desperately, ordering his men to focus their attention on the Swordsman, rather than the Leader—and to kill him; the final gesture, a slice across the throat, was unmistakable.

Sword's mouth tightened. His blade flashed, catching another spear behind the head and yanking it from a guardsman's hands, and this one he caught in his own left hand. He hadn't practiced with two weapons very often, but he had practiced. He had no idea how to use a spear as a spear, but as a big clumsy stick that vaguely resembled a sword he knew *exactly* what to do with it.

Less than a minute after the first blow had been struck he had worked his way along the entire line of a dozen spearmen; eight spears had been ruined in one way or another, three knocked to the ground, and he now held the twelfth himself. He had not harmed any of the men who had held them, though. Now, having completed the first step in his attack, he paused to appraise his position.

About half the spearmen were retreating, either empty-handed or clutching a broken stump; none were actually fleeing yet. The other half were standing their ground; three were retrieving dropped spears, and three were advancing with fragments of spear raised—one as if to use it like a javelin, the other two preparing to club their opponent. Their commander had turned his attention to Boss, and the two were talking loudly and rapidly, but Sword had no time to try to listen to what they were saying.

The row of archers had arrows nocked, all of them, and were looking for a clear shot at him, one that would not endanger their spear-wielding comrades. Sword smiled at them, then turned and dove toward the approaching spearmen.

The sword felt almost alive in his hand; he thought he could hear the cold *ler* of the steel singing, almost screaming. He danced past his nearest foe and drew a line of blood across the man's wrist, then turned his blade and sent the stump of a spear flying. The second man received a shallow but bloody slash across his forehead that would blind him with his own blood if he did not stop to attend to it, and then found his makeshift club split down the middle. The third was not cut, but suddenly found the Swordsman *behind* him, and took a good hard whack on the back of his head from the butt of Sword's spear; he stumbled, and when he did not immediately release his hold on the improvised javelin a second whack, this one on his wrist, sent the broken shaft spinning into the air, toward the archers.

And then Sword was up to the three who had tried to retrieve their spears, and each found his hand empty, his knuckles bruised and stinging, and each felt a slash across his tunic at waist level that cut through his belt.

Host People and merchants were staring in confusion and horror; some were running, others screaming.

Still none of the soldiers had actually fled; the few who had retreated after being disarmed were regrouping by the palace wall. The battle so far had been fought in eerie semi-quiet; no one but the arguing leaders had said a word. Despite the shouting and screaming of the watchers, the only sounds from the participants had been the thumps of blows landing, the cracking of spear shafts, the grunts of startled men, and the whoosh of Sword's blade slicing air and cloth and skin.

Sword decided that would not do; with a wordless bellow of rage that he hoped might penetrate the earplugs, he charged at the nearest archer with sword and spear raised.

As he had expected, the archer loosed an arrow at him from no more than twenty feet away, a yard-long shaft that could pierce an inch of oak—and Sword's blade knocked it out of the air in two pieces, sending the two halves spinning in opposite directions, arrowhead to one side of him, fletching to the other.

Then the archer's bowstring snapped as Sword's blade cut through it, and the man stumbled backward, almost falling, staring at his own thumb, where the snapped bowstring had whipped across it hard enough to break the nail and draw blood.

Sword could not spare any time to deal with him further, though; four of the other archers had loosed, despite the proximity of their own companions.

One shot was wild, and Sword did not worry about that one, but he brought the spear up to intercept two of the others; they thumped into the wood with enough force that wood splintered and his hand stung, but he did not drop his weapon.

And the final arrow was sliced from the air in two pieces, just as the first had been.

That finally penetrated the guards' consciousness; three of the remaining archers dropped their bows and ran. Others backed away, but kept their weapons raised.

Sword spun down the line, slicing each bowstring as he passed. Two more arrows were released; he ducked one, and just for the sake of drama sliced the last *lengthwise*, sending it arcing over his head in two curling pieces..

By the time he had ruined every bow that had not been dropped, four spearmen had regrouped, and a swordsman had appeared from somewhere; Sword swept through them, as well, disarming them all, and making sure each received a single gash somewhere that would draw plenty of blood and leave a dramatic scar, but that would not cripple or kill.

By this point more than half the original two dozen had either fled, or dropped their weapons and retreated with hands raised in surrender; a few were snatching wax-and-cotton plugs from their ears and demanding to know what was going on.

The guard commander had stopped arguing; he was staring at his men in shocked silence, Boss at his shoulder.

And one final guardsman seemed determined to fight. This was a big man, black-haired, bearing a sword; he squared off facing Sword, taking up a proper swordsman's stance.

Sword had no patience for this; he spun, flung his spear aside, and danced around the sword-wielding guard, apparently ignoring the man's attempt to fight even while three sweeping blows were somehow diverted harmlessly. Then he sprang away.

The guard's pants had been slit up either side, from ankle to thigh; his belt had been cut from his waist in three pieces. A triangular notch had been cut into each earlobe.

"You really want to fight me?" Sword asked.

"A chance to take on the world's greatest swordsman? Of course I do!" the man rumbled.

"Let me explain something, then," Sword said. "You should hope you aren't as good as you think you are, because if you actually manage to challenge me, to force me to defend myself, then I'll kill you. You can't beat me, you know that, and I don't have time to play, not with so many of you here. If you're just a big strong fool who knows no more about a blade than a cat knows about cooking, then I'll just disarm you—so let's both hope that's the case."

The big guard hesitated at that—and that was what Sword had wanted; he ducked, thrust, and cut across the man's hand just above the wrist, on the fleshy part of the hand. The tip of his sword wedged against the guardsman's hilt; Sword twisted his blade and tugged.

The man's fist flew open, and his sword tumbled to the earth of the plaza. He backed away quickly, raising his hands in surrender. Blood from the fresh wound ran down his wrist.

And with him out of the way, Sword advanced toward the commander.

"Now," he said, "do you *really* want to make enemies of the Chosen?"

"I have my orders . . ." the commander said, empty hands held out, his gaze fixed on Sword's face.

"You realize," Boss said from behind him, "that you don't know where the Archer is."

The guard threw her a quick look, then raised his hands farther. "I'm just doing . . ."

". . . what the Wizard Lord told you to," Boss finished for him. "Fine. And we're doing what we must, and we are two of the eight people in Barokan who do not need to obey the Wizard Lord's orders. Now, take your men and go away, before someone gets seriously hurt."

The commander looked from Sword to Boss and back, and then gestured to his remaining men. He began walking toward the palace's central door, head down, beckoning for the guards to follow.

The surrounding crowd cheered, though Sword had no idea what they thought they were cheering for. He paid them no attention as he crossed the plaza.

"So much for secrecy," Boss said, as Sword walked over to her.

"I hope you aren't too displeased with me," Sword said. "Those earplugs worried me."

"No, you did fine," Boss said. "Obviously, the Wizard Lord has tried to prepare defenses against us. That's not good."

"I suppose so," Sword said, as both of them ambled toward the gate.

They had not yet reached it when Lore stepped through and stopped to look over the plaza, at the shattered remnants of several spears and arrows, and a few small spatters of blood.

"I take it I missed the excitement," he said.

"I'm afraid so," Sword replied, smiling.

Boss stepped forward, hand out to shake. "You must be the Scholar, called Lore," she said. "Call me Boss."

"A pleasure to finally meet you," Lore said, taking her hand.

"I'm sure. Now, come on—we have a great deal to discuss." And with that she released his hand and spun on her heel, leading Lore and Sword back toward Beauty's house.

21

"That was amazing, " Azir whispered again, and again Sword waved for her to be still; he was listening intently to Lore's description of the Wizard Lord's behavior.

All the Chosen were gathered in the front room of Beauty's home; Boss and Lore had taken the two chairs by the hearth, and Sword and Snatcher leaned against the walls nearby, while Azir sat on the hearth at Sword's feet. Bow was perched on the stairs, while Beauty and Babble moved about.

"But it must have been twenty men!" the Seer insisted.

"Twenty-five, not counting the captain," Sword told her. "Now be quiet."

"*Twenty-five!*"

"It's magic. Now shut up."

Azir still seemed eager to say more, but seeing Sword keep his face steadfastly turned away finally discouraged her, and she fell silent. Sword did not have the impression, though, that she was listening to Lore; she was merely waiting until Sword stopped ignoring her.

"I think he's sincere," Lore said, as he concluded his account of what the Wizard Lord had told him. "I don't think there's any pretense, or that he intends any harm; he genuinely believes that Barokan would be better off without magic."

"But with him ruling it, magic or no," Boss said.

"Well . . . yes."

"And no magic means no wizards."

"What?"

Boss smiled humorlessly. "He's been killing wizards."

Lore glanced from one face to the next—Boss to Sword to Bow to Beauty to Snatcher to Azir to Babble. "You're serious?"

"Completely. You hadn't heard anything? Not even a rumor?"

"No! Not a word. That is . . . not that I remember . . ."

"Oh, don't try that," Sword said. "You've been up in the Summer Palace, where our magic doesn't work. Whether you remember a specific detail you heard up there or not is meaningless."

"Fine!" Lore retorted. "I don't remember anything about killing anyone, and I think I would, magic or no. Farash and Artil and I talked about possibly doing something about places like Drumhead and Bone Garden eventually, and that it might mean killing the priests, but we decided it should wait another few years, to be sure. That's the only mention of any killing that I remember."

"What about a new member of the Chosen?" Boss asked.

Lore stared at her.

"Well?" she demanded. "Did anyone mention a ninth member of the Chosen?"

"I don't . . . there should be one, shouldn't there?" Lore's surprise and puzzlement was plain on his face. "Because we killed a Dark Lord. Whenever that's happened before, the Council of Immortals has added a new role. But they didn't this time, did they?"

"We were hoping *you* would know," Sword said.

"Well, I know how it happened with each of the others. When they first created the Chosen there was a Leader to decide when and how they should act, a Seer to find them and the Dark Lord, and a Swordsman to kill him. The Dark Lord of the Midlands killed the Leader before the Swordsman slew him, so they added the Beauty, to distract. Then the Dark Lord of Tallowcrane protected himself behind locked gates and barred windows, so after his death they added the Thief. The first Scholar was created when the Chosen who fought the Dark Lord of Kamith t'Daru repeated mistakes their predecessors had made. After the Dark Lord of the Tsamas was defeated it was decided that relying entirely on close combat was a mistake, and the Archer was added. I think they created the Speaker after the Dark Lord of Goln Vleys simply because they could, and adding a role had become traditional."

"Wizards are very fond of tradition," Sword remarked.

"Yes, they are, so they *should* have added a new role after you killed the Dark Lord of the Galbek Hills, shouldn't they? But I don't know whether they did."

"You don't know?"

"No." He shook his head. "No one's told me anything about a ninth."

"Who would have created the ninth talisman?" Boss asked. "Who would know?"

"The way it's worked for all the others was that after the new Wizard Lord was appointed, the Council met in secret and devised the new role. Then they collected the necessary magic, summoned the necessary *ler,* and created the paired talismans. They gave one talisman to the new member of the Chosen first, and then presented the other talisman to the Wizard Lord. The new Chosen then went to the Leader and informed him of what the Council had done. No one told the Wizard Lord, though usually the new role became common knowledge long before the next Dark Lord happened along."

"No one informed *me* of anything," Boss said.

"You probably weren't the Leader yet," Lore replied.

A sudden hush fell.

"Do you really think that's it?" Azir asked, breaking the silence. "Because then I probably wasn't the Seer yet, and if the new Chosen always carried *ara* feathers, that would explain why I never sensed him clearly."

"You haven't sensed one?" Lore said. "Then why do you think there *is* one?" He looked from Sword to Boss, and back.

"Because that's what his men have been questioning wizards about," Boss said.

"Questioning?" Lore visibly relaxed. "I thought you said *killing* wizards!"

"I did," Boss replied. "He's been sending soldiers to question them about the ninth talisman, and if the wizards don't answer, the soldiers kill them. We know for certain that they've killed the Blue Lady— hanged her—and we've been told that they've killed at least three others, as well."

"The Blue Lady? Liria vil Surulin aza Kilorim Nolaris ḣela Tiri? That Blue Lady?"

"How would *we* know her true name?" Boss demanded.

"That was her name," Babble said quietly.

"I thought they were *friends*, she and Artil!" Lore exclaimed.

"Well, his men killed her anyway," Boss said. "She wouldn't tell them anything about the ninth talisman. Reportedly she said she *couldn't* tell them, that there was a spell on her preventing it."

"And they killed her anyway?" Lore sounded genuinely horrified.

"Yes."

"Because of the ninth Chosen?"

"So it would seem."

"But that's . . . he knows that's wrong. He's allowed to kill wizards if they do anything forbidden, but he's not allowed to interfere with the Chosen."

Sword cocked his head. "You think it's worse that he's asking about the ninth talisman than that he's killing people?"

"No, I . . . it's not . . ." Lore stopped, took a deep breath, and began again.

"I'm not saying anything right now about what's right and wrong," he said, looking from face to face. "But part of my role among the Chosen is to say whether or not the Wizard Lord is following the rules set down for him, the rules that determine when we are supposed to depose or kill him. *Under those rules,* as set down by the Council of Immortals themselves, interfering with the selection, creation, or actions of the Chosen is indeed a worse offense than killing wizards who appear to be innocent of wrongdoing. The assumption is that wizards can appear innocent while actually being guilty of horrible crimes or posing a serious danger to Barokan, while interfering with the Chosen *must* be assumed to be an attempt to protect himself from us, which in turn implies he has a reason to believe the Chosen are a danger to him, which implies that he knows he's done something wrong. You see?"

"So we're never to give any wizard the benefit of the doubt?" Beauty asked. "Neither the ones he kills, nor the Wizard Lord himself?"

"That's right, we aren't. The wizards themselves set the system up that way."

"Seems foolish of them," Snatcher remarked.

"Wizards are traditionally more afraid of each other than of anything else in the world," Sword replied.

"Well, this Wizard Lord doesn't seem to be afraid of other wizards," Boss said. "He's killing them for nothing."

"Not for nothing," Beauty protested. "He's trying to find out about the ninth talisman."

"I'm not convinced there *is* a ninth talisman," Boss said. "And if there is, does it make any sense to kill people who *can't* tell you what you want to know about it? Wouldn't it be better to keep them around and try to break the spell?"

"Maybe he's just eliminating magic," Lore suggested. "The talisman is just an excuse. He certainly talks enough about wanting a Barokan without magic—killing all the wizards is a step on the way there."

"Rather a drastic one," Sword said.

"And he's not killing himself," Bow pointed out. "He's a wizard."

"I don't think he's ready to go *that* far," Lore said. "But he does spend months in the Summer Palace, where he has no magic."

"And he hasn't killed *all* the other wizards, so far as we know," Boss said. "The wizard I spoke to said he'd found two others still alive."

"The Wizard Lord's men might not have gotten to them yet," Lore suggested.

"You think he really wants to eliminate magic?" Sword asked. "That's not just an excuse?"

"You don't think he just wants power?" Boss asked. "If he can rule without magic, then besides the wizards, he can kill the eight of us without losing anything he cares about. Which might just be what he's planning, and why he's so anxious to find out about this supposed ninth."

Lore hesitated, plainly unhappy with the question.

"You have to remember," he said, "I didn't have my magic up there. I don't necessarily remember the entire truth. Even down here, I can't always tell truth from falsehood, and in the Uplands I'm no better at it than anyone else—perhaps worse, since I've had less practice. This is only my opinion, and I have no magical knowledge to support it. That said, I don't think it's *power* he wants, exactly. Not power for its own sake."

"Care to explain that?" Boss demanded.

"He told me this, late one night," Lore said. "He wants to *make things better*. He became a wizard in the first place because he thought magic could make things better. He grew up in Caper, where the *ler* are whimsical and harsh, and he heard the stories about Drumhead and Bone Garden, and he always had the feeling that things *ought* to be better, that people could lead happier, richer, more comfortable lives, if only the priests weren't catering to the inhuman forces of the natural world."

"I've visited Caper," the Archer muttered. "If he's from there, I'm not surprised he's a bit mad."

"So he became a wizard in hopes of making things better, but he found he couldn't really do much," Lore continued. "He could do miraculous things, but only in limited ways. He couldn't defy any of the established priesthoods—that would violate the rules of the Council of Immortals, and the Wizard Lord would kill him. He couldn't change anything important—he tried, but the priests were too afraid, the *ler* too set in their ways. He couldn't even set foot in many towns without first promising the local priests he wouldn't do anything to upset the traditional ways—the *ler* would recognize him as a danger and forbid him entry."

Sword remembered the first time he had ever seen Artil im Salthir, then known as the Red Wizard. The wizard had been hanging in the air above the village square in Mad Oak because the town's *ler* would not let him land. Sword had not thought anything of it at the time, since he had so little experience of wizards, but now he saw it in a new light.

"He concluded that because magic derives from *ler*, it's inherently opposed to change. The world as we know it is what the *ler* have made it, what we've made it by cooperating with *ler*. If we want something better, we need to impose it on the *ler*, on nature, by force."

"And the only one who might be able to do that is the Wizard Lord," Sword said, remembering how the Dark Lord of the Galbek Hills had forced *ler* into unnatural behavior in his attempts to deter the Chosen.

"So he arranged to become the Wizard Lord," Boss said.

"Or at least, seized the opportunity," Sword said. "I don't think he had anything to do with Galbek Hills' becoming a Dark Lord."

"Yes," Lore said. "Exactly. He grabbed his chance. And now he's trying to impose his will on the *ler,* pushing roads through the wilderness, defying the natural border between Barokan and the Uplands, setting up authority and organization independent of the priesthoods, so he can make Barokan better without magic."

"And you don't consider that wanting power?" Boss asked.

"Not power over *people,*" Lore said. "Power over *nature.*"

"We live in nature," Beauty remarked.

"We're *part* of nature," Boss corrected her.

"But he wants to make things *better,*" Lore insisted. "For everyone."

"Not like Farash, who just wants to make things better for himself," Sword said.

"Don't talk to me about Farash," Boss grumbled. "You realize that if there really *is* a ninth talisman, and a ninth member of the Chosen, it's *Farash* who probably knows all the details? If they informed the Leader, and it was before I took the role, then it was Farash they told. The Wizard Lord is sending his armies out interrogating and butchering wizards, when his chief advisor probably already knows all the answers."

"We don't know that," Sword said.

"Farash may be how he knows there *is* a ninth talisman," Lore said. "Assuming there really is one. Maybe the wizards didn't tell Farash enough of what Artil wants to know."

"So Artil's slaughtering wizards just to *improve* things," Boss sneered.

"He *does* want to improve things!" Lore insisted.

"I don't consider rainy days and crop failures an improvement," Boss said. "And I'm fairly certain the dead wizards wouldn't consider their removal an improvement."

"But the roads!" Lore said. "The canals and bridges and ferries! The Boar of Linden Corner, the Mad Oak, all those other menaces he's removed! And . . . and he has other things planned . . ."

"He can do those from down here, and do them without killing anyone," Boss said coldly.

Lore fell silent, looking around helplessly.

"So what do you plan to do?" Sword asked Boss.

She did not answer him directly, but instead said, "So killing those wizards isn't necessarily a reason to remove him?"

Lore shrugged. "Not necessarily, but we don't necessarily *need* a reason. We're the Chosen; the rules say we are to use our own judgment."

"All the same, I'd like to be able to point to a rule he's definitely broken," Boss said. "Lore, is there anything in all the stories, all the histories, about whether the Wizard Lord is required to stay in Barokan? Has it ever come up before?"

Lore hesitated, then said, "Not directly. The Dark Lord of Spider Marsh apparently fled from the Chosen at one point by sailing beyond the Western Isles, but then thought better of it and returned to negotiate. He had discovered that his ability to purify seawater so that he and his crew could drink it vanished if he traveled beyond Barokan's waters."

One of the more incomprehensible lines in an old ballad, about "he sailed where the sea's salt could not be cleansed," suddenly made sense to Sword, but it hardly seemed relevant. "That's it?" he asked.

"That's it," Lore said.

"But he is charged with protecting Barokan?" Boss asked.

"Of course; it's part of his oath."

"He's not protecting us from this heat and rain," Bow said.

"That isn't part of the oath," Lore said. "He's sworn to protect Barokan from rogues and madmen, and those who would use magic to harm others, and from other threats to the peace. It doesn't say anything about weather."

"Is he charged with using *magic* to protect Barokan?" Sword asked.

Lore stopped and stared at Sword for a moment as he considered that, then said, "I believe he is. The wording is not entirely unambiguous, but yes, his oath says that he is given the talismans of the Wizard Lord to use them in his task of defending the people of Barokan."

"Then he's in violation of his oath," Boss said, "and this needs to be pointed out to him."

"I assume you mean with an arrowhead," Bow said. "I believe I ought to be able to hit him as he comes down the cliff—he's fairly distinctive in those red robes of his."

"We don't really want to just *kill* him," Sword said. "People love him, you know. The roads have made everyone feel rich, they've made life exciting. I'm not saying we should just let him go on killing wizards, or do nothing about the ones already slain, but just putting an arrow through his heart doesn't seem wise. We should probably give him a chance to make it right somehow. At the very least, he should be offered the option of resigning peacefully; he said that he would choose abdication over death." He turned to Lore. "You were there when he said that."

"I was?" Lore replied. "I don't remember anything of the sort."

"But you . . ." Sword frowned. "You don't remember it?"

"No."

"Oh. Then he was lying." Sword glanced at Boss. "That's not good."

"If you're really sure I heard him say it, then yes, he must have been lying," Lore agreed. "All the same, I personally would be satisfied if he simply agreed to stay in Barokan and promised not to harm anyone else, or to pry any further into this talisman business. Killing him would not be popular. And frankly, I *like* him."

"I'm not eager to kill anyone," Boss replied. "I was thinking of a letter, not an arrowhead or sword point. We tell him that we want an explanation for the dead wizards, and that his oath requires him to be able to use his magic, and we go from there. If he says, 'Oh, I'm terribly sorry, I didn't realize,' and agrees to stay down here and leave the remaining wizards alone, then that's fine, for the present—though of course we'll keep an eye on his actions to make sure he's behaving himself. If he won't cooperate, we'll remove him."

"So I'm to pass up the opportunity to shoot him on the way *down* the cliffs, tempting as it might be," Bow said, "but if I see him going back up the cliffs, I'm free to take him down?"

"More or less," Boss acknowledged. "But I'm not sure I'm any more eager to see him killed than Lore is. As Sword and Lore have both told us, people love him."

"And for another thing," Sword said, "his successor may be worse—the pool of eligible candidates must be pretty small."

"Yes, I suppose it is," Boss said. "Why are there so few wizards left, anyway? In the old songs and stories there are hundreds of them."

"There are several reasons," Lore said. "Probably the most important is that wizards have such a bad reputation that they no longer attract competent apprentices. Nobody likes wizards, so nobody wants to be one. And among the wizards themselves, the masters worry about training someone who goes rogue, or is appointed Wizard Lord only to become a Dark Lord, so they're very, very selective, and most applicants are deemed unsuitable. Many wizards, *most* wizards, live out their lives without ever training a single apprentice, so for centuries, their numbers have been dwindling."

"*Have* they." Despite the phrasing, Boss clearly did not intend this as a question.

Lore continued, "The current Wizard Lord said that one reason he wanted to set up a system that doesn't use magic is because he believes in another century or so there wouldn't be *any* wizards to run things the old way, in any case."

"That's . . . interesting. It explains a great deal," Boss said thoughtfully. "So he thinks he's just hurrying the inevitable."

"But we aren't going to allow it, are we?" Bow asked.

"I don't know," Boss said, "but we aren't going to let the Wizard Lord make these changes unilaterally. If he wants to change the basic rules we operate by, then he needs to consult the Chosen and the Council of Immortals first."

That sounded sensible to Sword, but at the same time he did not think the Wizard Lord would agree to it; Artil's opinion of his fellow wizards was not particularly high.

"He accepts messages, doesn't he?" Boss demanded.

Lore hastened to assure her that the Wizard Lord did indeed receive and personally read a great many messages at the Summer Palace.

"Then we'll write a polite little note asking him to return to Barokan for a consultation," she said. "We'll set a reasonable deadline. We'll be completely reasonable."

"And what if *he* doesn't think it's reasonable?" Sword asked.

Boss shrugged. "We are the Chosen, and we know our duty."

"You killed the last one," Bow said, looking at Sword. "Now it's my turn."

"If it's necessary," Boss said.

"You're more than welcome to do any killing that has to be done," Sword said. "Yes, I killed the last one, and it was . . . not something I'd care to repeat."

"Regrets? Nightmares?" Boss asked, looking him in the eye.

"No," Sword said.

"Then what?"

Sword looked at her for a long moment, then answered truthfully. "A sense of futility, actually—and of anticlimax. Here we are facing a new Wizard Lord who may be going dark; what, then, did we accomplish by killing the last one? And it took months of fighting our way across Barokan to reach the Dark Lord of the Galbek Hills, but my final confrontation with him, the meeting that led to his death, lasted only seconds, not even as long as it takes to tell you this. The *ler* guided my hand so surely he stood no chance at all, so it felt not so much like honorable combat as like swift murder, and there is nothing I nor anyone else can do now that will undo any of it. A man is dead who deserved to die, and I am left feeling—almost nothing, only the certainty that I should feel more."

"Indeed," Boss said, eyeing him carefully.

"Is that why you didn't kill any of those guardsmen?" the Seer asked over Sword's shoulder.

Startled, he turned to her. "No, Azir," he said. "I didn't kill any of them because there was no *need* to kill any of them; they had done nothing to justify killing them. They were doing their job, not harming innocents."

"I like to think of myself as an innocent," Boss said wryly.

"And they didn't harm you," Sword said. "Their commander signaled them to do something, probably to capture you, but none had yet touched you, or threatened you. I wished them no ill; I simply wanted to make clear to them that they were outmatched."

"There were *twenty-five* of them!" the Seer exclaimed. "You were *knocking arrows out of the air!*"

"I am the world's greatest swordsman," Sword replied. "The Chosen Swordsman, defender of Barokan, gifted by the *ler* of muscle and steel with the skill to defeat any foe. And I had surprise on my side, as well. Disarming them was easy. I probably should have done it without drawing blood, but I wanted to discourage them quickly, and prevent them from regrouping before I got to them all. A cut on the arm or hand lets a man know he has been bested without making him feel he is fighting for his life. If they had had time to consider their situation and had come at me sensibly I might have found myself facing real volleys of arrows, too many to block."

"You seem to have given this some thought," Boss remarked.

"I have spent an hour every day for eight years practicing my swordsmanship and preparing for every eventuality—mentally as well as physically." He shrugged. "I assume you have given some thought to the best ways to use *your* magic. Especially after your memories of how it could be abused returned."

"I have," Boss admitted.

"Mine . . . doesn't work like that," the Seer said. "It's not under my conscious control—I just *know* certain things."

"As do I," Lore said. "When I'm in Barokan I remember every true thing I have ever been told, and it takes no skill, no thought, no planning—the information is simply there."

"I practice and plan," Bow said.

"I hear what I hear, whether I will or not," Babble said, "but what I say, to whom and to what, is mine to decide. I do no planning, give it no thought, but do as seems best when the time is upon me."

"I am always the Beauty," the Beauty said, "but I can control the pitch of my voice and the tilt of my head to strengthen or weaken my effect on men. It takes no real practice."

Sword nodded—and noticed that the eighth member of the party had not spoken. He looked at Snatcher.

"Oh, I practice," the Thief said, acknowledging Sword's gaze. "And I plan. And I keep my mouth shut about it—people have an entirely understandable distaste for thieves."

No one had a good response to that, and for a moment the eight were silent; then Boss clapped her hands together and said, "I suppose writing the note is *my* job this time. Beauty, where do you keep pen, ink, and paper?"

22

"I could hit him," Bow said calmly, as he stared at the line of tiny figures making their way down the cliff face. One of them wore red robes. "I'm sure of it."

"I'm sure you could, too," Sword said, "but we don't want to kill him."

"Speak for yourself; *I* want to kill him."

"Well, don't. Not yet."

It had been almost a month since Boss had sent a message up to the Wizard Lord, and half as long since she had received a reply saying that he would be happy to meet and discuss matters when he returned to Barokan. The Leader had made plain her displeasure with the delay, but had not deemed it sufficient to allow the Archer his head.

"Talk first," she had said. "We can kill him later if we need to. If we kill him first, talking isn't likely to do much good."

So they had waited, crowded into the Beauty's little house, running short on funds and food and getting on each other's nerves, until at last rumors reached them that the Wizard Lord's household was preparing to leave the Summer Palace for Winterhome.

And one morning not long after, the Seer had suddenly announced, "He's back! He's on his way down the cliff." Bow and Sword had hurried out into the street to watch the Wizard Lord's descent, while Boss and Lore and Azir made their way to the Winter Palace to arrange an audience.

"I really think we should just kill him now," Bow said. "If we wait, we're giving him a chance to make it difficult. Remember last time, slogging halfway across Barokan in the rain?"

"I remember," Sword said. "But Winterhome is not the Galbek Hills. This Wizard Lord isn't some murderous lunatic living out in the wilderness; he's a sensible man trying to make the world a better place. And people love him."

"Maybe," Bow said. "But he kills wizards, and he may have other surprises for us, as well. Remember the traps in the cellars beneath the last one's tower?"

"Of course I do," Sword said, slightly startled; usually Bow did not care to remind anyone of those traps, since he had walked right into one of them and been caught. He had only been freed after Sword slew the Wizard Lord.

"Can you honestly tell me that you are *absolutely sure* there aren't traps like that under this Winter Palace of his?"

Sword blinked, and turned his attention from the tiny figures wending their way down the cliff to the graceful facade of the Winter Palace. He had been inside there, of course, had even spent a day or two living in it when he first arrived in Winterhome, but he knew he had only seen a small portion of it, and that portion had not included any of the cellars.

He remembered how very cautious Artil had been about the Chosen, demanding that Sword be stripped naked before being allowed into his presence. And there had been his determined and lethal inquiries about the possibly nonexistent ninth member of the Chosen. Clearly, the Wizard Lord, no matter how good his intentions might be, feared that the Chosen might want to remove him, and if Lore had told the truth, then Artil did not intend to resign if asked. He presumably intended to fight to the death.

And equipping his soldiers with earplugs demonstrated that he had given some thought to just how he might counter the Chosen, and had implemented some of those ideas.

With all that in mind, Artil *might* have built traps and dungeons in there; it wasn't by any means out of the question.

"No, I'm not absolutely sure," he admitted.

"Then maybe he's not so very different from the last Dark Lord after all, eh? Maybe he's just better at disguising his evil schemes. Maybe he's trying to lure us in, make us trust him."

"Then he wouldn't have taken this long to come back down and talk to us," Sword retorted. "Or let us find out so easily about some of the things he's done."

"Ah, he doesn't want to be too obvious about it, that's all."

"How did you ever *stand* living under the Lord of Spilled Basket?" Sword asked, referring to the Wizard Lord who had preceded the Dark Lord of the Galbek Hills. "He never did anything that even the most suspicious mind could point to as indicating evil intent."

"But he was an old man," Bow said. "I knew he wasn't the one I was destined to kill."

"What makes you so sure you're destined to kill *anyone*? None of the *other* Archers ever killed a Wizard Lord."

"Well, then it's our turn, isn't it? Four Swordsmen, a Beauty, and a Leader have killed Dark Lords—isn't it about time someone got some use out of the world's greatest archer?"

"You're being ridiculous," Sword said, turning away.

Bow took one last look up at the cliff and said, "We're wasting a great opportunity here—I may never have a shot like that again." Then he shrugged and followed Sword. "But I trust Boss."

Sword nodded. He, too, trusted the new Leader, far more than he had ever trusted Farash inith Kerra. Farash had *looked* the part—a tall, handsome, powerful man in the prime of life—where little Boss did not, but all the same, Boss fit her role better than Farash ever had. She was short and not particularly attractive, to the point where Sword sometimes wondered how she could bear to live in the same house as Beauty without going mad with envy, but no one ever doubted who was in charge among the Chosen. Her wits were faster, her tongue sharper, than any of the others. She spoke with authority, made decisions swiftly and for sound reasons.

When Farash had been the Leader, Sword had sometimes wondered why the Chosen did not seem to work particularly well together; he had been uncomfortably aware that they did not often act as a team. Under Boss, though, they *were* a team, always.

Farash, of course, had been deliberately subverting his role in order to forward his own schemes for dominion. He had probably been actively *preventing* real teamwork. Boss had thrown herself into her role, determined to prove herself. . . .

Well, either that or she was much, *much* better at hiding her true intentions than Farash had been. Sword tried not to think about that possibility as he ambled toward the plaza.

And even when he did consider it, he couldn't begin to believe it. Like Bow, he *trusted* Boss.

When the Wizard Lord and his entourage made their grand entrance through the gate and marched on around to enter the Winter Palace, they found Boss and Lore and Azir waiting for them at the big front door. Sword and Bow and the others were absent, by design, so that the Chosen's delegation would appear unthreatening.

In fact, Sword was waiting quietly in the plaza outside, milling about in the normal crowds, dressed as one of the Host People. His sword was strapped to his back, out of sight, but if there were a disturbance he could have it out in seconds.

Likewise, Bow was somewhere nearby—Sword was not sure exactly where, though. They had split up, to make themselves less likely to be spotted. Part of the Archer's magic was the ability to go unnoticed, to simply not draw attention, and while the other Chosen were largely immune to this it meant that Sword could not hope to locate his compatriot by seeing where other people were looking. Searching the rooftops or scanning the crowd might have let him find Bow, but it would mean taking his attention off the Wizard Lord, his entourage, Boss, Lore, and Azir.

Snatcher was supposed to be somewhere nearby, as well, but Sword knew better than to think he could see Snatcher if Snatcher did not want to be seen. The Thief was a master of disguise, stealth, and misdirection.

Beauty and Babble had stayed behind, at the house. Boss had thought she had quite enough in reserve with the Thief, the Archer, and the Swordsman standing by.

Not that Sword could actually see or hear much from his post; the crowds and guards at the entrances kept him from getting close. He had no idea what Boss might be saying to the Wizard Lord; he could only hope that he would hear any shouting or screams that would indicate the meeting had gone badly.

He did see Boss and Lore and Azir accompany the Wizard Lord into the palace; he stood and waited.

After several minutes a secondary door opened, and Boss, Lore, and Azir reappeared, apparently uninjured and unhindered. Sword did not rush to their side, but instead followed at a moderate distance as they turned north and headed back toward Beauty's house.

He noticed that perhaps half a dozen others emerged from the palace a moment behind Boss and Lore, all in the attire of Host People. One of these men stopped to talk to one of the guards, and the others scattered in various directions.

One headed north, and Sword found himself walking almost side by side with this man, close enough that he wondered whether he ought to make some casual remark. But then the other man seemed to notice him, and veered away, crossing the street; he paused at a shopwindow.

Sword shrugged and continued on.

A few minutes later the Chosen were gathered in the front room of Beauty's home once again, eager to hear what Boss and Lore had to report.

"He'll talk to us in three days," she said. "He wants time to settle back in down here, and catch up on more urgent business."

"You agreed to that?" Bow asked.

"I would like to end this peacefully," Boss said. "The more reasonable we are, the less likely we'll have to kill anyone."

Bow snorted. "I'd rather get it over with," he said.

"Noted," Boss replied dryly.

Sword hesitated, then said, "I'm not sure I trust him."

"Of course we can't trust him," Boss said. "He's the Wizard Lord, we're the Chosen—it's our *job* not to trust him!"

"Someone followed you at least part of the way here," Sword said. "Stocky fellow in Host People clothing. He came out of the Winter Palace just after you did."

Boss turned to look Sword in the eye. "You're *sure* he was following us?"

"No," Sword answered. "But I think so. And he may have recognized me, as well."

"Did he see us enter this house?"

"I don't think so; he turned aside a hundred yards back, when he noticed me."

"The fellow looking in the shopwindow?" Bow asked. "I saw him."

"Did he see *you*?" Boss asked.

"Of *course* not!" Bow exclaimed angrily.

"He saw *me*," Sword said. "That might be enough, if he was follow-ing you."

"I suppose so. Interesting."

"What does it matter?" the Seer asked. "After all, the Wizard Lord always knows where we are, just as I do. Even if we were all covered in *ara* feathers, when we're all together like this, he knows where we are. One or two of us could be concealed by the feathers, but not *all* of us."

"Another interesting point," Boss replied. "Perhaps he was trying to learn something other than our location, then." She pointed at the vase on the shelf by the mantel. "I think we might want to start carrying those at all times, not just when we're outside Winterhome. Beauty, could you divide them evenly, please? And Babble, there are a few mat-ters I'd like to discuss."

Sword turned to see Beauty already pulling the *ara* feathers from the vase, and hurried to help.

He spent much of the next two days sewing *ara* feathers into the lin-ings of his clothes; he and Beauty also ventured to the shops and mar-kets to acquire more.

The feathers were, Sword discovered, far less expensive than they had been a few years earlier; after an initial surge, the new roads had reduced the demand, as the *ler* of the roads settled down and travelers realized they didn't need feathers. Furthermore, the increased traffic be-tween Barokan and the Uplands that the Summer Palace had created had enlarged the supply. Beauty and Sword were able to provide each of the eight Chosen with forty or so of the big white plumes, and one merchant threw in a box of pinfeathers, down, and fragments.

"Do those block *ler* as well as the plumes?" Sword asked, as he twirled a pink crest feather in his fingers.

The merchant shrugged. "Who knows?" he said. "I know they don't look as good on a woman's hat, but what would I know about magic?"

"Come on," Beauty said, pulling Sword away, the box in his hand.

On the third day Boss explained a part of her plans to the group.

"I don't know what the Wizard Lord has planned," she said, "so we

need to be ready for almost anything. He's had time to prepare, he refused to talk to us immediately upon his return, and while that might
be entirely innocent and I hope it isn't significant, it might mean he's
arranged a trap of some sort. Lore and I will go to the audience, as
arranged. The rest of you will be somewhat scattered, so that you can't
all be captured at once if this Wizard Lord has come up with the same
notion as the Dark Lord of the Galbek Hills and decided to take us all
prisoner."

"What worries *me*," Lore said, "is that *this* Wizard Lord claims to
be willing to relinquish all his magic—and he even did so, temporarily,
by relocating to the Summer Palace. That means he might be willing to
not just imprison us, but *kill* us."

"That's true," Boss said. "Though remember, he can't kill us directly
with magic—we don't need to worry about being struck down by lightning. He can't make *ler* harm us. He can, however, make *physical*
creatures—dogs, birds, rats, deer, anything—attack us. If things go
badly, you'll want to be aware of that. Babble has been working hard
for the past three days, arguing with certain *ler,* and she thinks she's
arranged for various small animals to carry messages for us. I'll go over
that with some of you. If something *does* go wrong, the rats and birds
and the like will bring you news quickly, you'll all know what's happened, and you can take whatever action you think appropriate."

Sword looked at Babble, impressed. Her ability to hear and talk to
any *ler* had been useful on occasion in the campaign against the Dark
Lord of the Galbek Hills, but only in a limited way. He had had no idea
she was capable of anything of this sort.

Of course, that assumed she actually was, which remained to be
seen.

It occurred to him that no one had discussed any of these messenger
animals with *him.* "Now, I'd like to have a few words in private with
some of you. Snatcher, would you accompany me?" She beckoned, and
the Thief—who Sword had almost forgotten was there; his ability to go
unnoticed was remarkable—followed her up the stairs.

A few minutes later Boss called Sword up.

"You," she said, "are our second line of defense. You'll stay near the
palace and listen; Snatcher is going to try to arrange for you to be

somewhere you can hear our audience with the Wizard Lord, and if that isn't possible then you're to stay close by and listen to whatever word the guards pass. Use your own judgment as to when and whether to intervene. If this goes badly, you have two choices—fight or flee—and I'm trusting you to decide which it will be. If you choose to fight, then do it; don't hesitate. If it comes to that, your goal is to kill the Wizard Lord, *not* to rescue me or Lore or any of the others, *not* to protect innocent bystanders—kill him and we win, no matter who else dies in the process. If you don't see any chance of killing him, then flee, and I really mean *flee;* don't stay nearby, don't come back to this house, don't try to regroup with the others. Get away, and wait your chance. If any regrouping is to be done, we'll reach you somehow—Babble's animals, maybe. We aren't providing you with your own animal because you don't need the distraction, and you're the one word will go *to* if we need action to be taken, not who the word will come *from,* but if you find a rat or a squirrel or a bird talking to you, listen, and hope the Wizard Lord hasn't been clever enough to imitate one of us. You've got your *ara* feathers, so the Wizard Lord won't be able to find you, but of course that probably means Azir can't find you, either, and Babble may or may not be able to. If we had more time I'd work out a system to deal with that; I should have done it sooner, but I didn't, and now it's too late, so don't worry about it. If it looks like you need to run, then you get clear, get away, and we'll find you somehow."

"I understand."

"You and the Archer are our offense, our killers," she said. "You're going to be the ones he's most likely to kill outright, if he can. He'll try to take me alive because I'm linked to the Talisman of Command, and that's the part of his magic he's relied on the most in setting up all these new systems of his. You, though, you're linked to the Talisman of Strength, and with all his soldiers he doesn't need that. You're expendable, as far as he's concerned, but for *us,* you're the most valuable part of the team. We need you to survive."

"You're talking as though today's audience *must* be a trap," Sword protested. "He might be sincere."

"It *may* be a trap," Boss replied. "We don't know. We know he can be treacherous by what he did to those wizards, though, and because he lied to you about abdicating. He may be reasonable, but we need to be prepared if he isn't, and either way, we need you and Bow alive and still a threat. So don't die."

"I wasn't planning to," Sword said.

"Good. Then follow Snatcher's advice on where to listen, stay nearby, be ready to help if I need it and you can, and be ready to flee if that's what's necessary."

"I understand."

"Good. Then go back downstairs and send Bow up here."

Sword obeyed.

An hour later Boss finally felt ready for her audience, and the scheduled time was drawing near. She pulled up her hood, tugged her scarf up to cover her face, and led Lore out the door.

A moment later Sword, Beauty, Bow, and Snatcher followed, though they scattered immediately.

Sword saw that Boss had not headed directly to the Winter Palace; instead she was talking to someone, a stranger in Host People attire, while Lore stood uncomfortably by. Then she broke off her conversation and headed south, with Lore at her side, leaving the stranger in the street.

Sword followed at a discreet distance. Bow headed up a side street, and Beauty hurried on past the Leader and Scholar.

Snatcher slipped away so quietly that Sword did not even realize he was gone until he was at the edge of the plaza. He paused there and looked around for the Thief, who was supposed to find a way for him to eavesdrop.

There was no sign of him.

23

When the two spokesmen were admitted into the palace, Sword took up a position in a corner of the palace facade, leaning against the red-painted wood of a shutter with a casual air, as if he were waiting for someone. His sword was strapped to his back, under the loose black tunic of a Hostman, but he reached back as if scratching an itch and loosened the bindings; he could have the blade out in seconds, should it become necessary.

But he couldn't believe it would be necessary. Artil was a sensible person, albeit an ambitious and idealistic one; he surely didn't want to tangle with the Chosen, or to hurt anyone needlessly. He would agree to stay in Barokan, and all would be well. He would swear to harm no more wizards. He would have some reasonable explanation of his interest in the ninth talisman, and for killing those wizards.

He wouldn't do anything to the Chosen—he knew better. In seven hundred years, no Wizard Lord had ever bested the Chosen.

Sword glanced around at the guards; none of them seemed especially alert or disturbed. They were standing at their posts, two at each door, watching the people of Winterhome going about their business.

Then he felt a tickle at his ankle; he glanced down to see a fair-sized rat standing there, looking up at him. The rat had climbed up on Sword's left boot, and his whiskers had been responsible for the tickle.

Sword blinked. He suppressed his first instinctive reaction, and did not kick the rodent away.

This was obviously magic; rats did not naturally behave this way. Whose magic, though? Was this one of Babble's messengers, or was the Wizard Lord up to something? Might some other wizard be trying to contact him, or one of the Host People priests?

The rat, certain that it had been seen and recognized, scampered up

Sword's leg. Even knowing it was there and enchanted, it took a strong effort on Sword's part not to shout and fling it off. He forced himself to remain still while the rodent climbed up his flank, from trousers to tunic, until it reached his shoulder. It thrust its snout to his ear, and said, "Around back. There's a way up to the roof, and to the windows in the audience chamber. I'll guide you."

It spoke in a squeaking, high-pitched, inhuman voice, but nonetheless it was recognizably imitating the Thief.

This, then, was Babble's magic—and quite an impressive feat, really. Sword wondered whether *all* the Chosen not in the palace were listening to similar vermin; somehow he doubted that Azir or Beauty would be pleased by such a method of communication.

Sword smiled at the rat. "Lead the way," he murmured.

The rat pointed with its nose, and Sword went where he was directed.

A few minutes later he found himself clambering along a sloping ledge to where Snatcher crouched on the tiles, peering in at a narrow window. Sword hurried up beside him, and peered over the smaller man's shoulder.

This was one end of one of the two rows of clerestory windows that let daylight into the Wizard Lord's audience chamber. The two Chosen were able to look down directly at the dais where Artil sat, with Farash at his right shoulder.

Farash seemed to be smirking at someone.

"Keep low," Snatcher whispered, gesturing. "Don't let your shadow be obvious."

Sword nodded, and knelt at the second window in the row. The rat leapt from his shoulder and scurried up a sloping roof, then turned to watch and await further instructions.

"Thank you, Wizard Lord, for agreeing to speak with us."

Sword could hear the muffled words well enough to understand, but it took an effort; he crouched nearer to the glass, putting his head to one side and peering down at an angle until he could see the Leader, standing before the throne. The pair of feet he could just barely make out behind her presumably belonged to Lore.

Boss was clearly the target of that smirk on Farash's face.

"Refusing to meet the Leader of the Chosen would hardly increase my odds of a long reign, now, would it?" the Wizard Lord replied sardonically.

"We are not going to turn on you out of mere pique," Boss said, in that surprisingly deep, strong voice. "We take our duty very seriously, and you have obviously done a great deal to benefit Barokan. However, there are matters of some concern to us."

There was a commotion of some sort in the plaza just then; Sword tried to shut out the raised voices and banging noises that echoed over the rooftops to keep his attention focused on what was happening in the audience chamber.

The Wizard Lord had said something Sword did not catch, and was waiting for a response.

"We are here," Boss continued, "to discuss three issues. First and least, we are concerned about your lengthy absences from Barokan during the summers. You are sworn to defend Barokan against outlaws of all kinds, natural or otherwise, and the oath says that you are given the magic of the Wizard Lord to aid you in this defense. To leave behind Barokan *and* your magic would seem to violate your oath—you were abandoning your sworn duties as Wizard Lord."

"No," the Wizard Lord said, as Sword shifted his gaze, trying to get an idea of how many guards were in the room below. He could see perhaps half a dozen, but from his current post most of the room was not visible. There could be an army in there.

He was vaguely aware that the Thief had moved away, up the slope of the roof. Well, he didn't suppose they both needed to hear every word.

"I was kept well-apprised of everything that happened in my realm," Artil continued. "If the need were there I could have had my full range of magic back in a matter of hours. My stay at the Summer Palace wasn't a violation of any oath."

"The Scholar and I have some doubts on this," Boss replied. "You say yourself it would be a matter of hours before you could recover the use of your magic; a great deal can happen in a few hours. The weather in your absence was . . . unpleasant. There were frequent daylight rainstorms, and many days were swelteringly hot. Talltrees reportedly suffered an actual thunderstorm. You gave the *ler* of wind and sky instructions before you left, but clearly, they did not feel constrained to *follow* those instructions in your absence. If you spend every summer in the Uplands, I foresee a time when we will have not merely unregulated heat and rain, but lightning storms killing innocents, hailstorms destroying crops . . ."

"Hailstorms?" the Wizard Lord interrupted. "What are hailstorms?" He was clearly interested—apparently he had never heard the word before.

Lore's voice spoke, though Sword could still only see the Scholar's boots. "Storms in which balls of solid ice fall from the sky," he said. "We only know of them from stories centuries old, from before the Wizard Lords took on the task of controlling the weather, but until seven years ago that was all we knew of lightning. The fact that I remember the descriptions of hailstorms in detail would seem to indicate their accuracy."

"Solid ice? Really?" the Wizard Lord said, and Sword saw Artil lean forward eagerly. "I hadn't known anything like that was possible; I'll have to have a few words with those *ler*."

"Lord, we want to *prevent* hailstorms from ever happening," Lore protested. "The stories say they can wreak terrible destruction if they come at the wrong time."

Boss said, "Wizard Lord, as Leader of the Chosen, I ask you to stay in Barokan from now on. Do not go back to your clifftop palace."

"Is this a demand, then?" Artil straightened up again, and stared at Boss. "Will you depose or kill me if I refuse?"

Something looked odd, Sword thought. At first he was unsure what was bothering him, but then he realized. The guards behind the Wizard Lord should have tensed at that exchange, and they had not.

Farash had; the smirk had vanished. He looked worried.

"No, Lord," Boss said. "It is a request, nothing more."

"Ah. I will take it under consideration. Now, I believe you said you had other concerns, as well?"

"Yes, Lord."

"Call me Artil."

"Yes, Artil. I thought it best to start with the least important. Our next concern is that we have heard it reliably reported that your men have killed several wizards."

"Rogue wizards, yes. Was I required to inform you of such executions? If so, then very well, I hereby inform you—I have indeed sent soldiers to attend to the disposition of several rogue wizards."

"May I ask, Lord, how many wizards, and in what way they were rogues?"

The Wizard Lord stared at her for a moment, and then said, "Shall we come back to that? I'd like to know what your third complaint is."

"It's related. The matter of the ninth talisman. You sent your men to interrogate wizards about a ninth talisman; I can only assume that you mean there's a ninth member of the Chosen. We aren't aware of any ninth. If you are, we'd very much appreciate knowing the details."

"You claim you don't know?"

"I *don't* know. If any of the others do, they've lied to me about it. Why do you think there's a ninth?"

"Because of *this,* of course," the Wizard Lord said, thrusting a hand into the collar of his robe and pulling out something small and shiny.

Boss took a step forward. "A coin?"

"Yes, a coin. A coin that one of my fellow wizards, a man called the Cormorant, handed me a few months after I became the Wizard Lord, a coin that I must now carry with me at all times, or else I become ill. *Seriously* ill. *Deathly* ill.

"Unless, of course, I'm not in Barokan. Then I can leave this coin aside—but I can't return to Barokan without it, any more than I could abandon it here in Winterhome." He tucked the coin back in his robe. "The Cormorant called it the Talisman of Trust, but would not explain why. I know it has powerful magic, that it commands strong *ler,* but even after these six or seven years I'm only able to use a tiny portion of that power, because I don't understand it—and because it's linked to another talisman, and that link is *blocking* me! How is that possible, Leader of the Chosen?"

"I have no idea, Lord. I'm no wizard." Sword thought he saw Boss glance at Farash, who now looked very seriously uncomfortable. The Wizard Lord did not seem to notice.

"I *am* a wizard, and I can't understand it," Artil told her. "This is like no talisman I have ever encountered before. The Great Talismans, the talismans given to the Wizard Lords, are supposed to provide power, the power to rule Barokan, to find and kill outlaws, to guide the weather and ensure peace and plenty, but *this* talisman does little but thwart me. The Council of Immortals created it, and by doing that they betrayed me—*that's* why I have treated them as rogues, and had them killed for refusing to explain it to me. They broke faith with me by giving me this so-called Talisman of Trust, and I have repaid them accordingly."

"It would seem they broke faith with the Chosen, as well, by not informing us that we have a ninth member," Boss said. She was definitely looking at Farash, rather than at Artil, but the Wizard Lord still took no notice.

"If I am to believe you, then I suppose they have. Perhaps in that case you will pardon me for having disposed of them."

"The four wizards you killed were the ones who made this Talisman of Trust, and its unknown companion?"

"Four?" The Wizard Lord looked startled; his face, which had been set and grim, suddenly broke into a smile. "*Four?* You only knew of four?"

"Four—the Cormorant, the Blue Lady, Brownleg, and Kazram of the Bog. Yes. Were there more?"

"Leader, in these decadent times a new Great Talisman can only be created by *all* the Council. Four wizards escaped my men, two are unaccounted for, and *eleven* are dead."

Sword's eyes widened, and the blood seemed to chill in his veins at those words.

"That's—drastic," Boss said, her voice somewhat strangled; Sword could barely make out her words. Her gaze was once again fixed on the Wizard Lord, his treacherous advisor forgotten.

"I have never believed in half-measures, Zrisha oro Sal thir Karalba," the Wizard Lord said, straightening on his throne. "Rather, I believe in being prepared. I have been thinking this over carefully for years, Zrisha oro Sal."

"Stop calling me that!" Boss snapped.

"It's your true name, isn't it?"

"You *know* it is! Stop it!"

The Wizard Lord was grinning now. "Ever since I first became the

Wizard Lord," he said, "I have feared—no, I have *expected*—that the day would eventually come when the Chosen would decide, in your arbitrary fashion, that my plans violated some rule or other. I had allowed myself to hope you would be sensible, but I never really believed it. When you made no objection to the new roads, I was guardedly optimistic. When you allowed me to build the Summer Palace, I hoped. But when you demanded this audience, I knew I couldn't take any chances—and sooner or later you would need to go, in any case. Barokan is *done* with all this complicated system of wizards and magic and Chosen. The time has come to wean the people of Barokan from their dependence on the whims of wizards and *ler,* and to run this land with common sense and proper organization."

"You mean you want to eliminate the Chosen, because you want to eliminate magic?"

"Exactly." He stood.

That was obviously a signal; the guards behind him, in fact every guard Sword could see, suddenly straightened up and raised his weapon. Some lowered spears into position, some drew swords.

Farash had gone pale. He was retreating, off the dais, and Sword lost sight of him.

"Does this window open, or do I need to smash it?" Sword whispered.

"You'll probably have to smash it," Snatcher replied. "But that's a long drop; don't be hasty. She may yet talk her way out of this."

"Artil, you are the *Wizard* Lord," Boss said, and Sword was amazed that her tone remained calm, with no trace of wheedling, whining, or desperation. "Magic is the very essence of your role and your power; you can't change that."

"I believe I *can*, though. I believe that humanity can rise above the need to coax and cajole the favor of nature's petty little tyrants. I believe cooperation, organization, and plain common sense can serve us all better than magic ever did. Magic is the power of the past, and we must escape it and make our way into a better future. No more wizards, no more Chosen, and in time, perhaps, no more priests."

"Lord, I . . ."

"*I'm not finished!*" the Wizard Lord screamed. Sword started.

"Something's happening in the plaza," Snatcher whispered. Sword glanced up, but quickly turned his attention back to the confrontation below.

The Wizard Lord continued, "The Chosen are magical, and while I had hoped to avoid it, that means that you, too, must be consigned to the past, and removed from my path like every other obstacle. I had entertained some thought that perhaps you might give up your roles willingly, but I suppose that was too much to ask. And once you're gone I can dispose of those pitiful last few wizards, the ones who escaped my earlier attempts, and I won't need to worry about hunting them openly. Those fools called themselves by the grandiose title of 'Council of Immortals,' but they die easily enough."

"Are you going to kill us?" Boss asked.

"I am taking you prisoner," the Wizard Lord replied. "You and Lore. The two of you are harmless and potentially useful, so you may live. I regret to say that the other six must die—or seven, if I can ever find that new one. I don't need their magic, and each of them has the potential to be a threat, however minor."

There were a few seconds of silence as Boss and Lore absorbed this. Sword, alarmed, tried to simultaneously follow what was going on in the audience chamber, and what was happening in the plaza that had so attracted Snatcher's attention. He could hear shouting and rattling and stamping feet out there.

The scene below was more important, though. He started planning his entrance.

It *was* a long drop to the floor of the audience chamber, and he didn't know how many guards there were in the parts of the room he couldn't see, but he was the world's greatest swordsman, and that woman down there was his Leader. He would have to rescue her before she was locked away in a dungeon where his blade would do no good. He started to shift position, to find the best place to strike the glass to shatter it. He hoped he would be able to fit through without cutting himself; the window was not very large.

The stamping feet in the plaza were moving away, he realized. Good; that meant he no longer needed to worry about them.

"You've blocked their ears, haven't you?" Lore asked. Sword saw a hand gesture toward the spearmen beside the dais.

"Solid plugs of wax," the Wizard Lord agreed. "They can't hear a thing, but they have their orders, and they know the signals I've taught them. When I stood up just now, that was the point of no return."

"And I suppose you'll use blind men to take the Beauty?" Boss said.

"No. If she escapes my initial attack she'll be killed by specially trained women. Archers will dispose of the Swordsman, swordsmen will slay the Archer, and I need no tricks to handle the Seer or the Speaker or the Thief."

"Are you planning to lure them into this palace, somehow? Use us as bait, perhaps?"

"Oh, that won't be necessary. I know the house you've all been living in, and my soldiers are on their way even now. As I said, when I stood up, that was the signal—not just to get ready to capture you, but to exterminate the other six." He raised an arm, and a dozen men surged forward, pinioning Boss and Lore.

"*What?*" Sword had not intended to speak aloud, but the word escaped before he could stop himself.

"*Shhh!*" Snatcher hissed from a nearby roof peak. "There's something happening, a group of soldiers marching northward." He gestured toward the plaza.

"Have you been listening to this?" Sword whispered harshly. "They're going to kill the others! Azir and Babble and the others!"

"Are they? What about Boss and Lore?"

"Prisoners. They've been taken prisoner."

"Then I'd say a rescue is in order, wouldn't you?"

"Yes, but . . ." Sword glanced at the window, then turned his attention northward. He could hear those marching feet, marching up the street. Those men were on their way to kill the Seer and the Speaker, and the other Chosen were scattered around the palace and plaza; there was no one to defend the two women, no one to warn them.

Below him the Leader and the Scholar were being bound, about to be dragged away.

He had no time to think this through carefully, no time to save them

all. "No one's trying to kill those two," he said. "I have to save Azir."
He tried to get his feet under him on the sloping tiles.

"You might want . . ." Snatcher began, but Sword was not listening.

As he stood and began to run, back toward the succession of walls
and roofs that had provided the way up to this point, he heard one final
exchange from the familiar voices below.

"They're immune to your magic!" Boss warned.

"And *that*," the Wizard Lord said, "is why, just as with the wizards,
I won't use any."

24

By the time Sword dropped into the alley beside the Winter Palace some of the soldiers were a hundred yards up the street, marching briskly.

The Wizard Lord's minions all wore the familiar red-and-black uniforms, but they were divided into several groups—archers in one, spearmen in another, swordsmen in a third, while one company of a dozen or so had an assortment of armament, but were all apparently women. After the fashion of Winterhome they had scarves and hoods hiding their faces, and wore clothes so loose that the shapes of their bodies were at best vague, and it was entirely possible men were mixed into the group, but they wore women's clothing, and averaged significantly shorter than the other groups.

That was obviously the party intended to kill the Beauty, and the Wizard Lord had said the archers were after Sword himself, while the swordsmen would kill the Archer. That left the spearmen to deal with the Seer, the Thief, and the Speaker.

The question that filled Sword's mind, though, was how they expected to *find* the rest of the Chosen; to the best of Sword's knowledge, all eight were wearing enough *ara* feathers to block the Wizard Lord's innate knowledge of their whereabouts. Boss and Lore were captured, but did Artil simply assume all six of the others would be in the house?

He might well have other methods, though. After all, he was the Wizard Lord, holder of the eight—or nine—Great Talismans, and he had possessed a good bit of magic of his own back when he was just the Red Wizard. Sword hurried along the side of the street, trying to stay in shadows.

Then he noticed a final party of soldiers, at the head of the little army advancing northward—a small enough group that he had not spotted them at first. He counted four of them, and these four were carrying lit torches, with bundles of what looked like straw on their backs.

Sword did not like the look of that.

The torchbearers were in the lead, followed by the women and the spearmen. The archers and swordsmen, dozens, perhaps hundreds of them, were still back in the plaza, gathered in rows and columns.

Sword had not realized the Wizard Lord had so *many* soldiers, and even as he ran he cursed himself for that. He should have known, he told himself. The group that had killed the Blue Lady had been a party of twenty or more, and had only killed one wizard; probably the Wizard Lord had sent a separate company after each of the seventeen wizards, which would mean three hundred and forty men, without counting the ones who had stayed behind guarding both the Summer Palace and the Winter Palace. Almost everywhere Sword had looked for the past month, he had seen soldiers—and not the same faces each time, either.

How could the Wizard Lord have assembled so *many*?

That company in the plaza was huge. Those were the soldiers who were to kill him and Bow, Sword knew, and he was suddenly certain why they were waiting there. He remembered the man who had followed Lore and Boss halfway to Beauty's house; obviously, the Wizard Lord had spies. Some of those spies had undoubtedly been watching the house, and now these soldiers were waiting for the spies to tell them where he and Bow were hiding.

That stranger Boss had spoken to on the way to the palace—was that one of Artil's spies, or did Boss have her own agents?

The torchbearers, the spearmen, and the women were going to Beauty's house, but what was the plan for once they got there?

A rat suddenly scampered up to him; remembering Snatcher's messenger he had left behind on the palace roof, Sword did not kick it away, but instead bent down to listen.

"We're being taken to the dungeons," the rat squeaked. "I didn't know there *were* dungeons, but there are. Snatcher knows what to do about that. The rest of you, if you get this message—stay alive, stay free. We're safe—prisoners, but safe."

Sword wondered whether that was Boss or Lore—the rat's voice was not distinctive, and the words were not unquestionably one or the other.

"Sword, Bow, anyone—if you get a chance, kill him," the rat added, and Sword knew that was Boss.

"Sword, Bow, if you can hear me," the rat continued, "I wanted to let you know—there was a spy watching our house who was supposed to follow you, whichever of you left the house first, and report your whereabouts to his superiors. I persuaded him not to do it, but the persuasion may not last, once he talks to other people. The guards here have their ears plugged, and think I'm talking to Lore. I'm not sure whether I'll be able to keep this up, though, so don't count on any further advice. There may be guards who can hear . . ."

The rat stopped, and fled. Presumably that was all the message Boss had been able to send.

Sword frowned, and began hurrying north, trying not to draw the attention of the archers. He kept expecting a shout, or even the twang of a bowstring and the blow of an arrow between his shoulder blades, but nothing of the sort came; apparently that sword on his back was concealed better than he had feared.

He passed several Host People who were standing here and there on the street, looking puzzled and frightened. Ahead he could see the spearmen and women and torchbearers, marching up the street; as he watched they broke formation and began rearranging themselves.

As he had feared, they were taking up positions around Beauty's house. At least most of the Chosen were not inside—but two were. Lore and Boss were in the palace dungeons, Bow and Beauty and Sword himself were scattered, Snatcher was still back on the palace roof for all he knew, but Azir shi Azir and Babble were still in there.

Behind him men were shouting orders; Sword could not make out the words, and ignored them for the moment. His attention was focused entirely on the soldiers moving against Beauty's house.

Sword felt the weight of the blade strapped to his back, and thought he could hear the *ler* of steel and edge whispering wordlessly to him. He was the world's greatest swordsman, and those people over there were trying to kill his friends—he should be doing something about it. There were four torchbearers, a dozen women, at least thirty spearmen; could he win against so many?

Yes, he thought he could. He wasn't certain; it depended how well organized they were, and how well they were trained in the use of their various weapons. He was faster than any of them, he knew, but if they managed to close around him, restrict his movements, and set up a solid line of spears . . .

Well, it would be an interesting match-up, certainly. And if it came to that he would not be able to avoid seriously injuring people, perhaps killing some of them.

He loosened his tunic and reached up over his shoulder, feeling for the hilt.

Then he stopped, as a new sound penetrated his consciousness—a steady beat, a tramping, overlaid with renewed shouting—not orders, but argument. He turned.

About twenty of the archers in front of the Winter Palace had re-grouped into a line, and were marching up the street, forming a solid barrier from one side to the other, herding the Host People ahead of them, out of the plaza and away from the palace.

For a moment Sword thought he must have been seen and recognized, that the archers were pursuing him—after all, the Wizard Lord had said his archers would kill the Swordsman. Then he realized that this was not *all* the archers who had formed up in the square; it was, he estimated, no more than a fifth of them.

The others were probably marching up the other four streets that led out of the plaza. They hadn't located him; they were clearing the area. Perhaps they had realized their spy wasn't coming, and had gone to an alternate plan.

If he took on those other soldiers now he would be exposing himself to the archers, and he did not think he could take on *all* of those soldiers and win. The spearmen could corner him and stand back while the archers peppered him with volleys of arrows, and he knew he wouldn't be able to block *all* of them.

He lowered his hand.

"Ready!" someone shouted.

Sword turned to see that the torchbearers had set their bundles of straw around Beauty's house, and the spearmen had formed up in a square surrounding the building as best they could, given its location. The dozen women had taken up positions around the front door, weapons poised.

"Light!"

And four torches were thrust into bundles of straw, which flared up with a roar.

Sword stared in horror; weren't they going to give the Chosen inside a chance to surrender? He knew the Wizard Lord hadn't mentioned any such offer, but Sword had assumed that surely, Artil would prefer to take the Chosen alive, to retain as much of his own magic as possible.

Apparently Artil was more serious than Sword had thought about giving up magic entirely. Sword's hand crept up over his shoulder once again.

The stamping of the archers suddenly stopped; Sword threw a quick glance back at them to see them ranged across the street, watching their comrades and the leaping flames. He turned his own attention back to the house, preparing to rush in and save his companions.

It was already too late. The fire had spread impossibly, unnaturally fast, and Sword realized that the Wizard Lord's magic was helping it grow. Wind was swirling unnaturally around the house, rippling the dust in the street and pulling the flames upward along the walls, and ancient sap seemed to be oozing from the wood and bursting into flame as well. Smoke billowed around every shuttered window and barred door. The crackling of the torches had become a great roar.

The house must be empty, Sword told himself as the fire spread and smoke billowed up, it *must* be. His companions could not be inside there. Azir and Babble would have fled when they heard the soldiers coming, wouldn't they?

But then the front door swung open and two women came staggering out, coughing and sobbing, hands raised in surrender. Sword started forward.

He had no time. He had barely begun to move when the waiting swordswomen cut the two fleeing Chosen down, chopping at them as if the swords were giant cleavers; there was no grace or skill to it at all, only butchery. Sword froze, and stared in shocked disbelief. Blood sprayed, some hissing as it scattered across burning straw. Azir shi Azir managed a single piercing scream as she fell; Babble was saying something, but Sword could not hear it over the shouting and the roar of the blaze.

Then both were lying on the ground, the swordswomen still hacking at them, and Sword saw Babble's head jerk and roll to one side in a totally unnatural fashion.

Sword saw that the head was no longer attached to her body, and knew that Babble, the Speaker of All Tongues, Gliris Tala Danria shul Keredi bav Sedenir, was dead.

And Azir shi Azir ath Lirini kella Paritir jis Taban of Bone Garden, the Seer of the Chosen, who had once been called Feast but had freed herself from that fate, was dead as well, after just six years in her role. Sword had not acted quickly enough to save them; he had not really acted at all.

His hand closed around the hilt of his sword, but he did not draw it; he tried to force himself to think rationally, despite his rage and horror. He desperately wanted to draw his blade and use it to avenge his companions, but the line of archers was there behind him, waiting for him to reveal himself. He hesitated.

And an arrow appeared in one swordswoman's eye; she dropped in her tracks, her bloodied sword falling from her hand as she crumpled to the hard-packed earth of the street.

Sword stared. He knew that just moments earlier he would have reacted to this death with outrage, but he had just seen the woman chop two of his friends to pieces. Even now, as the swordswoman lay on the dirt beside them, she was still fully human in appearance despite the shaft projecting incongruously from her eye, while Azir and Babble were little more than bloody meat.

A second swordswoman spun and fell, an arrow through her throat.

Sword had not seen where the arrows came from, had not heard the snap of a bowstring over the chaos of the fire and panicking Host People, but he knew whose arrows they were. He had seen that fletching before—and who else could it be?

A third swordswoman fell dead, an arrow through her heart. Someone was shouting orders again, and a few of the soldiers were pointing back toward the plaza, the direction from which the arrows had come.

A fourth swordswoman had ducked back, weapon raised, as she saw what had befallen her fellows; it did her no good, as a fourth arrow speared through her chest. She staggered back a single step, then slumped to the ground.

A fifth fell, and a sixth; the survivors were screaming, falling back, taking shelter behind the spearmen. A seventh took an arrow between the shoulder blades and fell into a spearman's arms.

But then the remaining five women were cowering behind cover of one sort or another—mostly their male companions—and the arrows stopped.

For a second Sword wondered if the Archer might be done; after all, he surely couldn't have enough arrows to kill *all* the Wizard Lord's soldiers. Then a torchbearer let out a shout and fell, an arrow piercing his chest.

The other torchbearers went down in quick succession after that, but more people were shouting commands and pointing; the Archer's position had definitely been located, and the remaining swordswomen were out of his line of fire.

Every beat of Sword's heart was telling him to draw his sword and spring to his comrade's aid, to defend Bow and avenge Seer and Babble, but his head still had those relayed words ringing in it—"stay alive, stay free."

And that last instruction: "Sword, Bow, anyone—if you get a chance, kill him."

These guards and soldiers weren't the real threat; they were tools, swayed by the Wizard Lord's power and magical persuasion. It was the Wizard Lord himself, Artil im Salthir dor Valok seth Talidir, who most deserved to die—and it was Sword's duty to kill him.

Which he could not do if he died alongside Bow.

He took his hand from his sword, and stepped back, trying to blend into the background.

The spearmen were forming up into three lines, two of the surviving swordswomen crouching behind them; the other three women, Sword realized, were in an alley just north of Beauty's house, where Bow presumably could not see them.

The line of archers had turned, and now Sword heard the snap of a bowstring as one of them loosed an arrow at Bow.

Bow's response was so quick it was almost as if the archer's own arrow had turned in midflight; it took him in the neck, and he let out an inhuman croak as he crumpled.

Three more bowstrings twanged, and then a dozen, and then at a shouted order the archers broke their line and scattered to either side as the spearmen began marching back toward the plaza—toward Bow.

When they had passed his own position Sword could see that those two swordswomen were still following them, half-crouched and uncertain; he could no longer stand it. Orders or not, logic notwithstanding, he had to act. He drew his sword and sprang forward.

It was much easier killing than disarming; there was no need for the sort of care and precision he had used before. He slew both women in seconds by slashing their throats, and then began on the back row of spearmen.

The others stopped their advance and tried to turn on him, but because he was in their midst the result was chaos. He could strike out with impunity, since he was alone, while the spearmen were tangling with each other and had to be careful not to stab their fellows. He had killed or seriously wounded perhaps half of them when the first arrow whirred past his ear.

For an instant he thought it was Bow coming to his aid, but then more arrows flew, forcing him to duck, and he realized that the Wizard Lord's archers were now shooting at him, untroubled by the presence of their own spearmen.

In fact, one of the spearmen went down with an arrow in his shoulder even as Sword recognized the situation.

It was time to go, Sword decided. It was time to flee, to stay free. He had done enough to give Bow time to escape, and he had helped avenge poor Azir and Babble. There was no point in dying here, no need to slaughter the remaining soldiers, even if he could. They were not the true enemy; the Wizard Lord was—and perhaps Farash inith Kerra, if he had had a hand in planning this, if perhaps he had poisoned this Wizard Lord's mind.

Sword whirled, knocking a lowered spear down and aside so that it tripped another man, creating a moment of utter confusion, and used that to cover him as he fled back up the street, running as hard as he could, bloody sword bare in his hand.

His flight was not random, though—he had chosen his route carefully. He was headed for the alley where the last three swordswomen had taken shelter.

He found them sitting side by side against a wall; three slashes of the sword disposed of them. Only the third even had time to lift her own blade in an ineffectual parry before he was done.

And then he concentrated entirely on running and dodging, twisting and turning through the back streets of Winterhome until he was certain he had, at least for the moment, outrun his pursuers.

 Sword sat in the dirt with his back against the stone wall of one of the immense guesthouses, and wiped the last traces of blood from his blade. Then he lay the weapon across his lap. Sheathing it on his back was too awkward while he was sitting, and he was too tired to get up.

The banner flying from the guesthouse showed a ring of five golden stars on a red background. Sword had no idea which Uplander clan that might represent, and didn't much care. Whoever it was, they were still up above the cliffs, and would not be arriving until the approach of winter; the Wizard Lord had returned to Barokan at least a month, perhaps two, before the Uplanders would.

That meant it would still be at least a week or two before the Host People came to prepare the guesthouse for occupancy, and until then it would be shuttered and empty. The only people who might find him here would have to be actively looking for him.

Of course, there undoubtedly *were* people looking for him. After all, he and Bow had slaughtered more than a score of the Wizard Lord's troops.

Sword shuddered.

He had trouble believing it had really happened. All those people, dead in the street. Azir and Babble, hacked to pieces as he watched.

And he, personally, had killed a dozen or so.

He didn't even *know* how many he had killed; that was so appalling he had trouble accepting it, but the thought of carefully working through his memories step by step to count his victims was even worse.

He remembered when he was first considering accepting the role of the Chosen Swordsman, how his mother had asked him, "You want to be a killer?"

He had told her that no, he didn't intend to kill anyone, that the Chosen had not been called upon in a century and there was no reason to think they would ever be called upon again—and yet here he was, eight years later, and not only had he killed the Dark Lord of the Galbek Hills, who unquestionably deserved it, but now he had hacked his way through a whole company of guards. The streets of Winterhome were red with blood.

How could he ever face his mother again?

How could he face *anyone* again? How was he going to survive this?

At least the question of whether the Wizard Lord needed to be removed was settled. The Wizard Lord and the Chosen were openly at war now, and the Wizard Lord had struck the first real blow, capturing two and killing two of the eight Chosen.

Capturing *at least* two, and killing *at least* two. Sword realized he didn't know what had become of some of the others.

Boss, the Leader, was captured. Lore, the Scholar, was captured. Azir, the Seer, was dead; Babble, the Speaker of All Tongues, was dead.

But Bow the Archer had still been alive and free last he saw. He had no reason to think the Beauty had been caught. And Snatcher, the Thief—what had become of *him*? Sword had no idea. He had still been on the roof of the Winter Palace last Sword saw; he had not followed his companion down to the street.

And, Sword realized, he had no way to find out where any of the others were. The Seer was dead. A part of her magic had been the ability to always know where the eight Chosen were in Barokan, and where the Wizard Lord was, at any given time. That had not been *all* of her magic, but it was the heart of it. It was the Seer's duty to guide the gathering of the Chosen, when it became necessary.

The Speaker had been able to ask questions of *ler,* and sometimes send messages through them as well, which had been helpful in locating and gathering the Chosen—but she, too, was dead. Her hold on those rats and squirrels that had carried messages had undoubtedly broken when she died.

So how would the surviving Chosen find each other now? None of the other six had any magic that would serve in any obvious way. He was the master of blades and sticks, with superhuman speed and strength in combat, while Bow was the master of projectiles and adept at stealth and the art of ambush; neither of those would help them find the others. Beauty could distract almost any adult male, and coax him to do what she wanted, but that was of no obvious use. Snatcher could move unseen and unheard, could get through locks and guards, but he still needed to know where to go.

Boss had made plans to regroup, but those plans had assumed that the Seer was still alive, and Beauty's home still standing. They no longer applied.

And there was the whole question of whether they *dared* regroup, with the Wizard Lord's men hunting them.

There was some very small hope in the knowledge that the Wizard Lord had no more magical means of finding them than they had of finding each other. His magic would normally have let him locate them all, but now they were doubly safe. Each of them wore several *ara* feathers, which would guard them against magic, and in any case the Wizard Lord's ability to detect their whereabouts was dependent upon the Talisman of Warding, one of the eight Great Talismans. The Talisman of Warding was magically bound to the Seer's talisman, the Talisman of Sight, and with the Seer's death both those talismans would have lost their power, at least temporarily.

The Speaker's death would have rendered her device, the Talisman of Tongues, inert, which would in turn have neutralized the Talisman of Names. The Wizard Lord would no longer be able to instantly determine the true name of anyone and anything in Barokan.

That was a *huge* part of his power—or rather, it would have been for any other Wizard Lord, but the Dark Lord of Winterhome did not rely on magic for his power. He relied on his servants and his soldiers, and the deference everyone automatically gave to his position.

The Dark Lord of the Galbek Hills would have been relatively harmless and almost defenseless without the talismans of Warding and Names, but his successor was another matter entirely.

Artil still had six presumably working Great Talismans, of course, as well as the mysterious Talisman of Trust and all the ordinary, lesser magic he had had when he was an ordinary wizard, before becoming the Wizard Lord. He had taken Boss and Lore alive, which meant that the Talisman of Glory and the Talisman of Memory were still working—he could not learn new true names without effort, but he could still recall every one he had ever learned previously. The Talisman of Glory gave him an aura of authority and power that made it hard for anyone—well, anyone but the Chosen—to disobey or defy him.

He had the Talisman of Strength, paired with Sword's own Talisman of Blades, which meant he had superhuman strength and endurance.

He had the Talisman of Health, the Talisman of Weather, and the Talisman of Craft, as well, though whether they still functioned depended on whether or not Beauty, Bow, and Snatcher, respectively, yet lived.

That was plenty of magic, even if he had lost one-fourth of his power.

And he had his soldiers and servants, and he probably had most of the population of Barokan on his side. His roads had brought wealth and wonders, he had removed several assorted menaces like the Mad Oak, and his talk of a brighter, richer future had enthralled many people. The Chosen had been cast as obstacles in the path of this beautiful progress. This Wizard Lord hadn't killed innocent villagers the way Galbek Hills had; he hadn't flooded out crops or blasted guides with lightning. He *had* allowed a hot summer and daylight rains, but really, how seriously did most people take that? Sword had heard several people say they found the rains a pleasant novelty. Artil im Salthir had killed most of Barokan's wizards, but who cared about wizards? To most people, wizards weren't really people; they were the monstrous villains in old ballads like "The Siege of Blueflower."

Whereas Sword and Bow *had* killed people—not innocents, necessarily, but men and women who were simply doing what they had been told to do. Those swordswomen had butchered two of the Chosen, but all twelve of them had been slain in return, along with the four torchbearers and an indeterminate number of archers and spearmen.

And all those dead men and women had families and friends, as Babble did not. Sword was not sure whether Azir shi Azir might still have half-siblings living back in Bone Garden, but if she did, it was virtually certain that they would not care about her death.

The dead soldiers would probably leave a score or more of grieving households. In the past the ordinary people of Barokan had always welcomed the Chosen, and on those few occasions when the Chosen had found it necessary to remove a Wizard Lord only those directly under the Wizard Lord's magical sway had tried to prevent the Chosen from carrying out their mission, but Sword wondered whether that would be true this time.

For centuries, Dark Lords had tried to find a way to subvert the established order and make their own power absolute, and the Chosen had always ensured their failure, but Sword wondered whether Artil im Salthir might have finally found a way to do it, simply by relying on popular support rather than magic.

If that was true, then *should* the Wizard Lord be removed? Maybe it really *was* time to bring the whole system to an end. Maybe Artil was right.

But the Wizard Lord's soldiers had butchered Azir and Babble without giving them any chance to surrender. They had taken Boss and Lore prisoner for doing nothing more than their duty. And the Wizard Lord had, by his own admission, *planned* for that. He had prepared troops with stopped ears to capture the Leader, female troops to face the Beauty. He had *intended* to destroy the Chosen, he hadn't just stumbled into it.

Sword wondered how much of this had been Farash's suggestion, and how much had been Artil's own idea. He was fairly sure Farash had contributed something, but Artil had said all along that he wanted to destroy the old system and run Barokan without magic. He was the one responsible, even if Farash had been there advising him.

Sword wondered just how Farash was involved. If he ever did get the chance to kill the Wizard Lord, he did not think he would spare Farash again.

The Wizard Lord had said he wanted to eliminate magic, and Sword had never really thought that through, never understood just how completely he meant it. Artil had spoken with Sword and Lore, treated them as honored guests and trusted advisors, and all along he had been planning how to kill or capture them.

Sword could imagine what Artil would have said to this—that there were inevitably going to be some awkward moments in the transition, that not everyone would be pleased with the improvements he was making, but that over all, it was for the greater good. Azir and Babble were just in the way, like the *ler* of the wilderness that had been driven out or destroyed by the road crews. Boss and Lore were resources to be guarded.

And the rest of the Chosen? More obstacles.

He looked down at the sword in his lap, remembering how he had cut his way through the Wizard Lord's soldiers with it—and how *easy* it had been. The *ler* of muscle and steel had given him superhuman speed and control, and neither the *ler* nor his years of practice had failed him; he had always known just where the blade needed to be, and how to get it there. He had not been thinking of those men and women as people, with friends and families, with their own lives and souls; he had been thinking of them as targets.

That was *wrong*, to ever think of his fellow human beings that way.

The Wizard Lord probably saw him as a menace, and Sword was not sure he was wrong.

He was still staring at the freshly wiped blade, seeing blood that was no longer there, when he heard voices, and footsteps—many footsteps. He froze.

The tramping drew closer, and he knew what he was hearing; this was a company of the Wizard Lord's soldiers, marching steadily closer.

Then they stopped, still some distance away, and he heard voices again as one man barked orders he could not quite make out. There were footsteps again, just a few this time, and then the sound of latches rattling and fists pounding on wood.

"Locked up tight, Captain," someone called.

"All right, then—back in line!"

The footsteps retreated, and then the captain's voice called, "Forward, march!"

Sword understood now; they were checking the guesthouses, to see whether anyone had broken in and taken shelter in one. Sword thought that was slightly stupid. It would take an ax or a sledgehammer to break through those massive doors and shutters, not just a sword, and the damage would be obvious. It had never even occurred to him to try to get *into* one of the guesthouses, and it had apparently not occurred to these men that someone might just hide *behind* them, out of sight of the road.

At least, he hadn't *heard* anyone looking behind the one they had just checked, but perhaps . . .

His hand closed on the hilt of his sword.

The company had marched up to the very structure he was sitting behind, and once again the main body stopped while a few men tried the doors. He waited, muscles tensed, ready to spring up and fight his way free.

But no one came around the corner of the guesthouse, no one spotted him, no one called an alarm, and after a moment the soldiers marched on, to the next guesthouse in the row.

He could not be certain who they were looking for, of course, but it seemed very likely that they were hunting for the remaining Chosen, including himself. And their intentions were not benign. He remembered Azir shi Azir screaming, her blood spraying; he remembered Babble folding and falling almost silently, and the blades chopping at her until her head rolled free of her body.

He knew that if he met any soldiers, death would result—perhaps his own, perhaps others, he wasn't sure, but there would definitely be death. He didn't want that. There had been enough killing—or almost enough; the Wizard Lord still had to die, and probably Farash with him.

Sword realized he could not stay anywhere in Winterhome; the Wizard Lord's people were everywhere, constantly moving around the town on one errand or another. He would have to go elsewhere.

And he could not safely use the roads. The Wizard Lord's soldiers might be patrolling those, looking for him.

He could not hire a guide, if there even were any left around here; guides could speak to some *ler*, and might recognize him as the Swordsman. While he doubted most guides would be very fond of the Wizard Lord who had built the roads that put most of them out of business, he could not rely on anyone's silence. He had to remain anonymous, wherever he went.

He looked down at his sword again, and turned it so the blade caught the afternoon sun. He would need to hide it.

He could not leave his talisman behind, though; he became ill any time he was more than a few feet from it. Fortunately, it was small and easily concealed. The sword could be hidden or buried. . . .

But he would need to practice for an hour every day; the *ler* required that of him. He did not need to use an actual sword in his practice, but he did need to practice, and that might be inconvenient. Surely, though, he could contrive an hour of privacy each day.

And he needed to get away from Winterhome until he could devise some method for getting at the Wizard Lord and slaying him. He could use neither road nor guide, but he was one of the Chosen, and more than a dozen *ara* feathers lined his garments; he could cross the wilderness on his own in reasonable safety. He would need to be careful, as some of the wild magic might be dangerous even to him—he remembered his encounter with the Mad Oak the first time he left his home village, and shuddered. The Wizard Lord had removed some such hazards, but others still lingered.

An additional complication was that he had no supplies; all his belongings save his sword and the clothes on his back were either back in his mother's house in Mad Oak, or had burned up when Beauty's home was destroyed.

Still, he could manage, he was sure.

But where would he go?

Returning to Winterhome would be suicide. He would want to go back someday, to kill the Wizard Lord, but he could not risk it immediately. Those soldiers would be everywhere, hunting down the Chosen.

He wondered what had happened to the others. Snatcher ought to be safe enough; stealth and concealment were his specialty. He might even find a way to slip into the dungeons and free Boss and Lore eventually, or at least talk to them—freeing them might be a mistake, actually, as the Wizard Lord would never kill them while they were prisoners, but he might have no such compunctions if they attempted escape. Those three were probably alive and well, and safer without the Swordsman around.

The Beauty might be alive, or might be dead. Sword was sure that the Wizard Lord *wanted* her dead, but his little squad of soldier-women had been wiped out, and Beauty could probably handle any males sent after her.

He realized he had no idea what she would do, with her home destroyed. He could not begin to guess.

And Bow—Bow was probably dead. Yes, he had the knack of not being noticed, but he wasn't invisible, and with a hundred men after him it seemed unlikely he even got down from that rooftop alive. He would put up a fight, certainly, but his magic was intended for use at long range, and his supply of arrows was not infinite.

If he had somehow escaped, as Sword had, then he would be just as lost and helpless as Sword was. Neither of them could hope for shelter in Winterhome, or anywhere they were known; the Wizard Lord's men were hunting for them, and the ordinary people would almost certainly choose the man who had built their roads over the ones who had slaughtered two dozen soldiers. Even in Mad Oak, Sword was not sure he would be welcome—and of course, that would be almost the first place the Wizard Lord would look for him.

Sword needed to find some village where he would not be recognized, some place he could be a harmless traveler rather than the Chosen Swordsman, but how was he to do that? If he simply set out across the countryside at random he might never find another outpost of civilization.

Or at least, that would be a risk in the northern vales—but he wasn't in the vales, he was in the eastern corner of Barokan, beneath the cliffs, and to the west lay fifty miles of flat, densely populated land. If he stayed in the thickly settled Midlands he should be able to find his way without road or guide; the towns were often in sight of one another.

And he might see smoke he could follow, or firelight by night.

He would manage somehow.

He pushed himself upright, still tired, and slid his sword into its sheath; then he took a bearing from the sun, and began walking, bound west by southwest, to whatever he might find.

26

There was one detail Sword had not initially considered; he still wore the distinctive loose black garb of a Hostman, and everyone knew Host People didn't travel, even now that there were so many new roads. This realization struck him as he peered across the twilight fields at the brightly clad people of whatever village he had found. The men he saw here wore red shirts, and the women wore brightly patterned yellow gowns; his black clothes would make him immediately recognizable as a foreigner.

Well, he told himself, he didn't really have much choice. He couldn't have passed for a native in any case; everyone in a village this size surely knew each other by sight. And perhaps he could pass himself off as coming from some far northern town that affected black clothes; he had a northern accent, after all, and surely the Host People weren't the *only* ones who dressed entirely in black.

But he was still only a few miles from Winterhome, and these people would know how their neighbors dressed. The gathering darkness and his accent would help, but not that much. He looked down at himself. He could remove the ties at ankle and wrist, perhaps roll the waistband up . . .

And then what? Walk in across the field? They would know something was wrong then; *nobody* just walked in from the wilderness.

He would need to circle around and come into town on a road—any town this close to Winterhome would surely have a road by now. And he really ought to do it before full dark. The sun was already just a narrowing orange sliver on the western horizon.

He began adjusting his clothes as he walked, trying to make them look as strange as possible without being silly. He unstrapped the sword from his back and tucked it under one arm, then detoured to a distinctive tree, shinnied up the trunk, and set the sword securely in the branches, some eight or nine feet off the ground, well hidden from the casual eye by the surrounding leaves.

He was fairly certain he could find it there when the time came. He had already done his hour's practice, on his way through the wild, so barring disaster he would not need the weapon again until morning. He dropped back to the ground, brushed himself off, and trotted toward the road.

A few minutes later he strode into town, looking for some sign of a guesthouse or inn, and found himself the target of a hundred astonished eyes. He stopped, realizing that something was wrong.

Could word of his outlawry have reached here already? Had he been recognized so quickly? He had thought that his route across country had gotten him here faster than any of the Wizard Lord's soldiers could have come by road, even if they knew where to go. Had he misjudged that badly?

But he didn't *see* any soldiers. . . .

For a moment no one spoke; then someone called, "Didn't you see the shrine?"

Sword blinked, startled. In fact, he *hadn't* seen a boundary shrine, since he had come cross-country. When he had found the road he was already well inside the borders.

"What do you . . ." he started, but he didn't complete the sentence; every person in sight had cringed, and most of them had clapped their hands over their ears.

"Don't speak!" someone called.

Baffled, Sword stood where he was, trying to decide what to do.

The village was arranged in a circle around a central green; brick buildings formed a broken ring around the grass, with seven streets—he counted—leading away in various directions. He had come in on one of these seven streets, and now faced across the circle toward the largest structure in sight, a brick-and-marble building that filled the entire space between two streets.

And as he watched, the black doors of this building suddenly burst open, and three black-haired girls in yellow dresses came tripping hastily down the front steps, each clutching a handful of brightly colored ribbons. The last to emerge also carried a small drum, which she beat with the hand holding the ribbons. They ran across the green toward him, their steps keeping time to the drum.

Obviously, the local *ler* required some sort of formal greeting ritual.

Sword silently cursed himself, he had been so caught up in his own situation, the conflict of the Chosen and the Wizard Lord, that he had not given local customs any thought at all. The Wizard Lord, the Chosen, and the Council of Immortals might determine the fate of all Barokan, but on a day-to-day basis, it was the local *ler* that mattered.

"Oh, *ler* of this place, forgive me," he murmured under his breath as the girls approached. "I meant no disrespect. I most sincerely beg your pardon."

And then the girls were surrounding him, ringing him in hastily strung ribbons, and dancing in a circle to the simple rhythm the drummer beat. He stood and waited, assuming they would give him a sign if he needed to do anything more.

They were pretty things, perhaps thirteen or fourteen years old—a little out of breath from their hurried arrival, but all dancing eagerly and gracefully.

When they had caught their breath a little, the drummer signed to the others, and all three began singing, first in a language he didn't recognize, and then in an archaic-sounding Midlands dialect of Barokanese.

"*Oh, stranger, who disturbs our order, who are you that comes to our border?*" they sang, in clear, sweet voices, though one stumbled a bit on the word "border," glancing uneasily up the road. The tallest girl, who was in front of him at the moment, beckoned for him to reply.

Sword knew better than to lie to *ler*, but he also did not want to announce his role. Fortunately, there was a simple alternative.

"I am Erren Zal Tuyo," he said, trying to give his voice a sing-song quality.

This was apparently satisfactory; the three girls exchanged glances, never stopping their dance, and then one signaled the others. "*You who speak a foreign name, what have you come here to claim?*" the girls sang. "*What brings you to our humble home, why have you seen fit to roam?*"

"I am passing through," Sword replied. "I just want lodging for the night, and perhaps supper and a bath, and I'll be moving on in the morning."

"*One more request we three must dare,*" the girls sang. "*We have an oath that you must swear.*"

Sword waited, but they did not continue; instead they were watching him as they danced, clearly anticipating a response.

"Tell me what I must swear," he said.

"*By sky above and earth below, you must vow in peace to go; by light and water and by air, now swear you will no weapon bare; by blood and sinew and your heart, swear you take no foeman's part; by sun's bright light and moon's soft glow, vow you'll strike no hostile blow.*"

Sword hesitated, remembering for a moment what he had done and seen on the streets of Winterhome, but then he said, "I do so swear and vow." His eyes felt suddenly damp; he blinked to clear them.

He hoped very much that he could keep that oath. •

"*Then welcome stranger, to our town; now may you lay your burdens down!*" And with that the girls broke their ring, twirling apart, whipping their ribbons into bright spirals above their heads before bursting into giggles and running wildly away.

With the ceremony complete, several of the villagers now approached, smiling. Sword stood where he was, careful to make no threatening moves.

"Good to meet you," one burly man said, holding out a hand. "Erren, was it? I'm Dal—my daughter's Second Dancer." He nodded toward one of the girls.

"Thank you," Sword said. "I'm glad to be here."

"You have us all wondering, though—why didn't you wait at the boundary shrine? Can't you read? You gave us all a fright, walking in without ringing the bell, and starting to speak to us!"

"I can read," Sword admitted, "but the truth is, the day was so pleasant and the *ler* seemed so agreeable that I cut across the fields a little, and missed the shrine entirely. I'm very sorry."

This was not exactly correct, but Sword doubted the local *ler* would care; people lied all the time in most towns. Names were special, the *ler* concerned themselves with names, especially during rituals like that dance, so he had not dared give a false identity, but now that he was simply talking man-to-man he thought he could stretch the truth.

Dal shook his head. "Dangerous, leaving the road like that. You young men think nothing's going to hurt you, but one of these days you'll step on the wrong ground and find yourself cursed."

"Well, I hope that hasn't happened yet, and I'll be more careful in the future," Sword said. "I've very sorry if I upset anyone, and thank you again for your welcome. Is there an inn here, perhaps? Or a guesthouse at the temple?" He glanced around and discovered that he was now surrounded by villagers, but none of the others were speaking; they seemed content to let Dal act as their spokesman.

"Nothing like that," Dal said. "We don't get enough overnight visitors to need such a thing. But there's a spare bed in my attic, where my son used to sleep, or Iza might rent you a room." He nodded his head toward an old woman, who smiled toothily at Sword.

"An attic will do fine," Sword said, smiling in return.

"This way, then." Dal glanced at Sword's back, and the complete absence of a pack of any kind. "You travel light, I see; may I ask where you're heading?"

"I'm not really sure," Sword said, thinking feverishly. This was a time to not merely stretch the truth, but avoid it entirely—he needed a reason to be traveling alone, with no goods or money, other than fleeing for his life.

Fortunately, there was an obvious possibility. "The priests in Ashgrove sent me to find an herb called widow's finger that's said to grow in the southern hills, and bring them back seven leaves," he improvised. "Would you know anything of such a plant?"

"No, but I'm neither priest nor herbalist. You'll want to talk to Mother Forrik. So you're from Ashgrove?"

"Not by birth, but I'm courting a girl there. I'm from Brokenbirch, in Shadowvale." He didn't think any such town existed, but he wasn't very familiar with Shadowvale, even if it *was* just beyond the eastern ridge from Mad Oak. He hoped these people weren't familiar with it, either. "By the way, I've been hurrying so, I forgot to ask—what do you call your town?"

Dal was startled. "You never heard of Morning Calm?"

"Oh, this *is* Morning Calm?" Sword replied, a trifle hastily. "I thought I had farther to go to reach it! If I'd realized, I'd have stopped at the shrine."

"Of course," Dal said, smiling. He clapped Sword on the back.

Sword was not sure whether he had ever heard of Morning Calm or not, but admitting that would hardly endear himself to his host. "So tell me about your town; are the stories true?"

"Well, I don't know which stories you've heard, but we like it here," Dal said, spreading his arms expansively. "Our *ler* require everyone who sets foot here, either visitor or native, to swear an oath of peace, so we have none of the difficulties of other places. . . ."

Sword let him ramble on, and never allowed any hint of his own doubts to show. What mattered to him was that the supper Dal provided was filling and reasonably tasty, and the straw tick in Dal's attic was comfortable enough and apparently free of vermin, though it did crackle annoyingly whenever he moved.

He did have to pay for his stay, which depleted his already small supply of coin, and that brought another issue to his attention. He had always earned his keep when traveling alone by performing sword tricks and passing the hat, and he could hardly do that if he was trying to remain anonymous. For his recent journey to Winterhome he had relied on funds provided by Snatcher and Boss, who were no longer available. He had a small purse with him, but it would not last more than a few days at this rate. That might be a serious problem, as he did not want to resort to begging or theft.

He supposed that the money Boss and Snatcher had provided probably came from begging or theft, but that seemed different. *He* had not been begging or stealing.

He lay awake on his straw mattress until late, thinking.

As well as money, he needed a real course of action, something that would lead to Artil im Salthir's death. It was obvious that the Wizard Lord had no intention of retiring peacefully, and after what had been done to poor Azir and Babble, Sword did not care to offer him that option in any case.

Farash inith Kerra had probably had a hand in what had happened, and would therefore also need to be killed.

To accomplish this, Sword needed to remain alive and free until he
could devise a plan. That did not seem so very difficult, given his protective garb of *ara* feathers and the loss of magic that the deaths of Azir
and Babble had cost the Wizard Lord, but he would need to earn his
keep somehow, and his old methods of supporting himself—swordplay
and barley-farming—were not going to serve.

But what else could he do? He was a healthy young man, stronger
and faster than most, but he did not want to settle down in one place,
which took most of the likely choices out of consideration. He had no
special skills other than his supernatural abilities with a blade—well,
and his alleged prowess in bed, but he could not see any safe way to
earn his bread with that.

Perhaps he could be a messenger? Though there was no great demand for such; most people other than traveling merchants had no
business outside their own villages. The other obvious occupation for
someone who could not stay in one place was trade, but he had no
funds to buy inventory, nor contacts he could use to acquire credit—
and it would mean using the Wizard Lord's roads, which did not seem
safe.

And where there were no roads, the only people who traveled regularly were bargemen and guides. He had no idea how he might go about
finding work as a bargeman, but perhaps he could be a guide? As one of
the Chosen he could travel far more safely in wilderness than ordinary
people.

That might work—but he would have to find a route where guides
were needed, where Artil's roads and canals did not reach.

The Dark Lord of the Galbek Hills had wiped out the family of
guides that had served the village of Stoneslope, and that was obscure
and distant enough that there might not be any roads yet. He might try
there . . .

But no, Galbek Hills had also wiped out Stoneslope, and as yet, to
the best of Sword's knowledge, no one had rebuilt it.

Still, that part of the southern hills might have some possibilities.

He would head south in the morning, he told himself, and hope that
he could stretch his money supply, or live off the land, until he found
some means of supporting himself. Perhaps if he got far enough from

Winterhome he would find areas where word of the conflict between the Chosen and the Wizard Lord had not yet arrived, places where he could use his sword.

Perhaps in such places he could even find allies. The Wizard Lord was popular wherever his roads went, but surely there were places the roads did not go, and where the traditional distrust of the Wizard Lord and favoring of the Chosen still held sway.

He just had to go *far* enough.

Of course, the farther he went, the farther he would have to come back when the time came to kill the Wizard Lord, but he would deal with that issue when the time came.

With that thought, he fell asleep.

27

"Erren?"

Sword had been dreaming of Babble's head rolling in the street, leaving a trail of blood while a bell rang in the distance, but he woke suddenly at the sound of his name, and lay blinking at sunlight slanting steeply through the shutters into the attic.

"Erren Zal Tuyo?"

"Yes?" He sat up, and reached for his boots.

"You must leave. Now."

"What? Why?"

"Because we do not allow violence in Morning Calm," Dal said, his voice unsteady.

"What?" Sword straightened his clothing as he stared at his host.

Dal swallowed. "There is a man here," he said. "More than one man, really. They have a picture of you, and they say you are the Chosen Swordsman, and that they have come to take you to the Wizard Lord by force."

"They have what? A picture?" As the words left his mouth he realized that he had, by his choice of questions, effectively admitted that he was the Swordsman. He tucked his boots under one arm.

"And they knew your name."

Sword was out of the bed now, standing over the ladder where Dal perched. "Did they?"

"Erren Zal Tuyo. Yes. Is that truly your name?"

"Yes," Sword said. "I would not give a false name to your *ler*."

"They say you went mad, and killed a dozen people in Winterhome."

"I don't think I was mad," Sword said mildly.

Dal blinked up at him and swallowed again. "You did kill . . . ?"

"I killed soldiers, who had just slaughtered two unarmed and defenseless friends of mine, two of the Chosen. Yes. But I swore I would not strike a hostile blow in Morning Calm, and I hope to keep that oath. Besides, I have no sword with me."

"You can't stay here," Dal said, obviously in great distress. "You must leave *now*."

"I take it your *ler* do not have the concept of sanctuary."

"I don't know that word."

Sword nodded. "Then get out of my way, and I will leave as quickly as I can."

"You'll let those men take you?" Dal said, as he backed slowly down the ladder.

"Of course not," Sword said. "But I'll leave Morning Calm; I don't want to cause your people any trouble."

"But they're waiting for you at the boundary shrine!"

"Then let them wait. I'll depart on the other side."

"But . . . but they came . . . they want . . ." Dal reached the bottom of the ladder and stepped aside, and Sword half-climbed, half-slid down beside him.

"You know something, Dal?" Sword said. "I don't *care* what they want. I have a role to play as the Chosen Swordsman, and I intend to play it. Now, which way are they?"

"On the Riversedge road." He pointed.

"Then I'll go that way." Sword nodded in the opposite direction. "Is there a road toward the southern hills?"

"Yes, but . . ."

"Then that's where I'll go." He leaned against the ladder and began tugging on his boot.

"I'll . . . I'll go tell them," Dal said, backing away.

"Wait," Sword said. A thought had struck him, along with the realization that he had left his sword somewhere to the northeast of town, not to the south. "Could you tell me something first?"

"What?"

"What do the *ler* of Morning Calm do to oathbreakers?"

"Ah . . . they say that if they do not repent, the earth itself devours them. But I've never seen it happen—no one ever . . ." He stopped. "Are you going to break your oath?"

"Not if I can avoid it, no. But I think your other guests might." The first boot was secure, and he pulled at the second.

"They haven't taken any oath. That's why they're still waiting at the shrine."

"Even better. What do your *ler* do to invaders?"

"I don't know; it's a matter of whim, I think. They decide on something appropriate."

Sword nodded, as his heel slid into place. He straightened up. "Let's see what happens, then." He strode toward the door, and the Riversedge road.

Dal hurried after him.

When Sword stepped out into the street it seemed as if half the town was waiting for him, chattering quietly among themselves. At his appearance they suddenly fell silent, and a hundred eyes turned to stare at him.

"Good morning," he said. "I understand you have more visitors?"

The silence burst into dozens of voices answering at once, while a score of hands pointed to the north.

"They brought us your picture!" someone shouted, holding up a sheet of paper.

"May I see it?" Sword asked.

He glanced up the street as he accepted the paper, and saw more villagers—mostly children—running one way or the other, presumably hurrying from one stranger to the other. Then he looked at the paper.

The drawing was not the best he had ever seen, by any means, but it did look like him, more or less. There was text, as well.

"This is Erren Zal Tuyo, called the world's greatest swordsman, one of the so-called Chosen Defenders of Barokan. He has betrayed Barokan and committed numerous murders," he read aloud. "If you see him, inform the Wizard Lord's staff at once." He handed the paper back. "Thank you. Have you informed the Wizard Lord's men?"

Once again, several people spoke at once.

Sword held up a hand. "Good people of Morning Calm!" he called. "Listen to me!"

The crowd quieted, and those who had been moving slowed and stopped.

"I am the world's greatest swordsman, one of the Chosen!" he announced. "It is my duty to depose the Wizard Lord if he turns to evil. Recently, all eight of the Chosen gathered in Winterhome to discuss the Wizard Lord's actions of the last two years—the Wizard Lord had killed several wizards, allowed the weather to go uncontrolled, and otherwise interfered with Barokan's traditions. We had not yet reached any decision when the Wizard Lord, fearing for his life, sent his men to attack us, taking the Leader and the Scholar prisoner, and butchering the Seer and the Speaker in the street. The rest of us scattered and fled, and I found my way here—and I am grateful that the *ler* guided my steps, for Morning Calm has been kind to me. Your laws have kept my pursuers from dragging me from my bed by force. Thank you, all of you, and my thanks to the *ler* of Morning Calm."

There was a brief babble, but Sword raised his hands for silence and continued.

"I do not want to bring violence into your home. I wish no one ill. I am going to go speak to the Wizard Lord's men, and I hope we will be able to reach a peaceful understanding. I do not want any of you to get caught up in our dispute, but I do ask one more kindness of you all. If I find it necessary to flee, do not block my path. I will not try to shelter here, but will pass through Morning Calm. If I am pursued, then let my pursuers pass, as well. There is no need for you to be involved."

He lowered his hands.

"Now, let me go meet my pursuers." He started walking.

The crowd parted before him, and he marched up the street.

As he had been told, soldiers were standing by the boundary shrine. He had expected two or three, from Dal's description, and was startled to see at least half a dozen men in the familiar red-and-black uniforms. There were also three or four citizens of Morning Calm.

Someone pointed, and a moment later the entire group by the shrine was watching him approach. One of the soldiers lifted his spear, but another gestured, and he lowered it again.

"Are you surrendering peacefully?" the soldier who had gestured called, as Sword drew near.

"No," Sword replied. "I am not surrendering. I am coming to tell you to go away and leave me alone." He stopped, still more than twenty feet away.

"The Wizard Lord has told us to bring you to him if we find you. He said he would prefer you alive, but dead would do. Going back and telling him we found you and let you go would not be pleasant."

"I'm sure that going with you would not be pleasant for *me*."

"You should have thought of that before you killed those people."

"They should have known better than to kill two of the Chosen."

"The Chosen?" The soldier spat on the ground. "A band of murderers the lesser wizards use to keep the Wizard Lord from accomplishing anything!"

Sword tilted his head slightly. The soldier, he saw, was young, younger than he was. "I have never before heard us described that way," he said. "But I can see how you might think that."

"What else are you? 'Protectors of Barokan,' bah! What are you protecting anyone from? Roads and jobs and trade and travel?"

"Have you ever heard of a place called Stoneslope?"

"I've heard the story," the man admitted. "But no one's ever *seen* this supposed massacre site, this village the Lord of the Galbek Hills supposedly destroyed."

"I've seen it," Sword said mildly.

"So you say. Do you know what *I* think, Swordsman? I think you made it up, and convinced the others somehow. I think you *like* killing people. No one had any problems with the Wizard Lords until you replaced the old Swordsman."

"I think you're a fool, to tell me that," Sword answered. "If you had cajoled me, apologized to me, told me you were sure it was a misunderstanding—but no, you tell me to my face you consider me a murderous monster. Did you think I would be shamed into surrendering when you told me my crimes?"

"I think we are six to your one, and that you have no weapon. The townspeople assure me you brought no sword past the boundary shrine, while we have our spears. What does it matter what we say? We'll take you back with us whether you like it or not."

"Will you? How?"

"By force." With that, he beckoned to his men. "Come on."

The entire party lowered their spears into thrusting position, and began marching toward Sword.

"No! No! Stop!" a man from Morning Calm shouted, holding up his hands, but the soldiers brushed him aside.

He didn't resist; the laws of Morning Calm forbade violence.

Sword watched the men coming toward him for two steps, three—and then he turned and ran, back toward the center of the town.

As he had expected, the soldiers ran after him, shouting, spears at the ready.

He did not look back, but simply ran.

Until he heard the shouts change from the enthusiasm of pursuit to puzzlement, then protest. He stopped, and turned.

The soldiers were no longer running; instead they were sunk up to the knee in the earth of the street, earth that had been packed hard and dry when Sword ran across it a moment earlier. Now it was still dry, but flowing and churning like mud. As Sword turned to look at them, one of the men started screaming, and flung away his spear.

The earth around his legs slowed, and then came to stop, returning to its natural inert state.

Most of his companions, as if in response, also began screaming. Sword watched as they struggled futilely against the ground's grip.

The *ler* of a town were not the wild, disorganized spirits found out in the forests; they were spirits that had been woven together into a great cooperative network, spirits that had learned to pool their strength to serve their people, spirits that had been strengthened by centuries of human support. In some places they could stop a wizard's feet from touching the ground, while in others they could suck down invaders. It was never, ever wise to antagonize an entire town's *ler*.

These soldiers had just discovered that.

Those who threw aside their weapons and held up empty hands found that the unnatural seething of the earth stopped, but by this time all were sunk so deeply that they could not immediately free themselves; instead they stood trapped in solid ground, the first to disarm himself buried to just above the ankle, the others to the knee or worse. The screaming stopped, and they stood in embarrassed silence.

Sword thought that most of them could have pulled themselves free with little effort, but they did not. Perhaps, Sword thought, they were too frightened.

The commander continued to thrash about, refusing to relinquish his spear, well after the others had surrendered. Sword watched him in horrified amazement as he struggled, sinking steadily deeper, and his men, as well, apparently forgot their own situation and stared silently.

Dozens of townspeople gathered to watch, as well, forming a large oval around Sword and the soldiers.

The commander churned at the dirt, clearly trying to find purchase somewhere, but only sank more quickly; the earth rose to his waist, his chest, his shoulders. Only when a wild swimming motion threw a clump of dirt into his mouth did he finally yield.

"All right!" he screamed. "All right!" He awkwardly tossed his spear away, almost hitting a villager.

Silence fell. The six soldiers stayed where they were, trapped by the earth on which Morning Calm stood; the people of Morning Calm stood around them, watching the drama unfold, and did not approach.

Sword took a step or two toward his disarmed foes, then stopped and addressed them.

"I will go now," he said. "I am going to retrieve my sword from its hiding place in the wilderness. While I'm sure you can dig your way out, and perhaps even recover your spears after swearing to leave, I would advise you not to attempt to pursue me. I won't be using the roads, and the *ler* of the wilderness will be no fonder of you than are the *ler* here. Remember also that the Archer and I took on perhaps a hundred of the Wizard Lord's men in the streets of Winterhome, and left the streets soaked in blood while we emerged unharmed."

"Ah! Monster!" the commander shrieked.

"I am a part of the magical structure of Barokan," Sword said. "Much like the *ler* of the earth beneath you."

That elicited a wordless bellow of rage.

Sword bowed politely, then turned and bowed again to the townspeople. "Thank you all for your hospitality," he said. "I apologize for any discomfort I may have caused."

With that, he strolled jauntily northward.

Behind him, he could hear people calling for the temple dancers, and the sound of girls' feet running, but he did not look back. He marched on, out of Morning Calm. As he passed the boundary shrine he could hear singing far behind him; he stopped to listen, and to read the inscription on the shrine.

"Traveler, ring the bell and stay close, and do not speak until we greet you," it said. "Let us bring you into Morning Calm in accordance with our ways. Our land does not welcome those who pass this point unheralded."

The message was repeated in several different scripts and dialects; no one literate could say he had not been warned. Sword glanced back.

The dancers were still singing, but one of the townsmen had fetched a shovel from somewhere, and held it on his shoulder, waiting until the oaths had been made.

Sword smiled, then turned northward and marched on. He found his sword where he had left it, and set off cross-country, well away from the road.

At first he had no particular destination in mind, but as he walked he thought.

If he was sending pictures and soldiers out to every village in the area, the Wizard Lord was clearly determined not to leave any of the Chosen alive and free—certainly not the two weapon masters, Sword and Bow. He was also clearly not relying solely on magic to find them; he knew about the *ara* feathers that hid them. He was using his loyal followers to search.

That meant that Sword could not simply wander from town to town until he got so far away he would be safe, as he had thought. The pictures would circulate, and people would recognize him. Sooner or later someone would report his whereabouts, and the Wizard Lord's troops would come for him. Oh, if he traveled far enough beyond the network of roads it might take years, but it would still happen.

At least he did not need to worry about being found by magic, not with the Seer dead.

Or rather, he did not need to worry about being located directly. Once Artil had some hint of the area where Sword might be found, he could send birds and beasts to spy on Sword, and to guide his soldiers to wherever Sword might hide.

When that happened Sword might be able to fight his way free—but he did not *want* to fight his way free. He did not want to kill anyone else except Artil im Salthir himself, and perhaps Farash inith Kerra. Even if he didn't mind killing soldiers, while he was fairly sure of his own ability to avoid harming innocents in a battle with the Wizard Lord's men, the chances that some poor villager would catch a spear through the chest were far too high to risk.

At best, then, he would either find himself fleeing over and over again as his hiding places were discovered, or he would find a new home where the natives would take him in and protect him, and when the information finally leaked—as it inevitably would—the Wizard Lord might well slaughter them all in retaliation.

He hated the fact that he could not only imagine such a possibility, but think it likely. Once upon a time the idea would never have occurred to him, but then he saw what the Dark Lord of the Galbek Hills did to Stoneslope, leaving nothing but ruins and bones.

Once upon a time he would not have thought Artil im Salthir capable of such an atrocity, but then he found him taking Farash's advice, heard him boast of killing eleven wizards, and saw Babble and Azir cut to pieces in the street in Winterhome.

He could not live among people. Even if none of them betrayed him, either deliberately or accidentally, he would be putting innocents at risk.

Wandering the wilderness was not appealing, either. He was a barley farmer by heritage, not a guide. He didn't know how to find food or shelter in the wild spaces outside the towns.

Eliminating towns and wilderness eliminated all of Barokan.

Which meant he would have to leave Barokan.

He shuddered at that, but forced himself to pursue that line of thought. There were two—no, perhaps three—ways to do that. He could scale the cliffs to the Uplands, or take ship and set out to sea in hope of finding some unknown land. Or, just possibly, there might be a way around the cliffs in the swamps far, far to the south; there were legends of such a route.

He knew nothing of the southern swamps, though. He knew the hills extended for at least a month's travel from the Midlands, and there were said to be lowlands between the hills and the swamps. Surviving so long a journey in hope of finding a way into some alien, unknown land—no, he did not think he would try that.

Nor was a ship a promising alternative. He had never even been on a real boat, only barges, and only while they were securely tied up. He had never seen the sea, never tasted salt water. And if there were other lands out there beyond the sea, wouldn't someone have found them by now? A ship blown off course in a storm, a fisherman venturing farther than usual—wouldn't at least a distant sighting have been reported, and legends handed down? Sword had never heard any such legend.

That left the Uplands.

For three seasons of the year that seemed reasonable enough; the Uplanders thrived, after all. The *ara* flocks provided their food, and their tents were adequate shelter. . . .

For three seasons out of four.

In winter, though, the Uplanders took shelter in Winterhome, safe below the cliffs in Barokan. They did not try to survive the winter storms on the plateau.

Which meant, Sword told himself, that the Wizard Lord would never expect anyone else to attempt to survive the winter up there.

Sword looked up to the east, at the distant line of cliffs standing there on the edge of the Barokanese world, and at the white clouds skimming above them, blowing across the sky.

No one sane would go up there to escape the Wizard Lord. It meant slipping back into Winterhome, somehow getting through the gate in the Winter Palace, and making his way up that long, winding path undetected. It meant surviving alone in that vast open country up there through cold and wind and snow and storms that the Uplanders did not dare to face. It meant giving up the magic that made him the world's greatest swordsman, the magic that bound him to Barokan, and living with his soul cut off from the spirits that made him whole.

No one sane would try it, but Sword no longer felt sane. The sanity of his old life had been washed away in Artil's schemes and Azir's blood.

No one would expect him to attempt it. It was the last place anyone would look.

And that meant that when the Wizard Lord returned to the Summer Palace next year, he would not expect to find his enemy waiting in ambush for him. An enemy with no magic, true, but an enemy who had eight years of daily practice with a blade.

Sword had no idea how he would survive the Upland winter, no idea how he would kill the Wizard Lord without magic to help him, no idea what he would eat or drink up there, but he knew, even as he pretended to debate with himself, that he had already decided. He would find a way, or he would die trying.

He glanced back over his shoulder at Morning Calm, then turned his steps to the east and began the long walk back toward Winterhome.

[EPILOGUE]

THE BALLAD OF THE CHOSEN
(as sung by the children in Winterhome Market)

When day turned dark and shadows fell
Across the broken lands
And madness turned to taloned claws
Those ancient evil hands
Then eight were called by whims of fate
To save us from our doom;
The Chosen came to guard us all
And lay evil in its tomb

[chorus]   When Wizard Lords of old would turn
          Against the common man
          These Chosen eight would bring them down,
          Bring peace to Barokan!

The Leader showed his bold resolve
Confronted every foe
His words would guide the Chosen as
He told them how to go

The Seer sought her comrades out
And gathered them to fight
Nor could their foeman hide from her;
She had the second sight

[chorus]

The Swordsman's blade was swift and sure
His skill was unsurpassed
If any stood against him, then
That stand would be his last

A lovely face the Beauty had,
And shapely legs and arms
She distracted evil men
And lured them with her charms

[chorus]

There was no lock nor guarded door
That could stop the Thief
He could pierce the fortress dark
To bring the land relief

Every song and story told,
The Scholar knew them all
He knew the wizard's weaknesses
To hasten evil's fall

[chorus]

The Archer's missiles never missed;
His arrows found their mark
He struck at evil from afar
To drive away the dark

The Speaker harked to every tongue,
Of stone and beast and man
She found the Dark Lord's secrets out
So no defense could stand

[chorus]

When in the Galbek Hills there was
A monster come in human shape
The Swordsman struck the evil down
To save the land from magic rape

And thus the last of evil's spawn
Was driven out of Barokan
Never more will madness come
To trouble Barokan

[chorus]

And now a worthy man has come
To keep and rule the land
And bring us all a better world
Safe from evil's hand

The Chosen we shall need no more
Their long service now is past
A better way to keep the peace
The Wizard Lord has found at last

Our Wizard Lord will never turn
Against the common man
The Chosen eight no longer need
Bring peace to Barokan—
Yes, the Wizard Lord has now
Brought peace to Barokan!